I0643218

TRAIN FOR HEAVEN ON EARTH

finding your path ...

A novel by Oneya B. Rajsel

2024

TABLE OF CONTENTS

PROLOGUE

What a wonderful quote! A fantastic life motto! That is what I want!

My purpose on Earth is to experience the beauty of life!

Does that hold true for myself? A professor, teacher, leader of the youth, whereas (in the past) my photo decorated a page in Playboy, I danced in a strip club, and left a trace in pornographic magazines?

Not at the moment, not yet ...

Usually, people do not prove to be what their first impressions show and what different titles suggest. And I am no exception. If the teenagers that I teach, or their parents knew ...

On the other hand ... What is there for me to teach them? Indeed, are commas, coordination, Realism characteristics, and similar topics so important that we need to devote years of brains polishing to them? Or, would it be better for them and for me if I sincerely acknowledged who I am, what I do, and shared the awareness of made mistakes?

That is, if they exist ... Maybe they are merely lessons, or as a 13 years old student wrote in her essay: Life is a train where people enter and exit, and stations present events and experiences on our journeys ...

STATION 1:

THE SEA

Here we go again … An old story. I am lying and waiting for something to save me from fighting with insomnia; however, the struggle only brings another defeat. Tossing and turning in a moist bed are accompanied by gazing at a brown ball on the ceiling made from numerous woven ropes which create a chandelier where a light bulb resides. Semi-darkness does not bring a tranquilizing effect, only the pictures from my past are moving through my head with light speed and hinder the arrival of liberating sleep. I feel like a princess on a pea grain which has been replaced by grains in the brains – and there are so many of them that they could fill up several baskets and be sown on one or two fields.

Tonight, among many other permanent topics, I am re-living the experience of a girl from twenty years ago who was unable to calm down her thoughts the night before setting off to the coast. Not much seems to have changed from that point of view. I am departing in the morning, but exciting and youthful planning of the future has been replaced by anxious rumination about the past.

Even the place of a sleepless night has not moved far away. I have moved from the room next to my parent's bedroom to my grand-ma's place a few meters away. Next to my so unwanted one-room apartment, right behind the wall, lives my grandma. At this moment I cannot feel any gratitude for the fact that I have my own space, a kind of temporary home.

And I have been trying so hard to move away from this village … as far away as possible. An entire decade of running from one wrong hug to another only to be saved from living here. And where am I now, after all those years ... years of suffering? A 27-year-old single teacher!

The Universe has an odd sense of humor if this is its award for persistence.

"Hi. Where are you, my honey?! Oh, my sunny, my loving child!" I am sighing while approaching a table in a pub. There in the corner Alex is sitting, and the subject of my enthusiastic greeting is jumping and barking around his legs.

My golden retriever instantly marks my white trousers with his paws, and almost knocks me down, but I do not give up the obligatory cuddling. Although he has been away for only ten days I have missed him enormously.

Odysseus is a golden Sun of my life – whatever this may sound like. I assume that I may seem totally nuts to those who do not share the same enthusiasm about animal beings. But at this moment I am not interested in the meaningful and scornful looks from those people sitting behind the adjacent tables.

Alex is smiling empathically, he knows exactly how I feel. After the first euphoria has passed I realize that I have not greeted him.

"Hello," I say and sit on an empty bamboo chair across the table.

"Hi, how are you doing?" asks my ex-boyfriend, and without waiting for my answer continues: "He was very good. I bathed him on Thursday, he got his ampoule, and today I have brushed him."

Alex and I have decided on a puppy for our first (and only) anniversary. Actually, it was my idea. In my romantic belief that two people who function so well and never argue will stay together for- ever and live a fairy-tale life I suggested sealing our love with a dog.

I have adored these hairy lumps of bones since I was a little child. My father gave me a German shepherd for my twelfth birthday. She was my only support during difficult teenage years when I had to fight different windmills. Four years ago she was put to sleep and I lost my best friend. I found a similar friendship with this golden-haired being, but the family idyll did not last long. Our community broke up last autumn when I picked up my things in anger, put them into my car in the middle of the night and set off towards south of Slovenia, to my parents' house. I left Odysseus in Ljubljana and spent many nights crying due to the loss of safety and comfort. What will I do with my life now? Alone?

Things worked out on their own accord. Alex and I agreed on mutual care which proved to be an excellent solution. Every day few-hour-long connection with nature during rainy days and snow showers, or at impossible early hours and uncomfortable temperatures can be quite exhausting. Odysseus accepted the situation very well. The change of caretakers is carried out every 14 days so he receives the best from both of us – a lot of attention and indulgence, and when the period of two weeks passes, one happily takes him to another. We both soon have enough of the dog-tailored life. The new caretaker accepts him willing to fulfill his every wish, and the story goes on with a touch of guilt. We know exactly how divorced parents feel, and the dog knows how to get the most out of it. Nobody can say that animals do not feel and think … and take advantage.

"When are you departing?" Alex asks and brings me from the retrospection of our relationship back to the present. "After we drink this coffee, I'll jump to the shop, and then we'll set off towards Dalmatia," I answer still absent, busy dealing with the dog around my legs and the feeling of guilt, because he must have missed me as much as I have missed him.

After I unglue myself from him, I manage to light the first cigarette today which makes me slightly dizzy due to the early hour - that was a few minutes after ten in the morning.

I inhale even with a greater delight and this takes me to the period of high school, to the beginning of my smoking career when each smoke of Marlboro I took got me stoned. Ah, the beginnings are always the best.

"Have you brought me the herbs?" I mumble, so that nobody could hear my words even though the closest person is sitting behind the table which was located a few meters away.

"Of course. Yesterday I went to Kranj, D. has something new. Outdoor skunk, you'll like it," says Alex and exhales the smoke of his vicious habit.

"Shhh, keep your voice down," I nervously say as the waitress has just walked past the table next to ours. In my world it is totally unacceptable for a teacher of the Slovenian language who works with children to be doing something illegal.

"You know that I would not let you go so far away without obligatory equipment, you would go crazy." Alex smiles, takes a plastic coil from his pocket and hands it to me under the table. "And besides, you really deserve to relax a little. You have been very hardworking, take a bow! Basically, this is an extra gift for your graduation so that you can reconnect with your nerves."

Not only hard-working (that is, obedient), but also persistent, I think. To finish this damn faculty, one needs the nerves made of steel – I really get angry when I remember the suffering I experienced before I was finally awarded that paper. How many unsuccessful attempts of proving the knowledge, waiting for people who do not respect timetables (be it a department secretary or a professor at his/her last office hours of the academic year), learning the theoretical facts by heart, getting up early, taking long drives only to realize that the journey was in vain and that it would have been better and in particular cheaper to have stayed in bed or drunk at a wine festival …

All those bitter memories prevent me from paying attention to Alex, so I only give him a sour smile and regret that I cannot drink a glass of wine bottom up.

"Let's forget it, it's a thing of the past. Thank you for this stuff," I lovingly pet my handbag where I have hidden the pack with herbs which I will experience and reconnect with when I am on the coast. Possibly tonight at the sunset. "What will this year's harvest be?"

"We need to have some in stock because he departs for Thailand at the beginning of June and won't be back at least for a month." Judging by his appearance, our dealer is an ordinary person, in his early thirties, with the family and a steady job, who has raised the concept of gardening to higher levels of comprehension and who cultivates nice but forbidden plants, as his hobby. He does not smoke; however, the hobby brings him enough money to afford luxurious travelling every year with his partner.

"Huuu, cool! Do they travel alone or with an agency? Alone, of course." I already know the answer to my question.

"Sure," Alex is nodding. "They are planning to visit the entire state, and if they like a certain place they will stop there and enjoy. I envy them a little, all those paradise beaches, atmosphere ..." He is dreamingly explaining. When we were a couple, we used to spend a lot of afternoons and nights watching Travel Channel and making plans for our traveling. Thailand always jumped to the first place among potential paradise holidays. Also because of constant advertisements regarding the tiger sanctuary which is led by monks. I am imagining myself surrounded by those beautiful wild beings, how I am tussling with their cute striped paws and big striped head, and how I am making sounds such as guchi, guchi, gu, gu, bu bu ...

"Odysseus and I were at the ZOO this week. He was excited about a seal. He was shy at first, but still curious. He was the most afraid of an elephant," Alex is explaining. Obviously his thoughts caught the animal direction when Thailand was mentioned. "At the beginning he even barked at her, the elephant, and then he got closer and smelled her from the distance."

"I believe you," I smile. Odysseus has never proved to be courageous. He becomes brave only when hiding behind the legs – preferably behind male's legs, women obviously do not have so hairy legs that he could feel safe behind them. Sometimes he barks at a towel which is moving by the wind, or he runs from the balcony into the room with the speed of greyhounds running behind a rabbit and jumps onto my head. I believe he gets scared by a pigeon or a shadow or something like that. I have no idea. I used to check what devil annoyed my dog but I never noticed anything.

"Well, elephants are shy too," I try to be smart to defend the dignity of my dog hero. "It is believed that they are madly scared of mice, and this is really funny. Look at them, how big they are, and how small the mice are. If an elephant steps on a mouse, it is gone. How can they be afraid of those little creatures?"

"And how big are insects and how tall are you? What is your reaction when you see a tiny bug, not to mention an evil moth?" Alex laughs.

"You are right." I look down remorsefully and we both laugh. All my love for animals ends with the tiniest ones. Creatures, smaller than ten centimeters, in particular those carried by several pairs of hairy legs, trigger panic reactions in me which resembles hysteria. Love is replaced by murder instinct and a wild hunt with a broom or spray starts after an innocent being which came into my space on a trip, to look around, to widen its horizons … When I am not alone, my most frequent reaction is to jump shouting and run to the closest shelter and then behind the door, I demand the beast to be killed at once and without compromise.

Alex does not have such problems. He prefers to catch the insect and send it to freedom. This of course lasts longer than smashing it against the wall - which I find to be an acceptable, quick and efficient solution.

The coffee has been drunk, the navigator is present and composed - as much as you can expect from a dog – the boot is full. I honk and wave in farewell to the guy with dark ruffled hair, wearing a grey jacket and dark blue jeans, who has just sat into his grey fiat punto.

Viiiiia Dalmatia. YEEEEY! My well-deserved holidays, finally!

Very excited, we are cutting the bends on the road full of holes towards south border of Slovenia. The wind in my hair is the consequence of open windows due to the lack of air conditioning in my car. The wind in my teeth is caused by an English singer whose weeping voice is coming from an old radio and who is singing about a wonderful dawn and about how high he is. This dude knows what he is singing about. *The* song is for me.

The drive through hills and valleys towards Bela Krajina hinders quality broadcasting of any radio station with the exception of catholic Radio. God's voice, they say, reaches the ninth village. It must be true, since you can always rely on this frequency – be it in the middle of nowhere, among the mountains and woods, or even in tunnels.

However, for an atheist such providers are not acceptable, so it is time for my party CD with the hits which always accompany me on my journeys. First, Red Hot guys take me to the Other side ...

Before the Customs I start to feel nervous. After short touching of my breasts I realize that this time the magic pack is too big to be stuck into the bra to create a Wonderbra. Because it is too late to stop and hide it into my luggage among my underwear or chicken steaks, I stick it in my trousers hoping that I will successfully take it across the border with the image of an early-stage-pregnant woman.

At the Slovenian border the custom officers check our passports and I drive across the bridge, still trembling. In spite of this tension I notice freshly painted fence on the first part of the bridge, while the second half of the bridge is decorated by a renewed sidewalk which runs under an old railway construction.

I was worrying in vain. Croatian custom officers are very polite. They do not check the passports, but a nice fellow asks me where I am heading alone and he offers his 'handsome' co-worker to accompany me. I express gratitude for his kindness, but with a wide smile on my face reject the company, before I take a deep breath and drive on.

I am on my way to Murter, a little island which I have chosen as a reward for successful graduation and seven months of hard work in primary school. Oh, my GOD, I hope I will never have to teach in a school again!

After a two-hour drive I exit the highway and continue driving among fragrant pines.

"Where the streets have no name, have no name ..." I sing loudly, backing the crackling melody coming from weak speakers - with a cigarette and steering wheel in one hand, while another hand is waving in the rhythm of the music. Fortunately, the road is rather straight, and I slow down before the arrival so that Odysseus and I do not end up unexpectedly in a bush or ditch.

Finally, the road descends to the coast and the movement becomes snail-slow as we are both sealed to the window. I do not know exactly where to stop, so I carefully observe the house numbers. First, I drive past the destination, although I have been here before – I have never found anything at my first attempt. I realize that a lot has been changed during the last five years. It is obvious that tourism in this little corner has been developing quite well.

I park by the road and see a lady who is waving from a red colored balcony above a terrace. Mmmm, the terrace is large, cooled by a large pine next to the stairs, just as I remember. The two garages under the terrace are new same as another big balcony at the top of the house. It seems to me that I and my doggo are about to have a quality and enjoyable holiday.

"Hi, how are you?" I am greeted by the lady with fair messy hair, dressed in white linen trousers and torn bright blue T-shirt, who was coming down the stairs to the car.

"Hello, I'm ok. Super, now that I'm here," I reply and shake her hand while smiling.

Then she showers me with a bunch of questions: "Have you travelled well? No problems? Alone? What if something was wrong? I would never dare, I'd rather travel by bus or ask Damir to take me to places …"

"Yes, without problems," I smile at Bilyana, a distant relative of my big high school love. "If anything had happened I would have called somebody to pick me up. I only had to be careful watching the exit signs. And I informed Gal who is waiting by the phone in case I need to be saved," I am explaining my heroic act – travelling 300 kilometers alone, with my dog. He, however, does not count as an equal traveler in such cases. Obviously.

"How is Gal? Is he still abroad or has he returned and found a steady job?" She starts asking about my ex-boyfriend, her grand-nephew or something like that.

"He will be in Saudi Arabia for another month or so and then he'll come back home," I reply and she is nodding with interest. "I believe he has earned enough money to survive without a new job for a while," I say, and it is half true because Gal has always been spending too much and it is not necessary to worry that this time he will be hiding the money somewhere for too long.

"Oooo, what a beautiful dog," she says when she sees Odysseus watching us from the driver's seat. He always moves there when he is alone in the car. Although he knows that it is forbidden for him to sit there, he constantly tries to prove that he can do whatever he wants. Even when I am standing next to the car where he can clearly see me I am still ignored – probably because of mild punishments. "This is Odysseus, a very nice and spoilt doggy," I open the car's door and try to introduce them to each other. I continue saying nice things about him: "There are no problems with him, he does not bark, only when we are playing, and he does not ruin the furniture." The dog is rather impatient, sniffing around and paying no attention to the landlady.

"Where are we staying?"

"Oh, how beautiful you are … and cute … yes, nice doggy…" Bilyana showers my dog with words of praise and does not hear my last question. Soon I am expecting excitement about his silky fur. "Beautiful dog, and such silky fur you have ..." Aha, I would be surprised if she had missed that part.

"You are accommodated in the lower apartment, so that you can have your entire terrace to yourself and the dog cannot escape because of the fence. She must have heard my question and answered with a slight delay.

"Great." This is exactly what I had in mind when I was deciding where to go. Gal and I spent a few days here years ago and I remembered the owner's knowledge of the Slovenian language – the lady that I am talking with right now – and the excellent location – only a few meters from the SEA! This means that I can smell the sea water, and the view offers almost fantasy picture of blue-green water, where the continental part

14

of the canal is decorated with a small marina with fishing boats, yachts and sailing boats.

Now I turn towards the waves and the marina, and I see that one of them is mine. A yacht. The bigger one. If you are dreaming, dream big, I always say. Maybe this is the reason for my disappointments?

However, now it is not the time for such thinking. Practical things have to be carried out.

"Shall I help you with the luggage?"

I nod and as soon as I open the boot my strong landlady grabs the luggage and the bag with the food for a month or so. Just in case the shops are understocked here. You never know how it is *down here*. And what the prices are.

With all the luggage and bags the comparison with loaded donkeys seems to be offered by itself. We climb the stairs, walk past the garage. Carrying heavy bags is even more difficult because of the dog on the leash who finds every plant and each corner interesting and zig zags left and right and turns me like a peg top.

Bilyana opens the door and we enter the apartment. After a quick tour I realize that the interior has not changed much. The kitchen is equipped with basic items, in the dark room there are a double bed, green two-seater and a wooden wardrobe. In the right corner the door leads to a small bathroom with bad odor. There is no air conditioning, nor a TV set.

Ooo, now I notice a little transistor with a diameter of ten centimeters, which takes me to the sixties, with its little screen and grey metal case. Suitable for listening to football games, if I were interested in them. It seems that I have everything I need for the following days.

"Will it be ok?" she asks. Seeing me nodding with excitement, she continues: "How long are you staying?"

"Time is not my master," I say. "I finished my job and won't be working for a while, a few weeks ago I graduated and this vacation is my reward," I mention my academic achievement. "I plan to leave on Friday. If I feel like it, can I stay longer?

"Now there are no guests, so you can stay as long as you want," she replies.

"Great, thank you." 12 Euros per day is not a big expense. I am more afraid that I will be bored, alone in the middle of Dalmatian wilderness, among strangers, among CROATS! I hope that not all of them hate people of Slovenian nationality.

While carrying a second round of my holiday accessories we meet a tall gay on the stairs. At first sight he seems to be older than me, but he has come by a black scooter, so he must carry a young soul within himself.

"Oh, Damir come here," she calls him, and a thin two-meter tall fellow approaches us. We introduce ourselves and shake hands. "This is my son. He can take you on a tour of the town."

"Oh? Really? This would be great, thanks." I look up at the green eyes although he is standing two stairs lower than me.

"But he doesn't speak Slovenian, so you will have to communicate in Croatian."

My excitement over socializing now fades a little. *Haaalo? How is this possible? B*ut ok, I will do my best and I hope that I will not embarrass myself with Croatian.

"What are you doing later?" Damir, who *does not* understand Slovenian, asks me.

"Shall we go to the town?"

"This would be wonderful. I'll be unpacking for a while so we can meet at eight. Ok?" I stutter my first Croatian words this year.

"Ok," he nods. "So, see you at around eight, I'll come here to pick you up, ok?" After my nodding he concludes in Italian: "Ciao." *Hm, he speaks Italian*? He goes up the stairs to the upper floor. The family lives in the middle part of the house, the lower and upper parts are intended for the accommodation of guests.

I and Odysseus push our way into one of the ground floor apartments – yes, push, because he is constantly winding between my feet as he is scared of the new environment. And my movements are quite a balance challenge as I am trying not to step on one of his paws. I hope that the neighboring rooms remain empty through the Labor-Day holidays[1] so I can have the entire terrace for myself; I express a few egoistic wishes.

I quickly put the stuff from my bags into the refrigerator and freezer. My luggage is still unopened, lying on the bed waiting for me to deal with it later. Now it is time for a long, long walk by the sea, finally, I feel at home again!

Outside I catch just the right lightness, my lightness. Light for which I long not knowing exactly what I am longing for. The time of the day when the sun starts getting ready to sail behind the hills – or sink into the sea – and everything becomes different. Slightly reddish, more beautiful … I cannot explain why but it is. Usually I feel the urge to sit into my car and drive somewhere. I do not know where and why, but something is happening to me at that time. But not now. I feel that I am exactly where I am supposed to be. Where I desire to be.

I attach my dog to the flexi leash which enables him eight meters of freedom and we set off on the path by the sea which takes us out of the town. I am inhaling the sea air, and April sun is warming me pleasantly, so long sleeves are unnecessary. Even a slight breeze does not take away the feeling of pleasant warmth which is hugging me from everywhere, from inside and from outside.

After thirty minutes of walking, observing, sniffing and marking all possible plants (not by me) we arrive to the beach. A concrete one, but the sea is calling, my sea is calling me. I sit down and remain sitting there for a while. Happy. Satisfied. Peaceful.

I unleash my doggo to allow him total freedom in exploring the surroundings and marking his highness, and I am only meditating and enjoying the area, the view. Suddenly I feel sorry for having made an appointment with Damir. I do not feel like suffering with the foreign language, even less charming a strange man. The company of people does not suit me, I like being alone more and more frequently. Since I got Odysseus, his company has been sufficient; human beings with all their

---

[1] In Slovenia (and Croatia) the Labor day is on the first of may.

misfortunes have started to bother me. I have had enough of my own problems. Nevertheless … On the other hand … I am starting to feel lonely.

And the appointment has been agreed, so we get back to the apartment after a smoke break. There is still half an hour for me to shower, put some perfume and makeup on for the first bum through a Dalmatian island town.

I am sitting on the terrace in semi-darkness listening to the evening sounds when Damir appears.

"Hi, are you ready?"

"Yes, we can set off," or maybe go? Leave? I do not know the right expression. This will be quite a difficult evening.

And it really starts with the battle with my dog who is again afraid of everything he sees or smells for the first time. So he drags me left and right, far away from the waves, to the middle of the road. Finally, we arrive to the town center when I unleash him so he can go around marking places he visits. My Hansel (a character) from a fairy tale. There is the answer to why dogs are doing that! Maybe it is not macho marking of the territory, maybe it is a way of marking the road back. Of course, he cannot throw stones with his paws. Have I discovered something new? New philosophy, dog philosophy?

After ten minutes of a short walk and easy communication mostly made of "Hmm, how do you say this in Croatian … you know what this means …" we approach a little café. We choose a table on the terrace overlooking the sea and continental lights on the other side. Damir sits on a chair from where he can look at all the beauty, so I sit down on the chair opposite him, but the position does not suit me. I will not gaze at the wall!

"Can we move? I would really enjoy watching the sea," I kindly look at him and blink my eyelashes for a stronger effect.

"Well, you can sit next to me," I hear a simple answer.

Ok, then I'll sit next to you. Now I realize why old Dalmatian fellows sit next to each other, facing the sea. Nobody wants to miss the view.

We order drinks, beer for him, wine mixed with fanta for me. The first round is finished in less than thirty minutes. A true

Balkan man, he pays for the drinks while we are talking about everything on earth. The guy is ok, and language barriers seem to be destroyed after several glasses of wine. With every sip, my tongue is running better. I cannot confirm the grammatical accuracy but I do not care as long as he understands me. If he does. Damir encourages me with saying that I am doing ok, but I do not believe him.

After a classical introduction which relates to everyday stuff, such as job, free time, tourism ..., we start approaching a more slippery terrain when the topic touches fishing and the Adriatic coast.

"What is it with you Slovenians and flowers?" he says.

"I don't know what you're talking about ..." I try to look surprised although I do know. I know very well what he is talking about.

"Well, you have an interesting fellow, your Josko," he says right into my face.

"Ah, the news about flower pots has reached Dalmatia," now I admit that I know of the Slovenian national hero.

"Pardon? I haven't understood."

"It seems that everyone here is talking about flower containers?" I ask.

"Well, of course." He loughs. "I don't know why you have so many difficulties with them?"

"How not to?"

"It's natural for us to have marked the borders, so isn't it better to do it with flowers?" He is laughing at the topic which is rather sensitive for Slovenians.

"I don't know if that is the right way. If you don't like flowers, to jump into the river? But I have to admit," he does not stop scorning," I really had a good laugh when I saw the clip on you tube. A true gymnast, are all Slovenians such acrobats?"[2]

---

[2]   Little peace of land Josko Joras calls home is only accessible by a road *between* Slovenian and Croatian border checkpoints. It is on the disputed piece of land, claimed by both Slovenia and Croatia. The latter enforced its claim by blocking the road with cement flower pots and during protest march Josko 'was pushed' (he fell) into the water.

"Ok, you're right," I mumble and make a sip of the beverage, and then start defending the fighter of the south border. "But the man cannot reach his house. How would you feel if somebody put something on your driveway so nobody could visit you? Croatia has such a large part of the Mediteranian sea, why do you need that little piece of ours?" I'm combining several languages to express my thoughts.

"Mhm, I don't know. You know what politics is? Haven't you heard that it is a bitch? I don't know what politicians had arranged, neither do you. I'm convinced that they have already agreed on who gets what. You've got the Gorjanci hills and we've got the sea."

"What do you have in mind? Where did you get this about Trdinov vrh?[3] It has always been ours." *What is wrong with those people? Do they really have to own everything around them?*

"It seems stupid to me to even discuss this," Damir changes his tone of voice. Obviously, I have made a face at hearing that offensive assumption about the ownership of the part of MY beautiful Dolenjska region.

"We were brothers in the past. Under The House of Habsburg and Austria we were one nation and fought together against others. And in Yugoslavia we were brothers, and now what? So stupid … Because of such a stupid reason we're fighting against each other."

Ok, the dude is slightly right. We were under the same authority for a very long time and according to my historic sources quite big friends as there were talks about associations.

"I know the man who parked his truck across the road when Serbs wanted to reach you, with the intention to stop them. And he was not the only one. There were more Croats who risked

---

[3]   The highest peak of Gorjanci - hills in the slovenian border with Croatia - As Slovenia and Croatia had not managed to resolve their dispute concerning the border on land and sea despite numerous attempts, on 4 November 2009 they, with the assistance of the European Commission, signed the Arbitration Agreement establishing an Arbitral Tribunal.

their possessions to stop the army with barricades.[4] Would they now do something like this? Me? You? No, of course, not. Now we are killing each other because of a flower pot ..." He shrouds himself in silence for a while and I do not say anything either.

"You know how it was in the army at the time? In critical moments?" he asks without waiting for an answer. "Many soldiers deserted, because they didn't want to fight against Slovenian brothers. You know that they risked their lives when they rejected the orders of their superiors? I know several of such people, and how many do you know? It was for your land, too ..."

"Hmmm ..." Good. He has pointed to several hard bones to chew on with his radical statements. But the sociology lesson has not ended yet. "What would happen if more people knew and remembered such deeds? Would they have the heart to make our accession to the European Union so hard? To hinder the people who defended you in those times?"

"Hmm ..."

"And if you were on our side and made it easy for us to access Europe, who would complain because of a few meters of border, fish and similar shit. I am convinced the politicians have arranged all of this to refocus our attention from more important matters."

"Ok, you're right about some things. People forget easily ... But you should not blame only us. Every year something happens. When I and my boyfriend were in Savudria last year, somebody stole our license plate. What am I supposed to think then?"

"I know, there is no simple answer... But I do not see myself as a Croat, I'm a Mediterranean guy." He lifts his glass, pours the last bit of the beverage into his throat and waves to the waiter to bring another round.

"OK, you're not a Croat, now I feel better," I smile.

---

[4]   The Ten-Day War, or the Slovenian War of Independence was a brief conflict that followed Slovenia's declaration of independence from Yugoslavia on 25 June 1991. It lasted from 27 June 1991 until 7 July 1991. It marked the beginning of the Yugoslav Wars.

"By the way, I have a Slovenian passport too."

"How's that?"

"My grandma is from Novo mesto. Didn't you know that? Yes, my mother is half Slovenian and half Croatian."

Ah, the things have started to become clear in my little tipsy head. That is why his mother speaks almost perfect Slovenian, and exhibits no frustration and expected hatred towards my citizens or me. For a moment I thought that I charmed him with my appearance and this is the reason for such a thorough understanding of the whole situation. No, the guy is half ours.

During the nostalgic rhythm of Dalmatian songs, we are still drinking so that I am blessed with the possibility to observe the reflection of lights on the sea surface, the best dog ever – after a few glasses I become very sentimental – and a communication-difficult two-meter tall guy next to me. From time to time I turn towards him to see his skin scarves caused by acne of the teenage years, green eyes, decisive nose and brown short hair, so that I rest my eyes on something else besides his long legs in a grey tracksuit. When the tower clock strikes one, we slowly walk towards the house. I fancy a joint filled with herbs.

"How long have you smoked that?" is an obligatory question which strikes immediately after I have sat down on the most comfortable armchair on the terrace.

"The first time ..." of course, everyone remembers his/her first ..." it was in the high school right after the school, I was 16 years old." I say, inhale deeply twice, three times, and then hand it to him.

"Well, I don't smoke ... but ok, I can do it today," he mumbles and takes the joint. As an amateur – as a cigarette – he inhales a smoke from a burning stuff and hands it back between my fingers. And there it remains, for Damir's face turns green after few minutes. Nevertheless, I hospitably and with best intention offer him another smoke which he rejects. "I don't like drugs. I don't feel good. This is really not the stuff for me."

I understand. It is not good to mix marihuana and alcohol if you are not used to it. What you can get is only vomiting exercises, and they were frequent occurrence at the beginning –

22

when I was sixteen, seventeen, when I was hallowed into the world of enticing substances. I believe that I could have been used as a test for the quality of drugs. If there was something wrong with the drug – if it was sprayed with rat poison for better efficiency, as they liked to scare us – my stomach became rebellious and happy hours were replaced by sitting on the toilet, lying in bed, praying for the quick ending of the agony, swearing that that was the last time. Resolutions accepted at such nights maintained till the next party, usually the following weekend, if I did not succumb even earlier.

However, in a ten-year tasting, the body becomes used to a lot of things and today with the greatest pleasure after the all-evening bender, before bed I smoke a singing grass which brutally puts me in bed out of which there is no return for some time. During such experience I do not have power for thinking about thousands of things which constantly buzz in my mind till the morning.

Damir tries to say something, but it is more than obvious that he has had enough for today. There is only snoring waiting for him which usually happens after drinking larger quantities of alcohol.

"Ok, see you," is everything I get from him before he heads towards the stairs, slowly but clumsy.

"Ok, see you. Sweet dreams," I say and then move inside. I am lying in bed and finishing the joint. What follows if the turn to my left hip, when the bell in my head will ring and the fairy tale will end for today.

"Aaa!" I groan, numb in the spasm of fear. I do not know why and how much later I wake up, but when I open my eyes I see a silhouette of a man by my bed.

Obviously, an unnecessary mistake, for when I blink a few times, I can see nothing and nobody. Nevertheless, I switch on the light on the bedside cabinet and look towards the edge in fear. Of course, there is nobody by the bed. But my body is still trembling, I am really scared. I look at the dog who is peacefully sleeping on the other side of the bed. The journey and the evening in front of the pub at the new location exhausted him and probably there is no thing or trumpet that would wake him up. I know that I could not employ him as a guardian, he has qualities in other areas. But I feel better because I am not sleeping alone in the apartment. I look at the clock, it is three in the morning. I have slept less than two hours. It is not surprising, new locations always cause me to spend some time adapting to a new place and bed. The first nights I hardly ever sleep, so alcohol and drugs are welcome friends in the nights of insomnia. Odysseus behaves in a similar way. When I fall asleep it can happen that he becomes restless, starts barking into the darkness and even jump on my head. But not this time. This time I am the only one to be awaken by a third party. I better have another joint, followed by a night rest – attempt number 2.

I wake up into a sunny morning, disturbed only by a knife-sharp pain in the temples. It is consistently throbbing on the memory of a litter of red wine which was circulating in my veins and it probably still is. But this can be relieved by two pills. It is not acceptable to feel bad at the seaside atmosphere. Even hangovers which would roar at home in the shape of a tiger and would stick me to bed for the whole day, here only meow as young kittens.

I and my dog set off for a short walk by the sea where we activate all our senses and enjoy the surroundings. Upon the return we meet Damir on the stairs. I greet him and ask him if he would have some time in the coming days to show me a hidden corner of the beach, not known to the tourists. We agree to meet the following day at four o'clock, after he has finished his work. Smilingly, he tells me, supposedly for the second time, that he is employed in a store in Zadar. It seems that parts of my brains or memories have sunk in alcohol as I do not remember this revelation from the previous night.

He leaves for some errands and I set my intention to prepare something delicious and powerful for my restless stomach. On the terrace, there are some guests. I greet the owner and an older lady who is introduced to me as grandma Liljana. Ah, I see,

Damir's mother and grandmother, my compatriot from Novo mesto.

They invite me to join them for a cup of coffee and I accept it. The cooker with accessories and preparation actions around it is not my favorite activity, so it can wait for a while. Besides, I will really enjoy talking in Slovenian, and let my brain relax.

"Have you been accommodated? How did you sleep?" Liljana asks me. Obviously, there will not be any communication in Slovenian.

"Good," I just do not feel like explaining my sleeplessness and its causes. "Do you happen to know the weather forecast for this week?"

"It will be nice. There will be slight breeze but sunny, around twenty four degrees. However, the sea is not yet suitable for swimming in it…"

Soon I realize how difficult it is to understand the grandma. She speaks a kind of language-mess, created from Slovenian and Croatian, which is neither the former nor latter, but I sense that the two of us are similar in this regard. Maybe she would be more understandable if she spoke in Croatian but I do not dare suggest it.

"Did you and Damir go for a cup of coffee yesterday?" one of the elderly ladies asks me.

"Yes, we were in the old part of the town. It is very nice and tranquil there."

"You are right. It is very peaceful. We often went there with Damir and Petar," says the older one.

"Who is Petar?" I ask when I take a first sip of the black beverage.

"Don't you know? Didn't Damir tell you?" the grandma asks while Bilyana is gazing towards the sea.

"No, he didn't mention him," I think.

"His older brother. He died last year," she explains without hesitation or embarrassment.

"Drug overdose."

"Uh!" I almost spit out the liquid in my mouth. *Dear God!* How does a person respond to that?!

"Oh, my condolences ..." I utter and turn towards Bilyana and then feel bad due to guilty conscience because of my offering him a joint. *Really bravo to me, very tactful!* I quickly light a cigarette and inhale deeply.

"He was the one who found him. He probably didn't tell you, did he?"

I shake my head and wonder why she is telling me all that. And so leisurely.

"Yes, he came home, and Petar was lying there. He tried to resuscitate him but it was too late. He doesn't like to talk about it but it isn't easy for him. Yes, that year was very difficult for all of us." She is nodding to her words.

"Yes ... khmm ... I believe you ... awful ..." I cannot imagine how painful this must have been for the whole family.

She looks towards the sea and I do the same while smoking my cigarette because I do not know what to say. Then, we start talking about fishing. This year the catch has not been good ...

After ten minutes the coffee break is finished and I return to the loneliness of the kitchen to think over what I have heard on the terrace. I feel devastated because of my drug seduction. And very scared. Is it possible that I actually saw something at night? The silhouette by the bed? Ghost of Damir's dead brother?

According to all the thrillers and horror movies that I watched this could be possible. The ghosts of dead addicts who continue their addiction by somebody alive.

The loud Relax's Take It Easy piece of music pushes away those terrifying thoughts and I start preparing my favorite meal, roast chicken, mashed potato and a large bowl of my mother's green salad. This will be followed by lying on the beach and sun bathing so what had been heard will soon be forgotten.

It is half past four but Damir has not arrived yet. Where do I always find guys who cannot appear at the agreed time??!! If there is something I hate, it is being late. I am never late; however, I am always accompanied by people with this bad habit.

Fifteen minutes after my mind quarrel with Damir, he finally arrives. Without an apology or explanation of almost one-hour delay, we set off towards new adventures by my car so that Odysseus would not litter his sports astra.

The first stop takes place in the capital city of the island where we order our drinks at the pub next to the coast promenade. White coffee and a glass of water. However, instead of using the Croatian expression for a glass, I somehow just modify the Slovenian one.

Damir laughs and explains the cause of his laughter after the waiter has left.

"Well, it's good that he has understood you. Did you want a glass of water?

Uh, my knowledge of Croatian is really poor. Maybe I am good at Fuzine[5] accent? Where did the 'kozarac' come from?

I cannot go long without discussing the family tragedy so I interrupt the discussion.

"Why didn't you tell me what happened to your brother?"

"Who told you about him?" he looks at me in surprise. "My mother or my grandma, of course," he answers himself.

"Yes, yesterday we drank coffee and they told me about it. I suck, offering you a joint."

"That's nothing, it wasn't the first one."

"How do you feel? Because of your brother? Are you ok? You probably don't like talking about it."

"What happened, happened … I wanted to help him but I couldn't … he didn't want me to … And then it happened …" He is not talkative, he needs quite some time to put these words together. I do not want to ... just that he knows that I know. And I understand him. Or maybe I do not, because I have not had similar experiences. But I can imagine the situation clearly and the feelings, and I feel tension in my chest.

The topic has killed today's mood and we shroud ourselves in silence while drinking the rest of the coffee.

"Did you finish?"

---

5   Neighbourhood with immigrants in Ljubljana.

He raises his eyebrows and smiles before he answers: "Eh, I haven't. I would like to but this is not the right place neither the time for it."

When I look at him in surprise, he asks: "Oh, you mean coffee?"

"Yes, of course. Didn't I ask correctly?"

"Well, I have drunk up my coffee but one finishes orgasm," he laughs.

Oh, MY GOD! My face must have gone red as I feel heat, but not from the sun. What will the guy think? I am not seducing him!

"I didn't learn your language from porno movies, you know."

Because he is still laughing I calm down and start smiling myself too. Everything is good for something.

We are driving on twisting roads and after several minutes he directs me to a macadam road or a path where my red thunder is beating deep holes and large rocks on the way. We arrive at a stony beach where we are sunbathing alone but I expected more from Dalmatian islands – if that is the best what Murter can offer. But I do not believe it. Maybe I should have seduced him so he would be willing to show me hidden sand beaches and the turquoise sea which must be somewhere on the island which is also named Door of the Kornati archipelago.

I spend the following days on the beach reading, sunbathing, pouring cold water on myself and dog for the sea is not suitable for swimming, and daydreaming about perfect life which is waiting for a fresh graduate. How will my heaven on earth look like?

A house with a swimming pool, three dogs, two cats – one black and the other one white –, successful husband who will take me to the theatre, dinners, dancing … I still do not know what my occupation will be but I count on obligatory help in household activities, and in walking the dogs as I would not walk them every morning. How could I earn money with cuddling animals, in particular the young ones? This is something I really like. Probably I would have to be a healer or something similar, so that is not going to happen …

On Friday evening I meet Damir again, this time he intends to show me the island night life. It is ten to seven, the time for me to decide. Most of the afternoon I spent thinking about how it would feel to have a new male body on and in my body after three years. The tall Dalmatian does not cause butterflies in my stomach but I am attracted by his height. Why? Do I feel insecure and I need physical safety? Or am I more interested in what he hides in his pants? I happen to be a modern woman, sex and exercise are supposed to be healthy for the body and soul, and they improve the skin too … I am at the seaside … Why not? Why would I pretend to be a virtuous virgin?

After a powerful inner dialogue I decide in the last moment and run to a little store which is open for another ten minutes. To buy razors, of course. My bushy mouse will need quite a treatment to be suitable for a new visit. One of the more favorable sides of being single is that nobody knows if you have not spruced up down there, what is good for my sensitive nature. I do not know if the irritated skin full of acne is more attractive than a vigorous bush, but in my case during the time of popular Brazilian depilation it reminds me more of a Brazilian forest, so I will need several razorblades to remove the entire mat. I hope the drain will not be clogged up as its flow compatibility seems to be rather low.

I have done it so I move to the terrace but a young gentleman – during our conversations I learnt that he is three months younger than me, so I can afford to be a little superior – is late again. Waiting is easier with red wine which I brought with me and spared for the last night, and with an enticing joint. So I have everything. I enjoy evening sounds, slight breeze, the view and the fragrance of the sea. Damir's mother surprised me with a delicious fish today so I am not hungry. This is real hospitability for already the price for accommodation happens to be very low. So I do not want to be angry with her son anymore.

Half an hour later than agreed he appears. First we go to the town center and drink a glass of wine. Some of his friends join us to whom he introduces me, we shake hands, and then I am ignored for the following hour. In the beginning I try to cooperate and say something witty (according to my criteria) but there is no response. Because I am a woman or because I am a Slovenian? I feel 'persona non grata'.

Finally, we drive away (Odysseus is lying on the back seats) towards the main city of the island. There is a cute pub by the beach where we park our bodies on the terrace. I keep forgetting that they have not passed an anti-smoking law yet which in my country has chased the smokers under the sky. The communication does not seem to get lively so it is not before the third round of beer and wine that we move from general stuff to private topics.

This time he starts talking about his friends firefighters: "Have you heard what happened last year on the Kornati?"

I shake my head.

"There was a fire and 11 people died. Didn't you know?" *Uh, why did he remember that now?*

"Yes, I heard. Very sad …," and a little morbid.

"Six of them were from my town. We were true friends, socializing and so …"

I open my eyes widely. *What is happening here?* First, his brother dies, after a few months also his friends and acquaintances, neighbors? I don't know what to say. I have found different heaven at the seaside from what I expected.

"You are not lucky. How are you dealing with it? Can you sleep? I don't know what I would do … I would probably end up abusing alcohol or hard drugs."

"It is better now, I visited a psychologist, and I use medication."

"Which?"

"I eat helexe." Ah, my favorite medicine.

"Aren't you sleepy after?

"A little."

"I know about them. I used to take them myself. I had difficulties with insomnia for a long time. And when I was 18, 19 I used to steal them from my father. And not only them. Also lexaurine, and sanvals were the best. After taking those you sleep like a baby." I try to explain my experience with medication. "He always had a drawer full of medication and I took advantage of that." First I stole 0.5-gram pills from him, and then my friend who used to work in Krka – medicine factory – brought me 1-gram helexe. "How many grams do yours weigh?

"I don't know." He shakes his head.

"What color are they?" White, pink or blue?" I know everything about them.

"I think they are white."

Then they are 0.25-gram, that's nothing," I wave with my hand and continue with the confession about the next level of intoxication in my intimate world. "I used to swallow two or three 1-gram pills, then smoke a joint and slept up to 15 hours." This, however, happened a few times in exceptional circumstances. During the period of repeating the second year of my studies when I was considering ending my miserable life without hurting anybody. I did not find a smart solution. I could not cut my veins, hang myself or drown – I am scared of physical pain more than the devil fears the cross or my Odisseus fears the waves and New Year's fireworks. I owned an old yugo which struggled on a smallest hill in the first or second gear and could not manage more than 80 km/h, so I could not count on a bad or fatal traffic accident. I felt closest to medicine, but it was my father's or my friend brought it to me so one of them would feel guilty. I did not want that, so I gave up such planning. Fortunately, I kept the delusions to myself and consequently did not end in a psychiatric institution.

Because I am driving tonight and I do not want any problems with the police, besides I have different plans with my companion, we return to the apartment before midnight. We continue drinking, but I cannot start seducing him. I sit close to

31

him, touch his leg or hand, lean forward and emphasize my chest attributes, but I do not achieve a desired effect.

"What about a kiss?" I ask encouraged by a liter of wine.

"Eee … ok," he says and while smiling moves a little forward so that I can reach his lips. So I get what I have wanted … If I can say that at all, because holding out the lips without passionate tongue involvement is not an erotic kiss, which I have had in mind.

After a few minutes I sit on his knees so that he can touch my body, but I still do not feel passionate. His response is mild, I hardly feel his touching. He does not know how to do it, he does not want to do it or the pills are to be blamed. Does he not feel comfortable with the situation? I am used to the men taking initiative and I adapt to their wishes, usually I remain without pants too quickly, with my legs spread in some weird places in uncomfortable poses. Tonight it is different, and I do not like it. I expected thunder, lighting from the Dalmatian lover. He suggests moving to bed but I reject him. I focus on my wine and drink a few more glasses but the more I drink the more repellent the whole situation seems to me. Nothing will happen. In one hour I say goodbye with an excuse of being tired and he leaves without objection to his home, one floor up.

The next day I intentionally miss his telephone call and in the afternoon for the last time with Odysseus visit the rocky beach at the camp with wonderful turquoise-blue water and the view of rocky islands. I stay in the sun so that the skin becomes reddish. It is a pity that the sea is not warm enough for us to swim in it, the temperature is high and we are both hot. Next time I will have to find a little bay and shadow – as a mother for her baby – on these rocks I am forced to get the water with my hands and pour it on me and my dog so that we do not get burnt. A few drops on him, a few drops on me – we are like two retirees. Anyway, before my departure to the continent this evening, this feels like a dream. For a few moments, I manage to forget about the whole world …

STATION 2:

SOCIAL NETWORK DATING

I am lying in my bed, tired and cranky. Welcome back to the real life. On the way home the news on the radio 'pleasantly surprised' me: tropical cyclone killed more than 100,000 people; an earthquake in China, with I do not know how many casualties, they are afraid of floods ... The world reality is similar to mine – job hunting, tolerating my parents and their arguments, dealing with friends and their problems, ruminating about what I want from my life, what I would like to do ... 'Encouraging' thoughts for the beginning of the magnificent morning after a week of isolation on a Dalmatian island without the news, newspapers, parents ... My mother enters the room early in the morning and wakes me up as she will do the laundry and I have to bring her the clothes immediately. She likes to appear at the door at most unusual hours. This is the price I have to pay for free renting. But she will have to wait; first I need to take my dog for a walk. And I am covered with a bunch of errands and duties even before I get up, so I become unwilling even to do so.

In the evening I open my gmail. There are several messages waiting for me, but nothing urgent or interesting: mostly chain messages promising mountains of money and eternal happiness – providing I forward them to at least ten naïve people – or eternal unhappiness if I become stubborn and ignore them. I wrote to my 'friends' who remember me at such important occasions not to send them to me anymore but without an effect.

I also received an invitation to a certain social network. In the last year I have not met a suitable single man for me, that is why I have already searched for attractive guys over the net. I have found several interesting dating sites with acceptable photos of men but I have never been brave enough to join and communicate with somebody. At this point I decide that I do not want to be alone anymore. I want a new guy and I want him as soon as possible!

So I run the invitation and start creating my profile in "the community of young people where the users can maintain connections with the social network and widen it."

First I enter my basic data:

Name: Freya

I decide for my internet nickname. Let me be the goddess of love in the social media.

Gender: Female

Town and state of residence: Novo mesto, Slovenia

What do you expect? Friendship, business contacts

I leave out the relationships. I do not want to be so obviously pathetic showing that, as a million other people, I am looking for my soul mate.

Love state: Single

I like: Men

Introductory text: I am a mischievous young lady who enjoys walking in nature or town streets in the gleam of evening lights. I like visiting sauna and soaking in the sea or thermal waters. If you have similar thoughts and actions, contact me.

Interests: night life, books, movies, friends, music, humor, internet, television, traveling

I live: Alone

I live in: Apartment

Which is not absolutely true, but the program does not have an option: at my grandma's in my apartment, in her two-apartment house.

Color of eyes: Grey

Although my eyes are bluish grey with brown spots – but this option does not exist.

Hair color: Red

Weight: 50+

Looking for: friendship, friends for partying, non-serious, serious relationship

What do you find romantic? Night walks down the coast, candles

Cliché, but sincere.

Outfit style: casual, urban, jeans, sexy

Your favorite brand of clothes: /

What are you wearing now? Shirt, trousers

Smoker/Non-smoker? Trying to quit smoking

Cigarette brand, if you are a smoker: Marlboro
Do you drink alcohol? Occasionally - in moderation
Your favorite beer brand: Heineken

Which is a lie, but my sincere answer would suggest that I hate beer! I do not want to reject most of the guys already at the beginning, so I tick the least awful beverage.

Your favorite non-alcoholic drink: Water

Another sincere lie. I do not like water either but I want to paint the image of healthy life – to improve the impression of smoking.

Your favorite Cocktail: Tequila Sunrise

In particular because one is enough to feel gentle and loving caress of alcohol in my brains and veins.

Your favorite event or party: Moto gathering Pula 2002

It has been six years since then but I want to point out my motorcycle experiences and attract a steel dragon rider.

Musical style: pop, rock, house, vocal dance, dance, trance, classic, drum'n bass
Your favorite DJ, singer, bend: Robbie Williams, U2
Home website: /
What do you dislike? Egoistic and hypocritical people
The most annoying question: When will you have a child?!?!!
Your least pleasant experience: /
What do you do when you are bored? I watch TV
Do you have children? No
Your favorite animal: My dog
Mobile brand: Motorola
The best thing that has happened to you: /
The coolest person you have met this year: ?
Do you have friends living abroad? Yes
Damir
The best holidays: ?

It is difficult to say. It has never been really wonderful.

The best traveling experience: /
The worst traveling experience: /
The best foreign cities: Paris, Venice, Athens, Florence

I have not visited any of those but I am sure I would adore them.

Do you go dancing: Sometimes

I adore dancing, but I dare dance in public only when I am intoxicated.

When do you go to bed? Between midnight and two

The best book or writer: Vinko Möderndorfer

The best magazine: National Geographic

I have browsed through it twice or three times, but I cannot mention Lady or Nova[6] (my favorite readings) because I would seem shallow and that is unsuitable for a sociologist and teacher.

Your favorite newspaper: Mladina (The Youth)[7]

Although I am not reading their articles I respect the topics that they emphasize. Well, that they are supposed to …

Your favorite performance: /

Which movie genre do you like? 3D animations, imagination movies, mysteries, comedies, horror movies, historic movies

Actor/Actress: Sean Connery, Johnny Dep

Your favorite movie: Dracula, Alexander the Great

I love Dracula! And Interview with the Vampire.

Your favorite TV series: /

Your favorite TV Channel: HBO, Travel Chanel, Animal Planet

Your favorite radio station: Radio Antena[8]

Your favorite games: /

Game pad: /

Car lover: Cabriolet, coupe

Car brand: Ford

Your favorite car brand: Audi

How many times did you take your driving license exam? Once

It is like filling out a form or official document only that SS and CR numbers are replaced by a bunch of more intimate information. I need one hour to complete most of the sections.

---

6   Yellow press in Slovenia
7   Critical thinking newspaper
8   Antenna - Popular radio station in Ljubljana with mainstream music

The next decision is about choosing suitable photos. For my profile photo I have chosen a photo where I am holding a little Odysseus in my lap and hiding my face in his fur. So I am not recognizable enough to be recognized in the street but it is good enough for a doggy to attract attention.

There is no guy or man (even in the image of Brad Pitt) who would interest me if he does not like dogs – only being tolerant towards dogs is not enough. I enter more photos into the profile among which is a photo of my upper part of the body. I am lying on the beach, hiding behind large sunglasses and covering my naked breasts with my hands. A book by Vinko Möderndorfer, which I was reading at the time, is lying on my belly. The photo is rather sophisticated, it does not show anything but it triggers imagination.

After two minutes the first response appears, followed by similar ones with hearts and comments, such as: remove your hands; cool baby; I would like to lie next to you ... A woman responds too, that a book does not belong on my belly because it will leave a stain ... I am excited. I feel uncomfortable by all the attention which I am not used to, but soon I start enjoying it.

In one hour my page is viewed by fifty people, and I keep improving my profile till three in the morning, answering comments, liking, commenting, checking other profiles of people who noticed and approved my on-line content. After a long time I am socially active again, this time on the computer. Much easier and less onerous.

The following afternoon I meet Nina whom I missed at the seaside at BS.

"Hi, what's new? How was it? Have you ordered? Coffee?" the dyed chubby blonde sits on the chair opposite mine while asking the questions.

"Mhm. How was it in Novo mesto? What's new?" My answers are mostly interrogative.

"I've fallen in love," she answers with a smile on her face forgetting about most of her questions. "This time, I think, I have found what I have been looking for."

Ladies and gentlemen ... tararatararartara ... fanfare please, here we go again.

"And who is a lucky guy who deserves your eternal love this time?" I ask with melodramatic voice and try to hide my skepticism about the romantic adventure. I would believe her if she were not in the habit of finding drunk losers who only use her and then without any sense of guilt leave her.

"My co-worker. We talk on the phone every day almost an hour. Well, I am the one who does most of the talking," she says and looks into my eyes, meaningfully.

I have never understood why people spend hours and hours talking on the phone. Aren't phones meant for urgent cases? At Sociology of Media during my studies we were taught that the use of phones presents an escape from the present because during the communication you are mentally not present in the room where you are physically staying. Besides, I do not like the idea of frying one's brains with radiation, and my Motorola belongs to the first three mobile devices considered to be the most radiant, I read the other day.

"And what are you talking about for so long, my dear?" "Last time I was talking about my traveling and my future goals. He was excited about my traveling on Bali. I told him about my last year vacation with Tine in Vietnam, and with Lojze in Turkey. He likes my plan to visit Vietnam again in autumn. I adore Hanoi. First Vietnam, then Cambodia and at the end shopping in Bangkok. Of course I'm trying to get him excited to travel with me."

"Aaaand, what does he look like? How old is he? What is his responsibility in the company?" At this point I am more interested in the man than in the possibility of traveling.

"He's thirty-two. I'm lowering age levels," she smiles. She used to pick at least ten years older guys; so thirty-two years for hers twenty-six is a great advancement

"He's responsible for supply. A cute guy, sportsman, well built, only a little short. He's as tall as me." That means that he is 163 centimeters tall. "I hope it will be proved that those who do not exceed in height, exceed in …," she says and we both laugh. We have not yet discovered a rule or a sign which would disclose how many centimeters men hide in their pants. The size of their nose, feet or fingers does not predict the wealth down there. The myth about 'the thing' being proportional with height is not true either. It is not necessary that short men have a big one, and that all tall men have a big one is far from the truth too.

Or maybe the two of us are not that lucky? Bold men do not make love better due to the excess of testosterone as it is said in certain articles. Most of the cosmopolitan guidelines proved to be total nonsense. But I am thinking whether the desire for big size penis is proportional to the hole in the soul of a woman …

"Where does he live?" The company where she has been employed for a month is registered in Prekmurje, as far as I know [9].

"This is difficult, yes. In Murska Sobota. But because of the meetings we date at least once a week."

"Does that mean that you'll be moving up there?" In spite of initial reluctance I start building exciting plans about love which survives all the obstacles, including the distance.

"Uh, no. We're only turning each other on. We haven't had anything yet. When he was in Ljubljana he was rather reserved. Maybe because of his co-workers."

After coffee and three beers and the intermezzo about my adventures with Damir – I have not mentioned his family tragedy – the girl tells me something that she intended to keep for herself. "Mmm, there is something else about my future boyfriend … He has a girlfriend. But they do not get along very well."

I roll my eyes that they almost hurt me. I knew it!

"He says that the relationship is about to end, because he does not know what to do with her. She's too childish."

---

[9]   The northeast region of Slovenia.

"How old is she?"

"Twenty."

What do men expect from younger women or girls, I will never get it. And then they blame them for everything, they complain that they are childish and similar shit.

"How long have they been together?"

"Three years." Excellent, so a dream guy exhibits half-pedophilic traits. But I do not want to comment, it is her life. She can feel what I think without my explanation. So we conclude the discussion about him and start talking about the people we know. Then, we slowly go home. We do not dare drink more than three rounds because we both are driving and policemen in Dolenjska[10] are very thorough at their work. If you are drunk when they stop you, you are doomed, without exception. I myself have not had such 'pleasant' experiences, but Nina was left without a license and she spent the whole year paying off the debt of that night.

After a successful drive home I sit in front of my computer. How many visits have I had? How many comments? Has somebody written how beautiful I am? Is there a new message? Who has been longing for me?

I check a few new visitors, nothing special. It seems that attraction or originality and humor are not the qualities of men on this page.

Ups, I have just received an invitation for friendship by a bulldog – that is, his nickname is bulldog. I hope the name refers to his dog and not to his personal traits. I accept his friendship and click on his page to see who I am dealing with. Finally, something promising:

Name: Good bulldog
Date of birth: 3. November 1974
Town: Ljubljana
Hobbies: Swimming, martial arts ...

---

[10]   Region in the south of Slovenia

The four profile sections disclose only a little about him. I find a few photos where the main king is his dog while he is always hiding in the background, so I cannot study his face nor his posture enough to create a satisfactory image. He seems to be acting on the same principle as me. I am impressed mostly by the photo where his dog is lying on the bed and hugging a baby. Oh, how nice. I am not a children lover who would melt at the sight of a baby, but I like the openness of somebody to put a dog of the breed known for its aggressiveness next to a little helpless being. Aha, there is a photo of an Audi where a little one (that is the dog) is lying under the steering wheel. Of course I comment at once.

Who is the best driver?

I cannot help commenting at the next photo. They are lying hugged on the white leather sofa, so that the gentleman is hiding half of his face in the dog's fur.

Cute

In continuation I receive a few likes and comments of my photos from him, but only those where the star is my Odysseus or where we both are shining in them. He did not comment my covered uncovered breasts.

After half an hour I send my first message on the portal.

Hi, what's going on? What are you and the handsome doing?

The response flies in after three minutes. I already got scared that my first attempt of internet dating would sink as Siddharta's ship on the dry[11] land and that he would not respond.

> *Uh, nothing special. I am at the computer, he is sleeping under the chair.*
>
> *He's snoring that the whole house is shaking.*

> *Iiii, then with Odysseus they could saw up the whole woodpile. Mine is a true lumberjack (or he has not decided yet to be a lumberjack or a garbage dog).* *What's his name and how old is he?*
> *Bye*

> *Rocky, and he's three years old. What about yours? You have nice photos. Especially the one on the beach but I didn't want to comment. I don't like slobbering ...*

> *Odysseus is still a baby. He's one year and a half*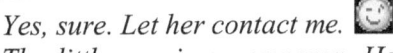
> *My friend is excited about bulldogs. She's thinking of getting one, do you have advice? With regard to breeders, maybe?*
>
> *And thanks for a compliment.* *You two have nice photos especially the one where you are lying on the bad. Everybody can see you love him. And the one with a baby. Courageous.*

> *Yes, sure. Let her contact me.*
> *The little one is an emperor. He's very gentle, so there's no panic. I bought him in Bela Krajina. The owner had them with him all the time so they got used to gentleness and cuddling, and now he can't be untaught.*

> *And you? Where are you? What do you do? How are you dealing with boredom?*
>
> *Bye, Matey*

Finally, I learn about his real name. Matey. Shall I trust him mine or shall I remain Freya?

> *Momentarily, I'm an unemployed teacher. If you know somebody who would need a Slovenian or Sociology teacher, let me know. Especially because I landed in Dolenjska due to logistics difficulties but I really want to get back to Ljubljana.*
> *I get rid of boredom together with my puppy, but there's no panic.*
> *I enjoy not working. It was rather unbearable at school.*
> *Where are you from? What do you do?*

I have been waiting for his response for ten minutes but I have not received one. I look at his status and see that he is not on line any more. He seems to have canceled me. Another one to escape when I mention my profession. I go to bed, totally disappointed.

The answer arrives the following evening.

> *Oooh, a teacher, I have to be careful how I'm writing* *I apologize for commas and other mistakes. Are you a strict teacher?*

> *O, look who has responded? I thought I had scared you. When I mention what my profession is people usually become different, more careful.*
> *I'm not strict, I'm always kind. Sometimes too kind.*
> *But I don't like shouting and disrespect so sometimes I get really angry.*

44

> *But I don't want to teach any more. Nobody respects you, everybody pokes their noses into your business, everyone knows more than you do ...*
>
> *I really hate forcing people into something and in school you just have to do it because the Slovenian language interests nobody – this does not mean that the children are good at writing. Besides, I had to deal with the gypsies who belong to a different 'turned around' world. So in those seven months of teaching at primary school I had enough of anything connected to teaching.*

I ask the same question for the second time, but I do not receive any answer. Instead of this I check different profiles, but I do not find anything likable. I exchange a few messages with a guy who has the photos of the whole world. I get enough of him after the third message when the subject changes to sex. Is that all that men are interested in today? I am disappointed, so I roll a joint and lie on my bed. I am thinking about Matey. He seems to be one of rare men who are not interested in how to get between a babe's legs. While I am thinking about the meanings of his questions my thoughts soon change to school and previous months which I spent there, gathering my first teaching experiences.

The very first day at the introductory teacher conference at the end of August I experienced the first surprise – the timetable. I had heard about a nine-year school program and different levels introduced by a new education system, but the abbreviations DSP, ISDP[12] did not mean anything to me. Fortunately, I was assigned an excellent mentor by my headmistress who explained those to me later. The timetable decoded into teaching Slovenian in the seventh grade, the eighth – level 3, the ninth – level 1, the Roma in the sixth grade, additional and advanced classes and three hours per week of individual hours for children with special needs. I was surprised that children with special

---

[12]   Additional professional assistance

needs do not attend special schools but are included into 'ordinary' general schools.

I did not hear anything about that during my studies (I admit that I attended only rare lectures in my last years of studies). Neither did I learn about that during the fourteen-day traineeship at high school. What followed was a period of adjusting and crying when I was writing my lecture plans till eleven in the evening or even till midnight, and the next day it was practically useless because I had to spend my time getting children to open their workbooks or textbooks and listen to me or write notes.

I felt totally incapable and rude when I found out that I got nervous because of things that cannot be expected from the kids with special needs (according to the words of the school counselor) – that is reading the instructions and similar things about which I had not been warned before. I felt incapable because in spite of my effort the boys did not master basic information which one has to learn by heart at home. I had to forget about the stuff I had been taught during my studies and start from the beginning. Because I had already forgotten fundamental rules - I had to refresh my basic knowledge such as the use of capital letters.

The next lesson in school was brought by the Roma children. When I first entered the classroom 7 b, all the children got up except a boy with dark complexion in the last row at the desk next to the window who was spatially separated from others. During introductions he did not want to share his name with me so I kindly stepped to him, crouched, so that we looked into each other eyes at the same level and talked to him about the group and how it was to be a part of the group. I asked him why he wanted to be separated from others, but I did not achieve any effect nor response. An immediate loss of my naivety.

There were several reports in the media about the school and the discrimination. It was reported that they separated the Roma from other children. I agreed with that kind of thinking until I experienced the situation myself. The first challenge was catching those children around the school, they adored hide and seek. Next, I had to persuade them to go with me to the classroom, which they persistently rejected and only my threat that I would call the headmistress got them back to the class. So, what is the purpose of separated lectures of Slovenian (also Mathematics and English) which are criticized by the whole state and rebelled by the Roma? To teach them how to write and read in the sixth and ninth grades because they did not master the basics due to frequent absence from school.

I was not qualified for that either. I did not know how to teach the kids to recognize letters so I went to my co-worker teaching at the general level and asked her to explain to me some basic rules. It is logical that in the environment where they cannot read or even understand the language, they cannot follow the lecture and their self-esteem and self-respect suffer. I consulted an English teacher about the situation and she admitted that she had lost any hope in teaching them English. English was the third language while they had not mastered the second one. So she devoted her time to teaching them Slovenian too. One hour per day I taught them, separated from the others, how to read and write, but most of the time that ended in their running around the classroom, throwing books on the ground, quarreling, calling names – but not from my side. I felt 'the best' in the group of three boys who communicated in Roma and according to their laughs and looks they were making fun of me. What is there to do when a 12-year old boy tells you what he will do with you, for instance nicely fuck you? Does he already know why he has it? Probably yes, as it happened that a girl of the same age stopped attending school because she got pregnant and devoted her time to maternity.

During my teaching at school there was one case with two first-grade pupils who, in spite of their teacher's warnings that they should not leave the class, managed to escape, and the father of one of them was waiting for them behind the corner and took them home. Those in charge at school called the police immediately who found the kids safe and sound at home, in a Roma settlement, and the father complained that he would not send his kids to the school where they did not take good care of them. But he will continue receiving the state financial support for them.

All the children know, as 13-year old Samo, who repeated the sixth grade, told me, that at the age of 15 they will be able to attend Research Educational Center, where it is much easier to finish primary school education. And that nobody of them would work for 900 Euros/month. And that the teachers must be rather dumb to work for such a law salary.

I wanted to give up but I did not know how. I am not a person who would accept the circumstances peacefully and not do what I am paid for. I did not let them draw or color as other teachers did who had already learnt that it was no use hitting their heads against a brick wall. After one month of crying and terrorizing myself how incapable I was, I realized that maybe it was better for kids to spend some time at school, if it is not time for gathering mushrooms or iron – at that time only few come to school, and be in the so called social environment, regardless of the fact that we were not learning about nouns, verbs or adjectives.

It was good for the kids such as hyperactive Mirko, doomed to Ritalin, who said that he would never try alcohol because his step-father was drinking every day, going to striptease clubs and spending all his money there – though he did not ever hit his mother. Or for a little Esmeralda who communicated only with shouting, but who liked attending school. Once she was absent for a period longer than a month because her mother gave birth again, to twins. 11-year old Esmeralda took care of her, a younger brother, two newborn babies, and that was the reason for her absence – maternity leave.

The children taught me about their culture. I was surprised at the fact that they really ate dogs, but only the older members of the 'tribe', and at special occasions. I was horrified at cheerful explanation by a nine-year old that they skin them alive because the meat remains soft due to adrenalin. I was even more horrified when they told me that they collected the dogs through Salomon classifieds magazine. When I was not capable of listening to those gourmet atrocities any more I was taught how to prepare a delicious hedgehog. It seems that my openness to other cultures is not as great as I imagined.

I was not the only person at school to question the purpose and meaning of my work. Some other teachers were wondering why school and their aspiration when those kids were sentenced to home ghetto.

Next morning I wake up close to noon in a very bad mood, I fell asleep almost at dawn. I have lunch at my parents, and then I go to the Employment Agency.

There I agree that my counselor registers me for the computer course. It will be of good use as I do not master power point very well. Two weeks of the afternoon work will not harm me, and the certificate of computer literacy will be a good reference when applying for a new source of making a living.

In the evening I find Matey's message, apologizing for a late response. His computer was out of order. Now he is at work (*what work*??) and wants me to trust him my telephone number. I am skeptical about that because I had to change the number four or five times due to impossible calls at non-human hours. But this *hulk* is the first after a long time who is not initially interested in the number of my bra or the color or hairstyle of my coochie. Of course there is another profile of man such as Janez who sent me the following message:

> *Hello!*
> *I'm for a serious relationship. What about you?*
> *Greetings, Janez*

Of course I am for a serious relationship, but this does not mean that I will marry the first guy who writes that to me, before I find out something about him. Nice, but that is not all that is important, I think. Or is it? What would a person in a pub think if I came to him and said: I am for a serious relationship. What about you? Wouldn't he think that I am crazy? Or desperate? Which I am getting close to, as I wrote to Matey immediately and sent him my telephone number. I will change it again if he proves to be another freak. I am not attached to numbers, but if I do not try my luck I will never know if he is the right one …

The next morning I am visiting the second counselor at the Employment Agency who is in charge of education. Two unemployed persons are waiting in front of the entrance and after half an hour the lady lets us into her office where she is explaining education and constantly using the word *obligation*. With the signature on the contract we *bound!* ourselves to regular attendance of the course. I ask her if it is possible for me to attend the afternoon course because there are going to be two courses, the morning course and the afternoon course.

The woman looks at me angrily and rejects my request. The groups have been defined and *my obligation* is to attend the lectures REGULARLY. I am surprised at a strict attitude but I ask her what happens if I get sick. The woman does not seem to like my questions at all. I notice her hateful look and she strikes me with a much higher tone of voice. "If you do not intend to attend the classes do not register!" She continues a little slower. "You are U N E M P L O Y E D! And as such you will sign the C O N T R A C T with the Agency to P A Y for your E D U C A T I O N! Your O B L I G A T I O N towards the Agency is the same as it would be if you were employed here! And what do you do when you get sick in your permanent employment relationship?" She does not wait for my answer.

"Every employed person has to visit a doctor and bring a medical certificate for the absence. This is how I do it!"

The hint is clear. Humble because of her shouting, I nod. I do not want to explain to her that to me it does not make sense that because of a few hour absence at a course I, an u n e m p l o y e d person, spend money, which I d o n o t h a v e, to drive ten kilometers far to visit a doctor, wait in the waiting room for several hours, to get a medical certificate for my education because of cold or fatigue or something similar. That seems to be a waste of my and doctor time.

"For every hour that you are absent from the lectures you have to bring a certificate of excused absence, she continues decisively, "if not, then you will have to cover the expenses of the course by yourself!"

The system seems to be clear and logical, but I cannot settle for the worker's attitude. I feel like a last garbage in the world, useless leftover of the society. I have more questions, but I rather remain silent, I will get the information at the course. I prefer to sign a bunch of papers and then step behind the corner. I need a cigarette.

Angry as I am, I take the phone from my handbag. Look, look, my first bright point today. Matey's message telling me that he is at work, that we can write to each other and that I should take care. I respond immediately asking how he is, poor fellow. On such a sunny day he is sitting in his office. I ask him what he does, the third time. If I do not get an answer I will star nagging that he is hiding something from me.

The answer peeps after a few minutes when I am still smoking and getting angry with the worker, in my mind. He says that he will write to me in the evening on the computer because the thing is a little complicated.

Well, what does this person deal with? What does that mean? Is he a spy? Something similar? Do they still exist? KGB and similar? Slovenia has a Sova[13], I read somewhere, although I am not interested in such things. I start analyzing the known data. He works in shifts, also in the afternoon and at night; he has access to the internet at work, so he does not work at an assembly line; and that is all I know. A physician? A security guard? A waiter? He has a dog but this fact is not helpful at decoding the secret.

I go home, I have enough of people around me. It will be better for me to devote my time to Vinko and his new book which I have not read yet.

---

[13]   Sova (Owl) – Slovene Intelligence and Security Agency

Three hours later I am still in bed, reading the book. I adore him! He has connected everything that I like in his writing with the subject of insomnia, my actual topic. *Insomnia is like pregnancy*, he says. To be able to start with a new life you have to question the old one. The internet connection does not work, but I am not nervous because of that as I usually am when I get disconnected from the world. I do not bother at all, I am focused on the book, nothing else interests me, not even a male person. I do not stop until I reach the end in the middle of the night. I am very tired, but I know that because of what I have read I will analyze past events even more thoroughly, the events which have brought me back to my mother's lap.

I fall asleep towards the morning and wake up a little before twelve in the company of Matey's message on the phone. He says good morning and wishes me a nice day and informs me that there is a mail waiting for me on the internet portal. He hopes I will still be talking with him when I have read it. There goes my answer from my bed into his telephone mail box:

Kitty katty is a sleepy girl,
A real Paris kitty. She would sleep if she could ...
Good morning, I'll read your mail and write to you. Have a nice day,
Greetings

FINALLY I will find out what this person does that is so confidential. Before I exchange my bed for a chair I receive another message from Matey. I must be playing on the right strings.

Uuuh, you are a sleepy girl, aren't you? I like
the people who know how to enjoy life. ☺
I would like to come and lie by your side on this hot day. Take care, keep in touch.

Now I am sitting at my desk and opening the world network. Right to the messages ...

Well, he said it. One would expect more courage from a policeman. I have not been happy with them in my personal life. The first one I was in love with, hit me on my face in the disco. I dated him a few times in the period when I and Gal (my ex-boyfriend No. 2) were separating – when we met at weekends at the same bar we spent the time quarreling. The policeman must not have liked my positive response to his question if I would go to bed with him and another babe. He hit me and yelled that I was a bitch because I did such bugger to the man who was so good to me – true, Gal almost killed me by suffocation in Budapest one month earlier, so that the bruise on my neck was visible the whole week and I had to hide it. A slap from policeman was a punishment for 'my cheating'. Or it was a mare revenge because I admitted to his girlfriend, who I had not known existed, that we had sex a few times. I believe that the hit was more because of my sincerity than because of my behavior to an on-off boy, his acquaintance.

The second policeman I got involved with a few months later invited me to the seaside over the weekend. He suggested that I invited a friend so that I would not be bored when he and his friend would go around the vacation home. I accepted the suggestion and Ema traveled to Krk[14] with us. In the first evening I found them in his or our-never-to-be bed, but I stayed

---

[14]   Island in Croatia

53

with them and his nothing-to-blame friend to the end anyway. Supported by abundance of alcohol and marijuana I had a good time and the 'friendship' with Ema survived. Six months later we met again when my ex-friend Tasha and I were having fun in Novo mesto, but he ended up in bed with her too – although he was in a relationship with the woman who is now the mother of his child. Tasha admitted, quite intoxicated, that they dated for quite some time. We were talking about little dicks and she could not proceed without mentioning that the owner of one of the smallest that she had seen or felt was a pearl of Slovenian police.

After a short review of the experiences so far I feel a slight tension around my heart but I do not know how to behave in any other way. Although I know that I can get burnt I cannot exclude the fact that I like him. What if he is a perfect man for me? The one I have been waiting for my whole life? If I do not take a risk I will never know, so in the evening we meet at our portal again.

Aaah, a policeman, you say?! I didn't know we had a anti-terrorist department, is it that bad?

No panic, I will not cancel you, you and Rocky are too cute. I know that policemen are not popular. But I am a person who doe not judge someone before she gets to know him better. Regardless what he does.

Nooo, we do not have an anti-terrorist department, but we call it that way. Because we are dealing with the biggest Slovenia offenders.

Mostly we deal with the establishment of psychological profile

That's so interesting.   I am interested in psychology.
I have always liked observing people and 'reading' them:
I like analyzing why they do certain things ...

Mah, it's rather overwhelming. The schedule is killing me, I
Am here whole days and there are duties..There is not much
time for private life. It happens quite often that I have an
appointment with somebody, but instead of meeting them for a
drunk I have to run to work.
On 21st June I am in Novo mesto on business. Will you have
some time to meet me for a drink? I'd like to get to know you in
person.

Of course I will have time. I can hardly wait.

Yes, but there are two weeks till then
I will organize myself so that we can definitely meet. I'd
like to
meet you too. Now I'm going to bed. Tomorrow is an important
day, I'm starting my computer course, yeees. And I have to get up
urly.
Sweet dreams, Nighty

Keep in touch, take care,
Nighty

This second kiss which he has sent me will cost me one or two
hours of my sleep, but I feel great because of it! I go to bed, not
to sleep, but to dream ...

The next two weeks pass marked with Word and Excel,
constant writing of messages on the phone and internet and an
increasing love towards the man I have not yet met in person.

And also with attempts to quit marijuana. I doubt that the conscientious policeman wants an addict for his girlfriend.

There was no problem in my arranging to attend the computer course in the afternoon, but I did not learn anything new. The four modules do not include the use of Power Point. If I had known the program in detail I would have not registered for it. But it helped me stay away from enticing intoxication. I sleep very little because my thinking about the new man in my life keeps me awake till early morning hours when in the yard my mother's Turkish cock sings his cliché song. It can really get on my nerves with its morning exciting shouting. There are some beautiful and less beautiful obligations waiting for me in the following days, before the tires of my red Thunder take me to the seaside. This time Zadar, the beautiful Dalmatia again. Tomorrow will be stressful: first, there is a final exam at the course, and then in the evening there is diploma award celebration to which I invited my parents and for moral support also Alex and Nina.

In the morning I successfully concluded the course, and I am driving with Odysseus on the back seats to Ljubljana. In one hour and a half I have to be at the Commercial Exhibition Hall where the diploma award will take place. It is the end of June and the temperatures are high, so my windows are open despite the high speed so that the atmosphere in the car is bearable. On the hanger above the window there are a short black skirt and a matching black blouse which I intend to be wearing for the award. I am not a type of woman who would spend a lot on clothes – I learnt that and similar feministic notes when I was writing my thesis – but I wanted to leave an impression for this particular occasion. I even bought a new sexy black shoes with high heels. And I also realized that inside of me there still lives a little girl who wants to impress her parents. Although I try to persuade myself that I do not care what they think about me, I want them to be proud of me today. If not because of the successfully completed long studies then because of my good looks. I want them to see that they have a beautiful and smart daughter.

"O shit!" I shout when the blouse suddenly flies through the window. What now?

I step on the brake and turn to the side. I am wearing an awful washed-out shirt of indefinable color. I cannot go there like this! I look back and slowly drive in reverse on the emergency lane towards a black spot which is lying on the overtaking lane, fortunately, on my side of the highway. I open the door, check the empty road and run to the blouse and even faster back to the car. It can still be worn; it is good that it is black. It is marked by road dirt but this can be sorted out.

A little bit of rubbing and after a minute it looks decent. I hope this is the last unpleasant incident with regard to the thesis. There were quite some of them – waiting for a secretary or mentor, waiting for the books, later eaten by the growing dog, a collapse of the computer and a blockage of the printer when there were deadlines and I was in a hurry, postponed official hours without a notice, expenses in the amount of 500 Euros because of lateness (not just mine) ... And now this? It is enough!!

Odysseus and I arrive at Ljubljana. I have to wait for Alex and Nina as always, my parents, in particular because of my mother's gift to be at the scene forty-five minutes earlier, are already there. We join them a few minutes before the beginning, so that I can walk down the blue carpet at normal peace.

While I am waiting in the line at the Commercial Exhibition Hall for my educational seal of the Faculty of Arts and listening to Luis Armstrong's song I finally feel the feelings of victory. The light of success was lit by Milena Zupancic[15] with her speech which she began with admitting that she had graduated in her late forties I hope my parents were listening carefully. I

---

[15]   Slovenian Actress

am also consoled by Simona Weiss[16] siting in student rows. So I am not the oldest graduate!

The group is singing *What a wonderful world,* and they are right, the world is really wonderful! We conclude the celebration with my parents by drinking champagne. I, Nina and Alex are happily continuing in Golden Boat pub.

In addition, a few hours later I am walking barefoot, pleasantly intoxicated, through warm night old city center of Ljubljana to my car. I adore this city, I adore my life! We are advancing! The foundation has been set .... I feel that I can do everything ... The world is lying under MY feet!

At least till the following day when I wake up in Alex's apartment with the biggest hungover ever.

"I won't drink alcohol again, never!!!" I mumble to the still figure on the adjacent bed. It was practical to sleep in his place and I know that he will be the one to take the dog out to satisfy his needs.

"I have heard this before, but let's say that I believe you. I am rather weak too so I'm joining the promise," I hear a thick voice. Too many cigarettes.

"Can you take Odysseus out? I feel sick."

"He'll have to wait for five minutes," he mumbles as the dog has noticed that we are awake and is already warbling happily, or how can one name the sound: ruuuuuuuuuu? The old practice of pretending to be sound asleep and trying not to move or show any signs of being awake, does not work in cases of alcoholic after-party. The only thing I can do is to move from my right hip to left hip and vice versa and walk to the bathroom, to the kitchen to fetch necessary liquid and back to bed where I am trying hard not to throw up what I drank to quench my thirst a minute ago.

The only bright spot of the tabby cat day is Matey's messages in which he is checking how it went yesterday and feels sorry because he could not join us due to the nature of his work.

---

[16]   Slovenian Singer

Which is alright, because I do not know how I would have felt in the company of him and my ex. It could have been a bit unpleasant. The messages end with kisses and hugs. My constant checking of the phone and its state during the month of message exchange shows that I am getting used to his presence. Every morning I receive a message which wishes me a good day and, if there is no message, I keep the phone in sight so that no sign of activity can escape me. I act the same when I am waiting for his reply. Actually I am doing what I hate in others! This is how the availability addiction looks like!

Alex pampers me the whole day. He is so kind as when we were a couple. I am worried though, because I am wondering if his good deeds are a sign of friendship or maybe he is expecting more. Our relationship ended ten months ago, but during alcoholic delirium after we had been celebrating my thesis defense till morning hours we ended between the sheets. A mistake, I knew it immediately. The next day I went home and we never talked about the 'slip'. I invited him to the award celebration because I appreciate the fact that he took care of all the expenses for six months when I was working hard on my thesis. I somehow still feel that I owe him.

Towards the evening I come to myself, so that we can talk.

"And what are the plans for the future, miss graduate?" is the first question referring to the future. "I know that the title 'miss' is not used any more. I remember that you taught me about that, but I cannot call you Mrs. because I feel that I'll make you older by ten, twenty years."

I smile at his words. "Yes, no panic. I have already sent a few applications, also to various publishing houses, mostly to Ljubljana and its surroundings, because I want to come back to populated areas. I want to deal with publishing but if I do not find anything until the autumn I will have to work at school. There will not be a problem with that because I have a diploma and experiences. I have worked with almost everything, I only need to obtain experience as a class head teacher and I have to pass a professional exam."

"Was there a response?"

"Not yet. I assume it is because of the distance. I don't know … I am not in a hurry to anywhere. I enjoy the fruits of the work of previous years," I cheerfully wink. "I've saved enough money for me and Odysseus to go to the seaside on Friday, this time to Sukosan[17], and we are going to stay there for ten days. Who needs a job?"

I do not dare mentioning the correspondence between me and Matey. Even to me I seem rather childish with teenage behavior towards the person I do not even know.

"How is it at your home? Any news from court?" His father is the owner of a striptease club where the main barmaid was his mother, that is, Alex's grandma, and the two of us spent quite some cheerful hours there. I liked to dance around the pole and tease Alex when the club was closed. At St. Martin I even danced there with the father-in-law. Not by the pole, we only performed a few jumpy moves, similar to polka – both of us very brave, lively and supple, with a few liters of young wine in our stomach and supported by a singing and dancing company with which we were blessing the new yield - that is, we were drinking - all night.

"Hm …," first he coughs but answers in a thick voice anyway, "the trial started in April … Yah, they are accused of organizing prostitution and trafficking. Last week they interrogated the person who turned my father in. He stated that he and Ivana were very good friends and that he took her out several times and found out how my father and grandma were exploiting her, restricting her movements, forcing her into prostitution and similar things."

"How are they restricting her movements? Why? Didn't he say that he took her out? That they went on trips?"

"Yes?!"

"Ivana is that one … a Moldavian girl who has been in the company for five years?"

"Yes, we were talking with her in the club." During the time of our relationship we worked in the casino and exchanged day

---

[17]   Sukosan – a town near Zadar in Croatia

for night, got up at six or seven in the afternoon – sometimes with the help of an alarm clock – and then worked till the dawn. When we were living in Kranj their club was the place to go during night hours when everything else was closed. We spent some time there and talked to the girls. Well, I communicated only with Ivana, the girls from Columbia did not speak Slovenian, and I felt that the other Moldavian women did not like me. Well, I was a girlfriend of "ready to marry" boss's son and presented an obstacle.

"Ivana has three children and a husband at home, doesn't she? They believe that she is working here as a maid?" I ask because her story got foggy in my memory. But I remember very well what she told me when I asked her why she was selling her body. A classic or cliché story narrates about thousands of kilometers away from home where the kids and husband are waiting and cannot survive without her money. They cannot get a job in their state, the family lives with her parents, in a little wooden house without heating and running water. Every additional euro means a lot and it also shortens the period of her absence from home. When they finish building their house she intends to go back and find a job nearby or whatever will enable them to survive. She assumed it would be selfish not to take advantage of additional, fast and easy money. And what a person does not know, in her case her husband and children, cannot hurt …

Alex nods.

"And she is supposed to be forced into prostitution by your father!"

"Uh … well … that's something … She herself gave a statement and negated all the accusations. All the girls are on our side."

"Well, sure! You know I know? Don't you?" I look at him sharply. He nods but I feel that the matter is troubling him. "I remember what relationship they had with your grandma. Her chicken soups when one of them was ill, abundant watering of flowers for additional income when your grandparents were absent, when they could have escaped if there was something true about the accusations. Besides, I find it hard to believe that your father could frighten them, they didn't give a shit about him. Do you remember how angry he was because they did not want to learn Slovenian? Free of charge. Or when they didn't want to lose weight?" Thinking of chubby dancers with the fat on wrong places on the body and the fifty years old man buying fitness equipment and his unfortunate yelling makes me laugh.

"I know, don't even talk about it!" Alex is irritated, he does not take the family prosecution so easily.

"The thing is that the guy fell in love with the woman and wanted her to leave her family in Moldavia and marry him. When she rejected him, he started doing fuck up in the club, so my father threw him out and forbade him to enter, and he turned them to the police. Ivana for not wanting to return him the borrowed money from him, and my father for ... you know."

I get serious too, the accusations are serious. "What now? What do the lawyers say?"

"All of it is a total nonsense. They say there is no sound foundation for accusations; they also want to confront the two police officers who collected the evidence with the girls they were with ... we'll see. The trial started last week."

"How are the girls?"

"During this time all of them returned home, but some of them came back. Including Ivana, Erica and Shirley. However, the pub is empty. I don't believe my father will find this profitable.

"And your ma?" I respected Alex's grandma – called the oldest madam in Slovenia by the media. We drank coffee together a few times and I found out a lot about her anything but easy life, in which she experienced a lot of things, but always put herself together and started living again. I saw her on TV, this year, when she spent a few weeks at women prison. She got older at least by a decade.

"She is ill. I took her to the clinic last time. They found something ... it seems to be cancer." Alex scratches his temples. He seems to be very hurt by the family situation although he tries to give an impression that it is not his business.

"Oh! Will everything be ok?"

"Probably. They don't know yet. It seems to be in early stages."

I don't know what to say, so I clumsily pet him on his hand. "Everything will work out, you'll see. We all know that they are not guilty, the justice will be proven, don't worry!" I assure him. "Ma will also recover, you know that she is made of steel. She won't be defeated by such trifle." If she escaped holding her child, from a violent man who followed her with a knife in his hand, survived a severe traffic accident and established a small bar imperium, she will survive that too.

"Will see," he growls, not assured by my words.

For a few minutes we shroud ourselves in silence, smoking. Then I lift up my wrinkled ass and drive towards my native Dolenjska.

FINALLY, the D day is here. The day when I meet Matey. An hour ago we talked on the phone for the first time and I must admit that his deep voice stirred my imagination about a police inspector even more. Slowly I drive towards BS pub and park my car at the most distant space so that I can look at other cars in the car park. Aha, there it is! A black Audi with privacy glass windows and Kranj license plate. Didn't he say that he comes from the surroundings of Ljubljana? Never mind, I like it!

In my wide white trousers and silk blouse which reveals most of the push up bra lifted breasts I graciously walk towards the bar. I am pretending to be busy with my handbag while scanning the guests with the corner of my eye. There in the corner I notice a head with a sign of boldness. It seems to correspond to the unclear photo in his profile. I step towards him and the head with a wide smile stands up, turned towards me. Uh, the guy is shorter than me. My mistake to have put on my retro sandals with few centimeters high soles.

"Hi! Matey?"

"Yes, hello my flower, finally we meet," he says while we are shaking hands, followed by a clumsy kiss on my cheek.

"How are you? Have you easily found the pub?" I feel embarrassed. I do not know what to say, where to look. His muscles are well visible in a tight Tom Taylor shirt; his lower part of the body is dressed in nice three-quarter-trousers which match his shirt and flip-flops. His eyes are gazing at me and my cleavage, his square face is decorated with a decisive nose and small pinky mouth. I have seen several more handsome guys, but the appearance is not what usually attracts me to men.

"Yes, of course. I am often on business trips here, the station is behind there."

"Ah, of course. Is there a lot of crime in Novo mesto?"

"As everywhere," is his unclear answer. "It seems a nice gesture to bring something for beautiful girl, so ...." He pulls a little dog-shaped cushion from the bag. "This is for you."

"Oh, thanks, you needn't have ... but thank you, really." I hold a little soft lump to myself and smile at him sincerely. "I will gladly hug it with my hands."

"So that you are not bored. Something hairy for taking to bed."

In spite of obvious smiles we do not know what else to say. Fortunately, I see Nina who I activated earlier to join us.

"Hi, Nina," she gives him her right hand while putting her telephone and all the stuff for free hand telephoning into her black bag with her left hand.

"Matey," he stands up like a gentleman.

"What is that?" Nina asks when she turns towards me and sees that I am holding an imitation of a puppy.

"A present for me. First come first served." I am smiling while explaining why she didn't get anything.

"Ok, ok, I'll have a white coffee then," she sovereignly tells Matey who stands up and goes to the bar to order the drinks, and the two of us take the opportunity to observe his firm butt and exchange remarks.

"He is shorter than me," I complain.

"What did you expect? Don't you know that the owners resemble their dogs? So, what does bulldog look like? Small and chubby," she says seriously. It is easy for her and her hundred and sixty centimeters.

"And what does Matey look like?"

"Short and chubby." We are laughing. We do not have time for more as Mr. Inspector is coming back. Nina takes over the conversation which now turns around dogs, bulldogs, their breeding and traits, and I am satisfied with shy flirting and my 'unintentional' touching his hand or leg. After one hour he asks if we are going to eat something. Because it is a hot June day I suggest going to a village inn which is known for its excellent food, fresh air and beautiful view of the green Krka river. Nina has to be at work today at Kostanjevica, so we decide that I travel with Matey and help him navigate, and she follows us in her car.

"Where did you park?" I ask pretending not to know what he is driving.

"There." He goes towards his black Audi. Obviously, I was right.

"Didn't you say that you come from the surroundings of Ljubljana? Kranj is not really the surroundings."

"If you take highway you come to Kranj in a few minutes. I'm not exactly from there." He is vague about the location of his residence. Again this feeling that he is hiding something, but I do not interrogate further.

He opens it with a remote and I comfortably sit on the beige seat. I like traveling like a lady, finally, in a good car and not in some old or rusty vehicle, as I am used to. I ask him about his work. I cannot help being curious about his job, and his mysteriousness adds power to my curiosity.

"What do the police have to deal with most? So, that you have to come to Novo mesto?"

"At the moment we are mostly dealing with drugs and human trafficking." I turn to the window and hope that I have not blushed since I got really hot.

"I read something about a large shipment of marijuana that you seized, yes," I mumble but do not want to continue on such a slippery terrain. I am sure that our views of the benefits of this plant differ significantly.

"The largest activity is with people trafficking," he ignores my comment. "We found two big nests, one in Gorenjska and another here in your region." I look through the window again. It is still hot.

"The owners brought the girls from abroad, promising them high salaries and forced them into prostitution in their striptease clubs."

"And how far are the cases?" I ask with a thick voice.

"It's unwinding slowly. In Novo mesto the thing is still in the investigation phase while in Gorenjska it is at court."

"Yes, I heard, I was reading about it too. It is one of the main pieces of news in daily 'informative' program. But ... you see ..." I stop. Shall I tell him?

"Hmm ... I know the family from Gorenjska and I doubt that somebody there forced anybody into anything. Maybe vice versa."

He turns to me with widely open eyes, obviously surprised. "How do you know the family?

"One year ago I dated their son," I reply and look at him with my innocent eyes.

"With their son? How? He's still too young for dating." He is talking about Alex's half-brother. Obviously our police are not up to date.

"Yes, hm, ... Alex does not go by his father's surname, his mother divorced him years ago. He does not have anything to do with it. He is living in Ljubljana. Well, at that time we were living together, he is working at a casino and is not interested in his father's business, not a bit." I hurry with the explanation so that Alex will not have any problems. Matey takes his eyes off the road too often for me to feel safe, and looks at me in disbelief.

"We used to drink at that club which I like very much, by the way," I smile. "I met the girls and I really don't believe that the old man forced anybody into anything. Maybe vice versa! Ok, it's true that I wasn't on the scene when the fuck room was established," I become directly vulgar, "but Alex explained to me that the girls wanted it and that his grandmother and father were against it. He did not have a choice, either that, or they were selling their bodies in the woods by the car park."

Matey's glare shows that he does not believe me, so I continue. "Really! You must know that he is an ex-cop? Well, according to my information both grandmother and father objected to the girl's misbehavior. They wanted it. I myself talked with one of them and she said that that meant survival for her. She thinks about a hungry child of hers and makes a decision. She knows that she is a thousand kilometers away from her home and she makes a decision. Is this so difficult to understand? I am happy that I do not have to do something like that which does not mean that I wouldn't be in a similar situation." Maybe I am too sincere. Matey does not say a word and I continue. "The Columbian girl's behavior towards the old man was awful. When he asked them to learn the Slovenian language they rejected. Neither English nor Slovenian, the guests should learn Spanish, they said."

Well, body language has won over the language barriers, the attractive, later also well-fed, girls were surrounded by drooling guys who gladly took up learning Spanish.

"I was there when he ordered Shirley to clean the toilet. She ignored him and went on as that he hadn't said anything. How and with what could such a person scare the 'poor' girls'? The women from Moldavia were more polite, they called the grandma Mami. Would you call somebody Mami if she exploited or locked you?"

"Hm ..." the police officer seems unconvinced. "Well ... it will come out ... work out ..."

"Sure."

After silence the conversation about the topic is over. I do not dare to add anything else. I prefer to start a more neutral topic. "Where will you go on vacation this year?"

"In July I and my friends are going sailing on the Croatian coast. I can hardly wait. Fourteen days of total disconnection."

"Wau, good for you," I would go too. "How many of you? Only guys?"

"Yes, eight true men. There will be laughs ... We have known each other since faculty and every year we go somewhere alone, without our better halves or families."

"Where are you going to sail?"

"We start at Krk, then Losinj, continue towards Dalmatia, the Kornati and back towards Kvarner."

"I've never been sailing," I sigh, "It's interesting, isn't it?"

"Yes, we constantly do something. I don't like lying all day, I like to be active so such a holiday is my cup of tea. What about you?"

"On Monday I and my dog are leaving for Sukosan. My brother owns a camper there, so we are going to drive there and spend some time alone."

"Won't you be bored?"

"Not really. A few years ago my colleague, with who I was supposed to go there, let me down. So I went alone for the first time and realized that it was much better to enjoy alone at the seaside than to listen to nonsense which does not interest you, try to adapt and similar things. In this way I feel free and relaxed. If I am bored I will visit Murter where I was in the spring and I have a friend there, and my friends are going to visit me at the weekend, so no panic."

"Excellent, a brave young lady. How many kilometers is to Sukusan?"

"About three hundred. From the border on there is a freeway, so I switch on loud music, light a cigarette and step on the accelerator. I enjoy driving, really."

"I believe you and I envy you a little," he smiles and I feel encouraged to invite him to come with me.

"If you have time, you can join me. I would like a company."

"Well, I could have some time off, but at the weekend." He is thinking and looks at me once more. "Are you sure?"

"Yeees, we can leave on Friday," in three days, "there is nobody there yet."

"You know I would really like to go … I will ask at work if I can get a few days off. This would be great." He is rolling his eyes thoughtfully. "A good idea, really, I'll let you know tomorrow, ok?"

"Ok, boss."

We arrive and park the car. Nina is not there so we stay at the car park for a while. I cannot wait anymore, so I move closer to him.

"Together at the seaside over the weekend? Wouldn't that be nice?" I get closer to him seductively and hold his hand.

"Yes, it would be nice." He accepts the invitation and kisses me. Finally! I have been waiting for this the whole afternoon, that is, the whole month. In spite of shortness, boldness and secrecy he attracts me. The kiss is wet, long, deep, his hands quickly end up on my butt and it seems totally acceptable to me. Nina arrives to the car park, so we unglue from each other and we go to the restaurant.

Friday brings the freshness of the Dalmatian rhythm. Matey has been checking everyday if I am still in for the adventure, we have been in touch all the time. It seems that he does not have reliable people around him if he feels the need to constantly check up on me. Everything has worked out well. At this very minute we both arrived by our cars at the camp and we are getting ready to go for a walk with Odysseus. When I finally breathe the sea, I become a different person.

What shall I do with my swimming suit? I do not care, the upper part flies away while I am observing Matey with the corner of my eye and I can see that he likes my gesture.

After refreshing swimming we leave for the buffet close by. Dressed only in our swimming suits we are not permitted to enter the first one. In this heat at thirty degrees we do not approve of wearing uncomfortable T-shirts. We have arrived here for freedom, so we continue walking to the next pizzeria where they do not have any judgmental thoughts about swimming suits.

"Your idea for me to join you was excellent."

"Well, you see. A little time from work and obligations have never caused any harm to anybody."

"Uh! Good, that you've reminded me. I have to check how they are doing without me." He is looking for a phone in the pocket of his shorts.

The following minutes are devoted to his co-workers and a few short phrases regarding the importance, accuracy and discipline. The boss seems to have everything under control.

"Hey, what was really happening with that girl last month?" I jump to the opportunity and interrogate about the event that shook the Slovenian media public. He would know what is going on, I do not trust the media at all. "The Roma were believed to have raped her in the school toilet and the headmistress decisively rejects the news?"

Matey grimaces and nods his head, of course, he knows what I am talking about. "Hm, this is an unfinished story ...," he says and shrouds himself in silence. He seems to be thinking whether or not he can trust me.

"You know, what you tell me and what happens here, stays here, ok?"

"Ok."

He does not seem to be convinced by my words and remains silent, so I continue. "A few weeks they were talking about this every day, and then over the night everything quieted down. That is why I am interested. There were complaints regarding the work carried out by the school and by the police, not to mention the new hunt against the Roma. Forums on the topic of gypsies are blooming on the internet."

»Ahm ...«

"So, what happened? Did the Roma boys really rape the 12-year old girl in the toilet, and she confessed to her relative's girlfriend after a few days? The police had not reacted in the right way if the rapists attacked her cousin too?" I summarize what I heard.

"It was revealed that there were more rapes ...," he starts explaining. "But they were not caused at the school but in the family circle."

"OH!" Devastated I quickly light another cigarette although I have put the previous one out a few moments ago.

Matey lights his cigarette too. "The case is still under the investigation, but for now it seems that somebody from the family is guilty though the girl was afraid to admit it."

"Why they do not say anything in the media about it, why don't they bark on Channel A? Why doesn't somebody clear the name of the school and the Roma? Again, they are guilty of everything."

"Hm."

"I found it interesting when the news disappeared over the night, but before that there had been everyday accusations against the most vulnerable and all possible institutions. Awful! I don't believe anybody any more!"

"This is how it is here … in the eyes of the public, those people who are innocent become guilty ones."

He caresses my naked leg. "It will work out. We are not here to be solving problems."

He is right. I lean forward and kiss him. "Mmm, you're sweet."

"You too. You don't even know how much."

While we are chatting about the weather and sea sports we drink up the rest of the ice tea and then move towards the camper. It was enough of shocking revelations for some time.

In the evening we go to the restaurant for dinner. I order calamari stuffed with shrimp, and a glass of red wine. Matey affords gnocchi with lamb and water. Rarely does he drink alcohol. Although he is on vacation he wants his head to be sober. I notice how he is estimating the entire room and observing the guests, so I direct the conversation again to his job.

"Have you developed any professional deformation? Always on the guard?" I smile at him.

"Yes," he says. "I always want to know what is happening around me."

"What makes you nervous at your work?"

He is thinking. "Domestic violence … Women! I get really pissed off when they call the police because their husbands are beating them, and then they step on their side and even defend them. You can't believe what GEESE women can be!"

Again I feel hot. "And what do you do in such cases?"

71

"Because the most such "abused" women," he beckons with his finger, "go back to their husband, the torturer, nobody files a lawsuit. Only good beating would help."

"Really?" I lift my eyebrows in surprise. "Have you already beaten a wildcat?

"I tell you that anything else is a lost cause. The only thing that works is thorough beating with a threat of what will happen if we come again. Of course, the women who were beaten before are outraged by such intervention and reject it even more than their men. And then they threaten to file a lawsuit against us who have come to help them."

"You know, it is difficult," I say and feel a brook of sweat flowing down my spine even though the restaurant is air conditioned. "It is difficult to oppose the man you love … Regardless of how bad he is treating you."

"Then they should stop calling us and let the men beat them to death." He rejects my statement and puts a piece of lamb into his mouth.

"Mmm … it is not so easy …," I can hardly speak. "Believe me that they do this when they really don't know what else to do … I am speaking from my experience," I mumble silently, so that my words can be hardly heard.

Matey lifts his eyes from his plate and starts staring at me.

"I persisted till court, but the situation before the judge, interrogation and explanation … were one of the most difficult things I had done in my life.

"I beg your pardon?" Matey is looking at me with the eyes which reflect disbelief and amazement, and I am thinking in confusion whether or not to tell him the story which is still painful as I can feel a lump in my throat and a burning feeling in my eyes.

"I felt unbelievably stupid … I was ashamed … I was aware what chicken I was, but I could not help myself." My voice is thick, the lump in my throat is getting bigger and my eyes are roaming around the room. I cannot look him in his eyes, I still feel the humiliation of everything that happened.

"What happened?"

I gather some courage to look him into his eyes. And then I look down again. "My ex-boyfriend stopped me in the street, pulled me out of my car ... poured some gas over me to burn me ... He was on trial for attempted murder and unlawful deprivation of freedom, and because he had taken my mobile phone and car keys also for a theft ..." I disclose the information with a thick voice and many interruptions. "He was sentenced to two years of suspended sentence for unlawful deprivation of freedom, because there were two witnesses. Two men saw him dragging me from my car and pushing me into his car, and the rest of the story ... they didn't believe me."

Why is it difficult for me to talk about it? Why this sense of shame and guilt?

"When did that happen?"

"Five years ago."

"You are still young ..." He puts his hand on my palm. "It's good that you got out of it so early."

"Yes it's over, let's talk about something else. We are at the seaside, it's summer ..." I say pretending to be excited and pour all the content from my glass into my throat. I don't want to admit to him – or to myself – that I still feel like a pile of shit.

Matey agrees and the communication continues in more peaceful waters, about sports and reflexive massage which he is good at. Of course, I 'apply' for one. We eat our dinner slowly and then, in the company of my dog, we set off towards the beach. The camper is located by the gravel bay which we use for a nice walk in the moonlight. The dog is happily sniffing around and I am holding my companion under his arm. We are hugging a little, kissing a little, almost without talking ... I feel great and I do not care whether or not the sense of peacefulness has been created with the help of alcoholic vapors.

At four o'clock in the morning I give up my sleep and leave the bed with hot Matey's body next to me. I sit in front of the camper. I cannot sleep, my mind is attacked by a swarm of mosquitoes. They are stinging into different memories and I am scratching them till bleeding.

His pleasant massage did not help me relax and expected sex did not happen. And that is ok. I sit down on the chair, looking at the sea and the sheen of public light and continue scratching through my past memories. I couldn't admit to him that I smoke grass, which, however, I was trying to quit for two weeks, but gave up the night before the diploma award, that is why I did not take a joint before going to bed.

I carefully roll a narrow joint on the table while keeping an ear on gentle snoring coming from the bed. I do not want him to get me at the forbidden activity.

Finally I light it and inhale in delight. Tonight's mosquitoes are flying in the images of my ex-boyfriends.

So, what can I expect from love, based on my own experiences?

My ex-boyfriend No. 1 was delivered to me by the primary school, and he brought the first experience of holding hands, the first kiss on my cheek, then on my mouth, the first French kiss. I smile when I remember how I could not sleep because of the excitement over new touching although I felt awful having his tongue in my mouth and I accused him in my diary that he made me into an ordinary slut. He was four years older, I was in love with him through the whole primary school, our romance was continuing on and off through higher years of the primary school. We met in the evenings. He arrived on his red automatic motorcycle usually from a pub and was with me for an hour or two, hugging me on the bench by the woods. Dates usually stopped in autumn and continued in spring. He used to say that winter was not suitable for love – he must have had in mind sitting on cold benches. Of course, he had many other girlfriends beside me. My mother asked me if I did not have any self-respect to be dating a guy who runs after every female skirt. *No, mother, I don't*. The last date was marked by his caressing my breasts and my hint that he could caress me between my legs. He rejected my offer and never dated me again.

Getting over him was difficult and even in my first years of dating Gal I used to think about him. Thinking about it now I realize that it is good that he rejected me at the time, for thirteen years later he is playing the role of a scruffy unemployed village drunkard who is wandering around, mostly without the roof over his head – if we take out the years of his staying at the psychiatric institution. Recently I have found out that during our 'friendship' his male wealth was not ok – till his middle twenties he was not able to use it in bed. He seems to have had a similar difficulty as the French King responsible for French Revolution.

The next bomb in the image of a man was brought to me in the first year of the high school by Gal – my ex-boyfriend No. 2, the biggest rascal in our small town. The mothers used to warn their daughters about him. Mistrust and blaming by my parents, that I smoke and drink and the limitation of my freedom encouraged my rebellious nature and I gladly started dating him. I thought it would only be a short romance to get even with my parents, but it continued for the following seven years. My family was devastated at my choice. They expected their daughter to have different friends, for she was a good girl, participating at all competitions, who was a chess champion in the municipality, who led school performances, who practiced the piano and played the organs at church concerts, and sang in two choirs – one of them was a church choir. They took measures and I had to spend most of the evenings at weekends at home in my room, until I was 17. While other school mates partied at various pubs and discoes I was at home, alone.

I rebelled only once, at the beginning. The first week when I and Gal started dating I escaped through the window and joined my school mate who was driven to the disco by her father. We didn't invite Gal and there I met a ten years older man whose name I do not remember. But I do remember his black golf, my begging, fighting, and the pain when my virginity was lost. I could never stand for myself and be assertive when saying 'no'. How my parents learnt about the event, that I do not know. But the following evening me and my father were crying and my mother was so disappointed that the only thing I got from her was her blameful shouting.

What followed was even stricter supervision and attempts of bribe with clothes and promises of a car for my eighteenth birthday, but I did not give in. At the end of the first school year I made a mistake and relied on my brother hoping he would stick with me. Encouraged that at least somebody understood me I lied where I had been, but my brother told on me to my parents. Consequently, I was grounded in the house for almost entire summer holidays.

When they took my freedom away I felt like they had taken everything from me, but I persisted in the relationship. Gal was an excellent company and he was the only one who understood who I was. I, and not a good and exemplary girl, who wants to please everybody. I made up for drinking, socializing and doing teenage nonsense during school weeks when we skipped school, stole a liter of wine and got drunk before catching a bus home. I became the master of excuses, covering, and lying. As did he was doing. It proved that he had been lying for years about which school he was attending and which year. I was convinced that he was attending the third year of Electro orientation, but one wine evening between vineyard houses, when he slapped me, I realized that he still hadn't passed the second year and enrolled into a three-year Engineering school to become a car mechanic – that had been his wish since he was a child, but his parents were too ambitious. As all other lie I forgave him that one too.

The relationship became falling apart when I started my studies. I was growing and he was stagnating in the same environment, with the same to-be-good-for-nothing friends who had not managed to graduate from high school, were unemployed, and were dealing with small frauds which started to get more serious. As far as he was regarded as a local one-to-blame, he actually started changing into one. Slapping was not enough, he did not care what others thought about him and actually started doing the things which he was accused for.

Besides, he started being more and more violent towards me. Occasional grabbing and pushing against the wall changed into strangling and serious beating. We were together, then apart, then together again, separated again, and the periods of separation became longer and longer. The last New Year eve together was spent in Budapest where he was, encouraged by large quantities of alcohol, strangling me for so long that I, leaning against the wall, closed my eyes and decided to let myself die. When he started shouting at me to open my eyes which were only slightly closed, I came back. He let go of my throat, so I fell on the ground because the legs could not carry me anymore. Then, instead of me, he broke the door and a window of the hostel we were staying at.

But that was not enough for me. I forgave him as I did the digging out the hole into which he planned to bury me after he would kill me. His following attempt was when he dragged me into his room and while I was crying on his bed, he was leaning against the door and sharpening his knife. My answer to his question where to stab me was: *Into my heart. As I don't feel anything anymore*. My friends knew what was going on but did not want to interfere. Once Ema jumped between us when we were fighting under the influence of alcohol, but he pushed her so powerfully that she fell down the stairs.

It was my decision to stay with him and I did not tell anybody about the happenings. The bruises were visible only once. During the business New Year celebration in a vineyard house I was jealous because he was dancing with his co-worker, but he never wanted to dance with me. His answer was his fist into my face and in few minutes I was lying on the floor almost naked as he had torn my sweater from my body. He kicked me strongly, several times, then he left the cellar where at the time we were conveniently alone. Feeling lost I got up, put on my winter jacket which was lying on the bench and ran out. I headed towards the town. I had no idea if I would succeed walking more than ten kilometers, but it did not matter. I had to run away. It was not long when he drove past me, pulled me into his car and took me to his home, where he ordered me to get undressed as we were going to bed. I was crying and silently obeyed him and lay by his side. After ten minutes he was snoring but I was waiting for another hour before I had courage to get up and put my clothes on. I looked towards the bed and saw his glassy eyes staring at me. Without words I put away my trousers and lay by his side again. Then I waited two hours before I carried out my second attempt. I slinked away in my underwear to Renault five which was parked in front of the house. The car was bought by him and registered at my name. The next morning I had breakfast with my parents, wearing heavy makeup, and I spent the whole day wearing the 'mask'. Nobody noticed or commented the bruise on my eye and a broken lip.

I took revenge in a way that I once slept with his best 'friend', the second time with a police officer, smooching with his acquaintances and former co-workers. But I had never flirted with them, for my even greater psychological poverty it was enough to hear their understanding and comforting words and feel their touches which wanted more and more … His pouring the gas over me a few months later was the final act of our seven-year game.

Less than a month after a grotesque happening Jan entered the scene – my ex-boyfriend No. 3. When I was working as a waitress at the buffet at the gas station, lost almost ten kilograms and started increasing my self-esteem. I realized why all waitresses think that they are beautiful. Beauty compliments were showering at me, the highest value was ascribed to one who claimed that I was a very talkative and pretty girl. Even the owner drinking with his rather intoxicated friend generously recommended that I should take advantage of my attributes – read: Show your breasts. The 22-year old girl who did not dare to greet and talk with an acquaintance because she taught that she was too fat, too ugly and too stupid for anybody to wish to deal with her, such allusion caused the breakthrough in her thinking and attitude.

I was warned to leave Jan alone when he came to the bar with his friends. If anything went wrong – ashtrays would fly towards the bar at such occasions – I was supposed to call security guard. Tall, strong, aggressive, unemployed, without a high school diploma, but it did not bother me. He had the most beautiful eyes I had ever seen and I fell in love with them at first sight.

Powerfully. Totally. Already when he touched and kissed me for the first time I longed for the confirmation of love. We waited for a week and the first "I love you" came in two weeks. We both were blooming, finally I felt safe and loved. There were no ashtrays flying across the pub, nobody was rude to me, everyone paid for their drinks. Even Gal did not break bottles as it had happened before. People who knew us could not believe how much we had changed. In particular he. He got a job and stopped everyday fighting at village pubs. I worked mostly in the afternoon, so we could meet after my work. After a year of abstinence I started smoking grass with him. So, first we smoked, than had sex, and I came home early the following morning. One morning my mother sat on my bed, worried about my roaming during the night, and asked me if I was selling myself. *Ough Mum, why do you have such a nice opinion about me?*

In the autumn when I returned to Ljubljana to study – I succeeded to enroll into the third year after I had repeated the second one and had a break – he returned to his old way and jealousy outbursts started. He was convinced that I did not get over Gal and that I was only using him to forget my ex. He was jealous at his friends who I was accused to be flirting with. And even at my kitten which I brought to create a mini family. I could not think about a bigger nonsense as I was totally addicted with him.

I was dying when I was not able to see him for two days in a row, or when he preferred to drink with friends than be with me. His wandering was acceptable while my friends were all sluts and my *offering myself to horny dicks in pubs* was totally unacceptable. I was forbidden to wear short skirts even when I wanted to wear one for him. He was constantly checking up on me when I was studying in Ljubljana. Throgh the whole year of our relationship my body suffered from angina and urinary tract inflammation, so that I had to take antibiotics. I had to have sex with him whenever he wanted it, otherwise he was convinced that I had it with somebody else. His 'work' was done so well that I suffered great pain till our next date.

Once I received a phone call from his friend who claimed to be Blaz whom I supposedly had met at a party in Ljubljana. Of course, I had never been at a party, so I was angry at Jan for doing such imputation. It could have been better if I had played to the end and convinced him that he had dialed a wrong number – maybe then he would have believed me – but I just replied gruffly to stop checking up on me and that I was fed up with it.

I had no life any more. After the lessons at the faculty I returned to my little room at an old lady's house who did not allow visits. I did not have any friends. At weekends I drove from Ljubljana to Jan's vineyard house where we spent every weekend in isolation. I did not have any money, he did not take me for coffee here and then it happened that a friend of his would visit us. I got pregnant after two months, and had an abortion, after six months of the relationship I was totally exhausted.

Well, at least I had lost almost ten kilograms, but I still was not thin enough for him - I had cellulite, my pussy looked as a tram would have driven across it and I should have been embarrassed at how I looked like down there. Of course the jealous attacks were joined by one which was the most efficient and the most frequent: I had killed his child. I could not assure him that he presented the whole my world and that I was not his mother who cheated on her husband, an alcoholic. All accusations, explanations, bagging were always followed by rude, painful sex.

Soon an old story repeated itself. I was careful which words I was using, I thought carefully about my every move, I apologized for every minute spent without him, but pushing and strangling started again. I know that I was also to blame, but an offended Scorpio strikes where it hurts the most. If he was going around pubs and I was supposed to be waiting for him at home, I allowed myself to be taken for a drink, by my male subjects from my past, what was enough for a jealous outburst – but the truth was I would rather have a part of my body cut off than allow somebody else to touch me, except my obsession.

This caused the separation. During that academic year I had passed 16 exams and I wanted to celebrate the enrollment into the fourth year but that afternoon he did not return my call. In the evening I drove to his place and seeing the parked car I knew he was at home, but he did not respond to my knocking. For almost one hour I was standing there, knocking on the door, calling him and begging, so finally the door opened. He had been sleeping. I instantly smelled alcohol and noticed the ashtray on the table, with some grass butts and I realized that I could not live like that anymore.

I was picking up my things, crying, and Jan got back to his bed and did not pay any attention to me. He said that he did not care if he would not see me ever again. So I left. But my departure did not bring the end. Every time he called me I modestly went back to him so he could have me and then dismiss me. This lasted for half a year. The last evening spent at his home was on 13 February. I came in the evening. After one hour of violence which bought me his closeness I started to feel pain in my throat. After two hours when he was sleeping and I still could not leave him I was not able to talk. When I came home in the middle of the night I had high temperature and the following day I stayed in bed due to angina. So I spent Valentine's day, day when the whole world celebrates love, in my bed, crying. I did not receive any message or call which would show me that somebody cares for me. Only my mother yelled at me that I should be studying.

After one year of silence I met Alex, but I had not got over Jan. The day I left him, I called him and we met. We continued where we had stopped. When he felt like it he called me and I ran into his bed. Metaphorically, because he would not let me in his parent's vineyard house where he still lived. I was looking for love in dirty rooms of surrounding private hotels. We met once a month for the period of six months. According to his words he did not have either time or will for a serious relationship but he prohibited me from seeing somebody else. He does not share. *Whom? What?*

I had enough of humiliation only when he came to me drunk and intended to hit Odysseus. It was the first time that I did not beg him but I yelled at him. He was surprised but would not leave. He was sleeping for three hours with the dog on his chest while I was drinking the wine. After I had finished the whole bottle I woke him up, dismissed him, and the silence followed again ...

It started dawning and I am still ruminating over old stuff which does not want to be forgotten. What is wrong with me?? Why am I looking for men who are on their way down? The men who do not even see me? Those who tear me to pieces? Do I not deserve at least respect if not love? Are my demands so impossible?

"Hi," I was surprised at the voice behind my back. "What are you doing? Why aren't you sleeping?"

"I can't sleep so I rather came out than turn and toss in the bed and wake you up," I say to a blinking Matey. He obviously does not notice the joint in the ashtray.

"Are you ok? Is there something wrong?"

"Nothing ... I often suffer from insomnia, so I fall asleep at dawn," I admit partial truth.

"Ayay, tell me, what is bothering you? You seem to be experiencing a kind of trauma." He slowly sits down at on the chair opposite mine and takes my hand. He is probably thinking about the court case.

"Which one? There are several of them." I smile at him. "No panic, really! I'm ok. I'm going to the rest room and then I'm coming to bed."

I go to the rest room and postpone my return for I do not want police interrogation. When I come back, he holds me tight and although the atmosphere got warmer, the muscular arms calm me down and I soon fall asleep.

I am awaken by his fingers caressing my breasts, hips, legs, so I am purring from delight. He turns me towards himself, kisses me gently on my lips, then my neck, he is getting lower until he reaches my groin. He lifts his body again and pushes it into my inwardness. After a long time I am feeling something inside me and although I am not taken into heights by the waves of delight, I am enjoying it.

"I couldn't hold back," he says when we are lying next to each other, tired out. "You were so beautiful."

I smile at him. Although I did not reach an orgasm, I am satisfied. I like his body, his movements, and I like his attention the best because I am not used to it.

"Would the lady like breakfast in bed?"

"Unfortunately, it won't work." I smile and point to Odysseus who is impatiently jumping by the bed. "The dog is demanding his walk so let's hit the road."

"Yes, you're right." He caresses the dog. "I'm going to the grocery. Where is it?" I explain the direction and we leave the wrinkled and sweaty sheets together.

The afternoon brings the burning sun and the temperatures over 30 degrees so there is nothing else to do except lie on the beach in the shadow of pines. Matey is incredibly gentle, he is caressing and kissing me all the time so that I feel fantastic, but I feel that the yesterday's conversation at dinner is still bothering him, and finally, he brings out the burning topic.

"What was happening as the case had to be brought to the court? I am interested and I can find out in any case. I can get the minutes of the trial."

I remain silent for a few seconds. I do not gather enough courage to start talking about it, but later, I swallow the lump in my throat, and while staring at the sea I start talking.

"We'd been together for seven years and when we finally separated he got a little crazy. He often waited for me in the middle of the night on my way home, stopped his car in front of mine so I could not pass and threatened me. Well, that time he did it in the town and because I did not want to go with him he took a gas can out of the boot and calmly asked me which I wanted him to burn first, me or my car. We were quarrelling and pushing each other so gas was spilt over me and then he dragged me into his car and drove around the town."

Matey is shaking his head, he must have heard about similar stories.

"First he took me to his place and called his uncle and aunt who he lived with and with who we had good relations. They liked me. He was calling me names, bitch and slut, and that I did not deserve to be living. Because he did not get any support from them he took me to the café where we used to spend a lot of time and there were his and my friends sitting at the bar. When I mentioned what was going on and asked also the waitress to call the police nobody took me seriously. They were used to our constant fighting. And they knew that I got it on my pussy from time to time, too," I cynically add and light a cigarette before I continue.

"At that time I really felt endangered, he did not let me go to the toilet because he was afraid I would escape. He kept asking me how I felt the last evening of my life and assuring me that I would got what I deserved. I did not go with him to another pub. As I was rather drunk from the afternoon drinking, and in the previous pub he paid for three dcl of wine with cola which of course I did not reject. I protested and said that I would wait for him in the car. He sat a few meters away from the car, on the terrace of the pub ... and ... At that moment something happened in me. I had enough. I jumped out of the car and started running away. The police station was on the other side of the road and without looking left or right I ran towards it. Of course he caught me, grabbed me from behind by my hair and pulled me back. Fortunately, there were two strangers close by who interfered so I managed to escape. To the station, but he came there too. He stopped only when the police officer who was standing behind the reception desk petted his handgun holster."

I stop and Matey does not say anything.

"It is interesting that I saw the same police officer at the bar where I was working the previous day and I asked him if he was a police officer. I wanted to ask him what to do because of constant threatening and breaking in the pub where I was working. He negated.

"Obviously he was not interested in helping anybody." Matey is angry and spits on the floor. "What happened then?"

"I spent the following three hours at the station because except the goalkeeper there was no one who could write the report. Then I was taken home by a police car, and the following day a criminologist came and wrote the report."

"What about the guy?"

"They searched his apartment, found the gun which he used to threaten me and even fired at me at one of night stoppings when I refused to stop my car. They also took a big knife and the following day they called me to the station where he was present too so that he could return all my stuff, and at the end we shook our hands, because that was the criminologist's wish." I conclude with a sour smile.

"And the problem was solved for them?"

"Yah … after six months we met at court." I do not dare admit that in the meantime I and Gal went for a cup of coffee quite a few times. We discussed the incident after a few days because I did not want to live in fear and drive home around the town which would take me 20 kilometers more. He was sorry and he invited me to the seaside which I cannot reject, never. I did not even resent the incident but after several weeks when I was in the relationship with Jan, he stopped me again in the middle of the night. Because of this and because of Jan's threatening that he would kill him if I did not persist – his threats were more serious – I went to the court. The story got even more grotesque when a year later he offered to defend me before my ex-boyfriend No. 3 with whom I had separated. I sensed that Jan's hidden anger was much more dangerous that his loud barking. But today I do not talk about this. It's awful what I can get into! *Surely, something must be wrong with you!*

Because I feel anxious I become courageous and announce that I will roll a joint. He is surprised but says that it does not bother him.

"Will you turn me in?" I smile at him.

"Why would I? My best friend smokes. I can say I know a lot of people who smoke. If you need it … go ahead …"

"I don't really need it … I'm not addicted. I just enjoy it, it relaxes me."

I roll one and light it.

I smoke in silence and when the grass has sung its song, he lies by my side, hugs me and whispers:

"Everything is ok."

"I know," I reply and sit comfortably in the shelter of his firm body. "I'll take a nap."

"You do. I'm guarding you."

To make the idyll perfect, Odysseus jumps into the hug so that now I am lying in a loving sandwich and I spend the rest of the afternoon sleeping.

In the evening we are getting ready to go to the pizzeria behind the corner when Matey receives a phone message. He does not seem to be happy about it as he angrily says something and responds to it with grimaced forehead. Then he informs me about the unpleasant news. "I'll have to leave tomorrow early in the morning."

"Really?" I am disappointed. I thought we had another whole day for ourselves. "When?"

"I'd better leave in the morning to avoid heavy Sunday traffic."

"All right," I try to sound as that I do not care but I feel that my sadness can be smelled all the way to Ljubljana.

"We still have the whole evening and the whole night," he says gently. He must have noticed my reaction.

Sunday morning brings disappointment. He does not seem to feel with his whole heart about me, for he cannot stay at least till the morning coffee. I do not understand why his departure makes me so sad. It is not possible to connect with somebody so quickly, is it?

At half past six in the morning he is waving from his car and I can hardly avoid crying. I go back to bed where I stay till noon when I am forced out of it by dry heat. I feel that something is wrong with my throat but nevertheless I leave for the beach.

In the evening I cannot swallow anything, not even saliva, and it is clear to me that my 'favorite' illness has visited me again - angina – which I am used to having in winter months but not in summer. Gurgling salt and vinegar, lemon juice … nothing helps, I'll need to visit the doctor tomorrow. And for the first time in my life I have not settle my health insurance. How convenient.

My following days are spent in bed, surrounded by mugs of tea, lemonade, antibiotics, and pills for reducing temperature or pain. Who says it is bad to be ill at the seaside? It is great! You do not have to wait long hours at the doctor's, because there are no patients, you do not feel bad when moving from one deckchair to another as you need to rest, you do not go to the beach, because you should avoid the sun, but you succumb to perfect laziness. You do not need drugs or alcohol either, dizziness in your head and the feeling of intoxication are caused by the body temperature itself.

Hours pass quickly as I am reading, watching movies on my lap top, taking shorter walks with my dog, and of course reading Matey's messages expressing how great it was to be with me, how he misses me and how bad he felt when he had to leave, and other sweetened phrases that reach and warm my heart.

On Wednesday I find a pub which has access to the internet. It is rather expensive, one hour is 60 Kunas, around 5 Euros, but a long confession to my police inspector is worth it. I am in love, I feel as a 15-year old teenager. I like it and I want him to know it.

My Dalmatian friend from Murter must have sensed that I am somewhere close as he sends me a message in which he is asking me when I plan to visit him. I do not feel like visiting him; my whole attention is oriented towards another man although physically he is not near me.

It is not until Thursday that I set off to the beach again. Although there is a nice bay across the street, I drive with my dog a few kilometers out of the town to the beach hidden among pines. Our little space on the fine sand in the shadow of a green and fragrant pine is waiting for us. 50 meters left or right I do not see anybody so I take off the cloth which happens to be the braw of my swimming suit and I lie down on the mat covered by a towel.

After one hour, a few meters away from us, a yellow rubber boat anchors. It has been circling around for the last fifteen minutes along the beach. A dark young man steps out of it and is piddling around the boat for a few minutes before he turns and walks towards me.

"Hi, do you have a cigarette? Can I have one?" I hear an introductory greeting.

"Yes, I do. You can have one, here you are," I replay because I happen to be a very kind person, and it was impossible to hide a white Marlboro cigarette box lying next to my towel.

"Thanks. Where are you from?" It seems that the guy did not come only to get a cigarette because he sits next to the towel. Close to me. Too close.

"From Slovenia, Novo mesto. And you?"

"I live there," he points to the camp in the distance. "Are you here alone?"

"I'm not alone, I have my dog." I point to Odysseus who is sniffing around the bushes.

"Well, that's not the same. You need a male company," he soon discloses the reason of his visit.

"I don't need it, I'm enjoying like this," I reject him - I think it is a rejection. "What are you doing at the camp or do you own it?"

"My family owns the camp, I'm working there through summer."

"Can you make a living from that?"

"Uh, no, not at all. I have a wife and little daughter, so it is not enough."

"You have a daughter? How nice. How old is she?"

"She is six months old. She is very sweet. Don't you have children?"

I shake my head. "How old are you?" I ask him. He seems to be in the early twenties, not a typical father.

"24, and you?"

"You are not supposed to ask women that question. Hasn't anybody told you that?" I scold his curiosity.

"You have a great body."

Thank you.

"You need suncream, the sun can damage the skin. Shall I help you?"

"No, I'm ok. You can go to your family, I'm sure your wife needs you to put some cream on her body." I become nervous because the guy started to grab my shoulders without my permission. He does not stop so I look at him with my most hateful look and I remove the intruder's hands from my body myself. He realizes that there is no willing *merchandise* here so he goes back to his boat.

"Ayd, bye,"

"Bye," we greet each other.

I am enjoying my music for another hour. It echoes on my middle ear because of mp3 headphones. Besides music, my total relaxation is achieved by my favorite joint.

"Hi, do you have a cigarette?" I am surprised by a strong voice. I open my eyes and in front of me there is a man's posture with fair complexion.

"Yes, here it is," I offer him a box. "Nobody buys cigarettes here?" I laugh at absurdity. A guy at the pay toll station also scrounged one while I was making the payment.

"Why?" He does not understand my words. Because I find the whole situation a little funny. I cheerfully explain to him that he is the third Croatian guy who asked me for a cigarette. He is not disturbed by my words and sits next to my towel.

"Where are you from?" A well-known conversation is taking place, it concludes with an offer of spreading the cream on my beautiful body. He admits that he does not smoke and he tells me the cream is not the only stuff which he would use to massage my skin, but I easily reject his offers. I do not get rid of him until I promise that we will meet at a local bar with lively night life.

Finally, he leaves and I refresh myself in the wonderful sea. After swimming I get back to the beach and open my book through which I learn about sex life of a very freethinking lady. I enjoy the images in my head, of course they include my lover, when I notice another man looking at us from between the trees. After some time of hesitation he decides to approach me.

"Hi, you have such a nice dog," he has chosen another tactic and pulls a box of Winston cigarettes out of his pocket. "Can I smoke here?" A nice change – somebody has brought his own cigarettes.

This 'admirer' is a little older, around forty or forty-five, I would say, so a more skillful tactic of seducing is a consequence of experience which comes with age. My decision not to get rid of him immediately is supported by his own cigarette pack and the fact that he is an ex-cop.

"Julio," he introduces himself.

"As Iglesias, the singer?" I ask. He nods his head in confirmation and then we both laugh. He does not resemble Iglesias at all. I am looking at an average man with short dark hair showing signs of boldness, with yesterday's stubble on his face, and a smaller beer-caused belly.

We are discussing his work. He left the police because he had had enough of negativity in his life. Now he is working at the road pay toll station. He does not look like a psycho so I trust him where I am staying and my plans for the rest of my holiday. After having smoked his cigarette he leaves on his own and I return to the hot madam.

After a few hours I have enough. On the beach there is almost nobody else but two boys in their early twenties are placing their stuff for night drinking a few meters away from me. I have had enough of conversations for today as well as potential grabbing hands so I gather my stuff and leave the beach. Fortunately, tomorrow morning my three friends are joining me at the camp, so I will not have to defend myself from horny Dalmatian squirts alone.

"Heeeey! My playful babes are shouting and waving through the windows of a grey caravan.

"Haaaaallooooo," I am shouting and waving back at them. Finally they have arrived. My friends.

Behind the wheel there is Nina, of course. The other two do not drive cars except to get to shopping malls. I see Ema being a navigator and at the back seat there is Katarina, the most reserved of them all.

"Hi mousy, we have hardly found you," Ema is the first one to hug me, a short and mischievous monkey who I have not seen for months. Eva, her one year old daughter, has limited our relationship, but at this time she has taken three days away from the family obligations and I can hardly wait to see my old Ema, always cheerful, positive and always smiling.

"Olaaaa … It's important that you are here now! You know that even a blind squirrel finds a nut, and three of you came so it was that much easier." I cannot avoid a little of friendly teasing.

"Hey, how was the journey?" I hug and greet Katarina, my martyr from the period of studies.

"We've arrived fast. I thought we would be driving till nine in the evening, but it took us only three hours to get here." Zadar has benefited a lot with highway; the traveling time from Novo mesto to Zadar almost halved. "Nina is awful, we have never driven within speed limitation." Katarina's life style includes strictly obeying all the rules.

"But we are here, luckily alive and healthy." She tries to soften her complaining. "Where shall I put the luggage?"

"There, for now," I point to the big table with two benches by near the canopy of the camper.

"Halo, who is the strongest driver, WHO?" Nina is shouting. "I hope that you have something for me in the refrigerator."

"Of course, my dear. There is a box of six ice-cold beer tins for you, and the other two ladies will have to share three bottles of home-made wine. If that is not enough, the town has many pubs which are, with their Dalmatian atmosphere, calling for numerous visits," I announce it in a theatre-like manner. "And now let me invite you into your humble home for the following days." With my hands I move the ropes decorated with dolphins which are preventing the view into the interior of the summer complex.

The canopy is hiding an improvised kitchen with the fridge, a few cupboards, counter and a burner on one side, and a bunk bed on the other.

"You have to decide which two will sleep here, Odysseus and I can accept only one in the camper," I open the door into the stuffy room with two large beds, a few wardrobes, kitchenette with a fridge, and a bathroom which use has changed, due to the lack of space for my brother's four-member family, into the pantry for various things, mostly fishing stuff. As I have assumed there is no quarrel they are unanimous, as the place inside belongs to Katarina. The other two would be able to sleep in the car or on a deckchair, under suitable conditions (read: after a sufficient amount of alcohol) also on the biggest pile of stones by the road.

"I say, once you go black you never come back," Nina is laughing when we, armed with alcohol, sit at the table and light cigarettes. "Is there any suitable merchandise for me here?"

"Of course not," I roll my eyes. Are we immediately with guys, or what? "You've come to Dalmatia not to Africa. Well, I did not notice anybody dark-skinned but the locals are rather courageous," I say and review the situation from the previous day on the beach. The girls are laughing and then we start criticizing the opposite gender. I am not the most active this time, the average of bad experiences has been lowered by Matey's loving messages. We will not see each other for more than three weeks. On Monday he and his friends sail to the Mediterranean islands and he will not be back for at least fourteen days.

Ema is quite talkative. "To catch my man ... seducing women ... I would strangle his neck! I can't get any help from him anyway. I have noticed that men do not know what to do with babies, but he could change the baby's diapers at least once a week. I don't ask him to be with the baby whole days, but a few minutes would be nice. For Eva too, not only for me!"

We all know that she is getting less and less happy in the relationship with Daniel. When I asked her why she wanted a child she said: "That I am not alone." I was introduced to her by Katarina. Both Nina and Katarina are her neighbors in the center of the town. During the period of my establishing new friendships I was repeating the second year at the faculty, so I returned to Dolenjska, was living with my parents and working four hours per day in a store selling office chairs. Ema did not work anywhere, she did not graduated from a high school; she slept during the days and spent nights in nearby pubs.

Both of her parents are psychologists, but their daughter was on her way to alcoholism at that time. We both used to laugh at her trembling hand which tried to get some soup from her plate to her mouth without spilling some on the table. And it was four o'clock in the afternoon. She was great company although constantly without money. I did not care, I gathered a few banknotes for a couple of drinks, the rest was paid by male guests. Of course, she and Nina who was working as waitress in one of Novo mesto dumps knew all potential alcoholics who spend days at the local bars.

But she has changed over the years. She met a man, with his private business. She stopped going out, was prequalified to pre-school education high school and finished it. She also graduated from Pedagogical Faculty of Maribor. She graduated before I did – but I am not a traditional example of a hard-working student. She got a job as a kindergarten teacher, moved to Daniel and gave birth to Eva. A few months ago she returned to her job, but she is not happy in the life she had always longed for. Daniel does not pay attention either to her or to their daughter, as most of the day he is driving his truck and spends his free time with his friends. We all knew, I am sure she did too, what kind of man he was. He is a mom's son who has never washed his dirty clothes by himself or cooked lunch. Washing dishes is a special event, mostly reserved for holiday days, that is why we did not like the idea of her having a baby and moving in with him and his divorced brother-in-law, but we supported her as friends. I am happy that she is here with the other two girls. I am sure she will enjoy the weekend with the ladies.

"I cannot imagine my Tadey in the role of father although it is time to start considering it." Katarina joins this professional discussion about men. "But how can we afford it with rented apartment and a job for a limited period of time? How?" She fires through us with her green eyes and desperately removes blond locks of hair from her forehead.

Katarina, our 30 years old playing-it-safe girl cried when she failed two exams at the faculty – but she passed them with A's at the next attempt. She started working in a high school when she still had pre-graduation status. That is why she has graduated this year. We have told her several times to relax, but she postponed relaxation to the time when she has passed an exam, finished the year, got a job, graduated. Now she feels inferior at the school where she is employed because she has not had a professional exam yet.

"It is difficult as it is. We've been paying off the car loan for three years now, there are still two years left. I don't know if they will prolong my contract at school. How can I have a child?"

"Well, nobody is forcing you," says Nina.

"They all are talking only about furnishing apartments and kids. Everybody is asking us what we are waiting for." Katarina is unlucky that most of Tadey's friends are wealthy, with good jobs and own new apartments which were bought by their rich parents. She is a child of an unemployed dressmaker and partially disabled father who is only sitting on the sofa and making life miserable for everyone around him. In spite of her constant complaining about the shortage of money, I have never mentioned to her that she had much higher monthly income than me, considering her living at the student home, having a grant and child allowance, while I was living on my parent's expenses and occasional jobs. Their so poor parents enabled her to go skiing every year and be accommodated in hotel rooms of different seaside resorts for 14 days, which I still cannot afford.

Repeating 'life' conversation is boring, that is why I head towards the fridge to open the second bottle of wine and fetch the third beer tin for Nina. The first bottle flew down our throats as it that it contained the most precious Dom Perignon - which, however, I have not had the opportunity to drink- and not our country wine. I do not really like it, it is too sour, but one does not look into the gifted horse's teeth – in particular, if it is the fruit of your parents' one year work who you still live with at the age of 27.

Through the following half an hour our conversation does not move away from standard topics about men and work-related problems. After that the girls become more cheerful. We start reviving our memories of all-night benders, dancing on the bar chairs and tables, fleeting men whose names we do not remember...

The open third bottle makes us run towards the beach and we run into the cold water, screaming. There is no end to splashing and shouting and I feel alive. Young, playful, and happy because I have everything I need. On the telephone line there is a new age knight who is saving the world from wild fools; in my physical dimension there are friends who I can share my intoxication with; and the future which will bring me an excellent job where I will develop my full potential and show my talents to the whole world.

Saturday morning brings the heat which makes me get out of the stuffy camper, and unbearable hangover which is tearing my head apart, bit by bit, and changing it into a ball of a painful untouchable mass. The babes are, on the contrary, unbelievable. The working ladies, they could not sleep till eleven. I am the only one who prolonged the sleep, and during this time they put up a roof by the canopy to protect us from the sun, made breakfast which is waiting for me on the table, and my doggy, who has already had his morning walk, is lying under it.

"Have I told you that I love you?" I manage to ask them during my nicotine coughing.

"Several times. Yesterday at least fifteen times." Nina is smiling at me. I must have been in a very loving mood.

I get down to spreading delicious butter on a soft piece of white bread and drink a cup of warm fruit tea. There is coffee too, but I reject it.

"Don't feel very olympic today," I complain at my nausea which is manipulating my body.

"A jump into the sea and you'll be as a new one," Ema is comforting me. "The water is wonderful!"

The girls are amazed at the warm sun, so we get into the car and I take them to the beach where I intend to sleep through the whole afternoon to cure my hangover.

I wake up into a not very pleasant conversation. The topic is the last descent on the Sava river. Already on Thursday evening Matey's message struck me with a brutal reality when he had to go to Sevnica where some important municipality persons had drawn in the Sava river. I received it still dreaming so I consciously pushed it away. I am at the seaside, I'm having a great time, enjoying … I did not want to deal with the tragedy of others. But it seems I cannot run away from Slovenian routine.

"How many were there on the boats? I ask.

"31 people participated in the descent, in four canoes and one fire-fighters' escorting boat," Ema is the one most up to date. "13 of them died including the mayor and deputy-mayor of Sevnica, and the director of public utilities." She does not stop reporting.

"They were going down the building site which is forbidden; they did not wear life jackets, the boats were not suitable and they were drunk," Katarina adds. "It is believed that they had agreed to walk around the power plant on the land, but they did not stick to the plan."

Nina also adds something interesting to the 'happy' topic. "Do you know that the mayor had named the expedition The Last Descent Down the Sava River? There were several unbelievable coincidences."

"Really?" It sends a chill down my spine even though a second ago I was considering cooling myself from alcohol and heat my hot body in the sea. Now there is no need to do so. The cold shower has been opened with coincidences into which I do not believe.

"And not only that. While taking a group photo, the journalist made a remark that they should take a photo before the descent so that they will see in the end if somebody is missing. They were all laughing at the remark.

"Oooo …" chilling in my body does not stop.

"The people who worked on the project died. The director of public utilities came dressed in an orange T-shirt with number 13, there were 13 casualties … One of the mayor's first jobs was a beach lifeguard. Can you believe it?" Nina says.

"Yes, it is covered by all the media: TV, newspapers, internet. Today I have been reading about it in a Croatian newspaper," Katarina says. "But forums are disgusting. It's unbelievable how smug people can be. Most of them are expressing condolences, but there are individuals who try to be witty by saying that they themselves are guilty because they were reckless and irresponsible. And the whole circus is created because they were politicians. Everybody should be treated equally," she adds.

"They are right, though. I don't believe that the political elite would be at the scene of the accident if ordinary people had been involved. They wouldn't express condolences to the relatives of casualties and they wouldn't consider announcing the mourning days as it had happened there," Eva says.

"Matey was there too. Already on Thursday I received his message that he was supposed to go to Blanca, and now he is afraid that he will not be able to go on vacation," is my contribution to the round table before I trip on sharp stones into the agitated water. I have had enough of morbid topic which is not my business at all. I want to enjoy my sea holidays!

This summer evening is offering warm breeze which hinders our simple management of barbecue. A sea fish is too done

97

while pork is still raw. Nevertheless, we gather around the table and in a good mood we pour our exquisite wine into the glasses.

The first glass does not go down the throat as smoothly as yesterday, but it makes it easier for the ones that follow. Nina does not have any problems with drinking, one tin with liquid hops was drunk already at breakfast. She continued drinking through the day and had a break at her late afternoon nap. Now she is happily opening a new one.

"Eeee, you see, this is life! The sea, good food, drinks, friends. Who needs more than that?" She lies down on the deckchair, satisfied, opens a few buttons on her too tight trousers and pets herself on white patch which has showed up.

I look at her and the only deckchair, and I reconcile with a plastic chair on which my ass is resting, exhausted from everything good. "Yes, I'm having a good time." I lean backward and put my legs on the end of the bench.

"I hope that Eva is OK," Ema says. "I'll call once again." She checked the home situation early in the morning, a few times through the afternoon, so this is the sixth supervisory call to her home today. Katarina is joining her. She has been texting with somebody the whole day. I suppose it is Tadey, but she is not revealing the content of the messages.

"How is it with Thomas?" I ask her about her co-worker when we are alone.

"Wonderful. He spent the last weekend at my place."

"What?" I look at her in amazed. "And you haven't texted me?"

"I did not want to disturb your sea idyll, and there is not much to tell. It was simply wonderful!"

"That is all? Wonderful? Haaaloooo! Details, please!"

"We went for a drink and I took him for dinner to Villa Otocec."

"Oooh, fancy!"

"Well, you know, the impression is important. High heels, a mini skirt, breasts happily greeting out of tight lace blouse ..." She is smiling. "He fell for it. The continuation happened in my bed, of course."

"Aaand? How did he do?"

"There is a need for more practice." We both laugh. "It is noticeable that he's short."

"A meter and sixty-three centimeters, right? Uh?! So if we meet someday together with Matey, I'll be the tallest," I'm laughing.

"And how was it with Matey?"

"Dream-like. It's unbelievable how gentle he is. He was caressing me, hugging and massaging me all the time. I had almost forgotten how it felt.

"Uuuu, so it is serious?"

"I don't know, I'm in love. We exchange at least ten messages every day, we're going to see each other in two weeks. This is it. We'll see what happens next."

"Nice. I want you to be happy after all those idiots you had around you. It is time for you to be spoilt by a modern man," she looks at me lovingly. "Life can be beautiful."

"Yes. I feel that our lives are beginning." I feel an enlightened moment. "Who knows where we'll be in ten years."

"Uh, I probably somewhere in Asia or Africa, with a strong Afro-American and little mulattos."

"And I on the sunny Caribbean, under the palms by the turquoise sea ... making a living with writing erotic stories!" I do not know where the idea came from. Except for child diaries, school and study writing assignments I have never written anything else, and I find it very difficult to say the word *dick* or similar obscenities. But we are both laughing at the visualizations of our future.

STATION 3:

EROTICS

"Huh, this one is talented!" I am reading a message sent by Matey, who has been sunbathing on the sailboat in July sun, somewhere between the Adriatic islands. He is writing about my perfect body and what he would do with it. I am rather excited about his imaginative selection of words; I feel the shivers, so I decide to sit behind my computer. A policeman cannot send better turn-on-messages than me.

I open my gmail, click on the new message icon and start typing. This work of art which I am creating now will need more space than a mobile telephone can provide. There are no problems with inspiration, I was reading teasing, erotic books and dreaming about him when I was lying on the beach last week. It is easy for me to fantasize so I intend to transfer my naughty thoughts onto the paper. My fingers start blind and smooth typing.

Summer Story

Coco was lying naked on the hot sand of an isolated beach and reading a book, full of lush erotic stories. After reading one of the sensitive scenes in which she vividly imagined how the actors unite in their unbridled passion, she put down the book and she started longing for a man's firm touch.

She looked around and noticed a man on the nearby rocks who was observing her. She liked the view of his tanned body, dressed in tight swimming boxers which showed his masculinity clearly.

So, she decided ...

She put on the most innocent and confused girly look and called him: "Mister, can you help me, please?"

He stepped closer and asked her: "Sure, what can I do for you?"

"The sun is still strong, I would like to sunbathe my bottom too, but I can't put the cream on myself." She said that with a seducing voice of an innocent helpless girl.

His blue eyes, full of passion, answered without words. She turned on her stomach, showed him her tanned little butt, and he sat next to her holding a sun milk. He started massaging her shoulders ... caressing her back .... She purred of comfort and enjoyment, and his hands continued gently, all the way to her butt, where they stopped in hesitation.

Coco already felt moisture which spread all over her crotch, so she purred even more convincingly and put her legs apart. Now, his fingers continued in a totally different rhythm. They did not caress her gently but they slid in an experienced way on the inner part of her thighs, over her wet pussy which screamed for MORE. In a certain moment she felt that she would explode. She wanted the man's hardness deep inside her body.

He must have felt it for his fingers stopped researching and she suddenly felt a deep, strong thrust into her. She got dizzy, she felt the heaven, and he was thrusting into her slowly, deeply. To achieve a perfect effect, her fingers started stimulating the clitoris, besides his stronger and stronger banging of his hard and demanding tool. All the way to a loud, heavenly, relieved orgasm. She felt that he was reaching his peak too, so she got out of his iron armor and took his club into her mouth. She drove it in deep into her throat, slid on it with her lips, and did the glans with her tongue, while gently pressing his eggs ... sucked it ... till it burst and spurt his juices into her mouth, on her face, breasts ...

She did not leave him alone, not yet. She licked his entire root so that she sucked in all the traces.

I find the photo in which I am lying on the sand, holding a book with one hand, and a finger of another hand is resting on my tongue between my lustful lips which are slightly open. Only my upper part of the body can be seen, naked breasts, eyes and a larger part of the face are hidden behind a big bzzz glasses. I attach the photo below my story and send it through the world network.

Send ...

When I see the window notifying me that the mail has been sent, electricity whisks through my body. My first story … My first thoughts about writing appeared one week ago … But as a joke … I was joking … Was I?

I read it quickly once again. Huh, I wrote this?! It is not bad at all … And I read it again. Now it seems worse. I notice that there are some commas missing, a few sentences are rather awkward … The more I am looking at the story and searching for mistakes, the more unconvinced I am becoming. What if that is a complete failure? What if he does not like it? Maybe he will find it unattractive and repulsive, what a vulgar nymphomaniac that woman is?

Before I lose all my will and a bigger part of my self-esteem, I send it to Nina.

The following hour I am walking to and fro in my apartment, smoking a cigarette after cigarette and waiting for the readers' response. The first to call is Nina.

"Halooo?" I answer the phone.

"Mooore," I hear a thick wannabe sexy voice and start laughing.

"Cool, babe, cool!"

"Isn't it?" My self-esteem flies to the heights again. "Did you like it?"

"Huh … If it doesn't lift the guy's …" I wrote her in the message what the purpose of such unholy literature was.

"It's excellent. I got hot too."

"Thanks, thanks. What did I say at the seaside? What?"

"Well … true." She remembers the prophetic words. "I bow. You're fast. Did you conceal something? Did that really happen?

"No, no. A barking dog doesn't bite. You know how I reacted to potential adventurers; I could not do that in reality. It's even difficult for me to pronounce the word dick," I whisper.

"Has Matey responded?"

"No, not yet. They are sailing during the day and it is difficult to get a signal between islands, even telephone. I sent him a message telling him to read the mail. He answered that in the evening they were going to anchor by the coast and he'd try there."

"Well, text me his response. I'm going now, a customer is waiting for me."

"Ok, talk to you."

"Ciao."

I remain sitting in front of the computer, looking at my half-naked photo on the monitor. I'm bursting with energy. If a woman likes it, he will like it too, for sure. Well, why he dared tease me with spurring messages ... Again, I am excited about myself so I send it to Katarina to see what a professional says about it. I warn her in a telephone message that she has received a strategically important mail. And that she should not laugh at it. Not too much.

I receive both answers in the evening. The first one is from Katarina. I breathe easier after I have read it. She likes the story too. The review confirms that a plot is smooth, no miserable attempts of high literature, and not too trivial either. She recommends that I should try with an erotic magazine, for she is sure that I will get a fee.

My appearance in erotic magazines so far is limited to one photo on the last page of Playboy, which is decorated by my image too. They took a photo of me as a croupier at the black jack table at the grand opening of a casino and my employer decided that the photo could be a good marketing approach for a new place of sinful fun. The photo focuses on the table and the crowd in front of it, but Nina informed me about it: "Hay, you're in Playboy!" And I really 'was'.

Matey's response is excellent. He is excited about it and praises a fantastic description of the happening on a beach. Of course he asks whether or not the story is based on an event from reality. I am lying on my bed while we are exchanging hot words. Huh, I can hardly wait for him to come back on Monday. Uh, wait ... I am reading his words asking me if I am free the following Sunday. He would like to come back earlier and spend a day with me. BINGO!

This night I need time again to relax and fall asleep. There is too much going on. The wheel of a new future has started spinning ... into the right direction ... I am going to be a writer!

After turning and tossing all night long in my sticky bed and dreaming about big dicks flying in the air and hunting me, I wake up into a sunny morning. My thoughts are directed towards Summer Story instantly. Odysseus is on holidays with Alex, so I do not have to go for a walk under the already hot sun. I immediately sit in front of the computer. I type *erotic magazine* into a browser, and 333,000 hits appear.

I have not read such literature for a very long time. I and my ex-boyfriend No. 2 did a thorough research in that field, but that was during the last year of high school. Once he sent me four editions of different magazines by mail because we were on bed terms, and then checked 'live' how I liked them. The reading of stories was completed with his mouth between my legs and we buried the hatchet.

I start thorough research into current erotic stories and newspaper activities in the area, it seems that there are at least five magazines with erotic topics satisfying our little state. I read the comments about the topic and a few boring not proofread examples, before I decide. I will introduce myself to the editors and ask for a job ... This very moment, before my will gets weaker.

I open my internet box and use an offer sample. I mention my education and my desire to write or proofread; and in my attachments I forward my Curriculum Vitae and a larger part of my story. I send it before I am won by fear. Today is Sunday, so they will probably read this tomorrow.

The next day, early in the morning I am sitting in front of my computer. After the yesterday's spending hours in front of the monitor and reading indecencies, surrounded by a smoke cloud, I am not that confident today. I am not at all. I feel quite stupid, thinking what on earth I was thinking about? Who do you think you are? A new or female Max Modic[18]? Pha, right!

I open my e-mail in fear and I am surprised when I notice the reply to my yesterday's offer. One of the magazines is asking how much I expect to be paid for 1600 characters, ~~and~~ as they plan to publish a strip cartoon in the future and will need a proofreader.

Fiyuuuu! I AM EXCITED!

I take a phone and call Nina.

"Say, babe," Nina answers at the second beep.

"I sent my story to some magazines and one is asking me how much I charge. They want to buy it!"

"Yes, really! COOL!" She seems excited but not more than me.

"Ahm, who is the STRONGEST? Who?" I shout. "Do you happen to know how much they pay for such things?"

"No idea … Hmm, I don't think I know anybody who does something like that. So there is nobody I can ask."

"And they will need a proofreader. For a strip cartoon."

"Excellent! Cool," I can hear from the phone.

"Yes. Palms, the sea, the sun, and here I come …" I find myself in the clouds again. But the very next moment I am thrown into reality by the photo of the diploma award which I happen to pass. I am smiling happily while my favorite professor is congratulating me and handing me a red folder with the evidence of the education achieved by hard work.

"Oh, my God! My parents would be so proud of me if they knew," it flies out of my mouth, "What they paid my studies for." I laugh although I feel tension around my heart. "For me to become a porno writer. Can you imagine?"

"Well …" Nina remains serious. "For the time being it is better to keep that to yourself. Let them enjoy the image of a virtuous daughter, teacher."

---

[18]   Max Modic was slovenian journalist, porn director, an apologist for pornography.

"Aha, I agree." I nod and stop staring at the photo. "Where are you?"

"I'm driving to Ljubljana, the meeting with my bosses started fifteen minutes ago." So typical. She is late again, as always. The average of her lateness is thirty minutes but she is not bothered by that.

"Can you buy a magazine at a gas station?" I ask her and tell her the title. "Nobody will recognize you there."

"Are you embarrassed?"

"Ahm, a little. I admit. It's difficult for me to buy condoms, and I've never bought a magazine."

I admit. *A sneaky sinner!*

"No problem, I'll buy it. Shall we meet in the evening? Will you come to my place for a literature evening? We'll be reading stories and commenting."

"Sure. As usual? I get six pack beer and a liter of wine?"

"Aha. I'll call you when I get back, ok?"

"Ok."

After half an hour there is another response. That magazine finds the story promising and they would like to see it in a longer version. The editor says that the magazine is pornographic, so I should use harder words, the fee is from 60 to 120 Euros gross price per story.

I inform Nina immediately and ask her to buy that magazine too. I need to share my excitement, then, I start considering the fee for the first one. They are interested in fewer signs ... 50 Euros net is an acceptable price. I am a beginner so I cannot expect high incomes ...

I send them my mail and I am waiting for their response. They do not respond promptly so I am afraid that I overestimated myself, but they reassure me in the afternoon. They confirm. I shall send them a story on the topic of my choice, and they expect hard pornography.

I start thinking about future masterpieces of somethig. Shall I look for topics in my own experiences or shall I use my imagination? They say that one should write about the known and comprehended topics. I roll a joint although it is too early. I lie on my sofa and light it. Let's see what sources I have ....

I can write about a swinger party which I joined. After a great disappointment with Jan – my ex-boyfriend No. 3 – I could not get rid of a sense of belonging, nobody interested me, so I said to myself: "If you do not want to be with another person one on one, then it is time for you to start one plus group. You've been interested in that for long, why don't you try it? Many dicks at once will surely convince you to forget a person who does not want you in his life." And besides, my 24th birthday was approaching, so why not get a somehow different present for myself.

Fortunately, I did not find myself in a stuffy club, but Ema's friend took me to a private party. The club was nicely arranged. In lower rooms there was a nice mini disco with a dance floor, where we met the other two couples. We were sitting on sofas, drinking cocktails and other drinks, listening to sexy music and talking. After one hour we moved to the upper floor with two rooms and a bathroom, intended for bodily plays.

We used the one with several mattresses on the floor, and by the wall there were white leather sofas, two-seaters and armchairs, next to a little table. I opened another bottle, and there was an idea, my idea – I was rather intoxicated at the time – where women take our clothes off while the men, already ready, encourage us from the mattresses. I was the youngest with my twenty-four years, accompanied by two women, the fair-haired woman was thirty-two, and the black-haired woman was forty-five. I do not remember their names but they looked great. We were dressed similarly so watching porno movies seems to be beneficial for I at least did not stand out as a clumsy beginner. First, we took off black transparent blouses, and then more or less long skirts. I was wearing a mini skirt with Scottish pattern – school version. With the skirt I threw away the image of a girl, and remained in a black lace underwear, hold-up tights and black boots with thick soles and even thicker heels. I found them a week ago when I was looking for suitable shoes for this particular occasion. And they were cheap …

Well, at the peak of seduction I was betrayed by my bladder – if I drink alcohol, my kidneys get crazy, as I become a toilet sister and visit it every ten minutes. That night it was the same story. When I came back the others were already streaming on the mattresses and I got scared. Instead of joining them I poured another glass of white wine – after two cocktails, three large bamboos, vodka, and an initial joint before I entered – I also smoked at least ten cigarettes.

I was watching and evaluating how beautiful body with the dark brown pussy the black-haired woman had, I did not notice a gram of excessive fat. No wonder that she got married with an eighteen years younger nice trader. The fair-haired woman was even more beautiful … While I was watching the porno movie live I was terrorizing myself with questions: Who will devote time to me? What if no one wants me? My 'friend' must have forgotten about me …

After a few minutes an initial crisis I was overcome by a man with a belly who I spotted a month after the party on TV Midnight Club where he presented the philosophy of Slovenian swingers. He took off my underwear, started caressing me and soon I was lying in an armchair with my legs wide apart, still with the glass in my hand.

The continuation of the evening stayed in my memory only in pictures … no feelings. I do not remember whether or not I was enjoying it, but I know that I did not reach an orgasm – that was forced only by Jan and his blaming, suspicion and hard work. I remember that the next morning I was lying in my bed and holding a soft teddy bear and longing for tenderness before I fell asleep.

The therapy *Forget your ex* did not work. After two days I found myself in Jan's bed but I did not find there what I wanted either. Although we used condoms, the next week I was able to enjoy the luxury of itchy fungal infection. Alone.

No! I cannot write about that … Not even in the framework of a made-up story … I start thinking about the visit with Alex in Amsterdam which happened for my twenty-sixth birthday.

After reading ticklish and bizarre adventures written by marquis De Sade, we were dreaming how we will try the in Red Light District. I proved to be a blabbermouth but without courage to realize my fantasies. I did not dare look at the charming ladies in the street, I only peeped towards their boots when we were taking a walk.

To be dragged to the erotic show I again needed several glasses of alcohol, supported by a number of enticing joints of white widow brand. Fortunately, the ticket included two glasses of spirits so I overcame initial shame at the bar where I remained sitting. The most plastic sex I have ever seen – a woman petted her built-up subject on his shoulder for a 'hot' conclusion of their play. I was relaxed by a fat older black lady, chubby big mama, who appeared to be more funny than erotic with her banana and happy Americans in the first row. The final touch to the merry atmosphere was supported by hang noses of most of the male customers when a dancing female miner's song was telling that she did not want any small dicks …

Yes, I can write something about that. What were we to do in the evening before my birthday, when we were accommodated in a reddish furnished apartment opposite the red street and through the window observing two friends of red lights dressed in red leather? Well, we found out that Viagra is inefficient if you drink large quantities of beer and smoke Dutch grass.

No …

Now I am thinking about a birthday party which would be slightly different from usual boring friendly dinners which I am used to … Slightly …

Birthday Party

I have not seen Tanja for a few years and I was nicely surprised when I received an invitation to her twenty-seventh birthday. We were schoolmates at the high school and we had our first fuck during the final excursion in Spain. One drinking night which we spent in one of discos, she pulled me from the dancing floor, where we were dancing by hot Latino rhythm and rubbing against each other, and took me to the women toilet, pushed me on the toilet pan, unbutton me and sat on my erect dick. At my eighteen years my little friend in my trousers did not need a lot of work to stand up and stay erected. She reached an orgasm already during the dance where I felt her hot pussy rubbing against my leg. In general, she was very hot-tempered, but obviously satisfied with me, for we became a couple and fucked till the end of high school. She was the one to teach me most of the bed skills and I was madly in love with her. When she started her studies, our paths separated, and we met occasionally for a cup of coffee.

No, this invitation came and I accepted it gladly. I hoped to taste her sweet pussy again, as I was interested in whether or not she had changed over the years, improved. If that was possible, for I have not had an opportunity to meet a better fucker.

The dinner took place in one of better city restaurants where they prepared and arranged a special room for us. Tanja greeted me nicely when I arrived, accepted my congratulation which was spiced with a kiss and a present; then, she introduced me to others. Most of them were her co-workers, and there was her room-mate who Tanja shared her rented three-room apartment with. Her name was Sanja and she looked older than us. She seemed to be around thirty-five, but she looked very attractive with her red hair and a short black dress. As well as Tanja, who has developed into a very tempting woman, with her black hair, blue eyes and model-figure, she was a true beauty and I was proud that I kneaded her and practiced with her in my bed, and even happier, when I realized that she seated me between the two of them.

The dinner took place in a nice, but for my taste a little too formal, atmosphere. While we were feasting with the selection

111

of dishes and strong red wine, I was bored listening to political topics and economy crisis of our little state. I was disappointed for I did not expect such seriousness from my former lover. But fortunately, her hand soon surprised me. It found itself on my leg and continued its way to the little friend. Maybe the night was not to be so boring, after all. I was even more warmed up by her room-mate's hand which was on my left leg. Hm, what now? I hope there will not be any conflict between the room-mates and that I will not remain empty-handed. Which one will you choose? It would be nice to have them both, but I did not dare think that Tanja was so freethinking.

A formal part of the dinner ended soon, thanks God, and the tie-people started leaving soon. Beside the host only, I and Sanja remained.

"Well, now you will find out why I invited you," Tanja goes to Sanja and kisses her on her mouth. I remained without words. Maybe I will have them both, I thought happily. They started caressing each other gently and kissing more and more passionately. I stepped towards them to join them but Tanja pushed me away.

"Be good, it's not your time yet." Tanja wagged her finger at me.

OK, I moved away and the girls continued. They were caressing all over their bodies, and then they got undressed. Tanja sat on the table and exposed her pussy to Sanja. When she buried her face into it, and the sighs became louder, I could not hold back. I stepped to Sanja's wonderful little butt, kneeled and put my tongue between her legs. She groaned and let me lick her for too short moments then she removed herself. She took a chair, took it to the wall, pushed me on it and sat into my lap. She stuck her tongue deep into my mouth and pushed my hands back to the chair. Before I was aware what was going on I was handcuffed to the radiator. "Now, that we know that you'll be good, we can continue." That was all she said. She got back to Tanja and buried her face between Tanja's legs again. I could only observe the swinging of unreachable Sanja's butt and sighing of Tanja who was looking staring into my eyes. I could not believe that there were two hot babes working on each other right before my eyes and I could not cooperate?!

Tanja seemed to have pity on me, for she got up after some time and joined me. She unbuttoned my trousers, turned her back towards me and impaled on my horny thing. Sanja kneeled to her legs, burrowed on her clitoris with her tongue and pressed my balls. Crazy!

Jumping in my lap got stronger, her sighs too, and I knew her well enough to realize that she would burst anytime. And she did. She wheezed and her body was shaking in orgasmic cramps.

"This is a present that I wished for," she uttered when she got off my penis. Sanja started swallowing her lover's juices off my penis and now I realized that they were not only room-mates. Kneeling, she dag it deep into her mouth, sucking it, while Tanja lied on the floor and pressed her pussy on her mouth.

A waiter found us when he came to ask us if we needed anything else. His eyes widened in surprise when he opened the door and caught sight of us. He apologized and wanted to leave but Tanja stopped him.

"One penis, please. "She invited him, lying with her legs wide apart. He stepped forward and was only looking at us for a while. We were not disturbed and we continued. Then, he went to the floor and started working on the horny Tanja's pussy.

Sanja got the horny dick out of her mouth and groaned loudly when my former girlfriend made her reach orgasm, then she got up.

"I think that the birthday girl deserves another portion," he said and helped dizzy Tanja on her feet. She put her on my horny dick, this time facing me. She was jumping on me alone for a while, then the waiter inserted his dick into her buttock. Her room-mate was caressing her breasts and soon she was shaking between the whirl of orgasmic cramps.

I and the waiter did not endure for too long anymore. I let my sperm into her, and the waiter abundantly filled the depth of Sanja's mouth ...

There! I am surprised at how fast I wrote it. It does not represent a masterpiece, but two hours later I am satisfied with the result. Quite. I will finish the details tomorrow. Now I have to buy enticing beverage for a lady evening that follows. I take a shower. Before I sit in my car, I take a shower and manage to send a teasing message to Matey. Then, I set on a cheerful and joyful drive to the town.

„Hi," I greet Nina who I had to wait for twenty minutes in front of her block, in spite of our pre-arranged time.

"Hi, I have everything," she answers, trying to reach balance with a box in one hand and the bag and magazines in another. The view of naked female genitals on the cover cuts my Scorpio plan of cruel revenge because of her not respecting my time.

"The best. Thanks! How many did you buy?"

"Three different magazines. And I can tell you that a sales person was looking at me rather meaningfully." She does not seem satisfied with the task that I put from my shoulders onto hers.

I smile. "What did you tell him?"

"Nothing." She smiles too. "I explained that I needed them at my study research."

"What do you study? It must be something interesting if you need such eccentric literature." I am laughing while I am opening the front door of a one-room apartment.

"I'm writing a thesis in Sociology titled Erotica in Slovenian homes." Her answer is serious.

"Hmm, interesting. Why I didn't I think of that?" I become serious too. What an interesting topic.

"Isn't it? But I don't believe it will be approved at the Faculty."

"What about tourism ... Why not? Erotic tourism in Slovenia ..." I find that title more suitable for tourism studies. "Do you think it exists?" Ideas are generated even before we fill the first glasses.

"Show me what you've brought." I reach for magazines after I put down my bag, open a bottle and mix bamboo – wine with orange fanta.

After a sip of cold drink, I start browsing through the first one. I am not attracted to the naked women in different erotic poses, alone, or in pairs, or triples. I do not find male bodies posing with erect penises resembling loaded fire-guns erotic either, maybe funny. I am interested in stories. I want to leave the pictures which will represent the contents of the stories to individuals' own imagination.

"Only two stories," I say when I check the content of pages.

"There are three stories here," Nina says. "But the photos are rather revealing." She is smirking and drinking her glass of beer.

We smile through a few erotic poses and comment grotesque facial expressions which are supposed to show ultimate enjoyment. Then we focus on reading again.

"Rather unrealistic," I decide for revision when I finish the first story. An ice-cream man, who was not suspecting anything, seems rather cute, but I cannot imagine how a naked horny tourist would attack him at his stand. What a woman would do such a thing? Maybe a retarded one ....

"I like this one," My friend shares her part of the research. "It narrates about a teacher whose computer broke down and a programmer assisted her. And after that also fucked her.

"Uuu," I reply, but I do not like the topic. Most men responded to my former teaching job by reviving school memories and an attractive teacher about who they dreamt. Wet dreams.

"Shall we have a cigarette?" She asks. "It's getting hoooot. Hooot!"

"Sure."

We take our glasses and a pack of cigarettes and head to the balcony. The owners of rented apartments do not allow smoking inside and Nina surprisingly obeys that rule. I have never been so obedient. If I pay for a place, most of the time a very high price, who cares what I do in there? Unless I am destroying their possessions, they should leave me alone. When tenants change, than – it is taken for granted that the place needs to be refreshed. I respect her subordination to invisible supervision and I light a cigarette outside, but I will avoid such circumstances in winter.

"I have a good topic for you." She says. "Miran and I once had sex in the cornfield by the road ... Or how Peter and I were observed by a neighbor ... Write about negroes and their enormous dicks ..." She is showering me with advice, but I ignore most of them. I think I will not have any difficulties with ideas, and what I have heard seems to have already been seen and analyzed.

"I've already written one. About a birthday party. I'll finish it tomorrow and send it via mail. Shall I forward it to you?"

"Yes, sure. If you experience difficulties with inspiration, you know where to look for an advice. Uh, did I tell you how Thomas and I had a fantastic sex?

"Yes? How are you two doing? Did he leave his girlfriend?"

"Non-officially, they have separated; officially, he is postponing about informing his friends and parents about that happy event." She has a sip of beer and lifts a cigarette to her lips.

"Aha ... And how do you feel?"

"Me? Great. On Friday I'm going to his town; I've rented an apartment on a tourist farm."

116

"You've rented an apartment? Why do you not sleep at his place?"

"He's living in the attics at his parents' house and he does not want us to meet yet."

"Ahm." I do not like that a bit. "Where did you have sex?"

"He had a meeting in Ljubljana, and we met in Ivancna Gorica. Well, on the clearing by the woods ..." She is talking about a hot date which to me seems rather cheap. But I hope I am wrong. Maybe he is a dream prince she has been waiting for. Maybe he needs a little encouragement to leave his unproductive life and recognize a loving woman in Nina who he will care for, protect ... *and similar nonsense* ...

What about Matey? Is he the one for me? My prince on a white horse who will redeem the waiting princess? It occurs to me now that I do not know much about him. He even does not want to tell me his home address. Whenever I asked him about his private life, he skillfully redirected the conversation back to me. When he returns, we will have a thorough discussion about that. He is probably shy, I understand. I find it difficult to talk about myself too, but it is time for changes. I do not want to pretend any more. He also needs a little of encouragement to open up.

I fetch the magazines. It is getting dark, but this summer evening is not cold. By the light of candles we can still read the stories which, according to my taste, are not the hottest expressions of passion.

The following day I am enthusiastically correcting my story. I read it at least ten times, before I press Send. Compared to the stories I read yesterday, this one seems to be of higher quality, but I am not totally satisfied with it. We will see.

And what now? I have not heard from Matey. Ema and Nina are at work, I am not in the mood of listening to Katarina complaining about the unjust life.

I will browse through Netlog to see what is happening in the virtual environment ...

117

Ahm, a certain multi-cultivator wants to be my friend. Of course, I accept you, my thirty-two years old friend. I check his profile.

"Ooo, a biker! Excellent!" I am excited. Single, 32 years, lives alone, does not like cash ladies ... Foggy photos reveal that he is a rather nice guy, according to the comments below them he must be a true joker. I like a few photos and write a few humorous insertions.

Then, I check the groups and connect with three dog lovers .... I instantly add several Odysseus's photos. Let them see how a beautiful doggy I have.

"Uh, and who are Lightworkers?" A colorful photo takes me to the page of a spiritual group. The members support coexistence of people and animals, search for the truth and unconditional love inside ...

"People have their guides? Where did I read about that?" I mumble to myself. "Ah, the Journey of Souls." It is the book I used to read during the breaks when I was working in a casino. Soul mates, past lives, life purpose in learning ... I remember what I read. One person needed approximately 400 lives to heal jealousy. The theory was appealing, but I did not deal with it more at that time. I did not have time. I am playing with a thought that I am accompanied by an invisible friend all the time and that he/she leads me through my life. However, the idea of never being alone is not pleasant. So he/she must see everything I do? When I pick my nose or scratch my butt? Even hears and smells my hidden and loud farts? Watches my masturbation? No ...

Different mystical things have always attracted me. I like the idea that after death we go to a place where we meet all the actors of the terrestrial play and we analyze the events that we played. Nothing in a sense of Heaven and Hell which I strictly reject. When I was a child I used to swallow books or movies about ghosts and witches.

"Ough, Wyndspelle." I remember my favorite book from the teenage period which narrates about a beautiful Pastor's adoptee who is unjustly accused of witchcraft. She runs to the castle

118

situated on the rocks above the sea. There lives a handsome dark-haired blind pirate in white unbuttoned shirt and manly dark fur under it. He drugs the girl so that he can marry her, so he actually takes advantage of her; but the story ends with a confession of true love. My favorite movies included those with vampires. I was in love with an unlucky Louis who was acted by Brad Pitt. I waited the whole month for the movie to come to our area and, with great vigor, I made my brother take me to the movies. Ooo, and Dracula, the most beautiful love story as far as I am concerned …

My dreaming about the dark attractive stranger with long hair, a cylinder on his head and piercing look, full of power … is interrupted by Matey's message.

"Iiii," I shout out when I read his words. He is announcing his arrival already on Saturday evening.

"Fantastic!" My parents are on vacation at the seaside, my hearing-impaired and almost immobile grandma will not disturb us, and we can watch Dracula together. Yesterday Pop TV announced the movie and made me very happy.

Finally, a great Saturday is here. My little apartment is clean and tidy. I have cleaned all the rooms: the kitchen is shining, on the table there are fresh flowers in a vase, a device in electrical socket is filling my room with fragrance of artificial roses, the fridge is full … All in all, my holiday man will be welcomed by perfection. My body has been waxed and shaved, so one cannot spot a hair; makeup and powder are applied on my face, and every lock on my head is in its right place.

It is eight, the time of arrival, but my desired suitor has not arrived yet. I do not want to be annoying, so I only send him a message with a question what keeps him so long. I receive a reply after ten minutes. He is driving on the highway and will be in thirty minutes in Novo mesto. Lateness again, but I swallow this always present lump in my throat. It is important that he is coming! Although this means that he will miss a part of a fairytale movie which I intended to watch with him. Well, probably he is not interested in the moving images on the screen.

I am sitting on the sofa in the corner alone, I switch on TV and light a cigarette. After a few minutes I am in the world of dark sucking of blood. Uh, why am I attracted by strong and powerful men, even though they are mean? Ah, Matey is not like them …

After several short impersonal words on the phone, where and at which crossroad he is supposed to turn left, I see the black Audi which is parking in front of the door.

I check my image in the corridor mirror, then, I run through the door to the yard.

"Hi! You've arrived …. Sailor …" I sing before I reach him and kiss him excitingly.

"Yes, finally, I'm here. Mmmm," He returns a wet long kiss and hugs me tight. Now I look around, fortunately, there are no neighbors in sight. And even if they were, I do not care!

"Come, let's get inside."

"Yes, let me just take a bag." He takes a black bag out of the boot.

"I take him past a rose bed, through the door into the corridor and then into my sanctuary.

"This is my home. You can put your things there." I point to the wardrobe in the corner and as a true housewife I ask him: "Would you like something to eat? Are you thirsty?"

"Yes! I'm thirsty of you!" He growls and glues to my lips again while his hands are kneading my butt fervently.

"Did you miss me?" I manage to ask a classic question before his tongue prevents us from communicating verbally.

"Hmmm, I missed you very, very much … You naughty, naughty teacher, you …" *Ok, I'll ignore that.*

"What a story you sent me! Another whole day I was hot because of you …" He mumbles while working on my left earlobe. Now I wake and slightly push him away.

"Later I sent it to some magazines and they liked it." I say with a shy smile on my face.

"Did they?" he is surprised. "Bravo!"

"Yes, I am discussing cooperation with two of them. I must be a new pornographic star in the area of writing." I say pretending to be proud and lift my head so that I look at him from above. He is shorter than I remember. I take him by his hand and lead him to the kitchen.

"Will you have wine? Beer? Juice?"

"Water, please," he says. "And what will you write about?"

"I have several ideas," I look at him naughtily, hand him a glass, and press my hips to his crotch.

"Yesss?" He grabs me tight so that I can feel something hard with my legs.

"This week I was writing about a special birthday party, and in my head I am hiding a lot of other ideas…"

I push him again, make a sip of red wine and lean on the counter seductively. He does not approach me, but is looking at me with his blue eyes reflecting dirty thoughts. "What were you writing about in the story? Is it based on reality?"

"Nooo," I smile and tell him a short summary of the content.

"Uh, hot." He nods and presses his glass against his forehead. "I would like to take a shower. Cold shower, so that I do not explode before I set myself to you."

"Sure. Let me get you a towel; the bathroom is on the left, through the kitchen." I unglue from his body and approach the wardrobe. I give him a towel and I sit on the sofa which is re-shaped into a bed during night hours. I light a cigarette and watch the plan for hunting a night bloodsucker:

"Oh, you're ready?" Before my joint changes into a butt he is standing at the door wrapped in a towel.

"You're smoking inside?"

"Aha."

"I'll have one too. Can I have yours? I left mine in the car."

"Yes, sure. Here." I throw a pack to him. I step into the kitchen to fill my empty glass with a new dose. I am a little nervous …

"What are you watching?" He asks from the living room.

"Dracula. My favorite movie. Have you seen it?"

"No. Vampire scenes are not to my liking." He must have seen an illustrative scene which instantly showed the essence of the movie.

"What do you like watching?" I ask him when I come back and sit next to him.

"You know, crime movies, thrillers, realistic stories and dramas."

"What about comedies?"

"Hmm," He shakes his head. "Not really." I am a little disappointed. Our movie selections are totally different. To avoid revealing my childishness I will not ask him about fairy tale movies and cartoons.

"Which movie is your favorite?"

"I don't know … I don't want to think about that now." He pulls me onto him. "I've been thinking about you for too long to be just looking at you now."

"Well, well," I push him away gently but assertively. "You've been waiting for two weeks, so you can wait a few more minutes, so that I can light a cigarette." This is my response. Before I light it, I drink almost a half of glass.

In the minutes that follow I try to find out more about his sailing but he is very taciturn about that. I learn that there were six men sailing on the yacht. They were not drinking much because you never know what can happen at the seaside. So, constant alertness is desired. They played tarocchi, visited several islands … Allegedly it was rather exhausting.

As soon as I inhale the last smoke and put out the rest in an ashtray, he jumps onto me. I indulge this time and soon I am naked too. I enjoy gentle, zealous caressing and slowly I am carried away … somehow …

In the morning I wake up in his hug. I did not sleep much. After two long body sessions – the guy is very persistent – I finally fell asleep.

"Did you sleep well?" I ask him when his hand starts moving on my leg.

"Ahm. It's a little uncomfortable for two, but it's endurable … And you?"

"Ok. But everything hurts me."

"Where is painful? Here?" He gently caress my swollen middle.

"Yes, this ..." I wheeze. In spite of pain I enjoy his touch. He must have sensed my positive attitude, for his caressing does not stop but it becomes more consistent, accurate, our breathing harmonious and deeper. The touching is joined by something harder and an avid play is blazed up. Still without the finale among orgasmic whirls. And that is normal, isn't it? For a woman to first get used to a man? Or is something wrong with me in that area too?

When we cool down, we get out of bed. He into bathroom, I into kitchen. I will prepare a dream-like breakfast for him. Tea, sausages, salami, cheese, yoghurt ... Well, only fresh bread is missing, but I am not willing to sit into my car and drive two kilometers to the only open store in the surroundings.

"Have you seen my phone?" I hear when he comes from the bathroom.

"I think that it is on the table, in the room." I say and go to the terrace holding a tray. We are welcomed by a sunny morning when it is not hot yet. Today it is going to be a wonderful day!

"Will you come to have breakfast?" I call him for he stayed inside.

"Yes, I only need to make a call. Job."

I start eating and thinking where I shall take him. To Otocec, is my first idea. I avoid walks when Odysseus is not here, but the island on the river is the most beautiful place in Dolenjska and I wish to experience it together with him. Then, maybe to Villa for lunch ... or Kostanjevica ... My thinking is interrupted by Matey'y wrathful look when he joins me at the table.

"I must go," he says. "There's a scene going on and they cannot do it without me."

"You're joking!" My facial muscles must have dropped. "How can't they? You're still on vacation! What would happen if you were sailing, as it was planned initially?"

"I don't know, but they reached me now so I cannot sneak." He is looking into his plate. "I'll make it up, I promise. We'll see each other in the following days. Soon. Ok?"

"Ok." I am really disappointed. But I will not give him a hard time. His job must be very responsible, I will not be an obstacle.

On the other hand, I really slept badly, everything hurts me … I will get into bed and sleep through the day. Nothing worse …

Breakfast lasts no more than fifteen minutes. He drinks coffee in one sip. Then he bids farewell with a tepid kiss and leaves. I remain sitting in the sun for a while, then, I take dishes into the kitchen and wash them. I roll a joint, sit in the massage armchair and light it. Then I turn on TV, Travel Channel. Excellent! The Caribbean islands!

The next day I receive a response to my story. The editor is satisfied with it and orders three more for the first edition. They want hard words, fetishes, farm and young boys on a fat farm lady with big bosoms. Fortunately, one topic is on me. I have time till the end of month. Good, I start generating ideas immediately. Although the genre is classified as trivial, they will receive a true masterpiece, I make up my mind.

I spend all day generating ideas and also waiting in vain for there is no call or message from Matey. I gain courage in the evening and write him a message which is not delivered immediately. Late at night I receive a notification about the delivery of the message to the owner of the telephone number. His answer arrives in the middle of the afternoon, the following day. He says that it is crazy at work and that he would like to see me at the end of the week. I reply promptly, I agree. I even mention that I can come to Ljubljana. I could visit Odysseus who is staying with Alex, and in this way I will kill two birds with one stone. Matey likes the idea, we decide for Friday. I can hardly wait …

While waiting I am passing the time with the creation of farm pornography. I have the whole story in my head, I need to transfer it to the paper. I do that in the evening hours.

Horny Mary

One of the summer storms left its traces in our village too. The worst happened to our neighbor Franc, for the wind blew away almost the entire roof off the barn. Of course, in a spirit of Slovenian generosity, we and other neighbors offered to help him with putting up roof tiles, and he accepted it gladly. After one week we went to his farm to do a good deed. I was accompanied by three old tough fellows, Lojz, Ivan, Janez, and also Peter, who I was on best terms with, but we had not seen each other for a long time because he was living in Ljubljana due to his studies.

Franc welcomed us with a glass in his hand and we had to try his home-made fruit brandy. Nobody rejected it. The older and more experienced men made a construction plan, as Peter and I, the members of a younger ignorant generation, were not allowed to participate in decision making.

After one hour the landlady brought us drinks. Mary, Franc's wife, was a true farm woman. She was short, chubby, with a wide swinging butt, and big breasts. We did not see her often, only at Sunday mass, or few times per month when she came to a village pub to get her drunk husband home …

I set a plot and describe the main characters. I do not forget about actualization. Then, I write about sucking, pulling, and fucking mouth, sighing, and groaning, banging, and the emptying of young studs … between potato sacks.

… So, everyone was satisfied with the work done. Franc, because his roof was repaired, Mary, because she was satisfied after long time and especially I and my friend. Since then, Peter has been coming home regularly, so that we can go courting together … I conclude the story.

"There, the first one is done," I say to myself loudly and look at the clock. To have transferred 6000 characters of fantasy onto the paper I needed less than three hours. What to write about now? I decide that it has been enough for today, tomorrow …

The following day I am gazing at the screen in surprise. I have received an invitation for a job interview. The editor of the third magazine decided to invite me into his offices near Ljubljana. *This will be interesting!*

I reply that I will gladly join the interview next week. Now I am even more excited about writing, so I continue with an unhappy young girl in a mini skirt who was thrown out of a car by a mean German guy. She is all lost and when is hitchhiking a macho man stops. Not only does he take her to the first station and leave her to his colleagues who are going in the right direction, he also consoles her. Psychologically and physically. I write about a golden rain and similar group – totally unattractive to me, or even repulsive – things. But fuck it, everyone has his/her perversions and fifty Euros is fifty Euros. Everything is better than teaching at school. So is writing this.

On Friday I drive to Ljubljana after lunch and first of all take my dog for a walk. Uh, how much I have missed this city! And Odysseus. He is staying with Alex for another week, after that the ownership and care for the dog will be transferred into my hands.

I and my ex are having a nice chat on his balcony, when a beep announces the arrival of a message. I hope it is Matey. I have not told him I am in Ljubljana already. Let it be a surprise.

"No!" I cannot believe it. The guy canceled me. He has to go somewhere, he states. An urgent task. But he wishes me a good time.

"What is it?" Alex asks me. He must have noticed my wet eyes.

"My colleague has canceled a date. We cannot meet today."

"Really? Why?"

"Job. He is on duty and got a call." I light a cigarette while Odysseus is getting into my lap. He senses when something is wrong and in this way he performs a suitable therapy of love.

"Do you want to join me? I'm going to a party?"

"Maaaah, I don't know." I don't like being in a company right now. I'd rather pity myself at home alone. Why have I come? Moron.

"A little of goa scene will not harm you."

"Won't I be in your way?" He is meeting his friends and former schoolmates who probably know that we separated more than a year ago. "Won't they be surprised when we come together?"

"No. They all know the situation with our dog, and that from time to time you come by."

"Ok, I'll join you." I give in. Probably the people around me, alcohol and loud music will not harm me. I assume they will be smoking a lot too. Up to now I have been to only one party at Metelkova[19], in early morning hours after we finished work at the Casino. It was nice. I was wondering why three unknown people offered me chewing gums within two hours. Alex explained that that was normal. Most of them smoke marihuana and they know how dry mouth you can have after that.

"Good. Here …" He offers me a joint which I rejected earlier. I accept it this time. Let the party begin.

Four hours later I am sitting behind a bar in an abandoned factory in the middle of the town. Immediately after we arrived, Alex started a hard debate with his friends who hardly greeted me. Drinks were ordered for everyone except for me, a joint missed me too. So I unnoticeably moved away from the circle and sat at the bar. I feel awful in a smoky dark room with dirty walls. I am drinking my sixth bamboo, but I do not feel drunk, not a bit. I am lonely and observing a few weird subjects in the corners, who are swinging in the rhythm of loud aggressive music.

I have to go to the toilet. I remove plastic which is used to replace a curtain and walk down the dirty corridor to the toilet.

"Fuck!" I shout when I open the door into the only free box and see a disgusting scene. In almost full toilet vomit is floating with shit. What shall I do? I step out. Behind an adjacent door somebody is having sex, according to the noise I hear, in the first box there is a broken toilet. That is all that is available. I cannot wait anymore so I will have to suffer the disgust below me.

---

19   Metelkova city - autonomous social and cultural centre in Ljubljana.

I get in again and try to lock the door. Of course, the lock is broken. I pull down my trousers and set my butt above the toilet. High above it. I close my eyes and focus. In my stomach nothing moves, so I pretend to be crouching above a toilet in the middle of a green meadow with the river running by. Nothing. I push. Nothing. I stop. Relax. Push again. Nothing.

After a few minutes of forcing and begging my bladder to piss the excessive liquid, I stop. That has never happened before. I have made up my mind, I am going back to Alex's apartment. Fortunately, he trusted me spare keys to his apartment before we departed. I almost run to my ex-boyfriend No. 4 and shout into his ear that I am leaving. Before he reacts I am already at the door. I walk towards taxi station but I must have missed the right road, for I find myself in a dark area where I cannot see any decent road, only blocks of flats and one-way street.

After fifteen minutes I see the lights. I reached the bus stop. I run to the taxi drivers who are talking next to their means of transport. Before I even reach them, the first one opens the door.

"Where to?" An older man with southern accent asks me.

I sit on the co-driver's seat: "To Siska."

We are fast, but the driver does not have any change so I run to an open bakery across the street and exchange a twenty-euro banknote. I get back to the car and thank the man as that he has saved my life. And he has.

Now I run to the building and into the fourth floor. I open the door and push the excited barking dog away. When I reach the toilet, my trousers are unbuttoned and after a loud spurt the unbearable pain lessens.

What now? Shall I wait here for Alex to return in the morning? I do not believe I will be able to sleep here where I never felt comfortable. And when I am expecting somebody I usually do not close my eyes at all, not for a moment.

I am going home and Odysseus is coming with me, although he is supposed to stay here for another week. I take a piece of paper and write Alex a note that I am taking the dog with me. I also ask him to give me a call.

I put two chewing gums into my mouth, prepare the dog's luggage and after ten minutes we are driving on the ring road. In less than one hour we arrive home. I switch on the computer in relief, take a half-full bottle of red wine from the fridge and fill a glass. Before I enter the virtual world I roll a joint of skunk and light it. Nothing new, nobody has remembered me through the whole day. I did not have any visits today even on the social network, so I close all my internet windows and switch off the computer. I get into bed and caress the being whose head, wishing some cuddling, is resting on my belly. "My dear doggy."

Through the following days my mood is not good. Matey's messages are rare and taciturn. Allegedly, we'll meet on Friday. Again. *How often have you heard that*? We will see. I try to focus on my last story which will be sent with the other two to the magazine. When I was at the seaside I was reading hot stories of a nymphomaniac - you see how everything is good for something – and an idea about cemetery indecencies came to my mind. To put it mildly. The story which is becoming alive under my fingers borders on sadomasochism.

But they wanted hard stuff and they cannot get anything harder from me, for I have not been able to get accustomed to the role of marquis De Sade.

I start with Eva visiting her grandma, and her wish for peace and meditation which she would like to experience on an isolated cemetery. A place which is covered with grey cold marble, and the inside which is filled with the remnants of human bodies, fills her with peace. So, she starts thinking about life and death. In particular, she is interested in the concept of making love – symbol of life – on a tombstone of death. At that time, conveniently, she notices two gravediggers. The scene that follows shows rough banging which includes the smell of soil, sticks, rope, impurity of all body openings, and forcing pleasure of a wild lust upon an unconscious woman.

Here, I managed to verbalize a few different humiliations of love, and with it, of human soul. Another masterpiece.

A week later I am driving nicely dressed to Ljubljana, where in one hour I am having an interview with the magazine. In the evening there is another drive. Matey will be waiting for me in Ivancna Gorica. So my heart is singing love melodies in spite of the stage freight which I have before my prospective employers. I am wearing black shoes with high heels and straps, in which I can walk only few meters – and I always get some blisters –, a short black skirt and a grey blouse which offers a quality view of my Baroque balls, supported with large pads.

In spite of few delusional circulations I arrive at the destination which is located in a building resembling a factory in the middle of the business zone. My facial makeup is smudgy due to heat. I refresh my face, check my perfect look in a mirror, and then I look for the entrance. I walk through a printer's room and down the stairs to offices. There I am met by a nice blonde wearing a white blouse and colorful skirt. She introduces herself, but I do not remember her name. She appears to be a secretary. She leads me through the door and a man in his fifties approaches us. He is wearing black trousers and a bright blue shirt with short sleeves. While smiling, he shakes my hand, introduces himself and invites me to have a seat at a big office desk.

"Did you experience any difficulties finding the place?"

"No," I lie.

"I hope that the time is not too early," he smiles. "I know what the artists are like. I cannot reach ours before four in the afternoon!

"It's really a little early," I comment twelve o'clock. "But, no problem. It's nice that you understand our working hours." And I mean it. Usually everyone is harassing me because I do not like getting up before ten.

Now a formal part of the conversation starts. "I've read your story and your CV. I think that we could cooperate. Have you been writing long?"

"No," I compress my lips. "I have just started. I did not have time for that. First, my studies, next, the thesis, then teaching. But I have always wanted to write," I say.

"We already have one expert on Slovenian writing for us. I think that he's satisfied with his job. And we publish books too. We are considering fairytales for children." He says.

"Interesting," I am surprised.

"We could not survive by only selling the magazines. Also the CD sales have been rather low lately."

"Erotic movies?" I ask.

"Yes. How is your English? The basics would suffice. We translate movies and if you could manage translations, with proofreading, we would kill two birds with one stone.

I nod. "I can do it. I understand most of it. I watch English movies without captions." Fuck me. Hard. More … more … more? Nothing easier. I watched a few porno movies – mostly on German satellite programs -, special interpretation of the activities was not necessary.

"Have you worked with the programs for captions?"

"No. However, I'm sure that I will master the science soon," I say, smiling.

"Excellent," he replies and opens a drawer. He hands few CDs with illustrative covers across the table so that I can watch them at home, and he writes a note about what programs for subtitles free of charge are available on the internet.

"Let's get back to writing," he says. "The magazine includes the news. Well, our author finds them on internet; usually he collects them from foreign sources, so the knowledge of English is welcome there too. Would you be able to write or translate such things?"

"Mhm," I nod.

"Yes?" He smiles. He seems satisfied. "Good. Can we agree that you first submit two stories and then we will see how to proceed?"

"What about the fee?" Now I remember to ask about the information which is very important to me.

"Ah, yes, of course. At the beginning, 20 Euros net per 1200 characters, and 50 Euros per movie. Is that acceptable?"

I expected a lot more, but I am satisfied with the opportunity that they are offering.

"It's acceptable," I nod.

"Excellent. Let's go on a tour so that I can show you our kingdom." He stands up and walks me to the door. Outside he shows me a pile with the most recent editions of the magazine and gives me one so that I can put it into my bag next to the CDs. He shows me various books, more movies, then he takes me down the stairs to look around the printer's room. After the tour he takes me back to the office and orders his daughter, who is introduced to me now, to exchange the data. He wrings my hand and bids farewell.

It is eight in the evening when I arrive at the place where I am to meet my policeman. I see the black Audi parked in front of the pub, so I am not the first today.

"Hi, beauty." He stands up from behind the table and kisses me.

"Hi, Mr. inspector," I smile coquettishly. "How are you? Have you afforded some free time?"

"Uh, don't talk. Exhausting, exhausting is the labor of man," he sighs. "I'm on call today too."

"You're kidding." I am disappointed. "What does that mean?"

"Ah, nothing. Usually I spend a night at the station. I said to my colleague that I was going on patrol. He won't miss me," he says and caresses my leg seductively. "How are you?"

I press my naked leg in my mini skirt against his and smile.

"Alright. I've missed you."

"Yes?" He is biting my ear in response.

"You'll never guess where I've been today!" Now my energy turns from passivity into a state of active euphoria.

"Where?"

"Three deciliters of wine with fanta," I order my drinks for the waitress who has just come to us. Then, I start whispering about the conversation in the world of pornography.

Matey's look widens and he starts fleshing his eyes.

"Ooo, you bad girl! Excellent!" He is excited and confirms the importance of the event.

Now I start talking about the magazines. "Ok, the stories can be funny, sometimes even bizarre and not teasing at all. But I'm surprised at the number of ads on last pages, everybody is looking for someone. I asked the director about that and he said that there were so many of personal ads that they could not publish all because they ran out of space." I am surprised at Slovenian hidden passion.

"Tell me something. I've found myself in weird plots." He moves a little away from me.

"My good friend, who I have known for more than a decade, has a very open relationship with her husband. He sees other women and she is active in other men's beds too."

"Yes?" I encourage him when he stops.

"Well, now she's showed me that she'd like to sleep with me."

"Really?" I feel hot. "And you?"

"No, I don't feel like it. But I'm wondering what to think about all that. I understand that she doesn't want to be alone when her husband sees other women, but ..."

"I'd never go with a married man." I sound very decisive. "Don't do to other people that which you don't want them to do to you."

"They've agreed, obviously they're not bothered by that."

"Why are they together, then?

He is thinking. "Because of the house which they've built together, probably ... I don't know ..."

"What about love? And being in love? ... The feeling when you're lying in a hug of the man you love ... Respect ... Want him ... Belong to him ... Then you don't want to share that with other people. Isn't that so?" I do not wait for his answer: "I don't believe I would exchange that perfection with materialistic goods."

I may sound a moralistic dreamer, but those are my principles. Why would one be with a person whom he/she doesn't love?

Because they are comfortable? Aren't they deprived of the most beautiful things? Isn't being in love the same as unconditional love? Then you would do everything for that person, you don't care about his/her past, friends, family … Only that person is important.

I kiss him. "Isn't it nice to be in love?"

"Yes," he mumbles between the kisses.

"Don't you wish that it would be always like this? Isn't that the best feeling in the world?"

"Mmmm." Nice of him to agree with me.

"Have you written something new?" He changes the topic when I unglue from his soft lips and muscular chest.

"Ahm." I tell him about the stories I've written. My escort is excited at the contents. I keep the last one, about the cemetery, to myself.

"Do you have any plans for tonight?" he asks me.

"You're my plan," I blink with my eye coquettishly – at least I feel I do.

"Shall we go somewhere? Rent a room and spend the night together? I'd like to feel you next to me. But I will have to be at the station at six in the morning."

"Yes, sure." He said he would like to feel me next to him. "That's ok, I'll have to be with my dog." Now I remember Odysseus that will spend the night alone.

"Where shall we go? Is there a private hotel near?"

Because I do not know about night shelters in the surroundings. I order another glass while we're discussing options. The motel in the neighborhood will suffice for we cannot remember anything else and we do not feel like going around asking people about that. I and Alex once stayed drunk at the motel after the night spent at the casino, and the price was not too expensive, only 70 Euros.

At the reception, one hour later, he asks me if he can book a room in my name. I agree. Why not? He pays for it, so each of us takes a part of the responsibility.

We are both surprised when the amount on the receipt shows 130 Euros. Now I remember that Alex did not register me at that time. That explains the difference in price. Matey's smile is a little bit sour, but he shrugs his shoulders. I find the price high too, but I do not want to feel bad about it. He should have taken me to his home!

We go to the room, and because the only free room has two single beds, we push them together and do not beat around the bush. In less than a minute I'm lying in bed with my legs apart and the gap between the beds under my ass. With every hit the gap is getting bigger.

When we finish the first round I light a cigarette by the open window –I am not disturbed by a note which says "Smoking forbidden". We have paid a good price for that room and I do not want to restrict my freedom and walk outside as a prostitute.

I go back to bed to the man who follows my every move.

"Grrr," I snarl.

At that moment his telephone starts beeping in his trousers which are on the armchair in the corner.

"Fuck!" He gets up and takes a damn thing. "Yes? Yes … Yes …"

"Mother fucker!" another curse from his mouth and the phone hits the soft velvet of the armchair.

"What is it?" I know what it is.

"I have to go back to work." He says angrily. "Uh, somebody will be beaten today!" He seems really furious.

I get up and hug him soothingly. I do not like the idea that somebody will be beaten because of me. But I am surprised at his aggressiveness.

"Full moon." He lights a cigarette by the open window and is looking towards the sky. "Something is always wrong at full moon!"

"Really? Influence?"

"Yes, quite strong."

We are smoking and staring at the starlit darkness.

"We'll have to leave immediately," he holds my hand. "I have to be at the station in half an hour and I have to first drive you to your car."

"Ok." I am alright with the situation. Odysseus will not be alone tonight, and I will be able to roll a joint, have a good sleep, and tomorrow finish my stories.

We dress in record time, and after half an hour I already park in front of the entrance of my home where on the other side of the door I am welcomed by excited barking of the jumping lump of fur.

STATION 4:

DYING BY INSTALMENTS

It is cold. The autumn rain has brought rain and I am wondering whether or not it will snow tonight – in the evening of my 28th birthday, a week before the all Saints day. It would not be the first time that the sky's present is abundance of raindrops.

I am sitting in my room which I have heated in the early afternoon. I am expecting a call in two hours. I am going to meet the not-mine-any-more police officer. An interrupted love night at the motel was followed by the last date when he took me to a private hotel in the surroundings of Kranj. His leg was painful, he must have pulled a muscle during his martial arts training, but I was wondering why he did not take me to his place. *He doesn't want you near! He must be ashamed of you!*

After sex I was lying on his hairy chest and teasingly asked him if he was married. He mumbled something in reply, so I got up and asked again. "No," he said through coughing, got up and spent at least ten minutes in the bathroom. After he got back I managed to explain the reason for my question – to heal his moaning because of pain in his leg with a phrase which I hated the most when I was a child – "*It will be alright when you get married*!"

He got suspiciously silent, so I could not help asking whether or not we would see each other again. His answer was positive, but after that there were no messages from him for a period of more than a month. My message asking him if he was ok and to let me know so that I did not worry received no response. My computer notified me that he was regularly visiting his profile, but he was not interested in me. Our planned weekend at the seaside at the end of August did not happen, and there was no explanation for it.

I tried to forget him by dating a nice motorcyclist from Krsko. He made me laugh with his jokes on his part. At the introductory meeting when we were testing each other – verbally – he used a very picturesque image to explain how his little dick glows at night due to the closeness of the nuclear power plant. Of course I was wondering whether or not that was true. Not before long did I manipulate three days of freedom with him and his Yamaha at the nudist beach in an croatian camp – I, a responsible girl, who is keen on motorbikes, but is not so crazy to drive around with strangers whom you cannot trust.

But it was his steel machine that attracted me first. I adore the rides, the feeling of flying, crazy accelerations of speed, vibration of the seat when the engine roars with more than five thousand revolutions... I, however, managed to hide it and convinced him that I was not a babe longing for his silver moto-cultivator. After a fantastic weekend full of drinking, fast rides, naked lying on the sand beach and night sex our dates got less and less frequent until there were only evening visits. I soon stopped them as I was not in love with him. I spent a lot of nights wondering what was wrong with me that I did not like a decent, intelligent and funny man who can even be responsible and mature.

I stopped writing pornography. Both magazines (I did not respond to the editor of the third one where they promised the highest fees) bought my first stories – I had to change At the Cemetery into a story about two workers from Bosnia, because it was too 'hard' – but nothing else came out of such creativity. At the first magazine they told me to write by my own impulse because different energy is triggered in that way. The editor and his daughter did not respond to my third story which was written for them and I did not have courage to ask them about that, and I had not received a translation or hot news either. I concluded that I probably wrote shit which could not be published. So I quit.

I started looking for a job. The savings were spent and 180 Euros of social welfare support was not enough for my life style. Beside twenty applications for various jobs sent to different places in Slovenia, plus - I sent a few to schools. But nobody wanted me there either; the only responses were from the head of a local grammar school and the head of a hospitality school. After the first interview I was informed that at the grammar school they decided for somebody else. Katarina, who knows the teachers in the area, told me that a new professor was commuting from Ljubljana.

Neither the head of a vocational school where I was defending myself and my work last week wanted to hire me. A new professor for 8-hour employment per week teaching two classes was supposed to start immediately. But he never called me. I thought to myself that it was obvious that neither my knowledge nor my persona were sufficient for restraining, I suppose, not the most obedient and hard-working students?

My birthday rumination is interrupted by Matey's message. I feel a sharp pain in my chest, he is not coming. *But of course, what were you expecting?!* He had to stay in Zagreb. *Fucking politics*! Could it be that an urgent matter which is in all the media is only an excuse? After one month of silence and my motorist adventure he started appearing on my profile as a guest. Our texting started blooming again. He confessed that he wanted to forget me, but he could not stop dreaming about me so he promised to redeem himself for his conduct. Also with the invitation to dinner at my birthday.

But I remained empty-handed, that is, with an empty stomach, evicted out of his world. Alone, even without a dog, because I did not want any obligations this evening. What am I supposed to do now? I informed everybody about our date so that I would not seem pathetic because I was alone at my birthday. Nina is booked in Prekmurje; her last fucker got her for himself with his neglect, so she does not care about my birthday. It is not the first time that she has forgotten about me for several months. And it is not first time that I feel totally unimportant because of similar rejections. Ema too seems to have had a tiring week at school and she cannot find a baby sitter for her daughter. Her message was very taciturn. It is possible that she and Daniel are fighting again. The only one who took the time to meet me was Katarina, who I met yesterday. She too has a lot of urgent school work to do over the weekend and cannot take the night off. We were sitting at the bar, drinking martini and discussing the problems of Slovenian school system. I found out that a job at her school, for which I applied, was given to a young teacher without a degree who worked there with children last year. No, I will not tell them off to inspection. And I will not call anybody today and ask for attention. It has been enough.

I take a bottle of Cabernet out of the fridge and open it. I take a nice wine glass and fill it up. Then I sit down, open the internet browser and find my song on you tube. *With or without you* Beno is singing and I hesitatingly sing along. Before the song is over I successfully roll a joint, light it and make a toast to myself. "I wish you all the best, all the best, my dear, all the best for youuuu," I conclude with a prolonged vowel. "I wish you everything beautiful. To find true love, real friendship and great job!" My toast is short and brief. I take a long sip and start searching for appropriate birthday tune. U2 is replaced by Plavi orkestar[20] with the song about birthday waiting which takes me to my teenage years and I remember my ex-boyfriend No. 1. The next song is by Pink asking Who knew, which is a must in such circumstances, then sings an elderly red-haired rocker who refreshes the memories of my ex-boyfriend No. 3. The first part of the holiday repertoire is concluded by Anastasia. My voice is becoming convulsive and louder »*OOOO, left outside aloooone, left autside aloooone ... ALL my life I've been waiting for you to bring faaaairyyyytale my waaaay ...*«

Now my glass is empty, I have finished the joint, and my mood is much better. I do not care at all. Actually, it is very nice this way. I am listening and shouting into the air as much as I want: *When there's no love in town, this new century keeps bringing you down. All the places you have been trying to find a love supreme. A love supreme ...*« Fortunately, the old lady – my grandmother – in the neighboring apartment is hearing impaired. I get up and start dancing in the reflection of ten tea candles, exhibited around the room.

---

[20]   Pop band from Bosnia and Hercegovina

The morning brings a hangover, but I do not care for the pains in my body. The years of drinking have taught me to reserve the day after a drinking night for lying because scraping along with disgusting taste of a dead animal in my mouth is always accompanied by awful fatigue and even worse headache. I cannot cure it with some pain killer pills, the only medicine that my stomach can take.

I feel even sicker and in the following minutes the toilet becomes my only devoted friend who digests all my unnecessary excretion. I am thirsty as hell but each sip I take causes even worse cramps in my stomach. I swallow a few sips of chamomile tea and go back to bed. I force myself to a few smokes of a joint which I had prepared before sleeping. Now nobody can say that I am not responsible or that I do not know how to take care of myself! According to my experiences, the nausea will be even more awful in the following next minutes, but after that I will fall asleep and wake up hungry and feeling a little less exhausted. I switch on the radio and lie down for having rest again. Happy birthday to me ...

November has brought changes. I have just had two hours of teaching at one of Novo mesto vocational schools where I am honored to be able to get to know and help prepare the youth for life, in two classes – the last year of a three-year program and the fifth year of a prolonged program. Even though the employment is part-time I expect it to be diverse.

Besides teaching the regular program I will have to review the programs of all other grades because I will be preparing the former for the final exam and the latter for the vocational matura. The challenge is even bigger for I got two of the most problematic classes at school, but the first hour went quite well in both classes and there were no incidents. Nobody burnt a school desk or did something similar. With more or fewer comments they accepted my lecture which I supported with a threat of a very difficult final part of education – I used manipulations which were the most disturbing part in my teachers' education and that I hated so much. After we got

142

familiar with the education plan we introduced each other and started discussing the activities in the surrounding town cafés. Almost all of them come from the surroundings of the town or even farther away, so they have to commute at least two hours daily. That does not bother them. What bothers them more is the inactive local night life.

After my first successful day at school I am walking through the town square to the post office. I am not satisfied with myself. I feel unsuccessful. I would rather be doing something else. Why are my study-period friends employed at ministries or newspaper offices while I am, after teaching alphabet and restraining the nomads accommodated here against their will, wasting my life with the problematic youth?

"Miss!" I hear a known voice and turn around. Oh, there at the table by the stairs Jan is sitting – my ex-boyfriend No. 3.

"Hi," I join him and his friend. "What are you doing here?"

"I'm waiting for my boss to arrange the papers. I am supposed to go to Denmark but something fell apart," he says. His new job is a truck driver. "And you? Here, have a seat."

"Uh, I've got a job ..." I say and sit down although I still feel weak when I see him. Fortunately, he is wearing glasses so I cannot see his devil eyes.

"What will you drink?" He interrupts me before I am able to explain the surroundings of this 'happy' event, and lifts up his glass of bamboo. Considering his obvious cheerfulness which is not very frequent, I believe the glass is not the first one.

"Polka. Three deciliters." He waves to the waitress who stops talking to one of the guests to fulfill his wish. This is how it is with the locals.

"What do you do?" Do you teach?"

"Yes," I smile, light a cigarette and say that I am teaching at his former school.

"You are kidding!" he sounds surprised. He finished the first year, repeated the second one and then gave up because it was not to his liking.

"Yes, two classes."

Fortunately, the waitress is quick and a refreshing drink is on the table. Before I continue complaining at my unhappy destiny I make a long sip and stare at the bottom of the glass. He, of course, likes the idea. Before I drink the second round he is interrogating me, if I will invite him to the class. I know what is in his mind.

Round after round and it is four o'clock when the two men suggest moving. Fortunately, I do not work tomorrow, but on Wednesday and Thursday when I have three hours of teaching respectively. So it is ok if I get a little drunk. And Jan is getting more and more attractive after every glass. Especially because he has taken off his glasses and is looking me directly into my soul.

We continue our drinking in a dump next to the hospital, but this time with an addition that we did not dare have in the middle of the town. A high school professor is sitting at the corner table in front of a bar and rolling a joint. The person who should be an idol of successful and moral human being does not really care about it at this moment. I used to dance on the tables and I am sure I will do it again. This is who I am. There, at school, that is the expectations of others.

The darkness brings a shipment which my companions have been waiting for nervously. A few grams of cocaine together with a few acquaintances arrives just in time when a heated nationalistic debate regarding the third-class blood – which is assumed to be donated to Slovenian hospitals by the Hungarian Roma – becomes tasteless even for my intoxicated taste. I almost rebel against a primitive hatred, but I take two more smokes from the offered joint instead. I like that because of my soothing and begging hand on his trembling leg Jan did not attack the person who dared oppose his opinion. I seem to still have enough power to hold back his anger. Attractive! *Sick!*

Jan is wavering over something now, he seems embarrassed. "Will you try?"

"Oh, I don't know … Grass is one thing, coca is another. I am afraid I'll be doing stupid things."

"I am here. It's nothing, really," he is assuring me "You will feel good. Without tiredness or nagging."

He does not have to convince me for a long time. I have wanted to try this drug since long ago, but there has never been a right opportunity. I am wondering how it is to have sex without any restraint, will the ground shake and the sky open?

"Ok."

The first ones to go to the toilet are his friends, my ex is going after them. Alone, he must have forgotten about me. He comes back with a glassy look and looks embarrassed. After some nonsense remarks he remembers me.

"Hey, what about you? Shall we? Let me show you."

"No, I've changed my mind," I say silently and he takes me by the hand.

"Did I screw up?" he asks with a sweet tone.

"No, you didn't. I just don't feel like it any more. I should be going home. I have work to do," I say and stand up immediately.

Jan hits his forehead in response. "Fuck! You did resent, didn't you?"

"Ah, no. But look at the time, I'm totally drunk. I need to get some sleep to be ok tomorrow."

"Sure?" He does not seem to be convinced. "Are you able to drive?"

"Of course, you know me." In a state of intoxication I can be more focused, more careful and more alert that when I am sober. This compensates for the decreased motoric capabilities. My driving cab very school-like, claim those who have had the opportunity to drive with me and observe my total concentration on the road. This ability was developed by years of driving my parents' car – if anything had happened to the car, we would have had a great fuck up at home, much worse than any material or physical injuries.

"I'll call you when I come back from the ride. Ok?"

"Ok." I pretend that everything is really alright, but I want to leave as soon as possible. I kiss him on his dry lips; he holds me tight before I sit into the car and drive away.

When I come home I relax. I haven't met police control, so I still have my driving license, so all is well. I switch on my computer and connect to the virtual world. There is Matey's message waiting for me. He wants to know how the first day at work was. Since his unrealized visit we have been in touch through internet, so he knows what happened today. Partly.

I write to him saying that it was awful and my behavior after school when I met my 'old friend' and got drunk with him even more awful. I conclude my confession with a statement that my rejection of cocaine and return home was the only smart thing I have done today. Although I really wanted to try it!

The autumn brings heavy rain and a bunch of unpleasant errands. Monday mornings are the most difficult. Thinking that I'll survive the two hours with teenagers who do not take me seriously and that the following martyr of my pedagogical and human dignity will not happen before Wednesday I force myself to get up.

The beginning autumn lethargy regarding my friendship with the members of the same gender was followed by a dramatic turn. After a break of one year I managed to renew my contacts with Tasha whom I met a decade ago through Gal – my ex-boyfriend No. 2. Yesterday evening we met at BS where I was drinking with Ema. I had not seen her since the weekend at the seaside, but finally she managed to take some time off to compensate for my birthday celebration. Katarina was supposed to join us but she cancelled the last minute. I was really pissed off when Ema admitted that an urgent test and essay checking on the day of my birthday was only an excuse. That little liar actually went to her co-worker's party. Although I pretended to be cool I was offended by the news.

I was very happy to see Tasha. I immediately recognized short hairstyle in eternal black color although she is wearing new pair of glasses – the fashion changes every season, the same happens with the glasses without diopter. She has always got on my nerves with her perfectionistic fashion trends devotion, even though it would mean wearing the shoes number 42 with a pointed-toe platform. I cannot afford the clothes she wears and replaces it every season so I have been playing Cinderella in her presence wearing the clothes of third-rate brands. We had not seen each other for years till yesterday when we, both rather drunk, were hugging as best friends. We exchanged our telephone numbers, only mine was different, and decided to meet today.

Again I am sitting on the terrace of BS and while waiting I am keeping warm under the bright frame as a little chicken. Fortunately, she is on time and soon I see her getting out of an old Renault clio broken and scratched in many places. She is dressed perfectly, according to the latest fashion trends.

"Hi," she greets me and sits opposite me.

"Hi, babe," I say. "How is it going?"

"Huh, busy, veeery busy," she says and we both light our cigarettes. "Have you ordered?"

I nod and she stands up, opens the door and shouts to the waitress to bring a small tin of beer. It is rather cold on the terrace, so we are sitting there alone.

"Where are you working?" Last time she was waiting tables in a little dump next to the tax office.

"In a store at the health center. We're selling various health supplements."

"Ahm, through a Student Employment Agency?" She nods. "And how is it?"

"Ok, it's not too difficult. You know …" Tasha suffered from a stroke at 22. It is difficult to believe, but she is lucky to be alive so her job should not be too tiring. There are at least four blood clots circulating in her brains which can prevent this human computer from working and the girl can become paralyzed.

"How is your health? Are you well?" I ask her.

"So, so. I'm still taking pills." She is talking about the medicine against blood clotting which is usually taken by the elderly. "A month or so ago I went to hospital in the middle of the night. I could not stop gum bleeding," she sighs.

"Ah!"

147

"But I met a very cute doctor," she smiles.

"Oh, my!"

"Mhm. We liked each other at first sight. I have his telephone number which I can call if anything goes wrong."

"And? What does he look like?"

"Huuuh. Dark, tall, a basketball player, so I assume there are nice muscles hiding under a doctor's gown. A firm butt ... Sweet to eat." She munches with her lips. "He is married, but I do not believe his marriage is as it should be."

"Is that so?" I do not sound too enthusiastic about it.

"Considering how we were flirting. And that after five minutes he handed me his phone number ... And ..." She takes a moment to light a new cigarette. "One does not ask his patient such personal questions. Yap ..." She is nodding, "Something will come out of it."

"How long has he been married?"

"Seven years. You know what they say about relationships in their seventh year?" She does not wait for an answer. "They separate or they get married. And this one heads towards the second option. Yuuh, he is so cool!" she whistles. Fortunately, we are still alone on the terrace. The waitress opens the door and brings her drink.

"O, my God, you don't know what bugger I had. How long is it since we saw each other the last time?"

"A year and a half," I say and almost continue in this direction. I want to make clear why we stopped seeing each other, and she interrupts me with another story.

"You know that Bostjan and I separated?"

"Yes, I met Tanja," her neighbor, "who told me. What happened?"

"Eh, you won't believe it. You know that he has started working at his uncle's?" I shake my head. "The one who has a big furniture store in the town?" Now I nod.

"Yes, they are doing very well. Money in abundance, his cousin is building a new house. Well, but he lost it one day. Everything was alright, we were talking how he would buy a new car in autumn. Peugeot, probably cabriolet. We were already browsing, a black one would have been great. He would have to apply for a bank loan but it was feasible. Well …" she stops for a while, takes a sip of her beer. "One morning he lost it. He started yelling at me how I always wanted something from him and that he could not afford that. He could not afford an apartment or house, a car that I wanted. He was throwing at me how he did not make me happy and that he could not live like that anymore. And that was it, it was over."

"Uh, really? When did that happen?" I act astonished, but I am not surprised. He was right, it just took him too long to get to know her.

"Six months ago. I do not know what got into him. Me? I did not want anything from him. I was satisfied with everything. I had been driving in that shitty renault for five years, sleeping in the attic at his parents' house. What did I demand?" She is calling for confirmation of something that I do not agree with. Tasha expects a lot from people around her. "Of course, after one month he got back, crying, but I was already in a relationship, "she winks with her eye.

"That was fast. Who is a lucky guy? Where did you two meet?"

"It was crazy! In a pub, where else? Tanja and I were at some concert and after that we went to a pub. He was there with my ex schoolmate. But we were just looking at each other … Ok, flirting a little … till I and Bostjan separated. And then it exploded like a bomb. After two weeks we started living together. "

"Really? Like a fairytale! Love at first sight," I swing. Why something like that never happens to me?

"Uh, no. Far from that. What a nightmare … the guy proved to be a true psycho."

"Why?"

"Obviously I didn't judge him well. First, he was smoking grass all days and I learnt from his colleagues what I shouldn't have. Considering that he was unemployed, with a lot of money and driving BMW, I should have realized earlier."

"What happened?" I am thinking about town mafia.

"Well, I believe he was smuggling drugs," she whispers. "His friend is in prison because of trafficking. And several trips to Zagreb were rather suspicious. I checked his phone and found some weird messages. About tools, halo? What does he know about any tools? He has never held a shovel or a broom in his hands. Don't ask how it was the first month after we moved together. An idiot could not learn how to put a mat under his glass. On my glass table! What a moron!"

"Ok …" Remember to put a mat under a glass when you are at her place. I do not use them; I do not even have them.

"Once I woke up and that weirdo was staring at me! Can you imagine waking up and seeing somebody staring at you? I was totally shitty. Fortunately, we registered the place on my name, so I was able to kick him out."

"So you are not at your parents' anymore?"

"No, I'm at the river now. A very cool one-bedroom apartment, 30 square meters, with a balcony, a newly furnished bathroom, a full cool kitchen and a large room. Hey, listen to this!" she continues her story. "He was calling me the whole day two weeks ago, but I didn't respond. And the next morning there was a surprise waiting for me. Broken windshield of my car.

"You're kidding!" I am really appalled this time. "Do you think it was him?"

"I am sure. I told the police."

"Did you call them?"

"Of course. And I told them what I know about him and his trips."

"A good girl!" It is right for her to stand for herself. What a life! Do we really need to put up with this manly shit? I remember that she was the only one who stood by me at Gal's last attack. I have always admired her assertiveness. She does not allow anybody to humiliate her. She sued a nurse who rumored about an abortion, although what was going on was the healing of her ovary and she won the case. She even threatened his father that he would take him to court when he wanted to hit her. He then put his hand down.

"And you? How are you?" Now she remembers that I have my life too. "Why didn't you answer the phone?" She looks at me under her forehead. "Too busy with Alex? And you forgot about friends?"

"There was one missed call." I start defending myself. "It's not that I wasn't answering my phone. And you didn't call after that. It's not important …" I stop and she does not say anything either while browsing through her bag. Aha, it must be her phone. "They told me that you were making fun of Alex who was hiding behind the corner and eating a Frankfurt sausage," I mention lies she was spreading about my ex-vegetarian.

"Not me!" She puts down her phone. "A weatherman was spreading rumors, not me." She mentions her friend from TV. "But I am not surprised. Ema told you, didn't she?" She is now leaning towards me, "I heard her talking about Nina too. That she forgets about her whenever there is a dick …"

"Well, it's not important. However, it didn't seem right."

"I wasn't the one talking about that and as far as he is concerned, he belongs to the past too. Since I and Bostjan separated he hasn't even greeted me. A hypocritical snake! How are you and Alex? Still together?"

"No, last summer we separated. I got a job here at the primary school and moved back …"

At the third round I start telling my story. In spite of a cigarette in one hand and a glass of bamboo in another I do not feel relaxed. I can hardly breathe and it is difficult for me to complete my sentences. I run out of air, so I put down a cigarette and my glass. Still short of breath I am talking about the children and teenagers at school, the problems with Alex, a longer part was devoted to Matey and our escapade. After my dramatic description of a new meeting with Jan and the happening at the bar next to the hospital we move to her doctor again. And the conversation sticks there to the fourth round after which we decide to go home. We plan to meet on Saturday to party.

On Saturday evening I receive Tasha's message that she does not feel good and would like to postpone the meeting to the following weekend. I do not blame her. I do not feel like going out tonight either. Odysseus is staying with Alex, so I have had time for aerobics, coffees, English course and internet dates through the whole week and today I do not feel so energized. That is all right. A peaceful evening in front of my computer, listening to the music I like, is better that sitting somewhere on a cold December night and freezing.

So, Netlog, two tins of beer in the fridge, music … this is it. I switch on the computer and open my profile. In the inbox there is a message from somebody I do not know. This time my on-line flirting attracted a 40-year businessman. I hope that photos in his profile are not too old as he looks rather attractive – in spite of his age. If he were one year older, he would not be able to see my profile as I limited the visits to people between 25 and 40 years of age.

I like only one of his photos then I answer to his compliment of my sexy posture with a naughty look by a little girl and a hint that the profile is hiding a lot more. He answers with a few cute words and soon I am writing about my life as a teacher, dog lover, I do not forget about pornography stories. Of course he wants the proof of the latter, so a few minutes before midnight the first erotic creation is being send. I spend the entire evening typing, slowly drinking beer mixed with fanta and wrapped in an enticing curtain of smoke. I do not know what I would do without it. It calms my tense inner world so that I can enjoy the moment.

Matey contacts me with his message too. He is at work and bored. So, after all, I am hugged by the attention of two men this evening. This is better than exposing myself to teenagers or drunk boors and waiting in long lines in front of the toilet because the girls are spending too much time in front of a mirror or toilet. The evening happens to be the best. With my not being interested and responding with short messages, I tricked Matey to show interest in me again. He is coming to Novo mesto on Tuesday to meet me. Excellent! It is time for me to get him out of my head and I know exactly how I will do it.

I meet him at the car park in front of Spar market, wearing white leather coat, underneath I am wearing a tight black blouse and a short red skirt which does not hide my knees. In my white boots with high heels I am shaking because of cold, smoking a cigarette next to my car when a black Audi arrives. I take one smoke seductively and look through the front window into his blue eyes before I throw the cigarette butt and sit on the leather seat.

"Hello, inspector," I say and put my tongue deep into his throat. "How are you tonight?"

"Excellent, young lady, mmm ..." He wheezes when I remove from his mouth so that he can breathe. "Huh, how beautiful you are today!" Of course I sat in a way that the skirt moved high up and uncovered the naked skin above the hold-up tights.

"You just do not know what is waiting for you," I smile naughtily. "Where shall we go?" I do not forget to caress the part of his body which is starting to wake up underneath his tight jeans.

"I don't know, you decide," he says although he knows that I hate constant decision making – which is, in my opinion, the shifting of responsibility. "Take us somewhere where we'll be alone."

"Of course. Take the main road to the center ..." I say. This time I am not bothered by this which was so disturbing in Alex and other non-decisive lovers. This time I am in charge.

I lead him behind the stadium where he parks under spruce branches. We immediately move to back seats. I pretend to be passionate, I grab his body, lick and bite his neck, chest ... the play is in my hands and he indulges in it completely.

Then the phone beeps. He lifts his head from my pussy and takes the phone from a trunk lid.

"FUCK!" he curses.

"Do you need to go back?" *Oh, so convenient!*

"This is unbelievable!" He looks at me unhappily. "Yes."

"That's ok, but we'll finish this." I pull him over me and take his soft penis into my hands. Although I am trying hard, gently massaging it, kneading or sucking I cannot get it into erect position. It hangs there half-hard so I try to push it into my body. I am sighing like a porno actress, but I do not feel it inside me.

"I can't." He moans.

"Why not?" I ask him in cold blood.

"I'm in a hurry, it's uncomfortable, and we're in a public place. Don't you know that we can get fined for this?"

"Yes?"

"Ahm." Now he gets of me and sticks his tongue between my legs. He tries to satisfy me with wild circling of his tongue and by pushing his finger into me which I encourage with loud voice, but I do not reach an orgasm. After some time, I push him away and say that it is enough.

"It's ok," I say. He looks rather unhappy. He probably knows that he has not satisfied me. While he is driving me to my car I am backing the song on the radio and he is silent. Before I open the door I kiss him.

"Have a good time," I say and caress his cheek.

"You too," he replies. "Talk to you. Ciao."

"Ciao."

I close the door and take a deep breath. This is it! I got exactly what I wanted. I feel like a cheap slut who has not afforded a coffee with her body. Not worthy of a comfortable room and bed, enjoyment or satisfaction. He rode me as the last bitch in the herd of stray dogs – the fact that he did not is removed from my thoughts. But I am satisfied. I acted perfectly. The feeling tells me that with this last act of humiliation I finally dispelled all emotions that connected me with him more than six months. IT IS OVER!

As a surprise Jan calls me after a few days. Instead of attending an English course which I registered for before I started my new job and is paid by the Employment Agency I decide to meet Jan in the pizzeria next to Spar.

"Hi. How are you?" I kiss him on his lips. I still shake when I look into his eyes. They are heavenly beautiful. Something in his eyes touches my soul every time he looks at me, in hatred or in love. Today he has chosen that latter version of communication.

"Uh, so, so," he replies. "What will you drink?"

"Polka."

He stands up and opens the door into the pub to order the drink.

"And? Where have you been lately?"

"You know ... I've been driving all weeks ... And the snow ..."

He is slightly stuttering when he is talking so I doubt his psychophysical abilities.

"It's been a cheerful day, hasn't it?" I ask him with a smile on my face, so that he would not understand my question as a reproach. You never know.

"Uh, don't ask ..." he sighs. I was at Andrej's home. He wouldn't let me out of the vineyard house. I had to escape so that I could have a shower at home," he mentions one of his interesting colleagues. Andrej's father shot to death another member of a local association and then killed himself. Both sons of the deceased are now good friends. What was the cause for killing I do not remember. Maybe a woman? Or unacceptable arbitrary determination of neighboring borders. In the hills where home-made spirit runs from large barrels, one never knows. The sons who were left without fathers at the same time can drink a litter of alcohol without showing it. Forty years old Andrej came to the bar where I was working before ten in the morning complaining that the police unfairly seized his car – at nine in the morning the alcohol test showed 1,5 promille. After he had slept nine hours on the bench in the vineyard house.

"But ... I wanted to see you ... I've been missing you, you know ..." he whispers into my ear.

"Yes?" I do not believe him. Why has he waited the whole month? I do not even want to think about previous dates and the entire love tragedy. It is over. I do not know what I am doing here. Am I looking for fun?

"You ... I have to tell you something ..." Now he leans back.

"Ok, tell me." I encourage him with a smile and drink from my glass in a flirting manner. Neither the pub nor the glass shows any sense of esthetics so I must have looked funny and not as seductive as I intended to be. Obviously, for Jan starts laughing.

"Oh, how beautiful you are!" He grabs and kisses me. "It's like this ..." Now he leans back again, sighs and looks at me. "Whatever I do I cannot get you out of my head ... I've tried many things ... it's like this ... I won't say that not a day passes without me thinking about you ... because not an hour passes. It doesn't matter what I'm doing, driving across Germany, reading a book, drinking with friends ... you're always on my mind ... Will you marry me?"

I open my eyes widely. I beg your pardon? "Are you serious?"

According to his facial expression he is serious; what is missing is a rose and he is getting on his knees. But I do not believe him.

"Yes ... I'm too late, aren't I?

I nod and reject him, feeling sad. "Uh, Jan! Where were you a year ago? I would have fallen into your lap without consideration." I grimace and look at him.

"But not now ... It was enough ..." I interrupt a long moment of silence.

"I knew it. But I had to tell you," he says with a foggy smile on his lips. And I cannot read his true thoughts from his glassy eyes. "Will you have another round?"

"Yes, sure." I light my cigarette and drink the remaining liquid from my glass. There was more than a half. Jan goes inside so I have time to think. It is unbelievable how the life is changing. I would have killed for those words years ago. Literally and metaphorically. I was so in love with him! How I was begging him to take me back ... Spent whole nights crying for weeks ... I could not bear anybody touch me for six months – if I do not take into consideration the swinger scene which happened for the purpose of forgetting him ... And now? NOW?!

When he comes back we do not mention his proposal, we start looking for another joint. It seems we will have to drive to Trska gora. We agree and soon I am sitting on a torn seat of his white Golf two and traveling to the hill by the town.

In a semi-built three-story house we are met by two persons who we have not met before. I cannot remember their names. Rarely can I remember the names of the people I am introduced to.

They roll a joint of fragrant plant immediately and start eating bread roll accompanied with wine. The conversation is about the rumors and the happenings of the people unknown to me. It is mostly about criticizing. When new age spirituality and healing come to the scene I become interested and surprise them with my support of discovering the new. Or the ancient – it depends how you look at it. I explain how I see myself in a yoga association in India. I have not given up reading esoteric texts; I only put them aside for a while. Unfortunately, they do not share the same opinion about the invisible and they reject me as a girl who spends too much time alone. I respond, that it must be the opposite – I am too active on the internet. They laugh and the topic is concluded.

We too end our visit, we got what we had come for. We are on the way to find a room for rent. Fortunately, I do not have classes on Fridays, but we will get up early anyway. He has to load the truck and drive it to the western Europe. Before we get to the well-known bed we have dinner. I have a Vienna steak and French fries and he orders plate of goulash. We eat more or less in silence, half an hour later we roll another joint as I wish to enliven the happening before bed time.

But it does not help; I do not fancy it any more. His body does not attract me. What once was so familiar that I could not fall asleep without, is now repulsive. Hairs, red swollen lump, hanging balls … It becomes clear to me that there is nothing for me, but it is too late to leave.

I finish the foreplay quickly and start the role of a porno star on her stomach. I do not want to look at him. I do not want to smell his breath. I do not want to kiss him … I just want it to pass quickly ... I am shaking my highly lifted butt and encourage him to press harder. It hurts but I suffer. After a long time, we turn to our hips and continue with the wild rhythm. Now I throw myself on my back and lift my hips which fall into his lap, so I feel his thing all the way up to my stomach. My weary crotch is dry, so he let go of me and starts with his tongue. He is not gentle, we are both crazy ... And although we are wildly mated the suffering does not end with orgasm. Fortunately, he gets tired too and I confirm that my pussy is more than satisfied and that I will not be able to walk properly for another few days. Then we stop.

Before I fall asleep I go to the bathroom to wash my painful middle. When I get back, Jan has already turned towards the wall.

"Let's sleep, ok? I'll have to get up early," he mumbles without turning towards me.

"Of course," I say and press myself to his back.

"Will you hug me?" he asks.

"Yes, sure."

I do what he wishes and press my hand on his chest. So we are sleeping like a couple, but the feeling is different, cold and strange. I do not believe I will close my eyes this night.

True ... I indulge in pushing out the ghosts of the past, present and future while I am listening to his loud breathing which however does not drown out the river and its rapids under the window.

After the day which started with an awkward departure from the bed at six in the morning and continued in my home residence, I get a message from Katarina. And this happens after I have removed her from the list of my close friends.

I got what I deserve!

Because I was rude to you and Tadey!

I'm pregnant and it is not Tadey's. I don't know what to do ...

I'm sorry!

Ough?! *Our good girl Katarina is cheating*? I had a feeling that the constant lack of time cannot be attributed only to the school work. And who is a happy father? I think she mentioned a waiter who took her to dinners when Tadey was playing drums somewhere in Serbia. And the waiter is his friend. Oh, how cliché … There have been misunderstandings between them for quite some time, they do not quarrel a lot, but she admitted that they have not been intimate between the sheets for several months.

I do not hesitate, I call her at once – I am always available when someone is in trouble. *Freya to the rescue … here I come …*

"Hi, are you alright?" I ask her with a soft calming voice.

Before she answers Katarina sobs into the phone. "No. I told Tadey. I couldn't wait …" she says.

"And …?" I am encouraging her while I am grimacing my forehead. Possible resentments have sunk into the infertile soil, of course, I want to be there for her.

"He called him and told him that he knows about us, and also, that I am pregnant. He's on his way here to talk."

"Really?" I am surprised at her sincerity and the cold-bloodedness of the cuckold.

"And what did he say? Tadey?" I do not want to interrogate why the waiter.

Katarina is crying into the phone. "How could I … Then he asked me who he was and I confessed. He called him and ordered him to come immediately. Oh, yes … and to bring six pack beer."

"Aha," I am not surprised. "When is he coming?"

"Any time now … Tadey is locked in the bathroom," she is crying.

We are both silent for a while.

"Did he say something else?"

"No … He didn't even look at me …"

"It'll be alright … When did you do a test?" I assume this is how she has found out the exciting news.

"Yesterday … Today I was at the gynecologist's …"

"Will you keep the baby?"

"No …" Her sobbing is getting more convulsive. "If the baby was Tadey's, yes … But not … Can you go with me on Monday? I don't know if I can do it alone …" The words coming out of her are wrapped in snuffle.

"When? I have classes till ten, but after that I can come there."

"I have an appointment at ten. Will you come after the classes?"

"Yes, I'll be there …" We are silent again. What else can I say …

"Does it hurt? What's the procedure?" she asks me. I told her about my two abortions which I did years ago. I had to do the first one because of my ex-boyfriend No. 2 who returned from the army; and I had the second experience with murdering unborn beings because of my ex-boyfriend No. 3, the one whose proposal I rejected yesterday.

"No, it doesn't hurt," I lie and do not tell her about consequent inflammation and bleeding which lasted almost the whole month. "You get anesthesia and you go home after a few hours," I share Nina's experience. In my case I had to spend two unslept nights in hospital, but fortunately, they let me go a day before Christmas.

"If you went to Ljubljana to have a hormonal abortion you would get a pill and go back in two days to lie there for few hours under supervision." In Novo mesto the nurses were rather rude to me, to say it gently. Listening to their words I felt like a pile of shit, none of them was kind to me, none of them helped me, one of the nurses even told her friend Ema about the event. So the next time I decided to have an abortion in Ljubljana without any consideration.

"No, I've already made an appointment with a gynecologist here," Katarina interrupts my mind jump into the past. "Must go now," she whispers. "Tadey is coming. Talk to you. Thank you!"

"Ok, I wish you luck with clarifying things today. Let me know how it goes, talk soon …Ciao."

"Ciao."

I hung up and remain sitting at the table. I do not envy her a bit. Physical pain is not worth mentioning but I am bearing a huge psychological load on my shoulders. But I do not want to think about that now.

I rather switch on the computer and check my mail. I am happy about the business owner who is coming to the city for a meeting and plans to come for a cup of coffee to Dolenjska. Excellent! I agree, of course. I respond at once. He is spending Friday evening at home, so we exchange our telephone numbers, define the time and location. Then, I sit in front of TV. I wish to escape into the movie world …

It is Tuesday and I am sitting at a café which is fifty meters away from Katarina's apartment, waiting for my friend. Yesterday Tadey took her to hospital and was there for her. According to the messages I got, they had a sincere conversation after a long time and decided that their relationship is worth to be kept and that they will not give up yet.

"Hi," the pale blonde greets me. She is wearing a long black coat.

"Hi, how are you?"

"I'm ok," she says but she does not sound very convincing. "Tired. Were you tired too?"

"Yes, I wanted to sleep all the time." And I still wish to sleep. "Are you on a sick-leave?"

"Only yesterday."

"And? How was it? How long were you there?"

She explains the whole procedure which has not changed much, they only send you home after a few hours of resting. Except for being tired she feels alright.

"What about in your mind? Do you feel guilty?" I ask her worried.

"Mah … I don't know … All in all it's only a fetus, it's not a being yet …" she stops.

"Yes …"

"You had two, and there is Nina, several acquaintances ... even my mother had two. We talked about that long ago. There was no other option ... It wasn't right ..."

"Really?" I did not know about her mother. "Well, you see. You know it wouldn't work for you otherwise," I hold her hand. I am not sure that I myself have released the feeling of guilt.

"Did you have any problems?" She asks me.

"Physical ... not worth mentioning .... Psychological? Huh ... I've been thinking about it frequently." Shall I tell her?

"One day I found my grandmother's edition of Family newspaper and one article was about psychological consequences of abortion. What can I say?" I inhale deeply and light a cigarette. I seem to be a chain smoker today.

"My story relates to that completely. The first year I was drinking, the second year I was smoking." The third year I got pregnant again. "The article mentioned the escape into work ... Well, that happened after the second abortion. The loudest reason in my head for the first abortion was that I was too young in my twenties and that I still had to enjoy life. I would have gone crazy. Diapers, worries ... I wanted to live." After teenage years when I spent most weekends alone in my room, I started enjoying at least partial freedom, sixty kilometers away from home.

"The reason for the second one was a necessity to complete my studies. And I did. I passed fifteen exams that academic year." Fifteen!

"I remember, yes," she nods. You are a phenomenon. Half of the students repeat the first and the third year, and you passed those easily, but you repeated the second year which is the easiest."

"Yes, that's me. I pass the most difficult exams at first attempt, and I repeat the easy ones."

"Do you feel sorry sometimes? Do you think that that was a mistake?

"No. Do you see me in the role of mother?" I smile, a little forcefully. "I'm not capable of such responsibility. I have different plans for my life. I want my life to be mine, but if you

162

have a child it is right to devote your life to him/her. I felt awful when I took a week of 'maternity leave' for Odyssseus. A week of constant floor washing, worries, if he was alright. Dogs cannot tell if there is something wrong with them. Teaching, patience … I am not sure I would have another puppy in my apartment. And you know that I find them cuter than babies and I like to look at them and spend time with them. I do not feel that I have an attitude towards babies.

Katarina nods. "Mhm, me neither."

"It must be because my parents bought me a baby doll when I was in the first class." I laugh. I felt rather excluded from the social life of children, in particular girls who had several Barbie and baby dolls. With my graduation I realized that an important part of socialization was missed because of that, the one which would create a social being from a biological female gender. I used to play with bears, puppies and other soft toys. Maybe that is a source of my loving attitude towards animals. If that is so, thank you mum, thank you, dad!

"You … I didn't want to bother you with this, but I have to ask you. How did that happen? I don't know … I don't see you as a type of woman who cheats on her partner …"

"I know … I'm not … But he is so different from Tadey. Decisive. He knows what he wants … You know that Tadey spent most of the weekends playing?"

I nod.

"Well …He was on vacation and we went for a cup of coffee several times. Then he took me to a fine restaurant. He really did his best. Of course I liked the feeling of just indulging. Everything was arranged … And with Tadey I have to do everything alone. Search for and call plumbers, book holidays, settle bills …" she sighs. "He cooks and tidies a little … But I don't know … That does not make him a man, but the waiter is a real man and I felt a real woman when I was with him."

"Didn't it bother him that he was his friend? Haven't they known each other since studies?"

She nods. "We both felt guilty. It was awful ... I don't like him from another point of view. He can be rather arrogant, totally different from my Tedy."

"How did it start? Did you get drunk and got off?"

"We all were out together, but Tadey went home earlier because he was drunk . The whole group was drinking since the afternoon, I joined them in the evening, he came after midnight. Well, when he arrived, Tadey left and asked him to take care of me. At two o'clock the bar closed and he took me home. Nothing happened. But Tadey locked the door of the apartment and left the key in the lock, so I wasn't able to get in. He didn't wake up. I was ringing and knocking for fifteen minutes then I called him to fetch me and I spent the night at his place ... This is when it happened, not after dinner, not after coffees ..."

"Aha ..." So, actually, he pushed her into the lap of another man. I am totally on her side. The guy deserved it. I myself would push antlers into his butt, hit him with them and get rid of him if it happened that I would not be able to sleep in my bed because of alcohol.

"And now? How do you feel about him?"

"No!" she nods her head decisively. "I'm angry with him!"

"Mhm," I nod. I know what she is thinking about. *How could he let it happen?! Pig!* He had a good time but she is the one who has to deal with the consequences. Although in this case it is a little different.

"I want to sort things out with Tadey. If I have a child, I want him/her to be his. I don't know ... When I'm with him I feel .... We belong together ... He is always by my side ... He understands even now and doesn't blame only me ... Maybe the things will change. I want to try..."

"Yes? Are you sure?" I do not understand why. I do not like mummy's boys who let women do everything. That somebody locks you out and you cannot get into your own apartment? And that I would have to arrange things with an electrician? Halo?! What can she lose if she is single for some time?

"Yes ... And ... if we separated, I don't have anywhere to go ... I don't want to go to his place, no way! Neither do I want to move back with my parents … I don't have a permanent job, so I don't know about the rent … But also, I don't know … I love him …"

"I know … You know, I'll have to go. There are some essays I have to check today," I lie.

"Aha, I need to get to bed," she agrees. "Tomorrow I will spend the whole day at school."

She insists to settle the bill for our two white coffees and enters the café.

"Shall I take you home?" I ask her when she comes out to fresh December air.

"Yes, please. I don't feel well."

She sits in the car and I drive in the opposite direction from my home.

"Take care," I say and hug her when I stop the car on the pavement.

"Yes, I'll be ok. I only need to rest." She returns the hug. "Talk soon."

"Talk soon …"

When she closes the car door I think about the situation for a while. She really is in a mess! Watch the contraception! I remind myself and remember the businessman who I met through the social media. I cannot wait to check my mail to see if he responded. The coffee we had on Saturday which ended with a long wet kiss seemed promising …

And here it is. Christmas Eve. I have been following the weather forecast closely for one hour as the snowflakes are becoming denser and heavier and my car has no winter tires. I called Tasha to ask her to come and pick me up with her old Clio which has winter equipment. Ten kilometers. But she rejected my request.

"You can do it. It's only ten kilometers," was her reply and she continued to order what I should bring for our Christmas dinner which she will prepare.

If Odysseus was with me I would probably stay at home, but I do not want to spend this evening totally alone. The businessman turned out to be an inappropriate groom who jumps from one bed to another. Literally, of course. During my attack of feminism I suggested I could drive to the northern part of the state and visit him. To let him know how independent and self-confident the women of the 21st century are. He accepted my idea, so my emancipation took me to a three-hour journey during which I experienced a snow storm. After a severe fight with nature I expected at least a welcome drink somewhere in the town where I have not been before, if not a castle dinner, before he gets me into his bed. I did not receive either of the two. I was put on my back immediately after the door opened. During a very tiring sex he boasted that I was the second one to have sex with him that day. I was deported from the apartment to the front of the block to have a comforting smoke, for a feeling of being a total harlot the snow shower was perfect. During the night I could not sleep. I even got hit into my head by his elbow. So I moved to an uncomfortable leather armchair in the living room. In addition, the following day I suffered from annoying hemorrhoids. Well, at least he prepared the breakfast before he set me off with good intention – in the afternoon it was going to snow again. And he already had plans …

This is about dreaming how I will not spend the holidays alone. This is the first time that casino let Alex have a few holiday days off, so Odysseus will be in Ljubljana until 30 December. He will spend New Year's Eve with me, and on 1 January he will go back to Alex who will be on vacation till the middle of the month. I do not agree with moving the dog at such short periods, but he cannot wait for the new year alone, Alex is at work. He starts shaking already before the night begins because of exciting firecrackers, and I am looking forward to some cuddling.

So I do not have to care for my dog today. Ema and Katarina are at their parents with their partners; Nina is spending the night with her mother. The only possibility of socializing during the placid night presents Tasha. It seems that I will drive there in one hour, alone … with summer tires on my car … but I can do it! *You can do everything!*

166

With a few smaller slips and an average speed of ten kilometers I arrive at the residential area above the Krka river. Tasha welcomes me busily mixing the French salad. She will prepare and fry chicken breasts which will obtain a celebration shape of a Vienna steak. I will be responsible for making potatoes and salad. Well, at least for the initial phase. The oven and Tasha who wants to serve the leaves of lettuce and chicory with exactly defined mixture of salt, oil and vinegar, will complete the pre-prepared dishes.

Soon I can sit down and relax with a glass of cooled wine which is placed on a nice blue mat, and the chef soon joins me on the balcony. "This will be wonderful, I tell you …" she starts expressing praise for her cooking abilities that she is very proud of.

"Mhmm," I confirm her monolog-directed eulogy.

Soon the monolog moves to the area of long white robes. She is talking about the married doctor who she was waiting for one night till midnight, prepared, manicured, with professionally applied makeup. Only then did he inform her that after a formal and boring dinner he would not be able to come to their date. I ask her a little more about this Saturday because I have a feeling that the rejection happened on the day when the two of us were supposed to meet but she canceled the party because she, supposedly, did not feel good. At that time I was not in a mood to socialize with her either. When it gets clear to me that the unsuccessful waiting happened at the first weekend of the month I am not awfully disappointed and I do not mention the friendship betrayal. She has no idea that I got her; she is so infatuated with the illusion of an important doctor.

During her speech about a perfect future with such a respected person (still married) we eat our Christmas dinner at a big glass table. The potato baked in the oven is fantastic, French salad is alright, I do not like pumpkin oil on a salad, but supported by a half liter of cabernet that I have brought with me, I do not complain, and the steaks are too well done. But Tasha likes them that way and everything is just fantastically prepared. She enthusiastically praises two crystal glasses which she has bought for similar occasions. Unfortunately, she can afford only two with her student salary.

The Christmas evening awards me with dish washing and later Tasha's two friends join us, fortunately, as I am getting sick of her self-prizing. I respect positivity, but in moderation.

"Ciaooo," Tasha greets them.

The first to enter the apartment, a wonderful one-room paradise turns out to be an average small studio apartment, is her former primary school schoolmate who I have known for several years. She is married and pregnant, but today angry with her husband, I learnt before they arrived. He got drunk by drinking good wine already after five in the afternoon. I am informed that the unlucky man does not want this child and that their life has been unbearable for months. She is worried about his non-seriousness and all their future, and he is spending more and more time with his single friends and bars which are really abundant in our area. The second to enter is a teacher-to-be, a part-time student, employed at a company which deals with matters.

What follows is compulsory kissing and prizing of new fashionable outfits. The black-haired pregnant woman is wearing a short black dress and glittering tights which are approvingly felt by our fashion enthusiast. The teacher is wearing fashionable tight jeans with a wide black belt and red blouse which seems to be made of silk. But the most exciting sighs are caused by new black leather boots with high heels, made by Gacho, the newest Tasha's article, which are placed by the door, but I, an ignorant girl, did not even notice them. I do not hear how much she paid for them; I am not the type of woman who can spend large amounts of money for her appearance.

Actually, I like the fact that I can do my own manicure with a minimum effort and the young and old are asking me which manicurist I go to. My hair is strong and thick, the skin is average. Well, boys say that it is very soft. Nobody complains but I have never used fancy gels or body milk. A lavender or rose hard soap will do. Not to mention exfoliations or anti-wrinkle creams which Tasha has been using for years. In spite of smoking, drinking and frequent keeping late hours I seem to look a few years younger, so I must be doing something right. Today I am not wearing anything sexy, warm and comfortable clothes are enough. I do not intent to freeze in this cold weather with intention of seducing somebody. I am wearing jeans, a thick woolen polo neck and a black shirt underneath in case I end up dancing somewhere, and comfortable boots with low heels. Well, it is snowing outside …

Unfortunately, nothing of my practical outfit sees standing ovations. They do not even mention anything about it, but I do not bother. I am happy to be in the company. The girls have brought champagne and presents. They did not know I would be there and I did not know about their presence, so the gifts are for Tasha. She is grateful for black silk thong which she gets from the pregnant woman in a gift bag. Then, she sees the book Goodbye Africa in the second gift bag, and she is very excited about that too. The first part, The White Masai, was gifted by me for her birthday and she liked it very much.

Now I take my gift bag out of my handbag.

"Ooo, look," Tasha lifts a steel coffee pot. "Nooo … I just bought one yesterday."

"Did you?" I grimace because my purpose is not achieved. Only a week ago she was complaining on her Facebook page how non-aesthetic it is to make coffee in a potato dish.

"Yes, I checked the entire Shopping center … but yours is prettier. Thank you, I will be happy to use it," she says smiling. "I am not a groupie of Santa Claus, so I have no presents today. You'll get them at the New Year. Will you have coffee or shall we continue drinking champagne?"

"Champagne!" the three of us shouts simultaneously.

She brings glasses and the ladies' chatter begins. First, we discuss our jobs which are rather boring and I get sleepy. Then, the confession of the unhappy love story by the mother-to-be is interrupted by the time. The time is fifteen past eleven and the guests want to attend the Midnight Mass, so we get ready to leave to town.

I take Tasha in my car and her friends are following me in their car. The old bridge and the old part of the of the river town are shining in golden and blue lights, surrounded by a soft white blanket. We park next to the movies and walk to the Franciscan monastery and the church next to it. It is only a few minutes past half past eleven but the seats have already been taken. We are standing at the back and listening to Christmas melodies which are coming from the choir above us. I am stretching out my neck to see a Christmas crib but I can only see white little sheep in the corner. Finally a giant in front of me moves a little so I manage to observe green blanket of moss with little houses and lights in them, sheep, the kings and of course a full barn.

I am pleasantly drunk, I feel nice. This time I am washed away to the past by the melody of Silent night. When was the last time I visited church?

In the first academic year, I remember immediately. Before the most important exam, with the purpose of testing the God. I prayed to pass the exam. If I pass - I believe in God, if I fail – I do not believe in God. I passed it, but I forgot about the promise and continued ignoring prayer, church and everything that it represented. In my childhood I went to Mass every Sunday, regularly attended catechesis, sang in the church choir, during Mass I even played the organ a few times. But I have never been convinced by the holiness of religious people. Where do hypocrisy, lies and wars come from … Who can be so naïve to believe that all the suffering we experience can have a meaning? Not me.

I gave up spirituality when I confessed the priest in the confessional that I had sexual intercourse with my boyfriend. We had been together for three years what I repented. The following minutes which seemed as eternity, behind the door my parents were waiting for their turn, I had to listen to the lecture about debauchery, obscenity and irresponsibility of the youth who are rolling in sin. I received remission but with a threat that that was the last time. At my next offence I would wait for the eternity in God's name in vain. I was supposed to send my boyfriend to the confessional too. I remember the educational film about abortion which was presented to us during catechesis by a catechist. While following the filmed procedure on screen we were listening to an illustrative explanation of the sinful work of mean doctors who first suck or tear limbs from the innocent beings and then they do the same with other parts of their body. In this way they kill human beings … the fruits of love … the fruits of God …

The singing of the choir which replaced the vicar's sleeping voice brings me back to reality. I do not feel placid any more. I want to go out. I notice that I have been absent quite some time as it is time for contributions.

I tug Tasha who is standing next to me at her sleeve. "Shall we go? Thirsty. And I need to go to the toilet. Urgently."

"Yes, let's go. I am freezing …" She leans towards the teacher on her left and probably tells her to meet us in the café nearby. I am on my way out. The people are searching through their wallets, singing to the angelic voices above them, but I am getting out of breath. Finally, I manage to get through the crowd, almost jump through the door and inhale the cold air deeply. *That much about God!*

Tasha is right behind me and we quickly walk towards the Well. The pub is full but fortunately the line in front of the toilet is not too long. My bladder releases the pressure painfully, and I sigh in relief while I am crouching above a dirty toilet. Uh, how I would like to sit on it … It seems that tonight I will miss the luxury of toilet paper too.

When I get back to the bar I notice that while I was emptying my bladder Tasha has found a co-speaker. I find out that a short and chubby man in his middle thirties is a local businessman, a regular customer in the pub where she used to wait the tables. They are communicating, but I do not hear their words because the music in the pub is too loud. I am looking through the window at the snowflakes which are gently descending from the sky. I am rather drunk and solitude in a completely full pub does not bother me. The White snowflake from the speakers inside the pub and white snowflakes outside the pub are enough …

A little later the two religious girls appear and we decide to move. What is still open today? Eternal BS.

"Of course, let's go there," Tasha says. "Freya will drive." She solves the problem of transport. The ex-schoolmate is not used to the white blanket on the road and is afraid of driving.

"Uh, my car has summer tires, and it has been snowing all the time. If the police stop me I will have to do an alcohol test, probably lose my driving license, and get fined because of tires," I say indecisively. Is there another option? No way, I cannot spend the night at her place, and I must get back to my village. A taxi home would cost the fortune.

"I can drive you there. But you will have to find the transport back on your own. I won't drive through the town once more," I say, this time more decisively. I see that Tasha is surprised.

"Why is this a problem today? You always drive when you are drunk."

"The problem is in driving conditions. If you haven't noticed, they are different today," I say sarcastically. I surprise her with my response and the tone of voice which she is not used to. Usually I agreed with whatever she said without any argument.

"Right. You don't have to be rude," she rolls her eyes, "Will you go by your car? And take me home too?" she turns towards the pregnant woman. She does not seem to be convinced. I feel she would rather go to bed, but she agrees, anyway.

It is crowded in BS. But I feel better there. We sit by the bar again and wait for our drinks. The music is perfect and soon we start dancing ...

After two rounds of alcohol, except the tummy, no one is shy, in the corner only a sober soul remains. The whole pub is dancing at Christmas melodies.

While I am waiting for a free toilet to empty the unwanted liquid again, for the tenth or fiftieth time, I think, and talking to the teacher, the idea of mutual trip comes to our mind. When we return to the still full pub we realize that none of us has any plans for the days to come. The office is closed, Tasha is not working, and we are all free. The pregnant woman's father is the owner of an apartment in Pula and we decide to go there for pre-new-year's holidays. I am excited! To the seaside, to the sea! What a beautiful Christmas present! The girls leave, Tasha is talking to an acquaintance and I am still dancing. I am not interested in anything around me. I indulge to the rhythm and I am enjoying … enjoying …

After two o'clock, when I am still in my trance, the pub gets a little emptier. Tasha is in the hug of a driver who will take her home tonight. I cannot drink alcohol anymore; I order water and step out for a while. Fortunately, snowing has stopped, so I am not worried about how I will get back home.

I cannot smoke either, so I get inside and indulge to the music. At four when they have chased us out of the pub with the silence and darkness, those most persistent ones, I walk across the almost empty car park towards my car. I stop by the door and start looking for the car key. While I am searching through my handbag I notice with the corner of my eye that a car is moving from the lot opposite mine.

The driver accelerates jerkily and the back right corner of his car hits my ford, before I manage to react he rushes off towards the exit. The situation clears my mind and I focus my eyes on the plate number of the moving away car. I keep repeating the combination in my mind and continue searching for my key. I find it, open the door quickly, grab the pencil and paper from the glove compartment. I write down the number. Is it correct? What if I have made a mistake?

"Hey!" someone calls by the door.

I look up. A guy. "Did you write the number?"

"Yes," I nod.

"Good. Do you need help?"

"No, I'm ok," I reply. My hands are shaking. I push the key into the slit below the steering wheel, turn it and switch on the lights. I step out to check the damage. Fortunately, the light is still on although the glass is broken, and the bumper and left fender are damaged too.

Fuck! What now? Summer tires, I've been drinking … Shall I call the police?

First, I light a cigarette with shaking hands. This cannot be happening! I have just improved my financial situation a little … With my part-time job … How can I pay for the repair?

I call Tasha who left the pub with me but the trader has already taken her home. I tell her what happened and she insists that I should call the police and that they will get back to BS immediately.

I listen to her and call 113. I repeat what happened and I state the location of the accident. Then, I light another cigarette. I would like to cry.

The first to come on the scene are Tasha and the driver, surprisingly we have not been waiting for the police more than fifteen minutes. It seems that the Christmas evening passed without incidents except for mine.

My friend knows them; both are customers at the pub where she used to work. One of them seems familiar to me too. I explain what happened, I tell them the plate number and I confirm that it was a white BMW. One of them fetches the camera from the police car and they start taking photos of the damaged car.

Then … I cannot believe it … No …

I see the BMW which arriving at the car park with the squealing tires – how can he do that on the snow? He starts spinning on the carpark, obviously with the help of the handbrake in spite of the police car parked nearby. We all look at each other, the policemen step closer. The car stops. I look at the plate … it is the same. I was right! I remembered it! Oh, now I see that the car is red. Well, at least it is a BMW. It is clear to me that I mistook the color because the car is covered with snow.

Before the policemen get to the car, a man steps out. He is laughing and a loud electronic music is coming from his car. The policeman tells him to sit back into the car and the offender obeys. He gives them the documents and then they all come to my car. He denies having damaged my car as he slept all night at the back seats of his car, drunk.

They enter the police car and close the door, so I do not see nor hear what is going on. I think he will have to do an alcohol test. One of the angels in blue comes out and takes photos of the offender's car and my car. Then he gets back into the police car without reporting to us, the waiting victims, about the situation in the police car. After fifteen minutes the one who seems familiar to me comes to me, hands out the minutes and orders me to go with him to the insurance agency where the procedure will be settled further. Tasha invites them to stop by her place and they accept.

When he stops the shift, after half an hour, he says. True, it is few minutes after five.

I drive to her place too to calm my nerves. I cannot believe what I saw. Who would believe that the idiot first drove off impudently and then came back to the crime scene …

After thirty minutes my heroes who 'caught' the rascal come to Tasha's place. One of them opens a beer, the other one asks for tea. We are talking about alcohol, parties … Tasha is totally drunk and is talking nonsense which does not interest anyone. Well, at least not me. But I am very grateful to her for the assertiveness that she showed earlier.

After some time, the familiar policeman turns to me and asks me if I have been to the police station before.

"Yes …. Why?" I say carefully.

"Aaa, you are the one who got almost burnt by a psycho, aren't you?" Oh! Did the whole station laugh at me and point their fingers at me months after the event?

I nod. "I took you home," he surprises me. Well, I got my answer why he seems familiar to me. It is true, two guardians of Slovenian citizens took me home in the police car.

The following ten minutes we are listening to Tasha and her criticizing of my ex-boyfriend No. 2. A real moron, worthless psycho … But she liked him when we were socializing. It must be because he used to drive her around and pay for drinks.

I have enough. I decide to leave and the policemen leave with me, only the trader decides to stay longer.

After six, before the night transforms into a snowy morning I open my home door. I feel totally exhausted but sober. My thoughts are buzzing with vertiginous speed; I am thinking about everything ... I decide to light fire in the stove before I go to bed. The old house does not have central heating, the apartment is warmed by a little stove which quenched hours ago. I like the lack of popular heating devices, I like listening how the fire crackles inside.

I jump under the shower and enjoy the hot water flowing down my body. It is so good! I dry my body with a towel and put on fresh underwear. I am cold, but I roll a joint before going to bed. In the stove it starts burning, so I lower the inflow of air to a minimum. It will hold for a while, I will have to go to the toilet so that the maintenance of the heat with new logs will not be a problem.

I switch on the lights on a little Christmas tree in the corner, two candles, so that the atmosphere in a soft light is comfortable and relaxing. I lie down under fresh linen and light a joint. All is well ... I arrived home happily ... I am warm ... The car will be repaired ... The fairy tale of Christmas evening is over ... *Happy Christmas to me!*

I am awaken by a severe headache and fatigue. I am thirsty like crazy, but each sip I take causes more fatigue so it is difficult for me to keep bile in my stomach. I get up and take two pills from the table and fall back into bed, and wait for the sharp pain in my temples to decrease. It is eleven o'clock. I still have half an hour to pull myself together before lunch which is waiting for me in my mother's kitchen. Fortunately, only few meters away.

I am not excited about the circumstances where my brother's family will be present at the lunch. I love the two and seven years old nephews, but their cheerful behavior does not help calm the hammers which are banging in my head.

When I'm there I start eating my soup in silence and ignore most of the conversation about politics. I miss a larger part of a minor quarrel between my father and my brother which always develops in similar family circumstances – this time about which fishing rod is more suitable for fishing on a boat. But I am disturbed by their ignoring of the housewife who prepared the whole dinner. Mother is standing by the table with a dish full of potatoes and is unsuccessfully asking them if they have enough before she takes the dish away. So that she can put another plate with chicken and steaks on the table as the roast beef will not suffice.

OH MY GOD! Why doesn't she stop that humiliation?! Nobody even notices her, nobody sees her! Everything is taken for granted. Nobody prizes her effort, nobody thanks her … nobody respects, appreciates her work ….

Me neither. I am silently looking at my potatoes and a little piece of meat surrounded by onion sauce and cooked carrots. I am the first to finish eating and I take the plate and cutlery to the sink. I rinse them with cold water and put them into the dish washer. I do the same with soup plates. Before I do something real, she runs to me and assures me that she will do that herself, later. I accept that gratefully and reject the dessert. I will get it in the evening. I return to my place … to lie down … to sleep … to vegetate… to wait for the pain to pass …

The next afternoon my mood is much better. Cheerfully, I put my luggage into the car and take out a lot of unnecessary stuff. I do not like the idea that the only possibility of taking us to the seaside is my car with the broken front light and summer tires. But the weather forecast does not predict any snow and the light is still working. So?

In Novo mesto I pick up Tasha and her red suitcase which takes a half of the boot. Then I pick up also the other two attendants of our ladies' days at the Croatian seaside. Fortunately, they do not have so much luggage, but they have to tolerate quite some junk by their feet in my ford escort.

I feel great. I adore the drive towards pines and breeze which has fragrance of salt. I enjoy cutting bends while thinking about the blue plain waiting for me. So, I am not bothered by a collection of CDs brought by my co-driver - I have to listen to

Slovenian music between the evergreens. I am accompanied by the sounds of Sasa Lendero where we all are shouting that we do not go on our knees. A deceased Macedonian singer follows with his song in our language, and then the last-year Eurovision winner of Slovenian hearts, Rebeca Dremelj. Between the music which is directing our pace when we are passing Reka city we find Freddie Miler too.

Under the shine of Pula lights we arrive at the obvious holiday resort for in the windows of white-yellow houses with red roofs only a few lights can be seen, the cars parked in the parking lots are marked by foreign coats of arms. Mostly from Slovenia.

We open the door of one of them and are welcomed by a large room. It combines the kitchen with beige cupboards, the dining room with a big oval table and chairs, and the living room where on one side there is a large LCD screen hanging on the wall, on the other side there is an air conditioning device, under it there is a black sofa made of leather.

"Alo, babes! Let the ladies' night begin!" Tasha screams so we hurry to the kitchen. On the counter there are beer cans, two liters of red wine, one liter of coca cola, Jagermeister and Bacardi rum. The following three days will be cheerful ...

I am disappointed. It is midnight already, the drink does not agree with me, and the atmosphere is totally down. First, the unhappy pregnant woman confessed her saga. She does not find any common ground with her partner anymore. Next, the teacher announced her furious battle against male gender. Her life philosophy includes an attitude that men are only unnecessary degenerate of human race. She has never had a boyfriend, she has never been in love and she does not want it. I am sure that she left out a part of the story but I do not make any remarks. They all agree with her opinion, including Tasha who supported her theory with her situation with a married doctor. In relationship, but flirting with her! What is he thinking, bastard!

"They are good, though, when we need to use them," she laughs. "In all forms. Cuddle with him then throw him out. That's the way to do it!" she shouts totally drunk. Alcohol seems to get to all of them, but not me. I have drunk a liter, and nothing. No dizziness, no energy, ... nothing ... I am only bored. Whenever I try to direct the conversation into different waters – we do not need to circle around male gender all the time -, I lose it. My period of heart matters is not brilliant either, but I do hope that somewhere lives a member of this 'useless' race who is worth to be loved by me. I do not know where to look for him and I have concluded the search for the time being but I do not want to agree with what they are saying.

I feel like that I have fallen down from another planet. I do not find anything common with any of them. Wine does not agree with me, the effect is not right, so I move to spirits. My head will hurt for sure, but I fill the glass anyway and drink it bottom up. I growl because my throat burns and I drink a glass full of water. I add both doses and sit at the table.

"Hey, how far is the sea?" As always when I am close to the infinite waters I start longing for the coast where the water and earth meet.

"Huh, too far away. More than half an hour of walking." My idea about taking a walk reaches deaf ears. Now they are focusing on the text that Tasha is going to send to the object of her seducing.

They have been creating it almost twenty minutes and during this time Jagermeister reaches its intended effect. I step to the music box and turn volume of Bonnie Tyler to the highest frequency. With this piece Tasha has made up for all Freddie and Sasas.

»Where have all the good men gone and where are all the goooods? Wheeere's the street wise Hercules to fight the rising ooooodds ...« comes from the speakers when I get up and with my eyes closed wave to the imaginary knight.

»I NEED A HEROOOOO ...« I am shouting together with the singer and accompanying her as the loudest back vocal through the whole song. I know the text by heart. One of my favorite pieces. EVER!

I invite others. Music wishes are showering; we switch off the lights, light candles and indulge in dancing and loud singing.

Realizing Tasha's wish, it is Sasha who is accompanying us most of the time, but this time I am singing with her myself, lively and from the bottom of my heart.

The next day is a torture. Till four in the afternoon I experience traumas in my bed with too strong hangover to be able to be a part of the company or even in a sitting position. I woke up in the morning and suffered through sobering process awaken. There is no feeling worse than that.

Late in the afternoon I recover enough to join them on the walk to the coast. The sea is wonderful. It was worth having come here! Dark blue sea is glittering in the mirror of a cloudy sky and it fills me with peace. This is all I need.

The girls do not fancy sitting on the rocks and observing the water width, so we soon enter the nearby pub. I try to fight fire with fire, but after a sip of Jager I almost vomit. It will not work.

The whole evening seems even more pathetic than yesterday's evening. The doctor answered Tasha's yesterday's message today, so now the whole drama is being performed about what to write him back. The guy is with his friends somewhere in Porec and he needs to be persuaded to come here. I decisively rejected the idea of me driving there. My psychophysical state does not allow it and when one is abroad it is not good for someone else to drive the owner's car – was my excuse.

Written correspondence is going on through the whole evening and a little before midnight it becomes clear that he is not coming. Instead of a hot date we are supposed to go to a local disco, but I reject that too. I'd rather watch TV than seek attention. I make all the party girls angry with my suggestion, and my preposition that they should call a taxi and go without me does not reach fertile ground. Instead, they go to the nearby café and I stay alone in the house. Thanks God! But the comfortable lying on the couch does not last long for they are back after one hour. The café is closed, and I go to the room. I can hardly wait to be at home again!

Next day we clean the whole apartment and as a gratitude for the owner's hospitality we wash all shutters. And those were really dirty. The closer we get to Slovenia, the better I feel. But not everything goes smoothly. I do not know what got into me, but I drove past the last gas station and now we can run out of gas. I hope that there is an open gas station on the other side of the border.

When Croatian custom officers let us cross the border, the radio plays Rebeca Dremelj's song. Tasha increases the volume.

"Hallo?" I shout. "Can you switch off that shit till we cross the border?" I look at her sharply and switch off the radio. I used to like the song, but in these two days I have heard it at least fifty times and started hating it.

"You're so annoying!" she says.

They let us enter the European Union in spite of a broken light and damaged front end of the car. The police officer asks about the circumstances of beauty imperfections, but he believes me and I do not have to show him the report.

A problem appears because we arrive at a small city a few minutes after ten and we do not find an open gas station, and the gas indicator has not lifted above the zero for quite some time. We are silent, nervous, wondering whether we will manage to reach the town or we will remain in the middle of the night somewhere in the woods. The second option only slips through my mind; I focus on visualizing my goal. I will reach a gas station, no doubt about that!

Carefully and taking into consideration all my knowledge about economic driving I manage to reach Novo mesto. Girls jump out of the car quickly but Tasha does not want to go with me to the gas station, so I make a short detour to let her out in front of her block. I do not know who to be angry with. With myself because I am henpecked to really take her right to the door of her home. Or with her because she is unable to consider someone else besides herself. If I run out of gas now I will have to manage everything by myself.

I'm a nervous wreck but I manage to reach the only open gas station three kilometers away. I think that the car coughed twice during last meters but it might have been my nerves' sense.

I am grateful to the Universe to have driven me here. I fill the tank, buy some sweets and pay a kind clerk at the cash register. Then I leave for home. I am gratefully thinking about a peaceful evening in my bed. My mother lit fire in the morning, so my warm room is waiting for me, maybe I will read a book …

New Year's Eve. The longest, I really mean *the longest* night is approaching. Plans?

It is obvious that Tasha is going to join me, but I would not mind being alone with Odysseus at home. In her apartment the dog's hairs are not welcome and other friends are busy. Nina will be waiting tables in a pub, Ema is spending the evening with her family, her older sister and her boyfriend, Katarina and Tadey are celebrating with his friends. First, I plan the dinner similar to the Christmas one, then, we will wait for the midnight at home and then go to town.

I am waiting for Tasha in my little kitchen of white-orange color, without windows, preparing potato salad.

"Holla," I hear when the door opens.

"Hey, come in," I invite her and step through the white frame without a door which divides the kitchen from the living room with a bedroom corner. Odysseus is circling around her legs and hospitably offering a slipper but does not let it out of his snout.

"I've brought cannelloni. It'll be ok, won't it?" she asks when she manages to pass the dog and close the door.

"Excellent, I'm preparing potato salad. Will you have a beer?"

"Yes, mam, bring it! I'm thirsty as a wolf!" she admits and sits down on the couch.

"Here it is."

I bring her a tin and put the glass on the table in front of the sofa, and sit next to her.

"Hey … can you believe … how pathetic …" she sighs. "the New Year's Eve and I have nowhere to go?! How could this happen?!"

"Yeh, I can't leave the dog alone at home. He'll be lost at midnight because of fireworks and firecrackers, "I apologize because we are not momentarily at the town square or a pub as we used to celebrate in the past.

"Mah … I know …" she lights a cigarette. "You, how do you like my new tunic?" she shows off and feels black silk fabric. Then she pushes the dog that is looking for attention around her legs. "Hey, puppy, go away! Shush, don't get me dirty! Yes, yes, you are cute but go there to the door," she is trying to direct him but he will not listen. He only moves when he hears my strict order and takes a place in front of the wardrobe.

"I bought it in Ljubljana, in Tom Taylor, it cost me a fortune but it is worth it. I had to buy a bag to match it," now she takes a big baggy bag. "Isn't it just fabulous?"

"Mhm," I nod. "Absolutely fabulous, just fabulous," I prize it although I do not like it. But if she is excited at her new item, she might as well enjoy it. It is a pity that in the big bag there is not a present from Santa Claus who was supposed to deliver a New Year's present instead of a Christmas one.

I light my first joint today and lean back. In my other hand I am holding a glass with red wine. "To the old year," I make a toast.

"To the old year. Beautiful was even more beautiful," she joins the toast and we cheer with glasses.

"What are the resolutions? What changes will you make in the coming year?" she asks me.

"I plan to stop smoking grass and decrease the amount of alcohol," I reply after a short break. I exaggerated the last month, that is, since November. I was around all the time, drunk during too many nights, or was stunned, or both, and nevertheless, in a bad mood. Something will have to be changed. I liked the last two days that I spent walking across the meadows, by the river, in the woods, far from everyone. I did not even think about alcohol and I lit a cigarette only with the morning coffee. Well, I have not given up evening joints yet.

"Really? Yah, right," she laughs.

"I have a few joints left and then I'll stop for a while," I reply seriously.

"And how does that feel? Cold turkey?" she laughs again.

"Mah, no. One is not physically addicted. The only problem is that I won't be able to sleep. During last intermezzo it took me two weeks to normally rest. I was tired all days, I could barely hold my eyes open, and when I got to bed in the evening it took me all night till dawn to fall asleep," I explain. "And after that, nothing special. I did not have any wish to start again. But I was unable to say no," I laugh now too, take the last smoke and put butt into the ashtray.

"Are you hungry?" I ask her.

"Not really. Let's wait a little longer. Fetch me another beer and I will set up music so that we don't fall asleep," she says. OH, NOT AGAIN!

She goes to the desk with the computer, in the corner of the room.

"But please without the knee girl, the late one or food processor," I ask her from behind the door of the fridge. "I had enough of listening to them last time."

"Really? Too bad. Ok, I'll find something ..." And she did ... OH!

Wine and beer are followed by dinner, dinner is followed by wine and beer ... Fortunately, Tasha came a little before ten in the evening so midnight strikes soon.

Together with a radio reporter we are counting the final seconds. And ... 2009 is heeere!

We kiss, wish each other an abundance of happiness, love, and similar stuff and then rise the volume of Silvesterski poljub (New Year's Kiss) song. This is not louder than firecrackers that started a few minutes before the peak. The dog is shaking and weaning in the bathroom and the two of us are dancing and drinking silver champagne from the glasses brought by Tasha for this special occasion – I would settle with 'ordinary' glasses for white wine. We wait for half an hour, then we drive to the town. She will leave the car here and return to get it in one of the following days.

I park on the parking lot next to the movies, and we walk to the center. There are a lot of people and the bars by the well are full. I do not feel good in spite of all my plans how I will relax and party this night. Fortunately, Tasha has found company soon. Two unknown men introduce themselves; we kiss on behalf of the new year. I do not remember their names; I only partially follow the conversation. I do not want to be here. I drink one plastic glass of cooked wine, and then apologize because I do not feel good and leave. I go home where my dog awaits for me jumping – crazily happy to see me – I am just as excited as he is. I put on some logs and open the window for the air to change; I can still smell fried food, onions and cigarettes. I fancy going for a walk and the dog is excited about that too. We start our short walk on the road which is surrounded by snowy landscape on both sides, so the visibility is excellent. I look at the stars and ask them what is waiting for me in this year. As a response I notice a black shadow in the snow approximately a hundred meters in front of me. I stop, and the dog's hairs bristle. He is standing next to me and looking in the same direction. Whatever that is, it is not moving.

My heart is bumping with fear and I start moving backward slowly. Now the shadow runs in the direction of a nearby forest. I feel relief, it might have been a lamb, there are a lot of those in the area, or a rabbit or a fox – I cannot estimate its size. Well, that was neither a bear nor a wolf, for sure. Or a ghost. It is believed that people used to see a kind of glittering globe which was moving above the meadows.

At home I close the window, switch on the computer and continue celebrating. Now with the music of my choice. The fist sip of champagne is accompanied by Viva la vida, the first cigarette by the Killers with their song Human, and the first joint by Rio with my wedding tune which makes me shine. With the music, wine and smoke I swim into a happy future where I will get married on a sand beach with a man of my dreams and we will dance at this very tune. The honey moon will be magic and it will last at least two months. After return to our perfect house, with glass walls through which warm sun will be shining, and with a big pool in front of the house, he will spend most of a day doing business, while I will be writing, reading or dealing with the family of dogs, twinned with a few cats. Evenings and weekends will be devoted to the fire of our love and research on the beauty of life. Every year we will go traveling and researching our mother Earth and we will happily live for ever …

On Friday I put out my last singing grass and this night, in search for the bliss of forgetfulness brought by sleep, I am rolling on the uncomfortable bed in vain, the third night in a row. Totally alone – I gave the dog into care before the last smoke of intoxication - I do not know how to dam the river of thoughts, fears and despair, which floods over me the moment I lie in my bed.

During the day I spend time reading, I have invited my friends for a cup of coffee but only Katarina and Nina responded to the message. The former is preparing material for school days and does not have time, and the latter is hosting a new sex friend. Ema and Tasha have not responded.

I hate my life! I hate people, I hate this world … the thoughts flood from somewhere. How can I live with it?

I do not believe in friendship anymore … *Those people around you? Those are your friends?* Then, why do I feel this way? *As a garbage basket for their problems*! Exploited and got rid of. As a plaster which is useful only when you need it … otherwise, without any impact on life … Unnecessary … invisible …

The first one to be analyzed is Nina. Is she there for me when I need her? *Does she listen to you when you need somebody to talk to*? Yes … if there is not a male subject around. When there is one I drop of the table as an empty plastic bottle.

I do not want that …

Am I selfish? An awful person who wants her only for herself? Am I possessive? *Would You behave in the same way*?

No … I have never let her wait when we had a meeting … But I cancelled our drinking. Once. Because of Jan.

How many times do we speak about my life? *Yes, how many times does a conversation involve you*? With Tasha around almost never ... Most of the time I have a feeling that I do not interest her, that she is not listening to me. With Katarina ... rarely ... And with Ema ... when did we talk about me? We did, but only superficially. My words only serve as initiation for her sharing her feelings or descriptions of events from her life.

How many times was not me the one who had to drive? We were all drinking ... a regular driver was me even though they all have a driving license ...

How many times did they visit you at your home? Each of them only once. I am the one always visiting them ... Energy flowing into one direction.

It is the same with men ... *How stupid you are ... You are searching, investing ... and what do you get*? A feeling of being used ... Why I do not think in the same way as Samantha from Sex and the City... as Tasha ... as Nina ... Well, the last two do not seem the happiest, but they are happier than I am. It is obvious that what I am looking for does not exist ...That someone loves you, appreciates you, respects you, wants to cheer you up, hugs you, spends time with you ... I have never experienced that, I do not see a relationship which would live love as the love I am looking for. Does that mean that it does not exist? Obviously it does not. How blind I have been ...

Something starts shouting inside me: OPEN YOUR EYES!
You are all alone!
Nobody will save you!
Nobody cares about you!
Do you care about yourself?
What do you do? How do you live?
Always well behaved, agreeable and obedient ... Rarely did you dare express your opinion because of fear that nobody would have liked you if you had been honest ... You are a hypocrite! You support and accept the opinions of others although you do not agree with them. You are a coward!

Look at yourself! Your life. What do you do for a living? You hate forcing somebody to do something that he/she dislikes, but that is what you are doing! Teach! Who do you think you are? To be able to teach somebody? No wonder they do not listen to you! They will never need the stuff that you demand they should learn by heart. You are not needed! Addicts are no use! You are no use to anybody or anything!

You could at least bring a new understanding to life so that he/she would change your mistakes. But you are incapable, a coward in this area as well! You had two opportunities to make sense of your life. And what did you do? You killed two innocent beings!

Now I start crying. The memory of sitting in the hall, staring at the wall and waiting for abortion is very alive. The bliss of the moment when after the days of sleeplessness I swam into the darkness under the influence of narcosis, not so much. I am re-living the disappointment and hysteric outburst accompanied by the flood of tears when I woke up from that bliss. I remember delusional walking from one corner of a hospital room to another to prevent me from going crazy due to tension in my chest and head while I was gazing into the air. The words by my love for whom I would do anything except kill myself with maternity: *"You've killed my child! You slut, look at yourself. What do you look like down there? Only a tram did not go through you! Shame on you!"*

If there is God, then I lost my place in Heaven. Fortunately, that is only an illusion …. delusion of pathetic people to justify their miserable life … the mask of spoilt perverts… the source of power and money … the tool of leadership …

No, I do not believe in God, I do not believe in love, I do not believe in friendship … I do not believe in people … Would God allow us to torture our dear ones? Would God allow what is happening now to innocent animals? Would God allow that which is happening on Earth?

Now I redirect my thoughts to events which I witness every day thanks to the luxury of having TV. It is proper for a sociologist to be up to date with the world issues but the news is not promising. The substitute for horror movies. Is there anything good happening at all? Is it worth living in such a world?

NO, the arrow whisks through my chest that I feel a sting. I do not want to live and persist in this shit? What for?

I do not want to! I can't ... I am not able to ...

The outburst of tears is interrupted by my urgent visit to the toilet. It must be the fifteenth time this night. I hate my body! I am disgusting.

When I come back from the cold bathroom, I check my phone. It is 5.55. At 8.50 I start my first lecture in the new year. I will be met by 'aspiring' students of 3 d.

OH MY GOD! I do not want that!

I try to calm down but I am even more overwhelmed. Now I remember a lullaby that I composed as a child to fall asleep easier. I am singing in my mind:

Sweet dreams my girl,
Do not be afraid.
We are all here with you,
Do not be afraid ...
Ninaninanana, ninaninanana,
ninaninanana, ninaninanana ...

The second time ... the third time .... I do not appear to be exhausted enough to fall asleep, but I calm down a little bit. Delusion is directed into blogs which I discovered in summer but started reading recently. They are announcing the new world, new thought, different values, return to Mother Nature and similar spiritual things. I found them interesting but I cannot chew on the mention of Christ, angels and similar imagination-related beings. The thoughts about illusions, created in dumps without exit, strike me again. I will have to see a psychologist or psychiatrist ... How will they help me? Studying Freud, Yung and their psychoanalysis did not help improve my mood. In spite of my knowledge of Thanatos, aggressive impulses, auto-aggressiveness and similar concepts, I do not feel good. What is wrong with me?

"WELL, angels!" I cynically speak into the darkness," if you do exist, why don't you help me?"

That very moment I hear a blunt sound by the table which scares me to death. I jump up. When I see that my schoolbag fell off my desk, the horror lessens and I lie back with my heart beating fast. I am lying on my back and observing the darkness of the room. I have never slept in total darkness or silence. I am afraid. I felt the best when I was living in a block.

I do not notice anything. Is it only a coincidence that the schoolbag turned on its side at that very moment? According to the material I have read recently, there are no coincidences. I am so overwhelmed that I switch on the light and look into the kitchen and bathroom. I look into the place with a toilet where I take a pea so that I get rid of unnecessary liquid caused by fear. I return to my bed carefully and lie in the pose of a fetus. It started dawning and I am starting to fall asleep because of exhaustion …

I spend the next day with the energy of a zombie. I avoid the ignoring behavior of uninterested students by playing a game instead of filling up their brains with grammar and vocabulary rules. With the game of hangman on the topic of literature I got their blurred attention and they became so attracted by guessing that the lecture passed without incidents. Fortunately, the following lecture is on Wednesday.

I try to fall asleep in the afternoon but I cannot. I am so tired that I can hardly move, but as soon as I close my eyes the thought mosquitoes attack me. Among other stuff also Tasha's boasting about her visit at an alternative therapist's who told her wonderful things. She noticed that Tasha was born under a lucky star, that her health was good, that she would meet somebody from abroad, move to live with him, and that she actually did not need the therapist's services. She only sold her some tea. The first visit is free of charge so maybe I should try that instead of visiting a psychologist?

I call Tasha and ask her for the therapist's phone number. She agrees. I am calling her but nobody answers. I sit down at the desk and start browsing through the internet pages to find the information regarding a lady of Russian nationality, a former physician, as they say. After minutes of searching I find the data about her company.

Less than half an hour later the telephone rings and after my explanation why I have called her a kind voice informs me that she is very busy till the end of the week, the only free hour is tomorrow at ten a.m. I gratefully accept it and my body is flooded with a wave of energy. I have always wanted to try that. Although it is difficult for me to admit I am interested in the world of clairvoyance, alternative healing, astrology, Greek and Egyptian deity … ghosts, vampires, witches, werewolves… No wonder I am so scared.

I can hardly wait to learn what she will see. But in a while I start worrying about what she will sense … I type a message to Alex that there is a possibility that he will have to deliver some herbs. "Depression has won," I write. "I'll go nuts."

The following night is easier on me. I fall asleep at two and I wake up at eight. I spend another hour in bed thinking, and then I get up and make some coffee.

I am getting ready for visiting the clairvoyant. Now I am really afraid. What if I am dying? Do I have an incurable disease? I am sick all the time, I have a sore throat, I am coughing. Blood and lung tests carried out at the beginning of December were bad. The physician explained that I was probably about to catch a cold but that did not happen. The urine test wan not good either, it is full of bacteria but I have been used to walking back and forth to the toilet since high school days. In addition, she noticed that the white spots on my back are not the consequence of my skin peeling after sunburn but are caused by skin mold. So I am molding – not only inside the body but outside my body too.

It is five to ten in the morning when I open a glass door behind the hotel. Blue oval pendants ring above me, and a red-haired woman welcomes me and before I respond she invites me to an adjacent room. The lady will arrive in ten minutes.

In a small waiting room I sit on a sofa with a floral cover and start looking around curiously. On the white shelves there are various teas and fruit and vegetable juices. In the corner there is an air cleaning device and a few different filters for water. No voodoo scenes.

According to what Tasha has told me I know that the lady is from Russia who moved to our town years ago. A former physician with formal education, she has turned to alternative medicine and is now offering healing and consulting services, massages and even prophecy. Besides, she is an active insurance agent. Tasha met her on one of the seminars where they were taught marketing strategies. I have not tried to find out more about her most recent business. I am not a person who would invest money, if I had a surplus, into fear so I am not interested in the description of a profile based on people's fear and I ignored her words.

After some time a little black-haired woman enters the room, wearing white trousers and floral tunic. She greets me with a smile and we shake hands.

"Come, let's go into the office," the voice with a foreign accent invites me.

The office is on the other side of the white-wall corridor. I walk behind her and I sit on a comfortable chair in front of a big wooden desk. I do not have time to look around the room. Her eyes are looking at mine, and I do not dare move my eyes to look around.

"Shall we start?" she asks me kindly.

"Yes …" I answer faintly. I do not know what else to say. Shall I tell her why I am here? If she is intuitive, she will sense it.

My internal monologue is interrupted by her words: "What is happening with your brains?" Now she is looking at something behind me. I assume there is a painting hanging there?

I lift my eyebrows and move my lips, but I do not say anything. After a decade of more or less regular marijuana smoking I am surprised that I still have them.

She does not look into my eyes; she is still looking at the spot behind me.

"You're very anemic … Drink read beat juice," she says and looks at me. Considering my blood test, she must be right. I once

192

had a treatment with that beverage of disgusting taste and I am not looking forward to drinking it again.

She notices sour expression on my face and smiles. "Don't you like it?"

"No," I say and give her an unhappy smile.

"Buy the one with apples. It's good. Look for it at a pharmacy."

"Really? I'll try it," I mumble. Maybe it will be more drinkable. Although I doubt it.

Now she is looking at something behind me again. I courageously turn backwards a little so that I can see a massage bed with the corner of my eye, and above it a large painting with a colorful ball.

"You are in a closed shell. You're suffering in it …", she surprises me. "You want to be good for people, but they don't see it … don't accept it … You're alone … Your parents, tell me their names," she turns her eyes towards me.

I tell her the names with a thick voice.

"Good people … Very sensitive, but they do not accept what they have not planned by themselves … They don't understand … Do you live with them?"

"Hm, yes … Not really," I hesitate. "I am living in the house next to theirs, with my grandma in another apartment."

"What's her name?"

"Mhm …" I start thinking ... but I cannot remember her name. I have always called her grandma or ma. OH MY GOOD! I cannot remember, so I feel embarrassed.

"I don't know, I can't remember," I say. Is she Antonia, Aloizia? Something similar.

"I've always called her ma …"

"It's alright," she puts down her pen and looks at me. "She's not a good person, she doesn't want good for you. She envies you that you are young and she's old …" she says.

"We're not on good terms and we don't socialize. Actually, rarely do we see each other." How can she harm me, then?

"Even though you're not physically in the same room, her closeness can affect you. She's miserable, she doesn't want to die, she doesn't accept illness …. She can transfer it to you. You have to move away from there."

"I want that more than anything," I respond. "I already lived in Ljubljana but I had to return because of my job. Now I don't earn enough to live independently," I explain.

"Where do you work?"

"I work part-time at school," I reply. She is looking above me again.

"That is not a good job for you. It's draining your energy."

"I know, I don't want that either. But I haven't found anything else. If I could I would leave. But I don't know how … where …" I look down, my eyes are filled with tears, I have a lump in my mouth getting bigger and bigger, and I experience difficulty swallowing.

"Would you like to be an insurance agent?" she surprises me with a question.

I move my lips. "I don't know, I'm not into selling … not insurance, no … But I can give it a try …" I am really desperate.

"Give me your number and I'll call you in the following days. I'll see if something can be arranged," she says and takes her pan again.

She writes what I dictate, and then continues: "When I find out, I'll call you to make further plans. "She smiles encouragingly. "Everything can be arranged with therapy. Everything can be changed. Death can be postponed too," she shocks me. What does that mean? That I will die? She is saying something else, but I'm not listening. When she mentions my boyfriend she pulls me back from rumination.

"No, I don't have a boyfriend," I say in surprise.

"There's somebody …" she continues anyway, "I can see him in your aura. He needs to process his fears. Face them and deal with them, or they will destroy him," she says. "The same as you. You have wonderful ideas, but they remain closed in the shell. Open up," she looks at me and leans towards in confidence.

"Do you have a question?"

Well, I will not ask her about my future, and I cannot think about anything else at this moment. Aha ...

"What's with my bladder? I am constantly in the toilet. Sometimes every five minutes. Sometimes I have to get up ten times during the night. I did all sorts of tests during my high school period but there wasn't anything wrong."

"Your bladder is alright. This happens because of sensitivity. You're very emotional, the body is cleansing itself in this way," she answers and reassures me.

"Oh, thank you," I say.

"Anything else?"

"Mmm, I don't think so."

She stands up and so do I. We have concluded for today.

"Good, I'll call you when I find out," she says and I give her a hand.

"Thank you very much." I am really grateful to her from my heart for what she has told me. "Goodbye."

When I leave through the door I look at her gratefully once again. The teacher conference is waiting for me so I do not have time for immediate analysis of the event.

A few minutes later I sit on my chair in the teacher assembly room and try to listen. But I cannot; my thoughts are buzzing about her words. I am trying to fight my tears and swallow a heavy lump in my throat. After an hour the salted brook finds its way out, so I take my pen and notebook into which I have not written anything, whisper into my co-worker's ear that I have an urgent matter to attend to and I leave with my eyes looking down. Before I get to the car my cheeks are wet. Fortunately, I do not meet anybody; I sit into my car and cry. How could somebody who I met for the first time sense my inner essence so accurately? The people who I live with, meet every day do not see anything.

I start the engine and leave towards my home. In spite of foggy visibility, I happily arrive home and park in front of the house. I enter the room and tears start running again. I sit on my bed and while trying to get some air I am re-thinking what I heard ...

NO! I cannot live like that anymore. Where can I find help?

I get up, take a paper handkerchief from my table and blow my nose. I wipe my tears and I decide. I am going home …

When I enter the kitchen, I find my mother alone, sitting at the table.

"Hi, where is father?" I ask her.

"In the vineyard house. He went to decant the wine," she answers when she lifts her eyes from the newspaper.

"I have to talk to you," I want to start seriously, formally, but I whimper.

She takes off her glasses and looks at me with her grey-blue eyes. "Is there something wrong?"

"No … Yes … I've never been so unhappy …" I barely utter. "I visited a healer today and she told me exactly where the problem was."

"Don't go to such people," she interrupts the beginning of my confession. "They will only mess up your head, the same as they did to my co-worker …" she repeats the already heard story about a woman who had cancer, left a fortune at a charlatan and died anyway.

"She was right … I am not like Gregor," I mention my brother. "I have not got married, I do not want to have children … I don't see myself living like that … I have a feeling that I'm doing everything wrong. But I wouldn't be happy … I can't be what you expect me to be …" I shout.

"Even though I'm trying hard …" I stop for a while to give way to the outburst of crying, and I blow my nose. I do not dare look at my mother.

"I can't be like that … And I'm sorry that you had to give your life away so that I could study. In spite of the fact that my father was sending me to the field to dig out potato as I was only capable of doing that … Do you think I felt all right when I fell one academic year? That I did not worry? I didn't want to come home. Do you know how I felt?"

Now I look at her, into her eyes, and I see that her eyes are wet too.

"As a pile of shit … The same as when I was a little girl and I heard my aunt say that I would not achieve anything … Or when you told me that you felt sorry that you had not had an abortion … That I was a bitch … Or when you killed Gaia and you did not feel I was worth enough to be told about it," I mention the unlucky shepherd who was euthanized. "I couldn't say goodbye to her … and she was my only friend here. You got rid of the cat also… nobody ever asks how I feel … It's only important that I do what you say …" My last words can hardly be heard. I cannot do it anymore. I do not want to.

"Whatever a person does, everything is wrong …" She is crying now too. "I've never been sorry to give birth to you! At the beginning of pregnancy, I wasn't sure whether or not I wanted to keep you, but I soon changed my mind … And when you were born … Everyone used to say that I was spoiling you too much, that I was harming you … Gregor … How often he blamed me that only you were important … How many things we made possible for you but not for him …"

What? Look at who is complaining. The person who did not need to cook or wash the dishes or tidy up the apartment because he, lucky man, was born in right gender. He was permitted to go out already during primary school period while my exits, a potential pregnant teenager, were limited until my studies. But he wanted me to become independent as soon as possible, and he was waving with a telephone bill and wanted me to settle it when I was sixteen.

"She told me about the grandma too." I continue with my confession and try to achieve that they will put her in a retirement home but my words end up in deaf ears. Although they are not getting well, the family responsibility prevails. What will the neighbors think if she does not look after her? Because she must.

I stand up and want to leave. I have said what I wanted although I have not been understood. But I understand her a little better so I feel better.

"I'm going," I say and walk towards the door.

"Wait," she stands up too. She comes to me and hugs me. "I love you," she says and tears come running down again. I do not know if I have ever heard those words from her before.

"I love you too," I whimper into her shoulder but do not stay like that long. I am not used to hugs. Nobody in our family is used to expressing love physically or verbally.

"Will you come for lunch tomorrow?" she asks me.

"Yes."

In my room I find a pleasant surprise in the form of a message. Alex has arranged the stuff for relieving my suffering and we meet in the evening, so I'll get to hold my dog for a while. I am exhausted, lie on my bed and curl up into a ball.

Fortunately, I set my alarm, so I am woken an hour before the agreed meeting. I have been sleeping for three hours but I still feel drained. I do not care how I look, I get into the car wearing my tracksuit and sports shoes.

As usually I am waiting for him. He is fifteen minutes late but it surprisingly does not bother me this time. We would fight about that immediately – I would be the one to be blamed because of my putting too much pressure on him, but today I do not care. He seems to care because he is nervously pulling the dog into the pub.

"Where are you, my doggy?" I greet, fondle and hug my dog.

"Hi," Alex seems curt. He apologizes for the lateness by numerating everything bad that has happened to him this day.

That includes a business meeting, his father's visit, unreliable dealers … As many times so far, I stop listening his talking, and cuddle my dog's snout in my lap. When he stops reporting I tell him my daily story.

"All that happened today?" he asks upon the conclusion of a brief summary. He is surprised.

"Yes. My idea about quitting smoking in the middle of winter does not work," I apologize for my unannounced bothering.

"Yes, it's not smart. The same as … I met my former schoolmate …" Now he is talking about someone I do not know. About someone I am not interested in.

When he finishes, I do not comment but get back to my topic. I tell him that the clairvoyant or healer, I do not know how to name her, senses a man in my life who is very scared. Is it possible that it is him?

"No. I am not afraid at all," he answers sovereignly and stops.

Unfortunately, only for a brief moment, then he continues to comment what I did wrong in the conversation with my mother.

This time I interrupt him impatiently. "Look! I don't need advice. Don't you think that it is possible that I only need someone to listen to me? I'm always the one listening to you …" I growl and drink my tea.

"I'm sorry … What else did she say?"

"Nothing." I am not willing to share the experience any more. "I am tired, can I get a pack? I'd like to go to bed as soon as possible, I have school tomorrow early in the morning," I lie, I am free next day. If he had listened to me, he would know.

"Yes, yes, of course. It's in my car. Let me just smoke this one," He answers and lights a cigarette. I do not feel like waiting at all but he did me a big favor driving all the way here so I lean forward and scratch golden fur by my legs. Alex tries to make me say more about the recent happenings but my answers are brief, concise, and curt so he starts talking about events in the casino.

Finally, he puts out the cigarette and we walk together a few meters to his means of transport. He opens the glove compartment, takes out a little pack and hands it to me.

"How much do I owe?"

"Nothing, a New Year gift," he says.

"Are you sure?" There seem to be at least two grams of skunk in the pack.

"Yes, I'm sure."

"Thanks," I take the pack and gratefully hug him. The feeling of unworthiness which usually outweighs gratefulness of accepting gifts is got rid of by the thought that I gave him the Raffaello box for Christmas, but I did not receive anything from him. So the pack somehow belongs to me.

"Bye, my golden child. Be good," I get to Odysseus on the back seat and hug him too.

"Enjoy, let's be in touch. You know, nothing is as bad as it seems, he says before I close my door.

"Yes, yes. Thanks. Ciao."

"Ciao."

Half an hour later I am at home. In front of the door to my room there is a pile of wood. It seems that my mother told my father what we had talked about. Normally, he does not do it – I am supposed to be responsible for my own fuel supply. This pile of nicely arranged wood is his response? This is his way to show me how he loves me?

I put some in the stove and sit at the desk. I light a fragrant stick and several tea candles and start a play list. Listening to Robbie Williams singing about a hole in his soul I am lying on the bed. Already after the first smoke I feel better. Less than twenty minutes later my mood sharply increases. I feel good in my skin. Finally, I found a bit of optimism, all is well; everything is going to be alright …

Suddenly I get an idea. I will write a book! Based on all my experiences! It is a popular idea, as everyone seems to be writing about something, but that is what I am going to do. That is what I want! I start thinking about the structure, the plot, main character, other characters, events that I am going to describe …. This time I am not only thinking. I take a white sheet of paper from the desk, a school textbook for the base and I start writing. The first chapter, the first station – graduation from school, Damir, Slovenian-Croatian relations … The second chapter … In less than thirty minutes both pages are full, I take another sheet to conclude with the topics of final chapters. I change music; the peaceful tunes do not correspond to my mood any more. It is unbelievable how one can change from depressive feelings saturated in suicidal thoughts into a winning euphoria. This is it! The end! The time for a new story!

In excitement I turn the volume up and sing together with the singer of Aerosmith …

The song reflects my inner happening. It is amazing and it is true, I left the good ones out of my life and welcomed in all the wrong people But fortunately the angel of forgiveness sees all my sins ... And yes, it is amazing when you finally see the light and you know that you are going to be just alright ...

STATION 5:

ASCENDING INTO THE SPHERE OF SPIRITS

I lie down at my roll-up mat, covered with a purple blanket, and cover myself with a soft thin blue blanket. I try to relax which is not an easy task in the group of lying like-minded people. The room looks like a gym, but it is about to receive the luxury of acoustic hall as we have gathered to be reborn by the gong sounds, crystal bowls, shaman drums and other old age instruments. I found the event announcement among the posts on Netlog page of Lightworkers and got enthusiastic about it.

I close my eyes and try to visualize the text which I have read at least a hundred times for it describes the promised experiences that I am about to try tonight.

EXPERIENCING SOUND INVOCATION
The participants are 'bathing' in the waves of abundance of energies of the Universe song which wants to be realized in a particular moment. Each person has a unique experience led by his/her intention, inner guidance, his/her current needs, as well as his/her willingness, assertiveness and openness for experiencing:
- Harmonization with his/her original vibrations
YES, PLEASE!
- Awakening of creative, behavioral … potentials
YES, YES, YES!
- Change and healing on any level
YES! EMOTIONAL!
- Insights, inspiration …
THAT IS WHAT I NEED!
- Freedom from old records, programs, memories
THAT INDEED!!
- Experiences beyond the time, space and matter
IS THAT POSSIBLE?
- Transcendence of consciousness which is followed by the transcendence of the entire Being.
WHAT IS THAT??
- SOUNDS OF CRYSTAL BOWLS cause the vibration of the brains' waves and enable the experience of higher

levels of awareness. The acceleration of secretion of body hormones causes:
- Rejuvenation
YES PLEASE!
- Strengthening of one's will and life energy
YES, YES, YES!
- Awakening of creative potentials
YES!
- Healing of addiction
OK, I AM NOT SURE ABOUT THAT.
- Pain relief
YES!

So ... here I am. Here I am now. All is well. Here I am and now ...

I try to relax, but I cannot. I am angry with Alex as hell. I invited him to come with me to this special event as I know that he is interested in such things. He used to meditate under guidance; he attended the course on emotional intelligence, so he should have showed some respect to the opportunity. But he did not. I arrived at his apartment in the last moment hoping to see him ready to go. But when he is involved nothing happens without waiting. Without a pillow, without a blanket, without twenty euros for the contribution. The instructions were specific about the exact amount so that there would not be any delays due to money exchange, but the gentleman's wallet was giving shelter to a 50-euro banknote. After five minutes of waiting and looking at my watch, so that we are not late for the concert, I slightly lost it when he entered the car.

I told him off as I had enough of playing his mum. Why he never happens to take care of me? No, it is always me who has to take care for both of us. Am I selfish? I, of course, came prepared very well. I do not want to be cold so I have brought two blankets, not to mention twenty euros. For this purpose I stopped at the gas station, filled in some gas and bought a bottle of water. So that I could exchange that damn 50-euro banknote given to me by the bank-machine.

Of course, Alex chided me too. I was listening to his blaming me that I was treating him as that he was a child, my verbal slaps then aimed at explaining to him why I was behaving that way and how fed up I was of that forced maternal role. Verbal fighting was continuing all the way trough Ljubljana. At the end of drive we both slammed the doors of the car and entered the hall separately. Well, at least I have my both blankets with me so I am not cold and I feel comfortable and cozy: even though I am lying among total strangers alone. Where is immature Jonny boy and what is he lying on – I have no idea, but I cannot get him out of my mind and shaman drums which announce the beginning are not helpful.

I am following what is happening with my eyes closed and trying to discern which sound belongs to didgeridoo and which sound belongs to Tibetan bowls…

The sound that comes after the overture of exotic instruments is a total surprise. I open my eyes and lift my body to assure myself that those are gongs. Between lying bodies in the hall there are ten big 'plates' and people dressed in white clothes are gently caressing them with coated stick-like accessories. But the sound that is filling my ears is totally different from the sound I heard on TV - usually in Asian movies. There is no loud noise. What I am hearing reminds me of winds wailing around corners during stormy nights. I lie down, inhale deeply and close my eyes again.

Wailing is intensifying; the sound is penetrating all parts of my body. At the peak I get the willies from my heels to the top of my head. The roaring of the storm is replaced by a peaceful female voice which is singing the text unknown to me, here and there I manage to understand an English word, but I do not understand the whole meaning. Nevertheless, it is relaxing in particular when she is joined by the sounds similar to the humming of a river. They take me to my childhood days, to the kindergarten, where I heard something similar for the last time.

A few minutes later the gongs appear again. I am trying to focus on my wishes for the future and the intention of today's concert. The instructions recommended that each participant creates the list of goals he/she wants to achieve with the help of today's sounds. Of course, the first place belongs to longing for love – to love and to be loved –, after initial blockade I am writing about willingness, abundance, courage, power, respect …. and I fill two pages. I am affirming in my thoughts and soon the drums reach the peak which is then again calmed by Tibetan bowls and other gentle sounds.

The third and I hope the last round is passing and I am hardly waiting for it to finish. One hour and a half without visiting a toilet is quite a challenge for my bladder. So the attempt to manifest my desired dreams is replaced by a simple longing for a cold plastic and drainage pipe under my butt.

Finally, rebirthing is over and I run down the hall. I assume that there are more cowards like me who did not dare go to the toilet during the concert, so I do not want to wait in front of the toilet. Not before a loud spurt flushes away the pain in my lower abdomen I am able to relax and sum up my feelings. In the toilet.

I did not experience anything special. There were no out-of-body experiences that had been described by some people, there was no crying while releasing childhood trauma. I feel a kind of peace but I am not sure whether it is a consequence of a sound experience or of a physical discharge of excessive liquid. But I like the experience. I have learnt something new.

I remember Alex and get angry again. Gongs' sounds did not flush away my disappointment in male gender which is personalized by him at the moment, even though they were trying loudly and intensively. I go to the car but he is still not there. It would be too much to expect from gongs to affect his slowness. Is there a slower person? Where is he again?

I light up my cigarette impatiently. Before I inhale the second smoke of nicotine I see him 'rushing' down the stairs.

"Hi" he mumbles and lights his cigarette. "There was no problem with the money" he reports immediately. Before the beginning I talked to the leader and she was surprised at my asking such a question. At the end I took 30 euros from the bowl and that was it." And if everyone had come with a 50-banknote? And took out 30 euros from the bowl? Would there be enough for all? Of course not. Fortunately, there are enough of those who respect the host's wishes so that those like him do not have any problems, I think to myself but do not say anything. It is a waste of effort or ignored words or another quarrel.

"She brought me a pillow and a blanket, even though I could have stayed on the floor. She was very kind to me," He continues babbling. Of course she is well prepared to take care for twerps so that they get something for their money. If he had been lying on the floor he probably would not have been able to enjoy the sounds. He is really smart! He pretends to be a poor guy and there is always someone who will help him get what wants.

"The only person complaining was you," he adds when he sits down on the co-driver's seat.

"Ok, it doesn't matter." I do not like adults who need to be taken care of by someone else; I continue my internal monologue while all the tranquility has been blown away by a cold winter wind.

Alex is now, for a millionth time, talking about the happenings in his casino although he knows that I find the topic from my past and his present repulsive. But my feelings AS USUAL do not interest him, what matters is that he can talk. During our relationship we used to fight about it, but I did not achieve anything. I do not understand why a person speaks and speaks about the same thing although he knows that the person next to him is bored and would like him to stop it. What is there for him? If he makes people around him miserable? I drop him off in front of the block of flats and I reject the offered beer and joint. For a change – I believe it is the first time. I am really fed up with him and the enticing substance. Neither Odysseus's presence would outweigh the feeling. I cannot imagine being in his presence for another ten minutes. Why did I even bother to take him with me? Yah … Of course I know … I was afraid to go alone.

A week after the big concert all positive energies, if there were any, flew away. I am at Katarina's thirtieth birthday between the walls of a friend's vineyard house, drinking sour wine. Approximately fifteen people are sitting at the big table. Beside the celebrating girl and her partner there are only Ema and her man that I know. Other guests belong to Tadey's friendship circle and their partners, mostly girlfriends or fiancés. I am sitting with Dajana, the only single guest beside me and consequently a good new acquaintance. We are sitting at the end of the bench and discussing Norway where she spent her two last holidays. I am attracted by her talking about untouched nature, cold nights under a tent and deer which peacefully eat their grass while not far from them one is walking between 100 years old trees.

"Oh, me to …" I sigh and lift up the glass for a toast to the following travelling. I am a little drunk, so it is easy for me to be in the wilderness with my mind. The lover of black, color of clothes and wine, cheers with me and takes a big sip herself.

Thank you God for her company. I do not know what I would be doing here tonight if she were not present. All the conversations at the table are about children, jobs and apartment furnishing. Am I really so childish that I do not have much in common with average thirty years old people? Dajana, Tadey's colleague from the time of studies is a real uplift of a boring 'party', that is, a light meal.

Till midnight we are exchanging ideas about the capital city where she lives, global attitudes, religions …, also friendship with ex partners. She is one of few people who is not surprised at divided guardianship of our pet, friendly coffee dates, and sleeping over on the sofa. She admits without hesitation that her ex-boyfriend is still her best friend and she does not pay attention to those who comment why they are not a couple if they spend soooo much time together, go to concerts, and spend holidays together in the north of Europe. They take care of each other when they are ill, and from time to time she visits his mother who happens to be a wonderful lady. I am excited about the little black-haired girl in a dark polo neck, tight worn jeans and old army boots. She joins me in front of the vineyard house where we are inhaling poisonous tobacco joints.

"I'm trying to quit, but alcohol without a cigarette … it's not the right feeling. The same is with coffee," she says when inhaling the first smoke of the offered cigarette.

"Isn't that true?" I nod understandingly. "How is your detoxification?"

"I managed to be without it for a week, but now I don't want to be under pressure because of this … non-smoking. I don't buy them, I can be without them for several days, but at some occasions as it is this one tonight, I give in," she laughs and continues talking. "It's important that you do not terrorize yourself, then you are halfway already."

I am nodding enthusiastically at what she is saying. "Ahm … Ahm … I promised myself at my 17th birthday that I would smoke till I am 30 and then I would stop. I am two years away from the turning point so it is wise to obtain information at this point. Maybe I manage to quit even earlier, you never know.

Katarina rushes in and drags me with her to the toilet on the first floor. I notice that she is quite drunk. While I am waiting for her in front of the bathroom to do what she is supposed to do in the toilet, I am listening to her talking about the present guests. I learn about everything that I wanted to avoid: who has bought a new car, who is thinking about a new suite in the apartment bought by their rich daddy, who is thinking about life insurance …

Fortunately, the water has flushed the gossip away too so we move to the empty kitchen. We have not seen each other for a whole month and now we are alone after the unpleasant event so I am interested in the situation at her home.

"At the New Year day we fought as never before," she says. Uh, we have not discussed that at all. Where was she?

"Where were you?"

"Five couples were celebrating in the vineyard house at Kostanjevica. Nothing special, we were drinking whisky, chatting, till midnight… And at midnight …" she laughs and drinks from her beer bottle before she continues. "Two couples … listen to this …" she stops dramatically. "Two guys proposed to their women!"

"Really?! How nice!" I say enthusiastically. I am always positively surprised when someone wants to get married these days – in particular men, to put their dear girlfriends on a pedestal of marriage. It is even more beautiful, but rare, if a man does not cheat on his wife! Or vice versa.

"Nice? I was so sad." Katarina is not enthusiastic about the event.

"And Tadey and I? Like this? For seven years now. And thinking about the last happening ... Where is our relationship going? Everybody is progressing, permanent jobs, part-time jobs ... children ... houses ..."

Ah, old Katarina again. "Why did you quarrel about?" I ask her.

"I was nagging how we do not seem to be progressing. And that no wonder what happened in the autumn. That I'm having a feeling that I'm marking time and that the life is passing by ..."

"What about him?"

"Classic ... as always ... That I'm never satisfied with anything. This is his answer to everything."

Hm, well ... "You want more from life," I avoid responding directly and have a last sip of wine instead. In one hour I am supposed to leave so to avoid spending the night at the police station after this glass I intend to change the enticing beverage with a liter of water.

"Well," she is continuing," Then we made up and last week we decided to buy an apartment."

I am so surprised that I almost spit. After all the drama, now this? Bounding oneself for another twenty to thirty years.

"Are you sure?" I look at her ....

"Yes, we've already looked at one, two-bedroom apartment. We'll see if he can get a loan, I've already saved enough for a deposit. If not, then in the autumn. I'm sure I'll get a permanent employment at school." She is strumming wrong strings, at least according to my opinion. She is excited at something that I would be crying about. Why would she stay with the guy who she is cheating on? Why would she stay with the guy if she

210

wants another man? Why to have a job where they do not respect your work and where you are not happy? Why would she want to limit herself and her future? Or is my thinking totally wrong?

"Yes, super. I'm happy for you," I say when I swallow all my second-thoughts, and lift the glass to make a toast. Maybe I'll have another one.

"I can't hardly wait to move. To our own place, finally!" She says and cheers with her bottle against my wine glass.

"Ahm, it'll be great," I say not very convincing. "I'm going to light a cigarette."

"Ok, after that come inside," she says and heads towards the door.

"Yes, sure," I mumble, take a ceramic bowl and pour some wine into my glass to fill it up. Just before I am supposed to stop drinking, wine is getting more and more tasty.

Outside Dajana joins me soon, so I quickly forget about Katarina. Dajana and I are now talking about diet. The girl is a vegetarian, she is also thinking about veganism bust first she wants to gather all the information about health aspect of this Spartan menu. I have considered non-meat diet several times, but at the moment I do not dare introduce radical nutrition into my diet. Alex and his vegetarianism was a great model. My parents accepted him without any caustic remarks. I had never brought a normal lover home so Alex's graduation from a higher school was enough for a welcoming acceptance. I, however, doubt that they will accept their daughter's deviation from the current norms so understandingly. There would be no meals for me free of charge any more.

I get inside the vineyard house to fetch a bottle of water and then I and my new colleague are bivouacking outside and continuing discussing the wisdom of life. It is very cold, but the drunken alcohol quantity is enough to prevent me from changing into an ice queen.

At around two o'clock I have enough and most of the guests have already left. Under the roof of the party only the hosts, Dajana and one couple who have come from Ljubljana will stay at night. Actually, Dajana has come with them. We exchange out telephone numbers and email addresses because she does not have a Facebook profile – she rejects virtual communication, then I drive home carefully.

I like, like, like this girl! After a few days I received Dajana's message asking me if I want to join her and her co-worker at shopping spree in Trieste. Fortunately, they planned the shopping for Tuesday when I do not work, so I was at eight in Ljubljana, and one hour and a half later in another state. Crazy prices! For only thirty euros I bought two dresses, a long skirt and two T-shirts from Asian sellers who substituted our south brothers who I remember from previous shopping.

They did not buy anything. "Ah, I don't like anything," I heard in every store.

Well, they were happy about my purchase so that the trip was not in vain. I invited them to the upcoming sound invocation at the next full moon which I am looking forward to. Dajana accepted the invitation, but the co-worker is not interested in such things. A rather boring lady in the middle twenties is not full of stamina and her one-syllable replies while we were strolling by the 'San Carlo Moll' were not exciting, so I will not miss her.

A few weeks later Dajana and I meet in front of the Biotechnical Faculty to listen to the sound invocation at the full moon. She has never experienced cheerful gong sounds so we enter the full hall. The event is happening at the same rhythm as last time, I cannot relax this time either. This time I am not dealing with anger at Alex, but I am worried if my new colleague feels all right next to me. At peaks there are some electric waves that shake my whole body. Maybe next time I should bring a quilt.

Sounds get slower again and I know that the event is coming to an end so I get up and look around. Everyone is stretching, hugging or moving in gentle sounds which are coming from several throats. Dajana gets up too and I cannot help myself hugging her while a tear of happiness slips down my cheek. I am at peace; I feel that all is well.

"It's alright, yes." She comments the event when we light our cigarettes in front of the car.

"I was cold a little bit, I did not reach any high revelation, but the sound is very interesting."

"Isn't it?" I agree. "Will you join me some time again?"

"Hm … yes … maybe. I wouldn't have this every week, 20 euros is quite a lot for lying down one hour and a half," she is hesitating. I myself know that I feel much better and optimism is radiating out of me.

Before we separate we agree to have a party around Ljubljana at one of the following weekends.

During the following months, with the exception of school labor, my life moves to the world network. I spend whole afternoons browsing through different articles and forums on new age, and the list of 'must read' books is getting bigger and bigger. I spend quite some time in social networking. But this time I am not looking for male samples, I have given this up for some time. My friendship with Matey is still canceled although I notice that he *checks* my profile from time to time.

This time I am reading blogs and forums of two groups - New age in Lightworkers. I was touched by Dusan's story about disaffected family life, his desire for change, and the next Pasman[22] Enlightenment.

How well do I understand his skepticism. I used to think that only pathetic incompetent people, who do not know how to care for themselves, meditate and believe in God. But I would never go to a camp full of weirdoes who communicate with 'invisible friends'. I do not believe in a Jesus Crist! Well, maybe only from the view that he was a cunning wise guy who twisted around his finger a group of mentally unstable barbarians who glorify him and in his name terrorize the world people millennia later.

---

[21]   Island in Croatia.

Through the internet pages I got into contact with a group whose name is Hanta yo gang. They are brother and sister, the twins, and their guides. Who knows if it is true, but now I am reading whatever I can find about reincarnation. I like the idea about learning here on Earth, about long-term goals, striving for pure life, and critique of short-term goals which brought our planet to what it is today. I like the idea about the place you go to after death and together with your guides you discuss the event you have witnessed. I like the idea about connection of our world with animal and plant worlds, with totems and similar things. His or her or their messages – I never know who will respond to my questions – are swallowed by me. Somebody is taking me seriously, finally!

Also when I ask why the dog is barking at the doll on the wardrobe in the corner. One Saturday night we were sleeping on the sofa in the empty parents' house when Odysseus started staring at the ceramic doll which he finds terrifying – it must be Chucky syndrome. I took it in my hand and showed it to him so that he could smell it but he continued snarling, so I took it to my former room. It was not enough and my next move was the tour around the house with a knife in my hand, but I did not find anything or anybody. I forgot about the doll till the last week when I found myself in the children room again and Odysseus started snarling at her again. I informed my on-line friends who beside energy painting, enthusiasm at gongs and similar instruments deal with a lot of things in the area of spirituality about it. I also wrote that due to all the thrillers I watched I am good at ghosts and other terrifying beings that are on the lookout in the dark. They responded the same day – to throw the doll away, maybe someone wanted to harm the one who the doll was given to. I do not know where it came from but I happily took it to the garbage container at the end of the village.

Further, I told them about the feeling of alienation, weirdness, and that I spend more and more time alone. It does not mean that I am not lonely but the old company does not suit me anymore. I mentioned a shared custody and an attempt to become vegetarian. ... For the first time in my life I had a feeling that somebody is interested in what was going on with me. The responses were always encouraging. They did not find me weird but special. After we exchanged mutual attitudes towards the world they suggested I do Gaia Initiation which would help me on my path. I would become the energy channel, similar to reiki, but stronger, heal myself in this way and help others, also animals. I was attracted by the idea. But I am not hundred percent sure, what if they are members of a religious cult of fanatics who would confuse me and took all my money. So I checked them on the internet but I did not find any forum which would disclose their scams.

I cannot even think about asking Katarina, Nina or Tasha about it. They stared with surprise even when I mentioned gongs and meditation. While Nina is somehow passively attracted to the conversation about energies, the others are totally against any spiritual spheres.

I sent email to Alex in which I confessed that I did not want any contacts with him, so the conversation with him is off. I received his reply in which he blamed my manic depression and irrational thinking but I stick to what I told him, I do not want to judge and I do not want to participate in his drama. Egoistic or not, I have a right to my unconcerned life. I have a right to deal with my own problems so that the problems of others do not take all my energy and willingness. Our contacts are limited to messages once a month regarding the location of the exchange of the dog and formal greetings suitable for the situation.

And there is Dajana. Feeling encouraged I start telling her about that side of my life. Of course, via email.

From: freya333gmail.com
To: dajana.pisnik@gmail.com
Subject: Abraham Hicks

Hi,

What's happening in Ljubljana? What about the cold? Everythir under control? ;-)

Well, if you are resting, I have found an interesting movie (auth is Abraham Hicks), which answers where my anger at Alex com from and why he is getting on my nerves. It must be a split betwe my old self which was dependent on others and was not autonomou ... and my present self, extended, which is trying to achie something in life. Peace, love ...

I'm interested in your opinion regarding the content. ☺

Have fun, take care, have a rest ...
bye bye

From: dajana.pisnik@gmail.com
To: freya333@gmail.com
Subject: Re

Hi,

My health is changing, but we'll manage. ☺

So the movie, hm, yes ... low of attraction ... There's a documentary abc it What the Bleep Do We Know, and also The Secret – if you haver watched them, I can record them for you. But my opinion is that it is wror ... it emphasizes wrong values. Ok, I won't go astray, maybe it's not the wrong, it brings to light certain matters, the basics.

Then, I don't know, I look at things in the way that everything is in me or me, we cannot change people around us but we can change ourselves and o attitude. We can play the role of a victim or we can grow, the choice is ou In reality it's not that simple. We have to first realize things before we acce them as ours. The whole point is in that we allow ourselves to grow fro and take the best from 'the worst' (which actually are not so bad, it's a mat of perception) situations. And it doesn't come by itself ... not by force ... maybe ... seemingly .... for a few moments ...

I don't think that I am something more or better ... no, no We all grow through different phases and even though we comprehend the theory we may not be able to realize it instantly. But we're on the way there ... we only need to mature (although we aren't pears, or are we?) purify our soul .

I can share something about vegetarianism. Last time two people (meat eater and vegetarian) were discussing it ... something ... I myself do not see any need for discussing benefits or disadvantages. Rarely do I talk about it, also because it's not often that you meet a meat eater who does not feel endangered. So I rather say nothing. I like vegetable eaters and meat eaters equally, we only have different attitudes. If somebody sees a steak just as something to eat, he is not any worse than any other person who doesn't eat meat. We are different souls ... I only say, let's share love and love will be born ... aaa, see, law of attraction. ☺ The same holds true with the opposite, when we share hatred, we contribute to its presence.

But who am I to judge???!!! Don't think that I am flawless. I do not want to force anything and I don't think that different people are worse. I don't care what anybody is doing in the world ... to a certain limit ... To the limit, if the things are done under external influence. I believe in changes that originate from the essence ... and that which expands from inner love cannot be bad.

Ok, this is a little scrambled ... but I'm ill ... ☺ It's the first time in six Years that I am on a sick-leave so I'm entitled to some buzzing from my bed.

Be cool!

From: freya333gmail.com
  To: dajana.pisnik@gmail.com
  Subject: Re Abraham Hicks

Nooo, you've put it great!

I understand, I agree with you in all respects. Law of attraction yes, I haven't had the opportunity to watch the movies but I've been reading a lot on that topic. I noticed a lot of things but I was always pulled back. I thought that I ended this unhappy circle of 'wrong' people around me with Alex, but I didn't. It is the same as before only in a different way. That's why I am angry, furious, in particular with myself.

He hurt me again (or I hurt myself??), when I sent him a mail that we could not continue like that anymore. I really tried hard, gathered courage almost for a month, tried to explain my feelings about him it's time for both of us to make a step forward, and if he really still loves me, we only prolong the agony by seeing each other.
His response?
As usually, he confirmed he understood me well - a constant problem was exactly his not listening to me, but trumpeting about his own ideas - and that I suffered from manic depression and should find professional help. What followed was fifteen minutes of reading about the things which had been discussed two years ago. But we don't come to see eye to eye.
So I was furious at him for the whole week for thinking that he knew everything. I just couldn't explain anything to him. Thank God I watched that movie, otherwise I would have written a nasty mail to him – I was already in my Scorpio feeling when I can blurt out Where it hurts the most. Sometimes I cannot help myself even though I know that I'll hurt a person. But this happens only when I defend myself or somebody close to me – and I'm not proud of it. But what I had seen in the movie kicked my ass at the right time, and I wasn't angry anymore. I won't even try to explain my feelings to somebody who is too much in his own truth to be able to hear what is being told to him. Waste of energy. ☺

Did you watch Zeitgeist? I've managed to watch only the first part but I liked it very much. It puts things in the right place. Now I've seen that in March there will be a meeting with an emphasis on the

fact that we want to make decisions about ourselves by ourselves…
In a sense of a documentary.

Enough of bothering … ☺ And you, go to bed! If you can't be
still, smoke one joint to relax … 😊 And lemon and other
vitamins, ok? 😊

From: dajana.pisnik@gmail.com
To: freya333@gmail.com
Subject: ReRe

Hi,
My attitude is a little bit different, as I wrote in my previous mail.
For instance, for me there is no such thing as a circle of wrong people …
but there is our perception of the people around us … and I believe that it
is totally up to me whether the words is beautiful or ugly, it doesn't depend
on anybody else. It is easier to blame others than to change yourself.
  Yessss, you see, this is similar to what I believe. I don't see a reason for
my explaining the things to people who don't seem open for them (or
vice versa). There's no point, it only creates bad mood with a sense
of trying to force something.
  Hm, that you want to hurt somebody … this is difficult for me
to understand for I don't want to hurt anyone regardless of what they
have done to me …. It happens, anyway, that I hurt someone
unintentionally … but everything can work out if we're willing to talk
to each other.
And you are … to admit it (you must belong to the minority), full cool! I
just love it!

  I haven't watched Zeitgeist, maybe I will if somebody brings it
to me. UAHAHAHAHAHAHA   …
naughty   girl!! ☺☺☺

> *It's so good to be at home! Six years without a sick-leave and I have always*
> *spent my vacation somewhere else. And now I'm at home, everything is 'take*
> *it easy', I'm constantly mixing brews ☺ Yesss, I've got to find a wealthy-o*
> *husband, a cook if it is possible, ☺ so that I can stay at*
> *HOME UAHAHAHHAHAHAHAHAA ☺☺☺*
> *Bye, bye*
> *P. S. Will you come to Ljubljana on Sunday? So that we can go ou*
> *together?*

Next week I get down from clouds into reality. First, my suggestion to take Odysseus with us when we go night-strolling around the city was rejected due to his sniffing. I admit, I am offended. I expected that such a big animal lover would be happy to have a dog company.

On Tuesday I get down off my high horse when the tutorial for final exam preparation was unexpectedly cancelled. I was ringing the bell of the house where the lady hired me to teach her son. I was phoning her, but neither ringing nor phoning bore fruit. The door remained closed, the call unanswered. My preparation for the tutorial, my reading of additional literature for explanation and exercises, was in vain. They had not paid my fee for the previous two hours for which I had not demanded the payment immediately for we agreed that I would teach the high school student all the way to examination for the school-leaving certificate.

On Wednesday I was disappointed by my yoga instructor with whom I had my first session of body stretching. During the meditation he went out for a cigarette. I did not expect that from a serious spiritual person. My question about Lightworkers was followed by a bunch of superior words about rays and fields which I did not understand, and about the exploitation of marketing …. He added that I should seek spirituality in the things which are free-of-charge. When I was walking home and thinking that I would not attend the initiation because no one would fill their pockets with my naivety, my knee started to hurt me. I had noticed similar unpleasant body symptoms before in similar unpleasant circumstances. Having read Louise Hay's book about the mind-body connection I know that difficulties with knees mean that in some area of your life you do not want to make a step forward. So I will think about the initiation a little bit more…

Saturday evening does not go according to the plan either. Dajana is very reserved, I am speaking about myself almost all the time. I am interested if we have another common point. Why does she seem so sad? The pain of her soul is seen on her face. It must be her relationship with her parents but I cannot get anything out of her. The feeling that she is rejecting whatever I say is getting stronger and stronger. She was not excited by Zeitgeist, nor by my clothes of bright colors, and as it gets clear at the end of the evening, she despises the music which makes me alive.

After a whole-grain pizza and a stop at a rock pub in the center of Ljubljana we get to her place before midnight. I get the willies when my favorite piece – Rio, Shine on – is evaluated as a total commercial crap, by her. And that happened after I had been very considerate about loud outbursts of anger, hatred and death with her hard metal hooligans, who do not have any sense of melody and synchrony.

When I do not have anything else to say I focus on book shelves where I notice The Destiny of Souls. I start reading and realize that it is the continuation of Journey of Souls, which I used to be reading during my breaks when I worked at a casino. Dajana finds it miserable and gives it to me as a gift. Excellent! I hardly manage to close my eyes on the bed which she generously gave me and she went to sleep on the sofa in the living room. I can hardly wait the morning when I go to pick up my doggy …

I cannot forget the Saturday evening with Dajana so I decide to let my soul out in an email. I have been writing it for more than two hours and during that time I have visited the toilet at least six times and smoked almost a half of the cigarette box.

I inhale loudly and press the button Send without reading it once more. I am afraid she will delete my mail. But this is me, this is how I feel, I cannot help myself.

I spend the afternoon outside with my dog and in the evening I switch on my computer in fear and check if the answer has arrived.

Here it is … in a form of a conversation.

From: dajana.pisnik@gmail.com
To: freya333@gmail.com
Subject: ReSaturday

Hello,

I need to tell you a few things and I rather do it this way, it's easi
I really do care that's why I'm spending time at the toilet so muc
so I need to let it out.

The people around us are our reflection and you're the reflecti
of me as I was six months ago. Now I can understand Alex w
wanted to help me but I always responded defensively, as that I w
the one who would know everything about me and that I didn't ne
him being a smart Aleck.

I believe that you don't know me enough to be able to judge about whose
reflection I am …

As for music, I will not apologize to anyone anymore if I listen
commercial crap, according to your opinion, if that crap gives m
energy and makes me cheerful, happy, joyful … and I can forwa
that energy to the people around me. There is nothing bad in that
don't blame, judge or look down on people who listen to accordio
Sasha Lendero etc … as long as that makes them happy.

But then, I expect from others to accept 'being different' in me. And you spitted on my favorite piece of music which makes me forget about everything around me and move to the island where there's nothing except the sun, the sea … and I'm satisfied … I don't like   someone looking at me as that I am a Barbie doll without the brains because of that.

Please don't project your difficulties onto me… at least not so sure that you are right …
I say what I think … but it doesn't mean that a person is inferior to me…
I'm not offended if somebody expresses his/her opinion about the music I like … or about a cartoon, movie …
As for the apologies regarding music … I don't need any … do you?
I don't judge people by music and clothes …

I don't want to watch for any word I say – as I felt uncomfortable about your expression and response when I asked you if you were tired. I didn't mean anything bad, I just wanted to congratulate you for your power and willingness – if I were working all day and went to school I would feel totally exhausted, I don't believe I would be able to go anywhere. But you seem to manage a lot more.

How can YOU know what I'm thinking about???
I really don't understand why everything on me seems to bother you … I'm VERY tired of people telling me that I look tired … I'm aware of it … It's obvious … so I'm not disturbed by your questions about it …

For instance: I will not be quiet and tolerant if a woman doesn't pay for my tutorial when I've been preparing for it and going to her place in vain … I hope she's not so irresponsible towards her son although we can conclude a lot from a person's relationship towards others.

This, too, is a product of your own thoughts ... We feel what we feel an
it's not about what we should or shouldn't feel ... it doesn't work like tha
...

I talk about such things to people who I feel comfortable with – b
obviously I've made a mistake in your case ... If I had known that you tak
such conversations as attacks, believe me, I wouldn't have said anything.
don't talk about it with many people (because of such reactions) ... By th
way, I didn't say that you have to accept things silently as it depends on
person, I wanted to point out that we can accept things with understanding an
not by looking for a escape goat ... It doesn't mean that I always stick to
in reality but I'm glad if someone reminds me about it in simila
situations.

As for Zeitgeist ... I had a feeling that you reject everything
forwarded to you. You probably didn't watch it carefully. Maybe
should have told you that it used to be forbidden in the USA and wa
not allowed on the internet for a very long time ... According t
responses it is supposed to be one of the best documentaries and ther
are meetings to support it ... Obviously you are the only one wh
dislikes it .... But you don't accept many practical things, mobi
phones, facebook – even though they don't have anything to do wit
dating as you seem to believe.

Such a documentary is good for people who don't watch Discover
and similar programs due to the lack of knowledge of English or th
lack of time or they don't have a cable TV – we already know wha
shit our media is showing, and there are no appropriate magazine
newspapers ... - in short, they don't have an opportunity to open the
eyes but are aware that something must be wrong.

No, I don't reject what YOU are forwarding to me, but I reject what
find uninteresting ... it has nothing to do whether someone likes it or not ... I
make it clear: I don't reject it as generally bad – who am I to judge what
commonly good??? But it's just my opinion, I don't decide for others – I don
have the right neither do I wish to.

224

*But I'm not a conformist to the level to hold my opinion about certain
matters to myself so that someone else would not be offended ...
No, I didn't watch Zeitgeist carefully because I'm not interested in theories
of conspiracy in detail. That we are manipulated is a well-known fact ... (as for
my rejecting everything you forward me ... I wouldn't have watched
Zeitgeist if I had known what you are now saying about it ...).*

*I'm sorry if you take such things personally, but this can't be changed by
someone else ... if you hadn't felt endangered at every second word I said you
would have noticed that our opinions regarding Zeitgeist were differed on a
personal level and not about the fact that it could open someone's eyes ...
I criticize The Secret too => the people who are not offended by my not
saying 'yes, yes', and the Secret is cool, notice what that means; those who
disagree with my saying so, don't notice it ... and for that movie too, I believe
that it is good that it has appeared ... but I dislike the style because it is has
too materialistic consequences ...*

I hope you are not offended, that wasn't my purpose. I only wanted to
clarify certain things. I have a feeling that you don't consider me equal,
so I'll stop being a smart Aleck. But I really see my relationship with
Alex in a different light …

*☺)) But this I find really unbelievable and funny at the same
time, you're comparing me with your relationship with Alex ... every
person is unique …
And this equality or inequality ... you're always talking about some 'being
smart'..... If I don't take everything you offer, it doesn't mean that you are
inferior ... or that I'm superior ... But the greatest miracle in a relationship is
not feeling endangered if somebody else perceives things in a different way...
And what is bothering me?
One and only thing (but it's not a little one, it's a **big** one), that you seem to
have the right to judge ... this mail is not the first one in which you're
telling me who I am and who I'm not and what I could be thinking or what
you would do if you were in my shoes ...*

I am shocked by her response. Am I really that awful? Do I judge? I have a feeling that everyone else is judging me. So, am I the one? According to the law of attraction, yes.

But I do accept her ... I only wish she were happier. Is that a judgment? But ... Of course I do not have the right to judge what is good for her ... However ... Don't we all want to be happy? Healthy? Vital? Or is it our purpose to struggle through life tired and sad? I do not know ...

After a few days of silence there is another long answer. "I knew that something was wrong!" I say when I read about the pains in her arms. I am not happy about her health state but my intuition has not become too foggy as she wanted to convince me. When I finish reading I start responding to her thoughts. Her reply, in which the confusion of thoughts is clarified by the line before the following paragraph, is received the following morning.

From:dajana.pisnik@gmail.com
To: freya333gmail.com
Subject: ReReResearch

same time that it's not you who's being criticized ... maybe I find certain
things self-evident and I don't explain them and then everything may seem as a
rejection.

In my case yes, because I am used to get it almost from everybody.
Aha, yes, in your case, I know ... wasn't it obvious 😊*)) But if you took
a better look, you can see that it's an expression of the problems of a
person who takes it this way ... it doesn't mean that there is
something wrong with the person, I only don't know what I'm
doing wrong if I don't go around explaining everything I think ... I
simply believe that the people who stay in our lives are those who see
something in us ... and you don't have to tell it with words (or there is an
alternative – to tell, as you told me ... you had a choice. you could sulk in
silence or you could tell ...and I myself had a choice – I could scold you,
or ...) ...*

---

*And maybe my response to your email wasn't the best ... maybe I should have
told you what I was offended by even though I don't know exactly (I admit,
I'm writing this unwillingly because I have explained our adventure to
someone and he told me to write to you about what had offended me ... I'm
not totally convinced about what he's saying but I've decided to write you this
even though I don't know why I'm doing it, maybe it'll do some good ...)*
t is absolutely right to tell me! I do not know where we would be
f we were quiet?

---

*In short, I was offended by your concrete descriptions and 'conclusions' about me,
and this is something I don't like ... I was hurt by you seeing in me only bad ...*

I have never considered you a bad person!!!!!!!!! If you have such
feeling you're wrong! Maybe it's projection as you see it - to use
your words?

Why have I got such impression?? Because I believe that I wouldn't have felt endangered at your every word if you had a good opinion about me ... I understand that there is more to it (We've talked about that) ... and of course, my opinion about me is also affecting it ... as I say, problems originate in ourselves and not in the people around us ...

The person I was talking to supports such explanation; usually it happens this way, we can try to change something .. here and now, in this world .. but not by myself ... What do you think about it?? That I shouldn't explain because I'm sensitive, or what??? What could have offended me if I had said 'the piece is awful but you're ok??? You must be the right person for the question because you were offended because I didn't say it ...??

Well, we're here to change something, aren't we? At this moment I believe in karma cleaning ... Yes, to be honest, I believe that you are a very sensitive person (so am I) and that's why there's this shield ...

Yes, that I'm sensitive, it's been clear to me the whole my life ... and people who have feeling for this can sense it (despite the shield) ...the people who think that I'm self-confident and strong are very wrong ...

And now I'm totally confused, because I don't know if I was really offended or am I just pretending ... I feel that I wasn't hurt deeply but just a little .. but I think we communicated it very well ... do you think that we communicated it well?

I think we solved it perfectly, at least I've solved my problem .. you weren't talking nonsense at all!

☺ *well, I hope it's like that ...*

Or, I was talking nonsense and you succumbed to it?? I'm really interested in this, so tell me the truth – because I don't want to be rude – you wrote it like that, didn't you? – but I'm wondering if you feel that I was rude??

No, my dear, I got my answers so I've clarified our misunderstanding in my head …
I'm so happy about you ☺ You may not believe my words …

I don't know … I know that I'm putting a bunch of questions and I feel weird and I'm wondering how you feel now??
I'm really relieved. I didn't believe you were accepting me as I was. I wanted to clarify it because my feelings told me that it couldn't be like that. And you proved it so I don't have any restraints with regard to you and I find it great, talking to you like this!!!

Wow, I'm glad … I think, that you are asking yourself (well if you hadn't we wouldn't be discussing now) ☺)) I don't rely on my feelings 100 % either. Because I know that my thoughts can trick me (because of my sensitivity … I believe you've written about it)

Well, this guy I'm visiting, says I should be writing about what hurt me in your mail (a hint maybe?), now I'm asking you about your feelings … He said I should write this email because of myself (I hope you understand) not because of you … I feel that I'm dealing more with you than with myself … but maybe I'm wrong …

At this moment I'm totally <u>confused</u> … but I don't know because I really don't want to change something or because I'm not sure about each person, or how can I express myself …
In short, either the guy gave me a too difficult task or I am confused by the approach …

I'm sitting here and trying to pour my feelings on this paper but I don seem to be doing a good job, do I?? And I don't know if it is because th event did not leave any seal on me or because I've put a wall around me??

I'm really wondering ... because when we went to Ljubljana it was obviou and clear to myself and to you that I did ... I'm defending my shield ... an this is why I'm confused ... because with regard to the story of the recent day I don' know if my response was the shield ... or it simply didn't touch me at a ...

How do you see it?? You know ... because I know very well that I have great shield around me (I'm a very sensitive person, someone once said the they have to deal with me in gloves) and that a lot of things affect me, but can't explain this with emails ...

Ok, now I can't help myself comparing you to me (although intended to let it go). I believe you have a shield, yes, I recognized because I had had one myself! I'm also too sensitive hence tha comparison with Alex and me... That's the reason for forcing you t tell me, trust me, what's bothering you...

Ok, we can throw a ball to each other, you that, and that, and that .. how can you be telling me stuff if you are doing the same thing ...
Don't you have the shield anymore?

Well, one confusion ... I don't know what I've been trying to tell, I only wanted to find a way how to discover if I had been really hurt.

You will have to discover it by yourself; you don't need to do immediately ... it will reveal itself. I just want you to know that I di not want to hurt you intentionally (maybe subconsciously?)!

That I know ... ☺)) You know what, I believe that nobody wants t hurt us intentionally ... and I support an understanding approach (no that you don't express your feelings but that you consider another option - e the event with tutorial) ...

.As I find everything weird and confusing I'm trying something, because you can't do anything with stagnation ... I've been trying for a while because I have to do something about my health, I don't want to have deformed joints at the age of 40.

I don't know if everything I do is ok ... about diet too, but I have to do something ... Whether or not I will achieve something, future will show it later, but there is nothing without nothing ... if there are 10 failures, maybe the 11th attempt will be successful, but if we don't try, we don't get anywhere ...

I didn't want to tell you earlier, but we are discussing such things, so I had to mention my terrible pains in my arms. I should hide them, but I don't want to ...

With my shield and with hiding my thoughts and feelings I did not come far. The healer I visited who I told you about her, told me that repressed things affect the body the most – this is where my problems with bladder come from and traditional medicine claims there is nothing wrong with it.

Now that I'm aware of it, I can start gathering evidence that it is like she said (the bladder is an emotional organ). When I was considering whether or not to tell you about our misunderstanding I was at the toilet every 10 minutes and then I was relieved. ☺

consequence: I believe - based on my experiences, I don't claim it's the same with you, it seems similar - **that in such sensitive people as we are there is a lot in the head ...**

YES!!

So the guy, I'm visiting for reflexive massage, told me to choose between:

> *a)   telling you about my feelings (offence) triggered by the mail you sent me,*
>
> *b)   telling you that I don't trust you that much to tell you anything ...*

My opinion is that friendship and trust come with time – only in rare cases when you meet someone who you tell everything when you first see him/her ... Of course I've decided for the first option ... I admit slightly unwillingly, but I wanted to try ...

Thanks for trusting me! ☺

It's obvious that I <u>must be doing something wrong</u>, or I wouldn't have these difficulties with my bones ...

I've been wondering if I'm pretending to be happy ... I don't think I'm pretending and I believe it's ok not to feel miserable but try to change something (although veeery slowly) ...

I used to cry a lot, now I don't, and I feel as that I'm fooling myself.

It's ok to cry, this is how the body cleanses itself, they say. And if you're holding your emotions, this doesn't lead you anywhere (this has not grown in my garden, I'm repeating after others, it has helped me – for the start) and I believe that you think that you're happy, but how it is deep inside you?

I think that we need to communicate, to certain limits, not that all life circles around it, but one needs to express his/her feelings. But tell it to somebody who will understand you, listen to you and no give you smart advice how and what should be done, what you're doing wrong ...

I think that only with total sincerity towards yourself and the others can you help yourself and others ...

Mhm, I don't feel that I'm holding my emotions with regard to my bones and that I'm repressing the problem.

Deep inside me it's not the same as I show it on the outside but I'm learning to make it so ... and I don't find it to be a 'punishment', but a gift from which I can learn a lot ...

And I'm talking about it ...

232

Last time I was discussing it with my colleague who was a little shocked and he told me that I was not doing anything good for him (Aha, don't mention such things to him?)

At that time I didn't find it ugly and I didn't take it as a rejection ... I don't know ... there are a lot of complex things here ... but we've never talked about my health state again.

When my arms were hurting me I spent every afternoon for three months at one of my friend's place (uh, it was so good not to be alone with the pain) ... but he later told me that he got involved too much personally ... he felt more miserable than I did (we exchanged roles) ... and now we're not discussing it any more (but it's not a taboo topic).

But I still regard them as my friends ... I don't know, don't expect people to be supermen ...

And then, this veganism ...

Marjan, the guy I'm having the reflexive massage at and who suggested this email, supports bio veganism and today I had a feeling that he's not ok with my not being in the action already ... maybe it only seemed that way. But he did say that I was enthusiastic with words but not in actions ...

But I can't give up dairy products over night. I had been reading about it before I visited him – literature and people confirm that dairy products are crucial in difficulties with bones, and he regards my hesitation as non-cooperation...

I don't know, am I really unwilling to cooperate??

I'd rather prepare slowly, so that I have proper food at home and that I prepare myself mentally. I went to him because I want to realize these things and I need someone to direct me.

The judgments of some people are about to follow, for sure they make faces even when they hear that you are a veggie and I don't know ... I can't do it so fast ...

How do you see this? As non-cooperation? I don' know anything anymo.
...

I know I'll have to cancel refined products, alcohol, dairy products, b
vegans cancel .... too, as this is in the last place at the moment and I don
bother with it right now, there is a lot before that ... a bunch of things th
an ordinary European has on his/her plate or in his/her glass.
aaaaaaaaaaaaa, I don't know ... hihiihihihiihi... ☺

I have similar problems: giving up marijuana, alcohol, cigarettes
meat. It's a great intention but people are human beings not
supermen, ☺ and we can't change everything (e.g. 28 years of
habit) over night.

And what is worse? If you're taking it as a burden and
consequently thinking that you're incompetent, you lower your sel
esteem. Is it better to light a cigarette? It doesn't need to be the who
pack of cigarettes or in my case of meat.

So, at your own pace, if the guy is expecting you to start
immediately, I find it rather unrealistic. I see you as a courageou
and persistent person but you're not a superwoman. ☺

Yes, you see, this is it ... I don't know, I was really confused with the
about nutrition ... because he actually said that if I decided to give up dairy
products I'd have to do it 100%.

I order food at Govinda's and I've changed into vegan meals ... He think.
that's not enough because they cook vegan food in the same dishes as dairy
and stir with the same wooden spoons.

I think, I find that absurd ... Maybe I'll look at it from his point of vie
in half a year, but at this moment I don't feel that I REALLY need to g
into such details... And I told him about it.

The first time I talked about this with him was on Thursday – till yesterda
there were 5 days in between and he immediately finds me to be 'enthusiast.
in words and passive in actions'? But I can't do such things quickly because
it would make me sick...

I don't know, I'll see what to do ...

He may have directed the conversation in that manner so that I responded emotionally (I was disappointed because I don't know any more if I am not ready to do something about it) and this mail is supposed to be an expression of emotions, those that I keep hiding ...
But I still don't find anything special in that mail that you wrote that I would experience emotional outburst (and conditional vulnerability ... I don't know, in that mail I saw the expression of your problems and I didn't take it as intentional attempt to hurt me ... I don't think that you wanted to hurt me – why would I be offended then?
Am I blind???

Uh, I certainly didn't want to hurt you! But you can hurt a person only when you ruin the shield, isn't that so?

It is ☺ as long as you agree with everything a person is satisfied. But I believe that you hurt yourself too (more than the other person). I would even say that you mostly hurt yourself ... although it doesn't seem that way ... but it is ...

Well, I'm about to conclude ...
What I've been writing (the questions that I've been asking) is not what he said. He only suggested I write you a mail about what had hurt me ... and that it should be because of me and not because of you ... and I've succeeded in the latter, haven't I? ☺

You know how happy I am (I admit, also honored), that you confessed in me??!!

Because Marjan said!!! ☺ buhahahahhha... no, I'm only kidding ... he must be everywhere ... and considering emotional matters I can be grateful to him – although you must have noticed how confused I was and although I told him that I wouldn't do it ...

that I didn't know you so well to start writing something out of nowhere ...

As for nutrition, I don't know whether to go to such an extreme ... I don't think it matters if they prepared cheese food yesterday in the same dish as today's vegan meal...

I'm wondering if it's about my stubbornness or his forcing of his belief. Before I got on this path I ordered two people to warn me if I fall under his influence – uh, I'm such a rebellion – because somebody else sees it more objectively ...

I haven't decided yet ... I know that I'll have to go there again to see if he is willing to deal with me, although I don't find dishes to be a problem ... And if he isn't willing ... I doubt I'll persist ... (I don't feel that way now but as I say, I don't decide by my feeling)

Nighty

I hope it helped...

Of course it did. I'll be able to tell Marjan proudly that I've done my assignment ... I'm kidding, I'm glad I did.

Ciao
D

Sweet dreams, and in the morning - Good morning and a beautiful day! I'm sure it will be!! ☺

Good morning!! And now it's time for me to start working, isn't it? ☺

236

I spend free moments of the following days reading the book Destiny of Souls given to me by Dajana.

"*... There are souls which regularly ask for the bodies which will challenge the character of their soul. Ray and Carl are souls who easily fall for unhealthy habits of taking different chemical substances. And why are they still asking for such bodies? The answer is: for practicing. Any obsessive state that changes behavior causes tension and Ray is assertive that he would beat it before he moves on ...*" I read and gaze at the butt of smoked joint in my ashtray. The words by a man with PhD in Counselling psychology and a hobby which grew into a profitable business stir up my mind. Studying Freud and his psychoanalysis did not help much with my feeling. I still do not want to give up aromatic grass.

Now I have come across a different explanation. So it is possible to look for the answers to everyday problems in previous lives?

I continue reading: "*Every life is a piece of fabric which creates the whole tapestry of our existence. If a member of a family is strict and inflexible, or maybe weak and emotionally cold this is only the outer part of the whole real character of the soul. If you were raised by very difficult parents, ask yourself: What did I learn from that person who gave me the wisdom which without her/him I would not have?*"

My parents? Let's see what they prepared for me:

1) The division of work into male and female activities, which means that I am sentenced to Sisyphus' cooking, washing dishes, sweeping, vacuum cleaning, floor polishing ... It would be much easier to repair something.

2) Every woman is given meaning and value by her family, that is, her husband and children.

3) Finding and keeping a permanent job as soon as possible.

4) Saving is perforce – for a new car (or two), your own house (with additional story for children), life insurances ... for Safety!

5) Respecting God and attending various worship services (such as mass, way of the cross, christening, confession) ...

It is not a surprise that my studies of Sociology turned me into an enthusiastic atheistic feminist who despises most of the male gender, with the emphasis on the father God, but there is still a tiny part in the chest which is still cheering for a black horse with a noble knight who will come galloping and will gallantly save the princess from all the difficulties of life.

"What the hell is wrong with me?" I touch my head.

Yes, yes, I am aware that such unrealistic expectations are the fruit of reading of numerous love stories of Madame Steel and similar soap operas which I used to swallow as a teenager when I was hallucinating about fairy tale future instead of working in the garden and hulling corn. But I cannot help myself – if a man cannot cook and clean after himself but needs the explanation why it is good to take care of himself and his existence, then in my eyes, he drops to the level of a five years old child, full stop!

In order to calm my disappointed nerves, I continue reading. The author writes about regression with Max, the soul, which is learning the skills of a guardian of animals, but he chose to have a butcher for his father on Earth. So he intentionally chose people with who he does not share life purpose? Similarly, I experience the differences of beliefs in my family. Since I was a child the lost animals have been finding me and I've been taking care of them happily, but my parents do not share the excitement about misunderstood beings. My father used to deal with livestock, a little bit with butchering too, so I cannot expect that they will accept my vegetarianism with joy.

"What do you say about these grass eaters?" my mother once asked me when we were watching a program where the association against torturing animals was faced with Slovenian hunters. "Do you think that everything is ok in their heads?"

And now somebody is claiming that I have chosen my family myself? Exactly this family?

The whole following week I'm browsing internet and researching the concept of regression. Although the indicator of financial availability in my e-bank estimates only 130 Euros, I am convinced by a Slovenian guru of this science. "*When our mind is peaceful and our thoughts silent, the screen of our inner life displays the pictures from the past which can help us the most in our present development. Emotions start vibrating in harmony with events and the energy which has been blocked is released and starts flowing freely*," claim the words which put the mind: heart wish on a scale and I decide to send the regression woman an email with a question about the first possible appointment. I inform Dajana about my intention. Her opinion is that what happened in the past does not matter and that it can even be dangerous and traumatic.

The lady's response which I receive the following day states that I can visit her the following Thursday and she apologizes for not being able to appoint me earlier. I reply that waiting is not a problem because I am sure that one of my life lessons is learning to be patient. I do not tell her that such learning gets on my nerves most of the time and that I am far from being used to it. So in one week I will know if in my previous lives I was a queen on the French throne or a witch during the times of dark-age or a prostitute in antique Rome or I robbed trade ships between the Caribbean islands …

I also inform my Hanta yo gang on Netlog about the adventure. Their response is focused on advice to avoid any negativity during this time and to watch a love movie – they have a feeling (correct) that that I disgust that genre at the moment. They are not surprised at 'weird' coincidences, for instance that during the time of waiting my kindergarten and school friend has renewed contacts with me after long years. Or that on Facebook a member of a royal family from Sri Lanka has added me as his friend. I asked him where he had found me and he replied that he had been dreaming about me and now he was curious when I would visit their island. When I mentioned that to them they confirmed my suspicion by greeting the princess (me). Regression has started …

These days do not pass as that the wind has blown them away; however, today is the Thursday when I am nervously driving to the capital city. I have been hardly waiting for this moment but now I am overwhelmed by fear of what I am about to learn. After one hour of racing I almost arrive at the destination, slow down and try not to miss the right house number. Of course, I cannot see a half-ruined dark villa with a squeaky note OCULT SERVICES anywhere, so I pass it at my first attempt. I continue driving to the crossroad, turn around and pass my destination once again on the opposite driving lane. At the first traffic light I turn back to carry out my second attempt to find the right house. The hedges make it very difficult for me to see it as the high cypresses are all similar, so I slow down and as a consequence the horns behind my car become really alive. With the corner of my eye I notice the right house at the last moment so it is too late to get off the road.

At my third attempt I manage to turn into the drive way of a typical Slovenian multi-family house. I park my car, climb the stairs made of concrete and ring the bell with the right surname. After long moments a grey-haired woman in slippers opens the door. She is wearing a white shirt and (not on purpose) worn bright blue jeans. At the first sight the lady in her middle forties looks like an ordinary woman. AHA! Her witch-craft is exposed by her right eye squinting into the right.

"Good day!"

"Hello."

We introduce each other and then she invites me in. I take off my shoes in the hall, hang my coat on a hanger next to the door and start looking around. I am interested in how the dwelling of such people looks like but I remain surprised and a little disappointed. I am standing in an ordinary city apartment; a slightly open door reveals a socialistically furnished kitchen with a small counter and a microwave on it. Next to the table with a lace-tablecloth there is a 'decorative' grey suite.

She takes me into the room opposite the house lady's temple, a little room with a desk, a leather chair and a narrow bed. It is furnished in a Spartan style and I do not notice any sculptures or images with angels and other invisible creatures.

She tells me to lie down, make myself comfortable, and she covers me with a violet blanket. She covers my eyes with a cloth.

"First we will relax, I will call our guides to protect and guide us and then I will be directing you through pictures and events which you will sense." Her words announce the beginning of my journey into the history of my existence.

"Are you comfortable?"

"Yes, I only need to go to the toilet." It seems that I can never proceed without these classical stops.

"Sure. On the right, next to the door."

I get up and after few seconds I am sitting on the toilet. The bathroom's appearance is ordinary, contrary to all my expectations. I cannot see any brews or glasses with suspicious substances. I push the unnecessary liquid out of my body and restrain my wish to open the closets. I rather return to the bed and put the black cloth over my eyes by myself.

"Everything alright?" the kind voice asks.

"Yes, we can start." As a sign of my readiness I inhale and exhale deeply.

"Good. Become aware of each part of your body that I mention."

Ahm, I can do that.

"My right foot toes are still and relaxed ... My right foot is steady and relaxed ... The calf muscles are still and relaxed ..." Before we get to my butt, my bladder starts cheering for a new encounter with the toilet. The lady starts relaxing my liver but I cannot follow her anymore because my whole attention is paid to the lower part of my stomach.

"Hmm ... I need to go the bathroom again ..." I whisper.

I get up quickly and go to the room next door. I feel relieved when the pressure passes. When I get back we continue with relaxing, however, the unpleasant feeling in my stomach returns when we were relaxing my back. Unbelievably, less than five minutes have passed. I endure till the relaxation of my forehead, then I say. "I need to go again." I take off the cloth and look at her miserably.

"Take it easy, that's ok." She seems to notice that I miss some marbles. "It happens."

When I return, the relaxation procedure is repeated from the beginning, but now in its faster version. This time I manage to the finish. That is, I manage to ignore the more and more painful feeling somewhere down there. But I do not say anything. I am peaceful and relaxed. The whole of my body is peaceful and relaxed. The heart ....

"In your thoughts open your eyes. Do you see a light? Brightness?"

Light? No. Maybe a little, there by my nose, but this must be due to the daylight because my nose is not covered very well. "Hmmm ... No?"

"Good. You are peaceful and relaxed ..." Yes, I am peaceful and relaxed, peaceful and relaxed. I AM PEACEFUL AND RELAXED!

"The heart is getting bigger, filling the entire room ..." PEACEFUL!

"Open your eyes again. Do you see the light now?"

NO, I do not see anything! Maybe with my eyes open? Yes, there by my nose! Is that what she means?

"Yes," I mumble not convinced.

"Do you see a window?"

Uh, I can see it a little. "Mhm."

"Slowly, walk towards it and look through it."

Yes, right. I get up and want to get off the bed to reach the window.

"NO, no, not like that! In your thoughts. Couldn't you do it?"

"No, I need to go to the toilet again."

I leave the room miserably. Well, what is wrong with me? Of course she did not mean physically, you fool!

When I return, even though I put the cloth over my eyes and press it tight on my nose bone, we do not start with relaxation – it seems that the guides are becoming impatient with me too, but she starts asking me questions.

"What are you interested in about your past? What do you want to learn about yourself?"

"Yess …" Do I need to tell her that? Why? How can I then know that she is not a charlatan?

"Mmmm, I want to know … who, for instance, is my soul mate … Why am I so attracted by the sea and also afraid of it …"

"Would you feel better if we talk by a cup of tea? Maybe a cigarette?"

"Yess! That would be great."

I stand up quickly and during my short walk to the kitchen I am feverishly looking for a pack of cigarettes in my handbag.

"Mint, green, chamomile?"

"Mint, please," I reply; my first cigarette is lit and I exhale dense clouds of smoke towards the ceiling. I am surprised when with the cups of warm tea in her hands she joins me at smoking too. And I have thought that spiritual people do not sin.

"So. We have somehow complicated the thing," she smiles at me kindly.

"Has this happened before?"

"Yes." She stops for a moment, and then she continues. "In some cases it is not good to browse through the past if you have not dealt with the present." She sips the hot liquid loudly. "Or a person cannot relax. Most of the time because of fear."

"Mhm," I nod. Well, at least I am not the only weirdo.

243

"What is your present situation in your life? What do you do?"

I complain about my not fulfilling employment at the school, about the students who do not listen to me, who have their own difficulties …. About how I want to stop smoking, but I am not doing it well, how I want to become a vegetarian, not really successfully. About my non-emphatic parents …

"What would you like to do in your life? What are YOUR wishes?"

"Maybe I would be a writer," I say. "But I am not sure I can do it. And even if I could my closest would not be excited about it. Most of them do not agree with my knowledge, attitude, perception. They would be hurt."

"Ahmm … Do you believe in the Universe?" I nod.

"Do you believe that the Universe is endless?" I nod in confirmation.

"Do you believe that the Universe is created from numerous parts, points? And one of them is you?"

"Yes." Of course. I am aware of the low of attraction. What is she aiming at?

"And who makes decisions for that point? Who decides where she will go? What she will do? How she will behave? If she will brush her teeth in the morning?"

At this point I hesitate, then I say: "Well, I do, don't I?"

"Of course! And why do you think that you can decide for someone else? Who will decide whether he/she will be offended or hurt? Who decides whether a glass is half empty or half full? You for someone else or someone else for you? Or each person for himself/herself?

"Ooo …" I feel that a bulb has just switched on above my head. The following words convince me that my wishes are supported by the Universe, it is only me who is blocking my path.

After three hours of chatting and a cigarette pack half smoked I still do not see that my expectation will not be fulfilled. Finally I bravely ask: "Can we do regression now?"

"No, not today. But you've learnt something new and it has to settle into your subconscious. You're not the same person as you were before the conversation."

"Right," I say although I am disappointed. "How much do I owe?"

She thinks for a while before she replies, but not too long. "Counselling is 37 Euros per hour, but because you've come for regression, 100 Euros will suffice."

With not as light heart as a few minutes ago I pay her, but I do not get a receipt. I start putting on my white boots. I am holding my handbag and pulling the boot with another hand, but this does not go according to the plan either. I start staggering down the hall.

"Let people help you from time to time," she smiles at me and takes my handbag. "You don't need to do everything by yourself. Life can be a real party, enjoy it!"

"Yes, thank you for everything. Goodbye. Good luck." Finally, I am ready to leave.

In the parking lot there is another car which complicates my departure. After a few minutes long back and forth movements I hear the sound I have been fearing. I look past my left shoulder and I see a column. I pressed my car to the fence. Excellent! Here I am, without my last hundred euros, I didn't get what I was expecting and I have caused the damage on my car!!! Bravo! Life is a party, isn't it?!

Disappointed, I arrive home. I enjoy a beer and a rolled joint. I am holding the smoke deep in me, when the phone rings.

"Hi, how was it? Are you ok?" Dajana does not waste time greeting.

"Mah, there was no regression. I'll send you an email." Neither she nor I like speaking on the phone.

From: freya333gmai.com
For: dajana.pisnik@gmail.com
Subject: regression

Ok,

If I had known it wasn't hypnotic I wouldn't have gone becau[se]
I'm aware that I can't relax by order ... Yes, she realized that I cou[ld]
control myself very well – nothing new, then, we were discussi[ng]
things I already knew (we're a point in the Universe, everythi[ng]
around us is our reflection ... bla, bla, bla ... how to work at scho[ol]
to be satisfied, to learn how to accept myself just the way I am ...
bla, bla, bla)

She charged 100 euros for regression (and she considered hers[elf]
gracious because she usually charges 37 euros for one ho[ur]
counseling and I was there 4), as the icing on a cake I scratched m[y]
car at the fence in the driveway because I couldn't get out.

So, I'm penniless, with a fucked car ...

I've had enough, I've opened a beer and now I'm ... the glass

P. S. I know that it has given me some benefits, but I have had
spit out because I've not received what I desired!!!

From: dajana.pisnik@gmail.com
For: freya333gmail.com
Subject: RE:regression

Hi, ☺

*Yes, true ... regression is not a type of hypnosis ... but don't worry, y[ou]
have one experience more, which will cause you to respond differently in t[he]
future ...*

*I understand you perfectly, including emptying your glass, ;-) we [are]
schmucks and try to solve things in that way ... I'm not supporting y[ou]
blindly, but our path is like this at this moment ... in time, maybe not
this life time it will be different ...*

> *As for forcing, I completely agree ... no 'must' leads to a root change because it is forced ... things happen when they mature...*
>
> *I hope you'll sleep over the event and smile in the morning ... expectations are not good, they often lead to disappointments ... Expectations are walls ...*
>
> *Bye*

Huh, it is great to have such friends, and beer, and ... I do not know why I feel much better, but I am at least able of cynical laughing.

So, reflection instead of regression:

1) <u>How is it with expectations</u>? Why are you upset? You received a lot of answers about your life which is happening here and now! Forget about the past.

2) <u>A glass is half full</u>, so change a perspective. In six years of driving, you damaged your car for the second time (and it is not anything serious), actually, you are an excellent driver! Considering where your head was wandering during the drive (everywhere except on the road), you can be proud that after sixty kilometers of drive you are still alive!

3) <u>You are not responsible for other people</u> and you cannot influence their emotions and actions. So, nobody else is responsible for your feelings and your life!

4) <u>There is no force that can create long lasting changes</u>. Everything happens at the right time, so prodding and impatience are not necessary!

Supervision is interrupted by another message in my inbox.

"Great!" I snarl at the monitor when I see that it is from Gasper, a high school student, who I am tutoring for the bachelor degree exam. He is writing a test next week and he is requesting additional tutorial which will bring me the needed gold coins.

I put the book that inspired me for an unsuccessful adventure into the unknown world on the shelf, and take the Collection of the Slovenian Language Assignments. Suddenly I think of another lesson:

> 5)   What matters is the present, and not the past nor the future. In English present also means a gift. *So enjoy it, for God's sake!*

The following day I encounter a page which offers an astrologic card free of charge. Well at least its basics, a detailed explanation costs 60 euros. Jenna, the astrologer, sends the astrologic wisdom in the evening and I am excited at her findings. How well she has read me! She notices everything: that I do not appreciate myself, she senses my positive energy which I do not utilize, she realizes that I am on the crossroad of my life where everything is changing, and how afraid I am of that, she encourages me to use my hidden talents. She has not missed my personality traits, she realizes how sensitive I am towards the emotions of other people, but strict and relentless towards myself, and fair ...

I am convinced by her findings and as excited as I am at her report I want to order a whole analysis immediately. I start filling out the form but the procedure enters the blind street – I cannot receive the map to the treasure without a credit card. I write to Dajana and in my exciting mail I ask her if she has a credit card and if she is willing to lend me. I realize by her response that there will be no such exchange of finance because she does not have one and she is also against such on-line services, moreover, she is a sceptic about the astrologer too. She believes the findings are too general to confirm her professionalism and skills.

Of course, what was I thinking of! Of course she is against it! She doubts everything I feel. Nothing, anyway …

The following day before the first lesson at school I am standing in line in front of the bank counter. A clerk takes advantage of my presence for which she has been waiting for several months – she has been waiting for my response to the invitation to change a student bank account into a work one. We quickly settle everything and I am to receive the card in the week that follows. So, nothing about my astrological report for now, I hope I will not be too late …

However, a slight obsession for astrology does not leave me. I look through Slovenian pages and realize that analyses are charged 200 euros each. And there only 60 euros? At that moment I remember TV reports regarding on-line frauds. The first suspicious thing that we were warned about by the authors is low prices for services or products. I decide to check on Jenna. I do not know why I had not done it before.

I type her name and service into Google. The first forum I open offers clear evidence that the lady is a crook. There is a letter whose content is the same as mine, and several other people reported the same reports. The person who ordered and paid for the whole analysis did not get a report of his/her happy future nor any other letter or response. There were other victims reporting about similar things but I checked the fraud on other pages. They all agree how wicked deed that is. And it reflects bad light on the innocent.

There will not be any analysis of planetary influence but I am still wondering whether or not to attend the Gaia light initiation. The records by a Slovenian master found on the internet do not convince me:

Eternal Light® is a very strong and at the same time very subtle, unique, holistic system of healing with the energies of eternal lights which were given to the humanity through the guidance of SANAT KUMARE, Assumption master, planetary logos and supervisor of all Light frequencies which are sent to the Earth during the exciting period of spiritual development – transition of our planet and humanity.

So I ask Tasha to take me to another fortune teller who prophesies in the mornings in one of residential areas. You can reach her through a phone call when she informs you about the location and time of the session.

"Strange," I say.

"Yes, but she's good, you know. It's strange that she has appointed us for the following week already, usually one has to wait longer," Tasha is theorizing while she is checking her eyebrow arches. "She's always sensed everything."

After half an hour chatting in the bathroom of the apartment it is our turn and the first one to enter is my colleague. I am waiting in the hall accompanied by a brown shoe case and a new customer. A younger red-haired woman, we do not say a word.

Fifteen minutes later I am sitting in the kitchen, opposite an older woman with grey highlights and messy hair, dressed in jeans and a tartan shirt. On the table in the mug there are beans, next to it there is an ashtray full of cigarette butts. The whole room is saturated in smoke in spite of an open window. The fortune teller lights up her cigarette, I take the pack out of my bag and take a first smoke in relief.

"Do you have any questions?" the thick voice asks me.

"I'm interested in general stuff. Job, life, love," I say and curiously look at the beans that she is turning between her fingers.

Now she shakes them out on the table so that they are arranged in some sequence that I do not understand, and nods.

"You're not satisfied with where you work. You don't enjoy … only for money," she says before her piercing grey eyes look at me.

I nod but I do not say anything.

"Parents, parents are a problem. They don't let you be who you are …"

Yes, it's true, they don't. I shake my head silently.

"You have to oppose and live your life," she comments and then arranges the next three beans into a scheme.

"You haven't completed something. Something in connection with learning? School?"

"I don't know, I've graduated from the faculty," I mumble and start thinking if maybe 'school' means the initiation. It is a school in a way, for healing. It's only that I haven't started it yet. Or have I? Or maybe she is thinking about my professional exam for teachers, which is not something I like, so I've been postponing the presentation in front of my mentor and the headmaster for ages.

"Well, whatever it is, it needs to be finished." She concludes the topic and takes the next group of legumes.

"Is there a guy that you like but you haven't told him about that?" She says and smiles.

How does she know that? It is true, on line I find a guy, who is born on the same day as me, attractive. He is actually younger by eight hours exactly: we are very similar regarding personal traits, he is a guardian of two great Danes, and he is cute. But that is it. I do not want to change a few witty remarks and exchange of dog-related experiences into a romance. Or maybe I have already knitted one in my head?

I do not say anything but give her a shy smile.

"You need to tell, you don't need to be embarrassed ... I also see a man ... a little older ... in a relationship ..."

Now I lift my eyebrows. Married men do not interest me, really.

"Well ... you'll see ... if you want to accept ... whatever you want ..." she comments when she sees disgust in my eyes.

I doubt I would get into relationship with a married man. Halo?!

"Is there anything else that you're interested in? Any questions?"

I am afraid to ask her about my future but I gather courage and mention the initiation.

"So ... I've met certain people through internet and they suggested I take something new ... Can I trust them? Shall I do that?"

251

"Yes," she says immediately, without a second thought. "Sure ..," she nods in confirmation to her words.

"Good. Thank you!" My gratitude is sincere.

"How much is it?"

"Whatever you wish to give. Whatever the heart is willing to give for the information ..." she replies and smiles kindly.

Ten euros seems to be a grateful price, and I cannot afford more than that, so I give her a banknote and leave.

Tasha is waiting for me in front of the block and reports about what she has heard, she seems excited – a brilliant future is waiting for her, everything will work out well with her lover. She paid her five euros. She does not ask me about my forecast, we sit into our cars and drive to a pub by the Krka river to have a cup of coffee.

When I reach the destination I am still wondering if it is possible for me to become a healer. Am I really a special person? Not just weird? I close the car's door when I hear Tasha's shaking glass asking when she can come to the hospital. In the following minutes I hear that her grandmother suffered a heart attack and they do not know what will happen next. I use all my skills to support her and remind her of good things, but I do not forget about what I have heard before. So another event where I can help someone with my presence? Coincidence?

Without hesitation and sharing of my opposing thoughts I conclude that I am a moronic goat and I decide to pay attention to my friend. Her situation is more important than my confession although soon she starts talking about her guy from Istria again ...

Next day I apply for initiation but my future spiritual journey will start this evening with terrestrial party which I am going to attend with Nina. As always, we meet at BS where we sit in our corner and order as usual. It is boring. It is almost midnight but the pub is half empty. Nobody is dancing and the music is not promising. Sometimes I like to listen to techno rhythms but this computer pounding is too much!

The atmosphere improves after midnight when our dose of alcohol consumption is full so we have courage to stand up and dance by the table following the electronic sounds. Soon we are joined by Nina's acquaintances, two handsome young men from Bela Krajina (White Carniola). One is tall, dark, unshaved, loud and witty, another one is shorter and younger, gentle, fair, smart and funny, but totally sober.

Together we close the pub and move to the disco. Classic, but I feel great. In spite of my continuous visits of toilet, the evening is fantastic. Absolutely relaxed I am dancing around the dancing floor, flirting with both escorts, but decide to focus on the older and more manful one. I do not remember his name but I like how caring he is in the morning when he escorts me to my car and covers me after I have remained helpless on the bench, and I put my head on his legs.

They bring me home after ten in the morning. Earlier I slept a few hours in the car so I do not fall asleep at once. Lying in bed I am awoken by a smell of something burnt. I get up and see a burning fan heater which I switched on to keep me warm in the room where it was not lit up during the night. I jump out of bed and pull the cable out of a socket. Fortunately, that is sufficient and the fire quenched immediately. Unbelievable! If I had been sleeping I would have burnt! I open the window to disperse the smell of burnt plastic and then I get into my bed again. How can one sleep peacefully ...

Tossing and turning in my bed is followed by afternoon sobering process and one of worse hangovers. Fortunately, a headache is bitten by few pills, but nausea not before evening with gentle grass. In my Facebook there are two invitations from both yesterday guys and in my phone there is a message from one of them asking how I feel.

Instantly I call Nina and ask her where he got my telephone number. She claims that I gave it myself but I do not believe her. I am fed up with constant changing of my telephone number so I am damn careful who I trust it even though I am drunk. I will check it with him too. Of course, I interrogate Nina about him too. I find out that he owns his own business, he deals with construction, he is a cool guy, and she does not tell me more than that. What were we talking about the whole evening and night?

I like his sense of humor, so I reply that I have an uproarious tiger and accept his request for friendship. During the following hour I like several of his photos and after that I roll into my bed again.

These days my life on the internet is oriented to Facebook where I do all the quizzes: Which nationality am I? (Scandinavian??), Which drink am I? (margarita), Which movie would I star in (Pirates from the Caribbean), Which domestic animal am I? (alien??) ... and I observe the responses by my friends. I am interested in particular in those from Bela Krajina. I exchange several messages with the guy.

Next weekend we meet for a cup of coffee. I come to the date before him and carefully watch the men entering the pub. Once, I had a coffee with a guy who smelled of garlic and looked much worse than my memory of him from the all-night blender. Actually I did not even recognize him but unfortunately he recognized me.

A dark figure who enters the pub is not an Anthony Banderas but I am not disappointed. He is rather cute. I see him observing the pub so I wave from the corner. What if this time he will be the one who is disappointed?

"Hi," I am greeted by a smiling person with one-day-old stubble, dressed in a blue sports winter jacket. He sits on the chair opposite me.

"Hi," I respond. "How is it going?"

The beginning of the conversation is very reserved but the second round of Jagermeister (after fifteen minutes – I do not want to wrap myself in a virtuous image) gets our tongues moving. I learn that he is a builder by profession who used to have a small company providing construction services but could not settle all the taxes, so he closed the business and now helps a local business man who deals with different services including building. We are talking about his work, he is sorry that he did not continue his schooling for carpenters, about mountaineering which he adores, difficulties with cars, life in the apartment with his divorced mother …

Only after one hour or so I remember to ask him where he got my telephone number. I am not surprised by his answer, but disappointed. Nina. And she knows that I do not like that! Besides, she lied to my face – well, not technically, because we were talking on the phone but the effect is similar. What else did she lie about? Does she lie?

Six hours of getting to know each other and seven rounds which we paid separately are concluded before midnight. We go to the car together and he shakes my hand.

"What about a kiss?" I say courageously drunk. "It must be my cap. You don't like it, do you?" I try to blame a piece of clothing for my own unattractiveness.

The builder responds without words, steps closer and sticks his tongue into my mouth.

"So, I got what I wanted," I say when I catch a breath.

"Satisfied?"

"Mhm, good night," I smile and go to my car as a winner, without looking back. I even forget to observe what car he sat into.

At home I start considering my future with the Carpenter. Did I like his kiss? I don't know … Do I want to get involved with the guy who has graduated only from a vocational school? I swore several times that I would not get involved with men with less than a four-year high school. Well, we think differently, I do not know why but this is how it is. How will one carpenter understand quantum physics which studies the energy of thoughts and creation of own reality? Or healing, angels; ok, I am sceptic about that too but I am definitely interested in the subject … The world of the invisible … He will probably laugh at it all …

No, this guy is not for me. I think that it is a waste of time and energy for something without future. Then I look at the table where I see Pride and Prejudice. I am reading the novel by Jane Austin again because one student needs tutorial for the matura essay and the novel belongs to the obligatory reading list. It strikes me that I do not behave much differently from the proud Darcy, only that the importance of material richness has been substituted by intellectual. I decide that I will not be like Darcy and that I will give the guy a chance to win my heart.

With that intention in my mind I plan to organize a picnic at my parents' vineyard house next weekend. Besides the boys from Bela Krajina I invite Nina who I still have not said anything about the phone number, Dajana, Tasha, also Katarina and Ema together with their partners.

The Carpenter confirms immediately, Nina is not sure she'll make it, Tasha rejects me because she will visit her partner in Croatia, Katarina and Ema are coming, Dajana does not know yet.

The evening is unfolding according to expectations. Nina is not present, she has not returned my missed calls, Dajana is not here either, the rest of us are peacefully talking by the glasses of red wine at the table full of roast meat which is eaten by others, for I have persisted with vegetarian food the whole month. This means that I am not welcome at the 'a la parents' lunches any more so I am forced to take care for myself, the first time after my studies. The menu is not varied – zucchini, potatoes, rice, for today I bought veggie burger, but it tastes of plastic so I have to improve it with plenty of cheese, mayonnaise, … and ketchup. To make it edible. At least.

The Carpenter's behavior is weird. Rather arrogant, commenting all the time. He indirectly criticizes my father who built the vineyard house himself. He points out all mistakes in the ceiling of the cellar, pokes his nose into the construction of stairs … A plain smart Aleck is stopped by the glass that I force into his hand and demand from him to drink it. I have not had a chance to get to know his cleverness but I believe that all of it is a consequence of his low self-esteem. I hope he does not get on the nerves of others but this is probably what he has achieved.

I am satisfied when I learn that he has nothing against marihuana. When he was younger he used to smoke it, traffic it and earned a good living by it. I realize also that Nina likes him. While she was ignoring my calls she spent quite a lot of time talking and having coffee with him. Obviously it did not work out well between her and the guy from Prekmurje if she is devoting so much energy to him and ignoring me.

Others soon leave and the two of us have our own party till morning. Great quantities of home-made wine are to blame for my brains' grim, so the next day I cannot remember most of the activities that happened after midnight and sex remains in vague memory. No ahoos, but it was not bad either. He reached an orgasm and that is important. I, as it always happens when I am intoxicated, did not feel much, but I practiced certain positions which are otherwise not typical for me. All in all, I took care for the diversity of the intercourse and satisfied my partner if I could not satisfy myself (*that is, I do not know how to do it or I do not want*).

In the afternoon I find out that his 33rd birthday is next Sunday.

"Would you like to come to the party?"

Uh, the moment of truth is here. The initiation workshop is taking place these days and I plan to stay the whole weekend in Ljubljana.

I grimace and say that I cannot manage. "Hmmm, I have this thing in Ljubljana …. It's taking place on both days, so I don't want to be bushed …"

"Can't you postpone?" He takes me by my hand. "I'd really like you to be there."

"You … I can't manage … Really, it's my wish, I need to do it …"

"What do you have?"

Shall I tell him? I inhale deeply. "You know … hmmm, how do you feel about supernatural stuff? Do you believe in healing, angels, energies and similar things?"

He lets off my hand and leans towards the back of the chair. For a few moments we are sitting there in silence. "I don't know, I haven't thought about it much so far … Why?"

"Yah, well … I've met some people through internet who deal with that and they suggested I take the initiation. Then I can

257

perform healing myself and heal people, animals …" I say and look at him skeptically. Will he think that I've gone crazy?

He shrouds himself in silence for a few moments. "Really? Is that possible? Aren't you born with that … gift?"

"Everyone is believed to have the gift but most of people repress it. Initiation would help me realize what is hiding inside … in my soul …"

"Interesting …" he is staring past me towards the valley. "You … what do you think about this …" He starts talking about a fortune teller he visited before he had closed his business. He described his personality traits and blockages which prevented him from succeeding very well and also that the little company would go bankrupt. I nod in excitement. This is it. Who would expect something like that? He seems more perceptive than I have thought.

Before I leave for mystic experience I trust my intention to Dajana.

From: freya333@gmail.com
To: dajana.pisnik@gmail.com
Subject: initiation

Hi,

One question. I'm interested in your opinion …

As I mentioned I had made contacts with some peop (Lightworkers) and through communication I mentioned how I ha taken care for lost animals since I had been a child. And last tin Odysseus brought a mouse which unfortunately showed only a slig sign of life – most dogs would just eat it.

Another strange event happened. Months ago, I was chatting wi my friend at my home and a big dog started barking under m window. When she was leaving, that big dog was standing in front of the door (although he seemed kind I escorted her to the car armed with a broom) and stayed there until the next morning. I was afraid of him due to his size, but nevertheless, I and Odysseus together with him went for a walk to the woods where this dog kept playing with me, smelling my hands … He was not interested in Odysseus at all. During the lunch with my parents I was thinking what to give him to eat when my father told me not to give him anything because then he would not want to leave. Well, I gave him water and snack and then he left. As that he wanted to check whether I would follow myself and not the fear … not the parents' advice …

Well, I shared my experiences with some people I trust on line – Hanta yo gang – including experiences with ex boyfriend who were problematic from the social point of view; similar happening with girlfriends – we started socializing when one of them cut her hand, another one was taking helex, Nina's boyfriend died … also you with your physical problems …
Their response suggests that my purpose is to help all living beings. They suggested Gaia initiation – Earth Healing Light - which would help me heal myself and eventually others … To become a healer.

Believe me, I'm very skeptical about it – I never believed in such things, but looking from this point of view all the events start making sense.

And believe me, I don't think I'm something special. I've been thinking the whole week that I have a big ego and that I'm imagining things … and that I've fallen into a cult … ☺. I, who think of myself as veeery open minded, now feel rather stupid … ☺

Well, the confession ☺ Believe me it wasn't the easiest thing. I don't want you to believe that I'm crazy … ☺
Greetings

I receive her reply in a nick of time.

From: freya333@gmail.com
To: dajana.pisnik@gmail.com
Subject: Re initiation

---

well, no, you're not weird ... nobody is .... It's only that we don
understand each other ... and that's why we seem weird to each other ... an
that's why we socialize with people similar to ourselves ... we 'get' each other
☺

and I don't think that you're crazy, you're courageous enough to have tol
everything clearly and loudly ... and if you believe this to be your purpose
your true essence, go for it ☺

maybe only (but I don't want to share advice) you can take some time t
reconsider those things. People are reckless beings and sometimes our min
fogs our soul and our ego takes the floor ... and when it gets what it want
it's very satisfied ...

but it all depends on what you feel that it's good for you ... don't listen t
other people, listen to yourself ... people can help you but a real change come
from within ... and it happens when a person is ready ... (meaning if
person does not want your help you can't help him/her even if yo
stand on your head ...)

ohhh, you don't need to convince me about yourself, you know the best who
to do ... be careful not to fall in the hands of manipulation (it can happen t
anybody, including me) ... today we can find a lot of fake spirituality ..
and I don't mean Lightworkers because (if nothing else) I don't even know
them ...

it's true, though, that in your words (I don't want to be judgmental) I ca
see longing for closeness and belonging ... that's why I say go slowly ...
hope I don't regret my words tomorrow ...

aha, fake spirituality ... real shit ... I saw an ad with that song from Enigma Return to Innocence and everything looks beautiful and ... and then advertisements for Klagenfurt sausages ... abuse ... how's that possible???? Isn't unconditional love intended for everybody and everything??? Not only people???

or the ad when one person is visualizing a car ... and tadammm ... he/she gets the car ... spirituality really is not intended for that ... that's why I don't like the Secret ... well, this is my view, maybe it seems strange to you, but in my opinion spirituality has nothing to do with any kind of materialism ...

but I hold it back a little because in a way it does improve the quality of life, I'm only wondering if it's not a delusion

ok, must go ...

p.s.: if anything bothers you in my expressing myself this way, tell me ... I'd feel bad if you got impression that I think something negative .... Because I don't ... you believe me, don't you? ☺

It's the day D. The Carpenter is celebrating his 33th birthday and I am starting the path of a Lightworker – whatever that means. During my drive I notice that I have forgotten a note with the address and instructions where to go, but it is too late to go back. Well, if it is meant to be, I will find it. I remember the name of the street, the crossroad where I am supposed to turn right. I am not sure about the house number, I am even less sure about the surname on the bell where I am supposed to ring. I reach the Commercial Exhibition Hall, turn right at the crossroad and part in the first road, as I remember the Google map. I am wondering around but I soon decide to ask somebody. A lady kindly directs me a few roads away from the center, I seem to have missed the right crossroad.

There are still ten minutes left so I run to the car. This time I find the right street, and a parking lot. The first problem is thus resolved, the second problem is the house number – 34 or 36? I do not remember which is right, so first I walk past the open door of the house number 34 to the last entrance. That one is closed, I cannot reach the bells in the hall, so I go back and pass two women talking by the column. Inside, on the right wall I see bells with surnames of the residents. I think it begins with 'p' …

I find the name which sounds familiar and ring. I inhale …

"Yes?" a male voice answers.

"Hi, it's Amadeya. I'm here for Gaia?"

"Yes, come to the fourth floor, left, the first door."

Oh, I feel relieved. "Thank you," I say and go to the lift.

At the door I am met by a grey-haired middle-aged man with who I shake hands.

"Welcome. You can take your shoes off here," points to the shoe case on the left next to which there is a pile of slippers. "Come in," then invites me through the door on the right.

I take off my boots, put on red slippers, and enter a large room divided into a living room on the left and a dining room on the right. Revolving doors probably lead to the kitchen. In the living room there is a sofa next to the wall, a comfortable grey armchair by the sofa, another one on the opposite side, and on the right side there is a wooden chair. It seems we'll be sitting in a circle. An old man is sitting on the chair. He stands up and introduces himself.

"Hi, Miran," he says kindly.

"Hi, Amadeya," I introduce myself and choose a space on the sofa. Someone else is ringing at the door, so the master T. goes back to the intercom and I start moving ….

"Where is the toilet?"

Miran points to the foyer, on my way to the toilet I meet the girls who were talking outside a few minutes ago. They are hugging the master, they must know each other.

"Hello" I greet them when I am passing them.

They both respond with a kind smile on their face, "Hello."

In the toilet I push everything out of my body – as always when I am nervous.

When I return I notice that my space is still free. Before I sit down I introduce myself to the rest of attendants. Next to me on the sofa is brown-haired Clara who says that I seem very familiar to her, and her name reminds me of a devoted friend of Heidi, the hero from a book, who steps out of her wheelchair somewhere in the mountains. On the armchair opposite me there is Maya, a slim girl with curly fair hair.

We look at each other in silence, with a smile on our faces. I have no idea what to expect. T. announces today's intention, that is, the Gaia eternal light initiation, level 1.

"It would be good that before the beginning you share your intention with us. Why are you here …" he says and looks at us. Who will start?

The first one to respond is the fair-haired girl. "I've been into spirituality for quite some time, I met Clara at one of the workshops," she beckoned my neighbor, "I want to help myself live a better life … I've been noticing slight improvements since the beginning, and now I feel that I want even more … to be a better wife, better mother …"

Next one is Miran. He is talking about frequencies, potentials related to human beings … I do not understand much.

Now it is my turn. I inhale and exhale deeply before I begin. It's difficult. Why am I here? I don't know exactly. Ok …

"One month ago I had a fantastic conversation with a healer. There was not a therapy involved but her words at the introductory session triggered a kind of process …. And …, well, I was shocked that somebody can see my essence so clearly … Such things have always attracted me but at that time I was absorbed … I'm reading the literature and I want to research, experience even more … So, this is a logical next step…" I somehow conclude and look towards the floor. I am not sure whether or not they have understood or accepted what I have just said.

"Yes … good …." I hear but there are no standing ovations for my courage and sincerity.

"And Clara?"

The brown-haired girl says that she has been having a therapy at her friend's who suggested she attend today's event. She is in particular worried about her relationship with her son, who seems to be too attached and she is actually triggering that. She does not want to hurt him so she wants to grow.

Now the master takes the floor. He announces the timetable: we stay here until twelve, then we have lunch in the restaurant nearby and after lunch we continue with the workshop until six. Tomorrow's schedule is the same.

He continues to explain Gaia. "It is meant for opening upper chakras: heart, throat, third eye and crown, and those above it, to the star of the soul and star door, to enable you to channel the purest energy frequencies all the way to the heart chakra." He is explaining slowly with his eyes looking into the air and only rarely does he look at us.

"Each person experiences initiation in his/her way. A lot of people see wonderful colors or lights, experience visions, others feel the connection with their true self as a peaceful arrival home, while some people feel how the energy is flowing through the body or healing a certain chakra ... the process differs depending on a person. This is followed by a 21 days long cleansing cycle when Gaia triggers healing process which is the most needed for your highest good ... during that period drink a lot of water, eat vegetarian food, fresh fruit, vegetable. Avoid tea, coffee, alcohol and cigarettes ..."

Uh, I am not sure I can do that. "What, nothing at all?" I ask.

The master looks at me. "Do you drink coffee?"

"Yes, and I smoke ... and something else too ..." I admit quietly. Will he throw me out now? A sinful soul?

"Well, as little as possible. Try to refrain. And in such cases afford a few minutes with Gaia healing." He consoles me a little bit. I will try, as little as possible.

While he is explaining further I see a cloud of bright dots in the air. Something similar happened to me at the seaside, but then I was lying on the pillow in the middle of the bay and rather intoxicated I assumed that I was hallucinating and that it would be best for me to get out of the sun. Today my psychophysical state is different. In one of the books (Was it Toward Enlightenment?) I read that anomalies that we sense around us are parts of other world which are opening to us. So, if there is nothing wrong with my eyes, what is that?

I do not dare interrupt the master during his lecturing so I remain silent and listen again. The description of energies which lasts about one hour is followed by initiation. Before initiation starts we all sit on the chairs, T. asks us to close our eyes because they could disturb him. We close our eyes, relax, then he starts with his work. When he is standing behind me I feel something happening above my head, on the vertex, upon conclusion he touches my feet but I do not feel anything special at that point. Maybe white light? Or it is only a reflection shining through the window? But I am surprised by the peace I feel, I am very peaceful ... all is well ...

After the main activity has been concluded we are asked to share our experiences. The fair-haired lady felt her heart chakra opening, the man felt the scent of roses, Clara realized that she was quite ungrounded. It was difficult for her to relax and the master who noticed her uneasiness spent most time at her feet, he removed garbage from her crown chakra. He noticed my peacefulness which is expressed by my sitting on the sofa with my legs in yoga child position, feeling very cozy.

At the lunch which we are having few crossroads away everyone is eating vegetarian meal and drinking water. I am surprised when the master mentions that he recently took care of a hayrack in my town so that it is in harmony with natural forces. I have not heard anything about it – in spite of Ema's regular informing me about the accidents that have happen in my surroundings; however, she did not tell me anything about the bind hayrack which was struck by lightning. T. says that I do not need to know everything.

In the afternoon the master continues the lecture about our etheric bodies, chakras and healing. The presentation model is Maya who is lying on the massage bed while we are standing around the bed, listening to the master's explanation and observing his movements and learning a healing practice.

We try what we have learnt on our own bodies. In sitting position we are checking our chakras on physical, mental, emotional, and aura levels. During the body scanning I feel pokes in my hands: this is supposed to be the dissolution of fears, triggered by Gaia. There is not a lot of time for questions at the end of the session, but each asks one. I ask about changing my name. Before I and Alex separated he had paid for my numerology analysis and it was suggested I add a nick name to my name and stick to it. That is why I am using the name Amadeya today. I like the sound of it and I always introduce myself with this name in situations similar to the event happening today. If that can help improve the shortcomings caused by my wrong birth name, and if it can contribute to my life balance and decrease my need for controlling and telling people what to do ... Why not?

I am surprised how difficult it is for me to tell this, and my voice is rather thick, the master comments that I seem to have serious problems with my throat chakra.

"Hence smoking and drinking coffee," he says. In my mind I add alcohol and marijuana but I only say: "And frequent anginas."

He agrees. "Problems - with telling your truth. The name has not settled into your subconscious yet."

Before we conclude, we are requested to be aware of special happenings, feelings or dreams that may happen this night.

During the night I have problems with falling asleep. Even though I felt rather tired, peaceful and satisfied in the evening and I did not miss a joint, I cannot fall asleep. The rumination of million thoughts is going on in my head, including today's experience. The master mentioned his recent divorce as a reason for his cold – this is how the body is changing and removing unnecessary energies.

Spiritual people are supposed to have these things sorted out, aren't they? That is the point, isn't it? Why then such shit as divorce happens in our life? And a child is involved ...

I have already known that we are not supposed to take the stuff thrown at us by other people because they are only their reflections. Alex taught me that.

He mentioned cracking in wardrobes and other elements. Those are supposed to be the energies from invisible levels. It is possible that our guides are sending us messages. Listening to the words I remember my student year where the wardrobes were cracking all the time. Even though they explained to me that that was happening because of different temperatures outside and inside the room, I was afraid. A crack was so loud from time to time that I was woken by it. And in general, if I was alone in that big two-story house I felt uneasy.

I try a method suggested by the master to easily slide into the sleep: you are lying on the bed with your hands on your stomach through which you channel healing energies and consequently achieve relaxation. Let's see if it works … If it does, it will be the first time for me to fall asleep on my back without being totally drunk …

The method is working less or more successfully, towards the morning I roll on my stomach and fall asleep. Not very soundly.

The first surprise in the morning is a little lake of sweat. I am totally soaked. I want to switch on the night lamp on the wooden shelf above my bed, but it flashes and switches off immediately. The ceiling light is no better, but I am used to it working or not working. There must be a short circuit because it sometimes surprises me with light at three in the morning if I do not remember to switch off the switch when the power has been cut off suddenly.

I turn on TV and switch on the lights in the kitchen and bathroom. When I am getting into the bath tub I look into the mirror and I notice a weird blotch on my back. I look closer and at the height of heart chakra I see that it has a shape of a human palm, red color. As that somebody has been scratching my body. MY GOD! What does that mean??? Well, although I did not dream anything, I will still have something to tell at the session today …

I am not the only one who is impatient and full of questions in Ljubljana. I notice that all women are dressed in something red, and both men are wearing something blue and I am excited. I was weighing between the two colors this morning and I decided for female. I mention this 'coincidence' and T. relates to my aura where he sees the light of awareness.

Miran wants to be the first to hear the explanation of his dreams. He was dreaming that he was driving in his car passing numerous pay toll stations and there is a roadblock at each of them. It starts descending every time he is approaching it, so he accelerates to prevent it from closing his path. He is in constant fear whether or not he will manage but he always does, narrowly.

T. explains his dream with a thesis that he seems to be in a hurry all the time. He advises him to calm down and slowly continue on his path. All is well; he will always reach the destination in time. We are always at the right place at the right time.

Maya was dreaming about her cousin whose mother died years ago. The explanation is that maternal energy is shining out of her. She would like to take care for everyone around her ...

Clara did not dream anything. She was very tired so she fell asleep immediately after she got home.

I am the last one and I start describing the 'scratch' on my back. The master harmonizes and asks the guides about it. The answer is that I did that myself. I am very afraid of something. He opens his eyes and asks me. "What are you afraid of?"

"I don't know." Of everything.

I have no idea. But I keep talking about the bulbs which are letting me down – this morning I noticed that a traffic light I was passing turned off too, a burning fan heater weeks ago, I remember another occasion when water boiler burnt out, that was last week.

"Well, this is how energies work," he smiles and adds: "Electricity is the most sensitive ..." Then he silently listens to the unheard.

"But it is not only that ... Is that an old house?" he asks me.

"Mhm," I nod. I do not wait for his answer but I start telling them about my grandma and about what I was told by a healer from Novo mesto.

T. closes his eyes but he does not tell me what he has found out, he only says that I will have to leave that place. That is exactly what I want!

We review the basics of healing and then have lunch. In the afternoon we are trying energies on each other.

The master tells us to harmonize, that is, to put ourselves in the light column and open our heart. We ask our guides who shall be the first one. I feel that I am the first one this time but I am not sure. Maya says the same. What now?

The master's suggestion is to ask again.

I do not feel anything this time but the pokes in my palms are getting stronger. I mention them and he decides that I am the first one. Energies seem to have started working.

"Ha, ha, nothing for you, today I'm the first one having an operation," I wink to Maya.

"No, no, not like this. You never know when you can hurt someone with your words," the master scolds my cheerfulness at the outcome.

"No, no, I didn't mean it like that, I was just kidding. Are you offended?" I turn to Maya, worried.

"No, not at all," she smiles. Thank you, God!

"We are serious and you're laughing," T. makes a remark and I do not know if it is meant to be a reproach. I do not take it as one and I say: "Well, that's why!" As that we are at the funeral. I notice that his eyes wander off.

I lie down on the massage bed; others cover me with a thin blanket and distribute themselves around me. I mention that I got menstruation half an hour ago and the master's eyes wander off again. Maya asks if healing is not recommended at 'those' days in a month, or if it is ring to perform healing at that time.

"Of course not," T. shakes his head. I think that I have read somewhere that women are even stronger at that time in a month.

"Do you have a question for your guides?" the master asks me.

"Yes. What is the purpose of my life? Why am I here on Earth? Why … What …"

269

He holds my hand and slightly smiles. "I asked Shimara the same question at my initiation ... Do what you love .... Be happy ... That's why you are here ..."

No clear answer which I would like but I feel slightly better anyway. I close my eyes and let the healing energies do their work ... Here and there I notice light shading from green to blue, but the experience of peacefulness is the strongest.

When they conclude I open my eyes and slightly lift up my body.

"Thank you," I put my hands in namaste position, feeling sincerely grateful. Others nod and we share our feelings. Somebody felt warmth on his/her palms, another one felt a slight breeze, different activities on different chakras ... We take turns and after each session, which lasts approximately half an hour, we share our feelings.

The master is observing and supervising the session from his chair, he is not participating in placing hands above the not moving physical bodies. He only joins when Miran is lying on the bed when I ask him if the aura carries the information from our previous lives. He caresses his aura and notices a ball which went unnoticed by the rest of us. He holds the invisible stuff and finds out that the dark ball of garbage is impatience dreamt by the future healer. When he mentions its presence it gets bigger but Gaia which is channeled through his hands breaks it and the body heals.

Before the conclusion of the workshop we sit on our places. It is time for questions and we start discussing soul mates. Maya finds out that her husband's soul mate is his mother with who they decided to have the present roles in this life. She nods at what she has heard because there is an inseparable link between them; they depend on each other very much. The second one receives confirmation that the attractiveness between her husband and herself which they have felt since the first time they met is a karmic connection. But I want to know more. The book given to me by Dajana, has enlightened that all persons who stay with you for a longer period of time are your soul family, but that you have only one soul twin. That is what I am interested

270

in. But when I want to ask about my relationship with the Carpenter, the master concludes the workshop due to late hour.

In the evening I feel energized although I am tired. Previous days I did not desire to be with the Carpenter; however, now I am missing him. I call him and ask him if he is bored – that he celebrated his birthday with a few beers and snooker I already knew. The party was postponed to the next weekend because of me, so that we both can be there and that he can introduce me to his friends. They are meeting today too. In an old house in the middle of their town they arranged rooms for fun, where they play snooker, darts and have beers from their refrigerator … The

phone conversation with Bela Krajina makes it clear that unscheduled cuddling is off, but I ask him to take some free time tomorrow in the afternoon. I would like to take him to the seaside, as a present for his birthday. Right after school.

The trip is great. First we walk through Portorose, drink coffee by the sea, and have dinner in in my favorite pizzeria. He is having calamari, I am enjoying gnocchi with shrimp and porcinis. I do not like shrimps as much as I used to, so most of them are eaten by the birthday boy. I am sweating all the time. I have changed two shirts during the day, and the third one during dinner. It is supposed to be a normal reaction to healing. The body is cleansing …

I have been in a good mood the whole week. I have no serious problems with falling asleep nor with my students. And without a singing grass, I have given up coffee, and limited cigarettes to three per day.

Until Saturday when I met the Carpenter's father and few hours ago also most of his friends. There are around 30 people at the party, they are sitting at the table, drinking, playing snooker, or being witty at the barbecue in front of the house.

I assumed I would miss smoking, so I have brought suitable accessories. The celebrating boy's previous crime activities seem to be handy as he easily finds and fetches a pack. Now that Alex and I do not keep in touch, he is very welcome as far as this area is concerned. In spite of large quantities of consumed alcohol and a joint with which I was hiding behind the corner I did not fit well in the group. I feel they are bothered by my accent. They do not feel good about somebody from the other side of the hills, they do not speak nicely about us. No panic, we also are happy to tell jokes about them. The fact that I am a teacher does not contribute to the relaxing atmosphere. But what bothers them the most is my vegetarianism. A few of them were laughing how is it possible that I am satisfied with zucchini and cheese while they are eating all those fragrant goodies. I must have gone crazy …

Anyway, I am offended by their comments about vegetarian diet and weirdness of people living to the north of the Gorjanci hills. My dear does not remain indifferent either, so we decide before midnight that we will not spend the night at his friend's but that we would like to be alone. So we have to drive to my place. The gentleman stopped drinking alcohol earlier, at his own party. That is ok - I have drunk enough for both of us.

The next morning I am surprised by his news that he is leaving at the beginning of May to Italy on business. And the next news, even sweeter – he has to go home at once for his mother is expecting him at Easter lunch. I cannot believe that with this intention he got up at ten and left my bed. After I had been listening about his ex-girlfriend with who he separated few months ago, now he is taken out of my bed by his mother's message? But I am glad that I will be lazy today …. And being apart for three weeks? Nothing worse … He can go to his mother, who needs him, anyway?

He has been busy the whole month so we manage to spend few days together at the end of April and we drive all the way to Makarska with the dog. But the weather is awful; it is raining constantly, so there is nothing to do. I cannot be drinking all days. I am also fed up with cheese. In those stores there is no food for vegetarians.

Nevertheless, I feel much better by the sea, in spite of circumstances. I have problems with electricity again: the first day a bulb explodes, the second one goes dead in front of the house, the third night a bulb in the bathroom starts flashing, when I return from the beach where I was sitting with the dog.

Before that it seemed that it would rain, it was thundering, lightning, blowing, so we ran to the apartment to avoid getting wet. But I did not stay there long, there was no rain, it stayed on the other side of hills. Encouraged by Jagermeister (at least myself) I returned to the beach with Odysseus where I sat down on the sand and let Mother Nature lash me. The wind was caressing my legs, I felt the tingling energy flowing up my calves, towards hips, on my belly … Then I stopped that weird but very likeable feeling. It was too weird – if I had surrendered totally I would have reached an orgasm. CRAZY! I can imagine rather lively how making love with Poseidon would look like. When after a few minutes after the experience I enter the room, all the bulbs surrounding me get a short circuit, and the one in the bathroom starts flashing.

The last day the weather gets better and we spend all day at the beach with the dog. After three days the Carpenter leaves but I do not think I will miss him. He is talking about his business all the time, how he will pay off his debts which are a consequence of his unconscientious settlement of contributions. He feels inferior due to lower education, and now that I seem to be a strange being with magic powers, I metaphorically cut off his eggs. This is how I feel by the unhappy boy next to me who cannot afford to pay our drinks. All the encouragement about better days and creation of fairy tale future, somewhere by the sea or even on Sri Lanka do not fall on fertile ground. Superficial conversations about classic things are boring so the initial attractiveness is evaporating. I miss conversations about spiritual experiences and he cannot help me with that.

In the middle of May we conclude teaching classes at school and we start preparing for the final exam. I attend weekly sessions in Ljubljana twice, as additional education, where the perspective and actual healers are mastering their skills.

It is the first time that I am unpleasantly surprised by hail on my way to Ljubljana, but pleasantly surprised by the group of women who have gathered for the workshop. Only women, except for the master. One of them shares her experience from the seminar on holy womanliness. She is telling us about a goddess who let male god make decisions, so that the world was guided by the logic, and now it is time of the power of goddess and her time is coming back. At the healing process we all ask for the cleansing of Isis's wound, inflicted on all women because they let their power go. When I am sharing my experience I mention the dilemma regarding my writing.

"Write, write," says one of them when I trust them my thoughts. "Even though you don't show it to anyone, it is good ..." Now she closes her eyes, but I do not agree totally with what she has said. Of course I would like to show my product to someone.

"Yah, their words ... Someone else can find himself/herself in your writing ... You can show him/her that they are not alone ..."

"Isn't that so? I share a similar opinion. Sometimes it is a book the friend who helps you find right answers and offers support and comforts you, when you realize that you are not the only one or alone in a mess that you have brought onto yourself.

At our second workshop I share my experience with lottery. Days ago I bought a lottery ticket for the first time and crossed empty spaces, and a day before I even dreamt about it. I found myself at Alex's and was telling him about my intention. He was sure that I would succeed but no numbers were mentioned during the dream and before I woke up we were playing poker. I was meditating the whole day on the subject of winning and before the lottery began I put myself into the column of light. I had cold feet and my hands were cold too. That was contrary to the happening during healing where I always felt hot and my hands got warmer. The balls had spoken and I almost cried from disappointment, I did not score a dime. No traveling, care for animals, normal life instead of vegetating. I mention that after the event I was reading Dalai Lama's wisdom who told me that sometimes what we wish for is not the best for us, and I felt a little better.

After my confession, T. talks about illusions among which is lottery. Numbers are an exception – if you dream numbers, it is recommended that you write them down immediately and play at the first opportunity.

I focus on my dreams. The last week was psychologically overwhelming, the Carpenter got back from his business trip, but there are no sparks between us. Nothing. What am I supposed to do with him now? I do not seem to be able of unconditional love. To add a negative point, I have stepped into the moors of hopelessness, I hate my life again. I will never write anything smart, nor have a good career, I will never get out of my grandma's dump, I will never have real friends, nor experience happiness with my husband … That is why I trusted my misfortune to the angels the other day before bed time. I complained that I could not and did not want to live like that anymore. I asked them to help me and show me the way.

I start talking with a thick voice. "I woke up in the middle of the night. Luckily, I remembered my dreams. I was here and the master asked us if somebody wanted to see his/her future. I agreed. Next, I was flying above a wonderful coast, the blue sea, and was happy that I would live there. Then the image of a man appeared, I do not remember him, but he was cute and he was not my present boyfriend. What does that mean? Are the dreams prophetic? Do dreams uncover what we want to know?" I conclude with a bunch of questions.

The master closes his eyes and opens his palms, but the questioning of invisible guides is interrupted by the man sitting on his right. "No. Sometimes the dreams are not the answers of our guides. It is important how you feel about them. Emotions …"

"I felt wonderful," I interrupt the explanation. "I've always wanted to live by the sea."

He nods and suggests meditation which can decrease our ego's power so that it would serve our soul and would not lead us to disappointing experiences. Did I talk too much? Did we devote too much time to me? Is my ego so big that it made him

275

suggest that? Is it leading me to experiences which will disappoint me?

I feel as that I do not know anything, that I do not deserve attention, guidance, anything ... so my intention before meditation is devoted to loving myself. We sit in a circle and the unknown man starts leading ...

After conclusion I feel dizzy in my painful head. I ask about a reason and find out that I am a little ungrounded – whatever that means –, a headache presents an increase in fear. T asks guides why but does not receive a response.

"Obviously it is not important, or you know it already. What are you afraid of?" I hear a well-known question. I am thinking about Odysseus, but I do not understand what I am afraid of in relation to him, so I reply that I do not know. Nothing.

My intention for the healing that follows is the same. I wish to accept myself the way I am, with all my mistakes and nonsense. While I am lying on the sofa I am thinking about the relation towards my dog. Few days ago he injured his ankle when he playfully jumped off the stone wall. I have noticed that several people around me are limping – also my mother who has a leg in plaster, I am limping due to my new, not-worn, still uncomfortable shoes. I feel guilty because it is obvious that somewhere I do not want to make a step forward – according to the philosophy by Louise Hay – and consequently I am hurting my dog. I assume that is because of a feeling of guilt because I did not attend Shimara's workshop at Bled, *which would open myself to divine energies even more*, but instead I used the money to buy a used lap top in which a world best seller is about to be born. While we are sharing our feelings the leader of the first meditation agrees with my opinion that we influence our animals with our energies. "If you want a feeling of guilt, your dog will take care of it ..." while I am fighting my tears and swallowing a lump in my throat.

When I was healing others I did not feel anything, I started to feel bored. Here and there a little bit of warmth, in particular when I was holding them above their knees, but no visions or insights. They are supposed to develop in one or two years of active research into etheric dimensions.

In the middle of June we gather on the second level of Gaia initiation. This time Miran comes with his wife, the others are joined by two women – a slightly younger one with brown hair, who mentions that I look familiar to her, as did Clara say, and a slightly older one with short hair.

The workshop starts with the question why we are here and our responses follow. I am talking how I would like to help animals. "People can ask for help, animals can't …"

"Yes, it's true." The master nods and shares his experience with a cat which was healed by him and his former wife, at distance. The cat was injured when it found shelter in a hole and did not let anyone approach her to help her. She was hiding without food and water for almost a week, but supported by Gaia energy which they sent her at distance, she survived and healed.

I interrogate about gurus who heal animals and get one address from England. Well, we will see. I can learn by myself too.

Everyone is talking about Gaia experiences during the last months; I encourage myself and tell them about pickling in my hands when my mother broke her ankle.

"Yes, if somebody next to us finds himself/herself in troubles, Gaia activates itself. If a person accepts it, of course," T explains.

"But my mother does not, in her opinion healers are charlatans and she used to warn me against them," I reject his words. Before he responds, I realize: "Well, then she must accept the energies on some level, otherwise Gaia would not activate itself?"

The master confirms by nodding and I am satisfied with what I have discovered.

"My father used to reject any healing and I myself received instructions not to interfere so he died of cancer," he shares his experience about his parents.

"What about healers? Can they take their patients' diseases?" Miran's wife asks.

"No, we're only channels. We are not the ones who are healing; we are only allowing universal energies to flow through us. But we always need to be grounded and put ourselves in our column of light.

I want to learn about the seller who sold me a lap top. In his presence I felt pokes in my palms. And I cannot explain it. Is it because of my fear that I was buying a broken device, or is it because there was something wrong with the person (or it was a sign of a good bargain?). I do not receive an answer; there is no time to harmonize. We have to continue.

The initiation into the second level is the same as the last time. We are sitting on our chairs with our eyes closed and our palms open, while the master is performing his work.

After it we are sharing our feelings and again I am the only one who does not have anything to say. It seems to me that I noticed a sign similar to ellipse, and a few white rings which were descending towards me. I do not mention that I briefly saw the blur of my dog's head. I really think that I only imagined ... What would Odysseus do in such things?

After lunch we continue with the presentation of symbols and distant healing. We harmonize and ask our guides who we are to practice our skills of healing-energy channeling on. I can think only of my Carpenter, the only person who knows that I am here.

I am visualizing him lying on the bed in front of me and my palms are walking above his physical body. I feel the most activity at the solar plexus area. But that is something I knew – he relieves his constant stomach problems with soda bicarbonate and similar substances.

During sharing I learn about the experiences of others. Miran experienced a few interesting minutes when he intended to heal his aunt but his dead grandma surprised him before he started, so he was healing a dead person. T asks higher realms about this and we learn that Miran is reaching the end of his karma cleansing. Bravo!

The next skill we are about to master is space cleansing. We select the right symbols, put ourselves in the light column and ask our guides which room to cleanse first. First, I do not receive any answer. The only one, the others have already decided where to start. Only when T modifies the question that it includes non-residential places do I receive a clear answer - it was a barn where our animals, particular bulls, used to live during the time of farming.

I harmonize and start cleansing the barn area with my thoughts. First, the inside, then I move to the ground. The ground, where they were dying and their meat was cut. I cannot see or feel anything but I can imagine a loader and a tractor, concrete floor ... Suddenly I feel a need to cry. After less than a minute I cannot hold it anymore and the tears start pouring out of my eyes. MY GOD! WHAT IS THAT?! I do not cry! Never! Not in public! *Stop crying!*

I cannot stop the tears, nor convulsive snuffling, I have no handkerchief with me, so I am hiding my nose with my hand and trying to dam the flood under it with my sleeve.

The session is finished, everyone is asking me if I am alright, I am nodding and hurrying towards the bathroom. There I blow my nose and try to calm down. I have no idea what happened, where has this feeling of sadness and guilt come from? I put myself together and return to other attendants.

The couple were cleansing their bedroom, where a black demon was absorbing their energy. The experiences of others pass unheard, because I start snuffling without any control. My visit to the bathroom did not achieve the intention. During the river of tears I only manage to say that I do not know what happened.

"Well ... I was walking and ... "I snuffle as that I am meeting all the Auschwitz prisoners. I do not mention the feeling of guilt for not helping the animals. I do not see any sense in feeling that way. I was a child, no one listened to me, no one listens to me

279

today, no one will ever listen to me. How could I have helped them?

T shares his experience with maternity hospital cleansing. He cried as a little child too, he felt the pain of all mothers who had lost their babies there ...

The youngest attendant (the one who finds me familiar) has been turning green in her face during this 'lively' sharing, and now the nausea strikes her with all the force. She wails about her state and the master sits next to her. He puts both his hands on her stomach, closes his eyes.

"Ridicule ... Did they laugh at you when you were a child?" she asks with his eyes closed. The dark-haired girl nods and starts crying.

"Migraine ...did you try to cure it with strong substances?" he continues.

"Yes" she says, "because nothing helps."

He opens his eyes for a moment and his eyes meets mine. They seem meaningful. Yes, I know that you know that I know that you know that I smoke and what ...

"Energies are very strong ... it is cleansing ... your body is cleansing ..." When he says that I hear a fart. Or did I imagine it? No, now the master burps. "It's cleansing in this way too ..."

"I can't do it anymore. I'm not ok." The girl stands up and runs to the bathroom.

"Yes, indigo children have very sensitive bodies ... So interesting ..." he turns to others and his hands are still hanging in the air. "Her physical body has gone to relieve itself, others are still here."

When she returns their healing continues. The others express thanks, hug each other, and then we leave towards our destinations. I am calm enough to drive but I admit that after so many years without crying, the tears present a real blessing. Therefore, I let myself cry in the solitude of my car on the freeway all the way to my home. I intentionally ignore a song from the radio commenting that I make drama by myself, and I stop only few kilometers before I reach my home.

STATION 6:

MATURITY EXAM

It is half past seven in the morning when I arrive at the school yard, still sleepy. This time I am early enough so that I can find a suitable parking lot from which I will be able to leave without first looking for an owner of a car which is blocking me. I close the ashtray and open the car door.

"Good morning, teacher," I hear a voice behind my back.

"Oh, good morning, Angelina. How are you?" I greet my former student of the third grade.

"Uh, I'm very nervous. Today we have a math exam. Oral." She explains that she is about to start the last scope of final exams.

"How did you do it at the written part?"

"Good, but now I'm shaking. Do you have a cigarette?"

"Yes," I look for one in my handbag. For a brief moment I am thinking that my action will not be a good example, but I still remember how nervous I was before similar exams. I do not envy her young years at all.

"Here it is," I offer her a pack, but look around anyway, to see if a moralistic co-worker is on a lookout from somewhere. "But you know that you are not allowed to smoke in front of the school, don't you?"

"Yes, I'm heading to the bridge before the exam starts. However, I saw our headmaster the other day, smoking in front of the entrance, and of course no one complained."

He must have been convinced that no one could see him.

"Thank you."

"It's ok. Good luck." I open a heavy door into the temple of wisdom.

"Good morning," I say to my two colleagues with who I share the place at the Slovenian subject part of table in the teacher assembly room. There are no teacher offices at this school.

"Good morning," says the first one and suggests: "Let's go to the class to prepare what we need."

I am following them up the stairs, carrying the box with keys, the registration list and other compulsory material which is necessary for oral examination of Slovenian at vocational program.

Today is my special day because the last class is mine, 5 d. The eighteen students who I have been preparing for this exam since November. I am interested in how they will do. How well I have prepared them.

I unlock the door and we enter the arranged room where on the table covered with a blue table cloth there is a majolica with water and three glasses. I am the chairwoman of the committee because I have not attended education to become an examiner, so I am not allowed to ask questions. Nevertheless, I am honored by my title although it only means that I will escort students to the class and supervise the selection of question cards.

One of the colleagues stakes the question cards from the bag and starts arranging them on the desk in the first row.

"Are they arranged according to the periods of the creation of works of art?"- I ask because I do not remember what happened at my maturity exam. I know that I was rather lucky with The Baptism at the Savica by Preseren, for there was a possibility to select The Freising Manuscripts or an even worse nightmare, contemporary Slovenian poets who I can understand only today. A little.

"No, of course not." Students would notice that immediately and would only study one work of art. Maybe (just in case) two. I forgot that a great proportion of successful teaching includes our ability to always be one step ahead of the students. To 'be wittier', because shortcuts and impossible excuses never end. Tests have to be prepared from the outset each year, it is popular to forward useful information to another class, so if you are teaching several classes of the same grade, you cannot have the same test in all of them. With regard to that the prospective youth have not lost a solidarity sense and I cannot complain at their resourcefulness either. When it is not necessary, really.

"Can you put the student list on the door? And invite the first one in so that we can finish as soon as possible. It is ten to eight,

284

a student is allowed twenty minutes to prepare, so we can start." Masha hands me the list with the names of today's martyrs.

I open the door and surprisingly, all of them are there. I put the list on the door and invite the first one in, Andrej. "Well, come in. You'll be the one to open the event," I beckon with my finger and open the door widely.

I look at other students. "Nervous?"

"Yeeees," they sing in one voice.

"It's not necessary. You'll do alright. We have, you have studied a lot, so I'm convinced about a happy ending. Good luck!" And I myself with healing energies will take care that everything will be carried out for the good of all, but I do not mention that to anybody.

"Thaank youuuu," I hear the sound of their voices before their heads turn down to their textbooks. Although, maybe a little late, I think.

I escort Andrej to the desk to pick one card and explain to him that he is allowed twenty minutes for preparation. He selects Ivan Cankar (the most important Slovenian writer) and his short story Chestnut of a special type.

"Are you satisfied or would you like to change the card? You can do it once, without lowering your grade."

"No, it's alright," he replies and scratches his head. I give him an empty list, as he has brought his own pen, and point him to the desk in the last row where he can prepare himself.

I sit at the festive table, open my palms on my knees and close my eyes. I call the beings that heal with universal energies and ask them to help the students so that the exam is carried out for their highest good and in harmony with the universal plan.

I open my eyes and look at my colleagues. "Oooo, look! We're all wearing skirts," I smile because I notice what we are wearing. Three goddesses of wisdom. Three Athenas? Hm, I would classify myself as Aphrodite, the goddess of love, Masha as Vestia, the goddess of home and family.

"Yes, as that we have agreed together what to wear," the long-haired Masha who is sitting next to me says and smiles while Tatjana remains silent looking at the papers in front of her.

285

Masha is an empress; I do not know what I would have done without her in that menagerie. She helped me with everything, lent me preparation lists and activity assignments, gave me advice and notified me about the events at school, love, work and general. One day at sports-school-day we were having coffee during the break when the students were playing games and she explained a few school's interesting things. I was shocked by a story about a mother and daughter who got pregnant with the same man, the daughter's boyfriend. The 16-year old girl had abortion, and the mother decided to keep the child.

She has taken over a non-written role of my mentor, while Tatyana has been keeping distance the whole year. The relationship between her and the rest in the teacher assembly room is very tense. It has been like that since the headmaster election when she phoned the president of the student council and tried to persuade her that her husband is (again) the most appropriate person for the position. It is said that she threatened to give her a lower grade, but one cannot believe everything one hears. Of course, the student reported the teacher to inspection eagerly. It is interesting how the youth are aware of their rights (but not duties) – and the elections will be repeated in the following months.

I myself have not poked my nose into school discords. But I was disappointed at her response to my question what to prepare for my students so that they would have all the literature well and systematically arranged for the maturity exam. She replied that they should prepare on their own although I saw her copying mini-collection at this very topic – a true goddess of intelligence and army strategy. Well, I prepared similar collections for my students. I will not let them be deprived due to my inexperience.

Andrej is prepared. I escort the next student into the classroom, Dejan, who picks a card with a poem An Island on the south by Kajetan Kovic.

Andrej has read the extract and then started answering Tatyana's questions.

"The author of the text is Ivan Cankar. What do you know about him?" is an introductory question.

"He's the biggest Slovenian writer, he was writing during the period of Modernism, he was born in Vrhnika …" The student mentions a few facts and then stops.

"Yes, great. Do you know when he was born, into what kind of family?"

"Mmmm … 1700?"

"No, 1876. When did he die and where?" Because there is no answer, she continues. "When does the period of Modernism end and at the same time World War 1?

"1912?"

"Nooo," says Tatyana, it is 1918. Do you know in which building he died, the same as Murn and Kette?

"In Cukrarna[23] in Ljubljana."

"That's right. What do you know about him and his life?"

The silence does not bring any answers.

"Can you enumerate some of his works of art?"

Andrej now discharges the answer as coca cola from a shaken bottle. "The Serfs, The Servant Jernej and his Justice, On the Hill."

"Yes, so what literature genre did he create?"

There is no answer.

"What mode of text is The Serfs?"

"A novel."

"No," she shakes her head, "Drama. What about the text that you have read today?"

"A short story."

"That's right. Can you summarize it?"

"It's about Marjeta who was dreaming about trees, chestnut and bugs which were crawling on it. She thought that there was treasure below it so she started digging but found bones and skulls."

---

22   Closed sugar factory in Ljubljana, the **birth place of Slovene modernism** as many young Slovene modernist poets found shelter in it at the turn of the 20th century.

"Yes, it's true, although a little bit too short, isn't it?" she smiles at him to encourage him. The student shrugs his shoulders.

"Do you know in what literature genre belongs short story?"

"Mmmm …," he scratches his head and stares at the paper with the text.

"Is it epic, lyric or dramatics writing?"

"Epic."

"Yes, this is an epic text. Why?"

"Because it narrates."

"Yes. Do you remember the year of its publishing?"

" Mmmm .. no," he admits.

The examiner looks through the window, inhales and answers by herself. "The Collection Images of Dreams, 1917. Why is it called short story? What are its characteristics?"

"It's very short … mmmm … it describes one event, mmmm …." He does not lift his head from the paper where he is trying to find an answer.

"Yes, what else? How does the narrator write about it? What is his attitude?"

"Mmmmm …"

"Does he include his emotions?"

"Yes."

"Is it subjective or objective?"

"Subjective."

"It's true! Where in the text can you sense that? Can you read one part of the text?" I notice that her face got a little brighter when she heard the right answer. And so did mine. He leans deeply over the text and flies over the text with his finger. "… Golden bugs are sunbathing as gold coins." He is reading and after that he looks at Tatjana hoping that he has guessed.

"Ahm, you are right, that is subjective," she nods. "And at the same time Cankar uses a lot of … what? What do bugs represent?"

"Symbolysm."

"Yes, can you find such a symbolic expression?"

Yes, one is bugs glittering like gold coins."

"Aha, and what do they symbolize?"

"Wealth."

"Any other symbol …?"

"Mmmm …," he is trying to find one but he cannot.

"What about a chestnut? What do we learn about it, already from the title?" The teacher crosses her arms and leans a little forward.

"That it is special?"

"That's right!" she nods happily. "It's the king of all chestnuts. Why is it so special?"

"It blooms earlier than others …. Its leaves are always dark green … Whoever was sitting under it left it in a cheerful mood, and the elderly always felt younger."

"Yeees, it's true! So, what is the chestnut a symbol of?

"… Mmmmmm …" Andrej is looking at his paper again, trying to find the answer to the question already answered at least hundred times during our lessons. But he almost never participated. The boy has a status of sportsman – he is said to be training football at a local level, nothing bigger, so he was never absent during the time of my teachings, but he was not active in the class in the sense of studying but very active in the sense of disturbing his schoolmates with rather stupid comments. I managed to motivate other students with being interested in their lives and also with threats about unscheduled oral exams which I was planning to carry out if they had decided not to follow or allow the explanation, but he remained untouchable due to his status. Unscheduled dictations which, by the way, they had not written since the primary school, did not help either. A positive grade for the first dictation was given to only four students – of course I did not have permission to write the grade into the gradebook, but it was enough to record the grades in my little notebook and my promise that five such grades make one for the gradebook. It is not allowed to carry that out either but they did not find that out and two dictations sufficed. Except for Andrej, as the status of sportsman brings several benefits such as mutual arrangement of the dates for oral and written examinations. Once I was totally furious when, after my ten minutes of persuasion to remove his mp3 and lift his head from the desk where he intended to take a nap, I still did not succeed in making him listen and open his notebook to record the lecture. I wrote into the class register that he was absent and told him that he could leave immediately, but he did not do it and instead continued napping. I broke 'God knows which law' but the class teacher supported me and marked his absence as unexcused. We agreed that he had been physically present but not psychologically and he never offered any sensible apology for that.

"Mmmm .... I don't know."

He does not know the answer, so Tatyana discloses the answer. "A chestnut is a symbol of vitality and power, the symbol of victory over death! Faith in goodness, love and persistence," she says. What about the image in the conclusion? What are bones and skulls symbolic of?"

"Mmmmm ...," no answer, only his leaning over the paper.

"The symbol of World War 1. Murdering that took place .... Cankar used short story and the entire Collection to condemn the war as the greatest evil of humanity." She inhales when there is total silence in the classroom. "In there we can find elements of grotesqueness. Where can we see that?"

"Mmmmm ..." Andrej does not lift his head. "I don't know."

"What is grotesque? What do the images look like?"

Because the student remains silent she answers herself. "The images are used by the author to point at the society's mistakes." She lifts her eyebrows and looks at me, I shrug my shoulders.

"What does Marjeta's face look like? What is wrong with her eyes?" She turns towards the student again.

"She has only one eye."

"Yes, it's true. Marjeta's ugly face is a symbol of horrible, ugly reality – wars, grotesqueness is noticed in the fact that the fairytale motive of the treasure under the chestnut is brought by one-eye Marjeta's dreams, so there is a contrast between fairytale and ugliness. The conclusion when a man with a ponytail and a bow appears, shows that a luxurious new life is originating from thousands of deaths. The war brings death, but

290

we can conclude that after the war the people can live a wealthy life." She concludes her explanation.

"So what is the main idea of the story? What is Cankar's message?"

"I don't know."

"What does he want to say with the words 'Now it can be seen where the power, love and youthfulness come from'?"

"Yes, out of bones."

"What is a prerequisite for life then?"

"War?"

"No, not a war. But the death, death is a prerequisite for life. What is his hint in the exclamation: Hi, friend, my dear friend, there will still be chestnuts blooming for us?"

"That there will still be wars."

"Hm, in a way. And what comes with the war and what is war followed by?"

"Death."

"Yes, this is an announcement of death brought by wars but after dying the life will win. Although the story seems pessimistic at first sight, its conclusion is optimistic."

With this statement the first part of the exam is finished.

"Good, let's move on to the second question, European Realism. What can you tell us about it? Its beginning, end, characteristics, orientations and members."

"19th century."

"Tell us the year or at least the decade."

"From 1800 to 1970?"

"No, Realism started in France in 1830 and lasted till 1880. What are its characteristics?"

"It emphasizes reason."

"Yes, what else? What does it show, what kind of language is used?"

"It presents reality, the way it is. The language is ordinary," he says and stops.

"Ahm, it presents reality and modern society, natural and societal laws with their opposites which the heroes wanted to change; the language is natural without romantic elements. Did the writers write in a subjective or objective manner?"

"Objective."

"Yes," she nods. What about the members of Realism? Do you know any?"

"Byron?"

"No, Byron is from the period of European/English Romanticism. Who wrote realistically?"

"I don't know." It is obvious that Andrej does not feel like answering the questions any more. He did not even blink before his answer.

"Balzac, Flaubert ... Who is the author of Crime and Punishment?"

"Kafka?"

"Uh, no. Dostoyevsky. There are other authors from that period: Stendhal, Gogol and his The Overcoat, then Ibsen, Dickens and others," she sighs.

"Ok, the third part. Read the non-artistic text loudly and point out the mistakes in the text." We start with the last part of the oral maturity exam.

Andrej is reading smoothly but he ignores most of the capital letters, commas which are missing or are not supposed to be in the text. He also has problems with the analysis.

"What text mode is that?"

"News."

"What register?"

"Mmmmm ..." He does not seem to have a clue about it so Tatyana helps him again.

"Is it a text that can be used in practical communication, art, professional or public areas?"

"Public."

"Of course, who is the news for?"

"The readers."

"Yes, wider public. Is it written objectively or subjectively?"

"Subjectively."

"No, not subjectively. How would it look like if the journalists wrote from their point of view? Each story has at least two viewpoints, so the most important characteristic of journalistic texts is a journalist's objectivity." I am not surprised at the wrong answer, objectivity has been very rare in the public media lately.

"What about the structure? What is the tense of the verbs in the text?"

"Past."

"Yes. What do you know about verbs? How do we define them?

"By number, gender."

"No, not gender. What else?"

"I don't know."

She waits for a moment and then announces the end of interrogation as she does not have energy to continue pulling the answers out of him. The student stands up and self-confidently leaves the classroom in his design clothes which are probably worth more than my garments. I do not believe that he assigns any meaning to the results. He drives to school in a grey Audi TT (my dream car!) which was his parents' gift for his eighteenth birthday. I am sure they will take care of his future very well.

The examination of the first student took forty minutes and Tatyana holds her head when she starts evaluating his knowledge. The evaluation list is divided into four main columns which are divided into few sub-sections. Loud reading can be graded by up to four points, the interpretation of artistic text fifteen points, language question at a shorter non-artistic text can get up to fifteen points, and the culture of dialogue six. I am really interested in how she will evaluate his knowledge. After a few minutes during which she changes points several times and consults Masha, she hands the evaluation list to me so that I can see the results of the first candidate from my class. Total score is 28 points, at which I am surprised, but it becomes clear to me why the hesitation and too high score, from an objective point of view. The results of the written exam are known and are not the best, so he needs 28 points to successfully pass the vocational maturity exam in the Slovenian language.

We both nod. I noticed at the final exam that teachers close one or sometimes both eyes to enable the students to pass the exam. The oral maturity exam was carried out in a similar manner. The results of the written test had not been available at the time but the teachers who checked the tests (school teachers) remembered approximate score of each student. Although the tests are coded each teacher of language knows their students' handwritings. *Let us help them get profession*, is a general motto of this school. Who cares about literature periods, comprehension of canonical texts and subordinate clauses? Such theoretical facts will be of no use at their jobs.

I invite the next student into the classroom, this time a female, Ana, while Dejan is already answering the questions. After she has picked up a question card, I sit down on my chair and listen to the questioning which has started well in spite of my belief that the period is rather difficult to comprehend. Dejan provided a correct answer about the Collection where the poem was published.

"It's Labrador."

"Excellent. What do you know about Labrador? Why the title? Why Island on the south?"

Tatyana directs the conversation, excited about his correct answers.

Dejan is speaking about metaphor for a country with many dimensions, metaphor of living, about symbols of clear leadership, possibilities of paths and new opportunities.

My mood is getting better with his knowledge too. If I have counted on someone to do well today, it is him. He is the only one with plans for the future, and willingness to achieve them. He was active through the whole school year, did his home assignments a few times (I tried to introduce home assignments but I was not successful and the teachers enlightened me that the twenty years old students did not have time for them). In spite of his good participation he reacted as an offended child when he got D for copying a book summary from an on-line library. He did not want to admit it. Only after I had asked him whether he wanted me to print the summary and bring it to school, did he stop playing a victim. But he was not the only one. With my optimistic expectations regarding the home reading assignments I got myself a lot of work. With one exception, nobody handed in the assignment in time, so I wrote 17 DRMS (did not reach minimum standards) into the gradebook and filled out 17 forms intended for such grades.

A teacher has to explain why that happened and fill out mini personal education plan how he/she will help the student improve the grade and in what manner. Four hours of preparation taught me not to write negative grades next time. Besides paperwork I had to check numerous summaries on the internet because I was naïve in believing that they would not copy the texts. I do not know who I was angrier with – them, because they thought I would be so stupid not to notice, or me and my optimism which proved to be naivety.

During my thinking Dejan was answering very well to the second scope of questions regarding the characteristics of Slovenian novel and story in the period of Realism. He is doing well with grammar too so a smile is fixed on my face.

Soon they conclude and Tatyana shows me the result. He got 36 points at the oral exam, together with his written exam this represents a C. I think we both are satisfied – the essay presents 30 % of the grade so regarding his talent we are clear that he probably will not become a writer.

Ana sits down on the 'hot' chair and I invite the next student into the classroom. I come back to the table very fast to cheer for my favorite student. Always kind, obedient, willing to participate, did all the (pilot) assignments and was the only one to hand in that damn home reading summary. She and Dejan are rare pearls who still value the right to education. I noticed that she did not socialize with most of other students. Several times she found herself in the role of a mediator between the class expectations and my wishful thinking. She touched my heart with a composition on wealth in which she confessed hard conditions at her home. She lives with her unemployed mother, an alcoholic, and her younger brother. They both work through a Student Employment Agency and care for food and expenses which 'bless' the house without hot water or bathroom. Bathing is performed by heating the water on the stove and washing in a barrel in the middle of the kitchen (when she is alone at home) or in a small place with a toilet bowl. In the composition she silently judges the schoolmates who complain about their parents not buying them new ski equipment, new design shoes or a jacket, worth several hundred euros and more, while she only wants rest, a warm apartment and enough time to devote to studies. The teachers discussed her non-attendance at school trips, last school hours, school activities ... Nobody ever mentioned her family situation which was disclosed to me by the composition.

I am glad that she is doing well with the questions regarding Green George. She comes from the same area as my former Carpenter – the home of the folk song on which the modern version has been created. I wish her the choice of the subject interesting for her from all my heart.

"The song is divided into three parts." She starts the explanation of the song/poem by Svetlana Makarovic. In the first part Green George is a positive character who is riding across the green field on his green horse, chasing winter away and bringing spring. The song is inviting people to open the doors and welcome him. But the people want George to become similar to them so they are giving him sadness and misfortune. In the second part human evil is increasing and the people want George to be as miserable as they are. They start hitting the boy with the rocks, so he goes away and does not want to be a part of this world. He does not return for several years and the people forget about him. In the third part the song asks people to close the windows and doors as the Grey George is coming to town. He has changed from a happy boy into an evil George and is now bringing fear among that evil people."

"You've summarized the song very well," Tatyana says and I just want to clap.

"What is the song's message?"

"That the evil gets even?"

"Yes, and not only that. Each evil gives birth to a bigger one and what you do to others, others will do to you. But it depends on each individual how he/she will behave. As Green or Grey George. Do you agree?"

She nods.

Her answers to the questions regarding the morphology and other language characteristics are good. They also conclude discussing the Age of Enlightenment in Slovenia and the interview analysis very fast. She gets 35 points, but because of her a little worse written exam she receives C.

The next student is Urska, and I invite Janez into the classroom. He was my greatest challenge, so I bet on diverse answers about Gregorcic and his The Soca poem.

When Urska starts with the summary of Matko's Tina, the pokes in my hands are becoming very strong. What coincidence that she has selected that very text! The student in front of us is highly pregnant and I have not experienced so profoundly expressed healing energy, which is flowing through my hands to her body.

"What kind of person is Tina?" Tatjana asks after Urska's successful summary.

"Tragic, in pain. She's longing for love, for her fiancé.

"So is it the body or is it the soul causing her pain?"

"Both, but the soul more than the body. She's falling apart inside. On one side there is her love towards Janez, on the other side there's guilt …. sin."

"Yes, it's true. Tina is not aware of her body until she meets Janez's corpse. Who else is important for her?"

"Father. Matko."

"What is he like? How does he feel about his daughter?"

"He likes her but is angry with her because of illegitimate child."

I am wondering how the parents of this unmarried teenage daughter accepted her pregnancy. We live in the 21st century but the church matters have not changed much. If a couple is living

297

together unmarried then a person is not suitable for a godfather or confirmation sponsor, and I have gathered from her composition that her parents would classify for radical catholic believers.

Urska is not that good with answering about Expressionism and the ideas from the text. "From the visit of Heavenly Mother we can conclude that there is a salvation coming from Heaven for the rude and unfair world. The new being presents hope for future generations, for injustice is calling for new rebellion. The world is calling for the redemption," the colleague concludes so that they can continue to talk about Social Realism and non-artistic part. As expected, she gets 20 points and passes maturity exam with D.

"No, Nino, you can't give up before you even start!" I stop a premature departure from the classroom. I am trying to motivate the next one who changed the card about Freising manuscripts for Black Boy – so from a frying pan into the fire, in his and my eyes. Holding his shoulder I direct him towards the desk. He holds his head and sits down in the last row and I return to the table.

I am listening to Janez, the oldest student in the class (he failed few years and re-registered) who came to classes intoxicated several times and diversified our school lessons with his 'humoristic' comments. I advised him to put at least a chewing gum into his mouth so that the classroom would not smell of alcohol; he accepted my advice. The next time we had a conflict was when I wrote in the class register that he was disturbing the lesson and he started shouting that he demanded to see what I had written, that this is his right. After that he went straight to his class teacher and explained the unfair circumstances and the teacher came to me that very day and asked for the explanation of what had happened. The third time we quarreled was because of my sitting on the desk – if I can do it why he is not allowed. My arguments that the students are supposed to be sitting and writing in their notebooks and I can observe them from a higher place, were not accepted. Next time I chased him away from the radiator where he intended to sit and watch the street only when I threatened to fetch the headmaster. Of course I did not continue breaking the school rules with sitting on the table – as he showed me the Regulations – but I did seize his crosswords. When he was doing them I was disturbed in particular because he did not even try to hide his act – I myself used to do the crosswords at school also but very carefully and discretely. Temporarily, I confiscated a few of his notebooks of other subjects and I prevented him from learning for other subjects during the Slovenian lesson.

In spite of that, I am glad that he attended my lectures (one of few) because his answers are excellent. A patriotic poem is his cup of tea and he is interpreting all its characteristics and he seems to have knowledge about classical literature. He summarizes the myth about the Trojan War understandably but he cannot remember the name of the goddess who wins the competition.

"Aphrodite," I shape the word with my lips when he looks at me.

"That's the goddess of love, Aphrodite," he says and 'innocently' looks at Tatyana. The third part is good as well, so we conclude fast and both colleagues are surprised at his knowledge. He politely thanks us and wishes us a nice summer, on the way out he goes to Nino, boxes him into his shoulder and says: "Break a leg, old man!"

Nino steps forward, sighs and sits down at the edge of the chair with his legs wide apart and leans backward. He looks like a very tired drunk at the table in a village pub.

"Well, tell us, what are your thoughts regarding the poem," Tatyana asks him when he finishes reading it.

"Well, a boy is standing on the yellow sand in the desert. He is holding birds on his lap. This is why he cannot escape. They flew away and fell to pieces in the sun. And then he holds birds again who fly away again and fall to pieces," is his sparing comment.

With mutual power and many sub-questions the comment expands into multi-meaningful image of a poet who is singing without perceiving any sense in it. Even though the boy is sitting in the middle of decomposition, where everything is covered with ashes, he is persisting in that passing.

"A sense of loneliness is prevailing," says Nino.

Tatyana nods and adds: "Yes! Loneliness of absurdity and rejection, we could say."

They continue to interpret the topic and analysis the style. Although it is obvious that 20 years old son of Bosnian and Serbian parents did not study that topic, Tatyana manages to lead him with sub-questions well, so that he gets to correct answers by himself. I believe this would not be possible if the boy were not so smart. After our initial power estimation we got together very well. At our second lesson I started gazing at him with the intention of making him take a textbook and start reading, but he accepted my look with an even more horrible one. His response reminded me of dog prompter's advice that you are not to take away your look from the opponent because you lose your respect and authority. Our contemplation lasted for eternally long seconds, but I won. Later he wrote a fantastic composition about pollution based on the documentary from Discovery, the channel which he watches on regular basis (besides National Geographic and similar programs, with similar orientation), in which he surprised me with his thinking about the connection between money and life and even teenager's love, cultural differences and prejudices. He was good at essays about different literature works. The boy, about who I had been warned because he could be very aggressive, started to surprise me in a positive way. I would not admit loudly that he belonged to the group of my three favorite students, the ones who I will remember for a very long time. He is successful too and I am becoming more satisfied with each presentation.

Next student is Matevz. He sits in front of us, dressed in black clothes, with dark colored hair and emo hairstyle. One of sensitive ones. His mother is making a living as a teacher, but he is not interested in school. The only one who did not write during the lessons, participated only in rare discussions, and mostly ignored everything around him, including my instructions, requests, roaring and raging. Once I went so far that I wanted to throw him out of the classroom (strictly prohibited!), because his answer to my question – why does he waste my and his time was "Bla bla bla …« and he showed me the most of his tongue. Nino helped me throw out his jacket and bag, but he did not dare touch him. I dammed my anger in time, so that I did not drag him out of the classroom together with the chair, and started paying attention to other students. I was thinking about him the whole weekend. The following week he was writing into his notebook without resistance. In silence.

Today he does not know much about The Parable of the Lost Son, the Bible and Existentialism or the philosophy of absurd in literature, but we manage to collect the needed points for a positive grade.

It is the last student's turn before the break. Anja, whose unlucky selection is An event in the city Goga, sits down in front of us. It is soon clear that she does not understand the text, she has learnt the text by heart, so she mixed the information and most of her statements do not make sense.

During the school year I was wondering how she managed to the fifth year. She seemed to take her notebook into her hands from time to time, but at this level it not possible to substitute the sense of language. Her grammar knowledge was acceptable, but essay writing did not make any sense. After five repetitions I gave her D. Once she tried a different approach. She wrote an essay one day after other students on the same topic (uh, I will never learn!) because she had been absent, but I corrected all essays at the same time. I noticed that her writing was different and I was not surprised when I later encountered another essay with almost identical content, there were only a few differences. I asked Masha and Tatyana about their opinion and we all agreed that the only grade we can give her is F (or drms). The following day their class teacher, whom they had complained, approached and their parents announced their visit. Unfortunately, they did not come to my office hours and the 'class father' agreed with my decision when I showed him the copies of their essays.

Sub-questions do not help her and it is clear that the results are bad. I check her writing test and see that she got fewer than 10 points. So, the first one from my class to fail the maturity exam.

After a fifteen-minute break we return to the classroom and the questioning continues. The nine students of the final grade are successful and I am excited about them. I miss the most perspective student who wrote an excellent poem – with a bunch of vulgar words, but who am I to judge – in which he confessed that he will become a father soon. Grammar and literature did not present any problems for him. If he had tried harder he would have got B, but he never handed in that home reading assignment and later the collection of text modes. Because of the two drms (F) which need to be improved he got an exam retake. He was absent during the last month of school. I met him only on the stairs when he was explaining to his class teacher that he would be absent for some time because he needed to find a job and an apartment – his father with who they do not have a good relationship, has thrown him out.

But I am not worried about him. I am sure that he will succeed in life. I am more worried about the fact that none of my students got a better grade than C.

"The students of the program three + two are taught in a different way in their first three years of schooling. They do not write essays as you must have noticed, so the next two years are rather concentrated, but a lot of things have been missed," Masha explains.

"In general, the students of vocational schools rarely get A's, also B's, there are many C's.

Janez and Anja are waiting for me downstairs. I promised to tell them, against the rules, how they did. I tell them the results; I praise Janez, and explain to Anja that her writing test was not successful so that today's oral exam did not play a decisive role.

They invite me to have a drink with other students who are waiting in the nearby pub but I do not accept the invitation. My Odysseus is waiting for me at home.

I open the car doors and want to get in but I notice Angelina, so I approach her.

"How did you do?"

"Good. I passed."

"Excellent! Congratulations!" I clap my hands happily.

"So, only Slovenian was problematic. Will you try again in autumn?"

"Yes. I decided to try, actually, my schoolmates persuaded me to continue the studies. To the program 'three + two' if I pass." She says, proud at her today's accomplishment.

And I am even prouder. "Excellent! That's the right thing to do!"

In the composition *How I found my way out of suffering*, she was writing about her sadness and the feeling of being lost after her mother, her aunt and her brother died – all of them in the period of six months. I was shocked because I was not notified about the deaths. If I had known I would have behaved in a different way, I would have been less demanding. In spite of Masha's advice to give her D because of the content and her courage, I gave her C regardless of many grammar mistakes. I even talked to her in private, lent her Destiny of Souls where one chapter deals with how to cope with the loss of our closest friends. She admitted that she intended to leave school and get a job. That is why I am so happy to hear her words today.

"Thank you for everything, teacher. Have a nice summer."

"Thank you. Enjoy the summer, and good luck in autumn. Have a nice time."

"You too. Ciao."

"Ciao," I am looking at the person who I wish all the best in her life, but I was forced to throw her at the final exam. She experienced a blockade at the written test and did not even start the last assignment testing the functional literacy worth the highest number of points. At that point it was obvious that she would not pass. The only one in the third year, the class where we first fought wars, continued with language and literature hangman games and personal conversations, and ended with having coffees in a bar where I felt like a queen between them. At the final teacher conference, also their class teacher praised my work. He is an old well-mannered teacher who started teaching decades before I came screaming into this world.

I sit into my car and run the engine. This is it! The conclusion of one period and the start of the summer which will bring the Employment Agency again and writing of job applications, but the tiny details are not important.

Last night the Carpenter came on a visit and told me that he did not feel good in our relationship and that he wanted us to separate. I was fed up with his constant lack of money and consequently decrease in his self-esteem which reflected in bad mood, not being interested, and total submission to my ideas and plans. But I did not dare end our relationship, so what happened yesterday was actually a relief. In few hours that were left to bad time I went through all the phases (without the third one) of unsuccessful relationship – numbness, anger, negotiations, depression and acceptance.

I am FREE!

STATION 7:

NEW BEGINNINGS

I am celebrating New Year alone. After Carpenter I met two members of the opposite gender, but the first one started grabbing my bra with his sticky fingers after fifteen minutes of our introductory date, which took place in a pub, the second one came to the date totally drunk, so that I needed to support him on his way to his car – he said he did not have difficulties with driving in such a state, only with walking. It is obvious that I need to cleanse my inner world more deeply and thoroughly if I am attracting such men, so I decided to give them up for a while.

I do not miss their company at all, I am enjoying in my apartment in the middle of Ljubljana. Finally! After two years of exile, I managed to come back to the center of life!

There is one hour separating me from the New Year and I am buzzing about the lessons of the current one. It started with a fall and continued with the research into spiritual spheres. In summer it was the last time when I attended weekly meetings of healers. The master was summarizing my experience with lottery, but he did not share with us the right method of manifestation – one-day workshop (charged) will be devoted to the subject. He received a message for me, from nowhere: Dreams are the processing of subconscious strain or blockade, my guides say. Crazy! It was in harmony with the events of the previous weeks when Katarina trusted me her night mare in which she was trying to save a box with a sign on it from the lake and was scared for her life, and in few days I experienced the worst nightmare ever.

I was hugged by something, first it felt good, but later I got more and more anxious. I wanted to get out of the hug but the thing held me tighter. I managed to get out, through a door, into the darkness. When I looked back if the thing was following me, I did not see anything, but I knew it was coming. Then I woke up, totally soaked, numb in fear. Fortunately, there was the dog by my bed, peacefully sleeping so shudder decreased. Then I switched on my TV which since then has been my regular companion during night hours. It was that night that after a long time I had turned off the device and fell asleep in total silence and darkness.

After a few days, I was talking with Ema, who admitted that she had often dreamt about a dead person since she gave a birth to her child. I related the content of her dream to her dead grandpa with who she was left alone in the room before the funeral. His arm slid down his lap where it was resting and she got very scared. She lost somebody she loved very much and now she is afraid something like that would happen to her daughter ... The words that were forwarded by the master confirmed my opinion regarding Ema's grandpa and her daughter, but I have no idea about the meaning of my dreams. Where did I feel safe at first and then escaped from there? What am I afraid of? What is hunting me?

During the healing it was difficult for me to hold my tears. I worked in the group with the master and I was very curious what he would feel. His words were comforting.

"You are a wonderful woman." He told me after the flowing of energies and held my hand again. "You have a very pleasant energy, it is good to work on you. But you were not treated nicely ..." he sighs and shakes his head. "They did not recognize you ..." Recognize as what? What am I?

"At this moment in life you need support ... Everything will work out, don't worry ..."

After the sharing, we agreed that he would send me a package of Bach drops which would help me in cleansing of fear patterns, salvation, and similar states, but I never received anything. I sent him another mail asking for the drops, and wrote my address, but there was no response, nor medicine. I do not beg and I do not like being ignored, so I stopped attending the sessions and I do not intend to attend them again.

From September to December I worked with an Association which helps the young Roma and immigrants' children, in particular of Albanian nationality, with education and integration. Another 'wrong' world. Neither former nor latter appreciate what is gifted to them. They were destroying things, ignoring instructions, and having their own fun. In that area, as in many others, financial support depends on the number of participants, so we suffered and took care of non-socialized kids. It's done kindly, not to discourage them from attendance. Some of the teachers even wrote essays instead of children and did their home assignments. Otherwise, the children would not bother attending the lessons.

Last month I started teaching at school again. I had not found anything else, so I traveled eighty kilometers every morning to work in Vrhnika. The first snow assured me that that was not the right way, so I rented an apartment in nearby Ljubljana – thirty square meters, without a balcony, one-room apartment, where the room in divided into the living room with an ugly old sofa and the bedroom without a window, and at the time without a bed. But it is my little sanctuary with friendly neighbors. A kind babe who I met on the stairs offered me her password for the internet, when I first met her. There are enough of parking spaces, and the owner seems nice. I moved in yesterday, at full moon, and the moving activities triggered the female cleansing period – a few days too early. It is a little awkward because an electric boiler is not connected yet and I am sentenced to heating water in a dish until 2 January, but I am grateful to the owner that he let me into my new home before 1 January. I will be all right as long as I have my own place! I am a little worried though, whether or not I can afford to pay 400 euros for renting, plus expenses. I am only working to substitute for a teacher who had brain tumor surgery in November and she is not coming soon to her workplace.

I and Alex reconciled when I invited him for a cup of coffee one day in autumn when we exchanged our animal child. He accepted the invitation (and later admitted that he had a déjà vu about it in the time when we were together), and we were nicely chatting about vegetarianism, spirituality, love. He has met a pretty girl but nothing is going on between them. From time to time we meet for coffee and today I have invited him for dinner. He stayed one hour, now he is celebrating with his friends. I am fine, the dog's company is enough for me not to feel scared, and

I am enjoying solitude and being lazy on my sofa. The cramps caused by my uterus during the bleeding are hardly bearable.

On the radio they start counting down the minutes, so I take a small bottle of champagne, open it and at midnight, pour it into my glass which was bought today, beside other dishes and accessories needed in my new home. I make a toast to me, my loyal doggy friend, and the future. I feel fantastic! I am ready for a HAPPY 2010!

1 January brings Avatar and the first view of 3D movie. Alex and I were crammed in the crowd at the big complex when we were waiting for the tickets. There were only front rows left so we are stretching our necks towards the screen from the second row. But it is worth it. I am fascinated by the idea of the planet, I am excited at the connection with mother nature, but disappointed again about science and the consequences caused by scientific advancement … regardless of everything. When I arrive home I start buzzing in my mind how careless race are people. In order to satisfy our own needs for comfortable life we are willing to walk over each other, not to talk about our attitude to nature and animals.

I have been thinking about it for the whole month, more and more each day, until positive impacts of moving disappear and I fall into slight depression again. I like Ljubljana that much that I do not succumb to it as I did in previous years when I was not able to oppose constant fog, cloudiness and general grimness of short days. I am grateful for little things, for having a job, even though it does not satisfy me, for living in the city of shopping sprees, in spite of lonely evenings. Nobody from Novo mesto visits me and I do not have any wish to search for something or someone there. Nina, with who I reconnected in autumn when we met in the middle of the night in BS – in a pleasant intoxicated state – is now traveling in Vietnam. I have no idea what is happening with Katarina, Ema forwards me a chain message from time to time, and there is no word from Tasha. Only Dajana and Alex who live in the neighborhood stop by from time to time. I do not know what is happening to me –

whoever I meet I can spend one hour top with them before I am fed up and wish to be alone again.

In February I receive an invitation for the Activation of Law of Attraction. I do not know where it came from but the text catches my attention.

… Today we will be led by Lady Guinvere, Marlin's student, he was the one to teach her everything she knows as an alchemist. She will be joined by Maria Magdalena, Goddess Jazebel, Kuthumi Agrippa, Archangel Mihael, St Germain, Solar archangels … All beings of light participating in the project Weaving of Lights. The Goddess of Water World Nimue will come to the room; we will connect with the Kingdom of 10th dimension. The energies will help us manifest everything we want 10 times faster.

Today the activations into the Water Door begins, bringing the blessing of cleansing and healing of our emotional body …

Today's 7 doors will reward you with seven qualities which will be different for each of you. Each of you will receive what you need the most at the present time: peace, understanding, liberation, clarity, hope, faith, courage.

Lady Guinevere will start healing collective record of sexual abuse and the second sacral chakra, the chakra of life. In the following activations the Goddesses will gradually take us through the healing of wounds because they know that they are deep. They will find the way for us to better understand our sexual energy and recognize how sexual and creative energies are almighty powers of light which enable love to penetrate through all parts and systems of our being and make everything in our life alive.

Activation into the law of attraction will help us release old programs and records and change that to what we are attracted. Not, what we are attracting, but to what we are attracted. Everything starts inside of us and with us. With this understanding we step out of the role of a victim into the role of a creator.

Maybe we were attracted to shortage, suffering … in the role of a victim. With the transformation of old records we make space for new intentions and decisions, to become powerful creators of new life and choose a new point of attraction; happiness, peace, harmony, balance …

My God! That is what I need! I adore mythological scenes! Before I register for the event, I check the detailed description of the woman who leads it. First I look at the picture and recognize one of healers from Gaia sessions. Aha, the one who was talking about the goddess and was healing Isis's wound. The creator of the group who channels the texts is very well presented; both of them have had many educational courses and teachers, so I believe they know what they are talking about and what they are selling.

I type my message confirming my registration quickly, and send it without grammar proofreading – before I change my mind.

The directions were accurate, so I find the one-story house with a wooden fence in the surroundings of Ljubljana immediately, as well as a car park a few meters away. The door is open so I knock and enter.

"Hello." I say loudly.

The answer resonates from the room on the left. "Hello, come in, slippers are by the stairs."

Yes, they are. I start taking the shoes off when a tiny fair-haired woman from the session and the photo approaches me.

"Hello, how are you?" She steps towards me and hugs me.

311

"Ok, ok," I say surprised and return a loose hug.

"When you put on the slippers, come in. The majority is here. Have some tea …" I do not hear the last part because she has already disappeared behind the door.

I find slippers of suitable size, I hang the jacket and step into the kitchen. On the left there is a counter with a cooker, on the right there is a cupboard with shelves and another door. In the corner there is a big oval table with little bottles. I do not see anybody in this room so I step through another door.

I see a big room with a leather suite of beige color, a wardrobe is behind it, a cowhide is in front of it, with a kind of altar on it – between the cards arranged in a circle there are crystals of various colors, sizes and shapes and one red apple. Wooden chairs and an armchair together with a sofa make a bigger circle with an altar in the center.

"Hi," I greet the five women sitting in different places. They all respond and continue chatting. I sit on the right corner of the sofa.

"Can I take one?" I ask and point to the blankets on the chair.

"Yes, of course. You can have a cushion if you need one," the fair-haired lady says. I will not need it, I only need a soft blue blanket.

After few minutes, five women and one man join us. Then we start. We put ourselves in the column of light, invite our guides, archangels and other beings of light, then the leader sets the intention for today's event, and starts channeling activation in which Kunthumi explains the principle of Water door in detail, wisdom is disclosed by Guinevere and other beings who I have regarded as mythological made-up characters, up to this point. We drink seven cups with various qualities …

Two hours later I feel relaxed. I felt a lump in my throat a few times and I wanted to cry several times but I managed. I like the idea that Avalon with goddesses, knights and wizards existed, that is, is existing in other dimensions.

I am waiting for the sharing of our feelings but most of the attendants are leaving. The rest of us are not that talkative so I stand up and say good bye. Before I put on my shoes, I wash my cup in the sink and look at what is there on the table. Bach drops, karmic drops, oils, protection sprays … I would like to take most of the bottles, I feel I need all of them, but I have to wait till I get my income.

The following week I feel rather light and I am not surprised that on Friday I am in the group again. This time is the Activation of the Law of Assumption.

First, the leader shares her experience when she left her body. It is not necessary that the body dies; we can experience assumption earlier, even several times, and continue with lessons in our body. We are sitting in the circle, today there are two men, she is talking about how she was having a bath, totally relaxed, and then noticed how she was lifting. She saw her body lying in the bath but she was not afraid. She saw a few important moments of her life and then came down.

During the activation we receive a code and principles of the law which will enable our self-love to grow – of course if we want that – and in that way we will let everything that does not support us die. When we are rising in self -love we get our power back which was given to our lower ego, and with that love we enable the healing of fragmented pieces of our soul. They come back to our body and we start feeling our true-self. Our wounds, suffering and fears are not us; we are the soul in a physical body which has come to feel joy and harmony of live on Earth.

With awareness I say Yes to self-love and remember who I really am: a being of love. When we remember that, fears and wounds with which we have identified ourselves can leave and we create place for new to come into our life. We can feel betrayal and disappointment but only because we are not able to love ourselves as much as we can love other people … Maria Magdalena is talking about how to love ourselves, how to go up the ladder without leaving the physical body, how to let go of karma (fate) and step on our true path (destiny) …

During activation we get an assignment. To set a date when we will 'die' on a certain level – let go of that which we do not

313

need any more. I get a clue that it is smoking both cigarettes and marijuana. I only need to define the date.

The following month is very exhausting. The colleague got back to school from her sick-leave and is working part-time but I feel awful. The children like her. She is very generous with good grades. Or am I jealous because they like her but they do not like me? I am kind of happy that I do not need to deal with the highest-grade children although I have to check twice as many essays and tests as the lady who took over the other half of lectures. Unpleasant feelings are not triggered by kids only; I do not feel that I am welcome in the teacher office either. She has the last health examination in May and then it is possible that she will return to work full-time, which is what she wants, in spite of the fact that she has less than a year to retirement and nobody expected her back to work.

With regard to the situation and possibility of my leave I do not remain passive. First, I sign a contract with a language school in Ljubljana for a part-time job, because my income is enough for my rent. At the end of March I start teaching foreigners three times a week. Excellent, I will earn additional 400 to 500 euros per month.

Next, Tasha persuades me to write her a thesis for the price of one rent. The girl is under a lot of stress and this can harm her sensitive nature and the clots in her brains can go crazy. She is worried so she asked me to help her. My future is unreliable and the money earned in that way will be very welcome, so I agree although not very willingly.

But that is not enough. I ask my guides if there is any future for me here and I receive their answer. If you do not know what you desire, the Universe delivers that which you are familiar with. The next day I got really angry at the kids, also the colleagues in the teacher office ignored me, so the answer was clear. Get out of there as soon as possible. I write a job application the very same day and send it. It is filling in for a worker who is on a maternity-leave, in the neighboring town. I get the call after few days, and after a successful interview I receive an invitation to start working after Easter. In fourteen days.

The headmistress is not satisfied that their children will be taught by the fourth teacher of Slovenian this year but she understands my situation and does not complicate with regard to one-month notice. I feel scared and I gladly accept an offer for DNA-therapy. Something that I really need!

The only free term is on Easter Friday which I find great. The next week I will start my new job totally renewed and I have registered for great sound invocation where powerful festive energies will be utilized. To make my energies even stronger I start bleeding at the full moon.

After I have reached the well-known house of Activations, I ask K. if everything is in order with me physically because early menstruation scares me slightly. She harmonizes and the answer is exciting. I am connecting and tuning with my female energy, feminine aspect, and that is why the cleansing started a week earlier. She explains to me that at the therapy today she will not be talking about what she is cleaning from my previous lives. I have been looking forward to the new opportunity of insight into my past so I ask her what is preventing me from researching my past. I am interested in history so much that I even wanted to study it. I am wondering what role I played in it. She asks the guides again and the answer is that I will mature in two to three years and research those dimensions myself.

Now I ask her about pictures and movies which I sometimes see under my eyelids before I fall asleep. And when I am not yet asleep but not awake either I am aware of my surroundings.

"Well, it is … it looks like a camera window …."

"Yes, exactly. As that I am looking through the camera. But then I get scared and it disappears. Usually I have to go to the toilet straight away."

"Yes, this is how the body is cleansing," K. nods in satisfaction.

Yes, I have heard about it. When I was on a similar journey for the first time, I was observing my shoes – they were man shoes – on a paved street, the second time I was observing a kind of mansion, and the last time I was looking at a beautiful lady with curly black hair, dressed in medieval clothes, I believe, in the middle of a church. When I approached her I saw evil in her eyes. Who was that? Me? Was I an evil? Is that the reason which is preventing me from finding more about my past?

Now we start with relaxation. This is interrupted by noise from downstairs where a big dog resides with exactly the same puppies as was my late dog. I caressed them several times before activation and today they greeted me as well. I felt a tick on one puppy. I hope it will be taken care of. But I am surprised at her attitude towards animals. She set a trap for mice, a cowhide is on the floor in the living room, but I do not want to think about that now. But I get a hint, what if animals are trying to warn me and prevent the happening ...

K. goes downstairs and calms down the noisy pets. When she returns we continue. In every case, it will happen for my highest good, so there is nothing to be worried about.

After we have put ourselves in the column of light, called the guides and other beings of light, we start the cleansing process of DNA record. I am lying on the two-seater with my palms open on the knees while K is reading a channeling text. I am listening about cleansing of the records of artificial substances, vaccine, medicine, drugs ... from the chakra system and from my physical body ... This is followed by the awakening of the universal nature through the connection with prime DNA which is carrying the record.

"When we awaken our universal nature and awareness that we are blessed, we are automatically connected with the source and start the universal journey. The whole Universe starts supporting us: we meet people who help us, counsel us, who want to co-create with us. We are led to places where we are awakening, learning, and growing joyfully. We are becoming more and more aware that as blessed beings we deserve everything: health, a beautiful and harmonious home, pleasant relationships, fulfilling work, money ... We are energetically communicating that to the Universe so everything starts flowing into our life …"

I am stepping out of a victim consciousness into the awareness of my role as the creator of my own life. I start living my purpose as we are the beings of light that are anchoring the source light on the Earth and bringing Heaven to it.

Now I have to ask myself which part of myself I do not trust. What map of my best life journey do I want to see?

Before I repeat the entire question in my head the answer is clear. Love! This is the area with a total destruction; I do not trust myself at all. How could I? What men am I choosing? That is, what men I am attracted to? I will do fine with my work, I have started writing my book – although I only typed ten pages. I am not worried about my future in that area. Oh my God? Does that mean that I will meet somebody? Now? Oh … I do not know if I wish that …. Now, a guy, when I finally stopped searching for one?

Among all the thoughts and feelings that keep flying in, the fear is the strongest. Am I afraid of love? I make myself unseal from not very romantic thinking and I start focusing on accepting the code for attracting everything that I need for success in my life. I am supposed to start feeling my soul, heart, intuition …

After the text has been read, I mention the fear of darkness and beings from other dimensions. I do not have enough money with me to cover the whole expense, but I leave the place lighter by 150 euros (I will pay the rest at the next activation), and wealthier by DNA cleansing, code anchoring, three different bottles of drops, spray and CD for space cleansing. Before I bought it, I asked her if Gaia healing was not sufficient for space cleansing as T had told us, but she said that the healing follows the transformation, and the knowledge of transformation is provided on the CD in my bag.

After therapy a lot of people do not feel well physically. The consequences of cleansing usually cause diarrhea, vomiting and similar troubles, but I only feel tired. I sleep through Sunday, and in the evening I meet Alex and his friends, who are playing poker and need someone to mix and share the cards. In the honor of my student work as a croupier I agree. I am wondering whether or not I can influence the result and decide by myself who to give good cards and who to give bad cards. In the casino our regular 'patients' (as we were making fun of them) often accused me that I did not want to share good card intentionally, that is why I marked them as grumpy nags. Now I am wondering if they were right. Even at that time I noticed that I was always winning and clearing the chips from tables and their pockets when I was really pissed off.

The evening and game is boring. They bet a little, no one takes risks, no one is bluffing … I notice, though, that I am in favor of the host. He gets good cards most of the time but does not risk, so he does not get higher wins. He should risk a little! What about me? What are my cards of life?

Easter Sunday and Monday pass during my tiresome lying at home in my bed, the evening before my first day at the new job I spend in the hall listening to gongs. This is the first time that I am not enjoying the concert. I am restless, I am tossing and turning, but no position suits me. I am thinking of leaving the invocation earlier and waiting in the toilet for its conclusion. But I do not want to give up. I wait, although with difficulty, for the Tibetan bowls to settle and the event to conclude.

On Tuesday I wake up even more tired than previous days and set on a journey towards my new life. I meet new colleagues in the teacher assembly room, no happy faces with the exception of two teachers of the Slovenian language. Soon I am informed that the most of the school will be demolished, on purpose, so that the foundation can be strengthened and a new gym can be constructed. That will cause the lack of suitable rooms, noise and similar unfavorable circumstances.

The children are mostly alright. I can notice countryside-fairness characteristics although they make fun of me a little bit, but I am used to it. The youth here are used to listening and team working, at least a little, for they have several brothers and sisters at home. It seems that in this little town an average family consists of at least seven members, so I do not experience any spoilt disturbances from children looking for attention.

In the afternoon I teach the foreigners. Something new. The group of fifteen former south brothers is totally different from talkative kids. It is difficult to persuade them to say something in Slovenian, but they seem alright. I feel that the course will run smoothly and the initial fear of adult participants disappears after few minutes.

I stay at the language school until half past eight in the evening. Then I fell into my bed. Although I am exhausted I cannot fall asleep. I am worried about the coming days. Can I manage? On the other hand, I am hardly waiting for Friday and new insights at the activation. I actually must go there, I owe K. money for little bottles. I feel that the Law of Attraction and Surrender suits me down to the ground and everything is happening at the right time.

I am getting used to the school circumstances successfully. I do not like a clogged and crowded dining room, where we have our lectures because most of the classrooms are unsuitable, but I will live. If nothing else, I am grateful that I can earn for rent and independent life. I will not have to worry about finance for the whole year.

The drops have not had any effect yet; it often happens that I am lying in my bed in horrifying mood because I feel that a lost soul is standing by my bed. Regardless of abundant insertion of liquid with alcohol into my throat, I still feel fear.

I cannot fall asleep tonight either. The closeness of the largest cemetery in the state and daily walks around it do not contribute to my sense of security. Even though I fear those spheres like a devil of cross – I fall asleep at night with the blanket over my head so that only my nose is sticking out –, I notice that I often find myself in the places somehow connected with death. I used to live in the house where the Germans killed my grandpa's brother, the parents of two teenagers who committed suicide have moved into the neighborhood, the events taking place in a Dalmatian island, and now I am living next to cemetery. Not to

319

mention constant cracking in the wardrobes or TV. I asked K. about it the other day, but she explained that causes and meanings should not be explained because in that way the development of the soul could be hindered. I will have to find the answers by myself. She only told me that I was safe.

When I am scared I feel today my kidneys get crazy, so I stand up and go to the toilet to relieve my bladder. On my way back I notice the Destiny of Souls on the table in the living room. I never paid detailed attention to the front cover, but now I am wondering what the foggy picture above the title represents. I take it into my hands and I feel electric shaking of fear when I recognize the image – a kind of creature similar to ghosts. A dark unrecognizable face, implicit arms – three –, a strange body, everything transparent, interwoven with reddish mist. Horrifying! But it probably presents a soul and not a poltergeist (which is only a trapped energy of a soul)? So I am scared to death of myself?

My initial week in my new working environment is successful and I arrive to K. The activation is taking place as usual, we relax, put ourselves into the columns of light, and then we start receiving the lessons and wisdom.

"When we consciously or unconsciously deny that we are divine instruments through which the Universe works, we start suffering because we experience the dying of our soul's parts – our spirit. We deny ourselves, say no to the laws of attraction and surrender, we say no to life …"

Soon tears start flowing down my cheeks. Fortunately, I have a handkerchief with me because I am neither the first nor the last one to cry in that room. There is at least one person who leaves with messy mascara and red nose, and today it is my handkerchief which is soaked so soon.

While I am pressing it against my nose, K. is reading on. "Acceptance does not mean that we give up. It is not capitulation. Acceptance takes courage. To accept the circumstances of our existence. When we accept them we can let them go – we free ourselves and make space for new resolution and creation in a new manner. When we accept what we need to face, we allow higher energies to flow into our life … Acceptance opens creative mind and we attract creative solutions. When we surrender and allow solutions to reach us, and we have all the knowledge, we do not feel fear … We become aware that it is safe to be free and that with acceptance we allow our spirit to serve us …"

She continues to talk about a dragon and my last brakes loosen, I am crying. I imagine hugging the dragon and cuddling him so that he puts his head on my shoulder and hugs me with his wings … CRAZY! Did I fly with that magnificent being? So my childish watching of fairy tales, my belief in myths, silent longing for magic in life … is not so unconvincing. So it is nothing wrong with me if I believe that such beings do exist? I have been *terrorizing* myself all my life how childish I am and that it is high time for me to grow up. I am moved to tears and the relief continues during the dolphin dancing. I continue crying till the end of the activation, I am not the only one, and then leave the house totally tear-stained.

I have spent the whole month teaching the school kids and adult immigrants, I have been writing Tasha's thesis, but I do not seem to get far with my book. That is why I accepted the invitation by one of regular attendants of activation sessions – who has been traveling with me to the sessions because she does not own a car –, to go with her to Braco's[24] session.

First, I wanted to cancel the Sunday visit because I believe that I do not need a magic help of a third party to help me manifest my desires and intentions, but I was convinced by a night coincidence. I am so tired when I come home from work that I fall asleep around eleven in the evening, but on Friday evening I was piddling around till midnight when a report about him surprised me in one of night TV programs. Because I do not believe in coincidences any more I decide to take her there and join a group of 'who-knows-what-kind' of people.

---

[24]   Braco – croatian faith healer.

On Sunday afternoon a great number of people gather in front of Hotel Mons. Me and my colleague's – an elderly retiree – turn is in one hour. At the entrance into the hall we hand out our roses which bedside 5 euros intended for the rented place, present the price demanded for Braco's magic insight which is supposed to make your desires for health, love … come true.

In the hall we arrange into several rows, as I have no idea how many of the attendants were squeezed inside. Maybe around fifty? Some of them are holding photos of their relatives for who they are asking health and the others are praying. First, someone from Braco's company comes to the stage and tells us a little about his work, books, and CDs that can be bought in front of the hall. He requests total silence in the hall so that the folk hero can focus on his channeling during we are not supposed to remove our eyes from his. Before he leaves he tells us to think about our wish and surround it with the intention to manifest for the highest good of all.

I admit that it seems funny to me, but I think about getting assistance with my book writing, with intention to inspire many people – I must have slipped into a saver's role again – and I look into a little fuzzy face of a grey-haired figure coming to the stage. It is high time I ordered glasses. I try not to remove my eyes because I could miss his healing power which he is about to channel through his vision, but I anyway observe the happening in the hall with the corner of my eye. I am surprised by the movement – swinging – of others which is getting stronger and stronger. His looking at the attendants lasts for a few minutes – I cannot tell if or when he looked into my eyes, then he leaves without saying a word.

In front of the entrance his associates are sharing the flowers. I have brought a red rose, the symbol of love, and I have received a flower pot with an unknown flower. I hope it will not die as many have already; I am not good at being a florist, really.

I am losing my mind over all the work, so fortunately the last week of April I have vacation. I wanted to go somewhere for the Labor-May holidays and one night before the beginning of my new job I asked my guides for finance and advice where to travel. The next morning I woke up thinking about Murter. It would be good to energetically clean the house where I used to stay and in that way help Damir and his relatives get over his brother's death. Or the deceased to find his light.

Do I dare? Despite all the drops and sprays I still feel the fear of the intangible. Yes, it seems that I do, because I managed to save the money with doing part-time job and I also proofread one thesis.

Therefore, I and my dog find ourselves on a little island during first May holidays, the same as the year before, only that the landlady accommodates us into one of the higher apartments offering even more beautiful view of the sea and marina.

The first evening I meet Damir in front of the house, but I lie that I am tired and that I want to rest, although my real desire is to enjoy birds' night singing and the moon reflection on the smooth surface in front of me, so we soon say goodbye.

The following day, first, I go for a walk over the rocks and observe the Kornati islands, and then, I lie down on the warm sand of a small beach and offer healing due to my excitement about all the beauty. Under my eyelids everything turns green, and in the evening, when I look at the photos I have taken, I see a few green circles – in front of the house, at the beach and above the sea. I am amazed but I still feel the fear of realizing my intention – cleansing and healing the space.

Regardless of what I feel I set to work in the evening. I put the CD into the computer and set the sound at low volume so that I can barely hear it. I put myself into the column of light and call the angels of violet flame and transition to help the deceased enter the other world. I remember the deceased firefighters and expand my intention to include them, the entire house and the whole island. Next I do Gaia healing – just in case the first approach did not help, better more than nothing. I do not feel anything special at that time, but after one hour a terrible headache starts. In the middle of the night, when every thought hurts, it becomes clear to me that I am experiencing my first migraine. On top of that I am not sure whether the cleansing and healing was successful and I am paranoid that all the deceased are standing by my bed in spite of the CD which has been playing the entire evening. According to K, the sound on the CD itself is supposed to help. The night is unbearable and I fall asleep at dawn.

In the morning the pain decreases a little bit, so I decide to go to the center to find a pharmacy because I do not want to experience something similar to the previous night, ever again. Before I leave I meet Damir on the stairs. I do not know why but I ask him to fetch me a pill against headache and he agrees, so I put a hundred kunas into his hand. I return to the kitchen where I put a dish with water onto the cooker.

He comes back after fifteen minutes, just in time for coffee, which has cooled down on the balcony. We both light a cigarette, I take two pills just in case, and then we tell each other about the happenings through the year. I learn that he has left his job and is now working illegally – he is a computer programmer, so there is always work for him, even on the island as small as this one, and at the weekends he is playing music in the only mini disco on the island, which he has always longed for. I tell him a lot about my happenings, in a slightly shorter version, I do not mention the healing. I feel that it would be good to mention what I did the previous night but I cannot get the words out of my mouth. When we have almost finished our coffees, I manage to tell him a brief revision of my spiritual journey and the possibility of energetic healing.

"That's interesting," Damir says while looking at me with his eyes wide open. "Last year I read The Secret. Have you heard about it?"

"Of course." It is a fundamental work of manifesting what you desire. "But I only watched a movie. How do you feel about the book?"

"A fascinating idea, I like it a lot and try to live it …" He says. Now I feel encouraged and provide a brief review of a healing practice. "Well … With regard to that … A person can do everything, even heal himself/herself if he/she is ill …" Then I continue to talk about the souls of the deceased. I tell him about a horrifying mirage by my bed last year and about the yesterday's performance.

"I think … I think that your brother does not want to leave unless he is sure that you are alright …" I conclude, whispering and coughing. "Maybe it's on you … your pain …. to let him go … so that he can enter the light?" What the hell am I talking about?

Damir is silent and I light another cigarette. This is too troublesome. It is the first and the last time that I am poking my nose into something that is not my business!

"Do you think a lot about him?" I try to interrupt the silence.

"A lot … sometimes I feel that he's still with me …"

"And he is … this is it …. He will always come when you need him … You can always call him …"

"Mhm …" he nods while gazing at the sea surface.

"Are you ok?" I ask him.

"Yes, I'm ok, but I have an appointment, so I must leave." His eyes swim back and he stands up. "Thank you." What for?

"It's ok. Be good, see you." I say and wave.

"Yes, I'll call you later. Bye."

"Bye."

Damir did not call, the last two days I am spending on the beach with a book in my hands, entitled I exchange enlightenment for a quick vibrator. The headache has passed, now I am suffering from stomach pains, I feel nausea all the time. On top of that, the words I read about the masks we wear, even to hide before ourselves, make me cry. What is it in me as I am so afraid of, that I am hiding even before myself? Fortunately, there is no one on the rocks so I can empty the stock of salted water from my eyes or sinuses or wherever it is coming from.

I leave the Island without seeing Damir again. He called me yesterday, but I missed the call and sent him a message telling him that I am dealing with something and cannot meet him for coffee. I think it is over with the house and the people in it. I feel that I will not come back. In spite of the exciting happening I feel relaxed. It is time for a new adventure!

In the middle of May I leave through the wooden door in the suburbs of Ljubljana once more and head towards my car. This time I feel great, no crying. I have experienced a great event. On 15 May, the day I set for quitting smoking, the activation into the law of unconditional love has just been carried out. I could not miss that one. So this morning I lit the last cigarette and the last joint, but after what I have heard I am not sure that that was the right plan. All my feelings through the last months and preparation for today ... everything seems to be a support for activation which somehow continues DNA-therapy. One hour ago I let a part of me die and transform into love. The part of me that had to do with relationships has died, but it will not harm me if I realize the primary intention too.

The abstinence attempt has been successful for two weeks. But the afternoon came when I shared my life with too nervous teachers, and in addition had to deal with the ninth-grade children where I was filling in for a colleague who is on a sick-leave. They started throwing paper planes at each other and pouring water all over the classroom. Powerlessly, I went to fetch the headmistress deputy and then spend the time till the end of lecture writing All is well All is well ... to prevent me from crying. After the hour of torture I ran to the store to buy a pack of cigarettes. With the greatest relief I lit a cigarette the moment I stepped out of the store and finished it before I got to the car. In the evening I smoked a nice joint, thanks to Alex.

The weekend is not glamorous. Fortunately, I have my dog with me. Former friends do not suit me anymore; Dajana's energy has become too heavy for me. I cannot stay in the same room with Alex more than half an hour and that is felt by Odysseus too who starts barking, snarling, and similar. During the last month I have only connected with the reviser living in the apartment above mine and with the business woman living under my apartment. I like that in the line of a two-story block of apartments, three independent women of different age are living. On the ground floor there is a 41-year blond lady who is living in habitual relationship with a younger man, me on the first floor, and a 36-year runner on the second floor. They do not like each other, but I like both of them, so I happily join one or the other for a cup of coffee.

I do not attend activations any more, but I carried out one yesterday by myself. At home. I bought an English original from K. and connected with creation and magic. A person can find them in sacral chakra; the love relationship is the one that opens the doors to magic, so I connected with the Atlantean priestess whose sacral ritual has been disclosed to me. I enjoyed the company of my twin soul for the first time, but Odysseus who came to scratch on my legs, interrupted my excitement about the energetic meeting.

Today I am focusing on summer vacation. I will earn enough with teaching immigrants to afford longer holidays or further away. Finally, I am able to afford a travel, but I do not have a company and I do not fancy staying alone in a hotel. Anyway, I am surfing the internet to find the right place for my escape.

My browsing is interrupted by Odysseus who wants to go for a walk, but I do not like the idea. I am excited about 14 days on Bali which I noticed last week. Spiritual journey, so it is with good intention, but in a luxurious version, for 2000 euros. Too much for me, so I have been thinking where to earn additional finance. In spite of attractive beaches and comfortable beds on the photos, I take the leash and go with the dog for a walk. It is cloudy but it has not been raining for several days, so I am surprised by the rainbow above me. From this angle it seems that my block of apartments is right below its end or beginning.

"Yah, sure," I say in a low voice. It is really possible to be living at the beginning or the end of the rainbow where the treasure is hidden, in Ljubljana.

I am walking in the park on the grass and when I am passing cemetery I look up towards the sky again. From this angle, too, it seems that my block is at the beginning of the rainbow. Weird …

Upon my return I meet the neighbor who is living downstairs. She is holding the book that I was reading in Murter. We both like it, but I do not comment the parts that made me cry.

Then, in my apartment, I connect with the world network. I check the activities of my friends on Facebook, known and not known ones. One of the latter has commented the post by the writer whose book has just been returned to me, and reading her words I remain breathless. In summer she will be staying at the Canary Islands for a month, at yoga holidays, in a house with a pool. Dream like! There is a link to the yoga teacher page, the organizer of the event. I click on it and I am satisfied when I see that her profile is public. Excellent!!! I can see that for the amount of approximately 1000 euros I can afford the whole month of recreational enjoyment. I send a message to the yoga teacher asking her about a free term and remain waiting impatiently by my computer. I feel that I want to, that I need to go there. Thinking of the possibility that there is no vacant position I shiver down my spine.

The answer comes in the evening. I shall book a flight and confirm my attendance, for now all the terms have vacant positions. I spend the whole following weekend searching for air tickets. I start at school during a free hour, but I become worried when I realize that I can spend a 1000 euros or even more for the flight. And besides, I will have to spend a night at one of the European airports. Finally, I find a flight for 400 euros, leaving from Venice in the morning and arriving at Fuerteventura at six in the afternoon. Return flight is acceptable too, departing from the island at two in the afternoon and arriving at Venice at ten in the evening. So somehow I do not have a choice, I would have to pay a lot more for any other flight, but I do not complain at the chosen term. It is perfect! So I depart on 14 July! Before I book a flight, I check with Alex whether or not Odysseus can stay with him during the four weeks. No problem. And if I need a drive to the airport, I should let him know. I send a message with arrival and departure dates to the yoga teacher and check the availability once more.

OH MY GOD, I am so scared that something may go wrong and prevent me from going to the dream holidays! I have never been at the airport or flown by plane or travel further than to the Netherlands and Spain – well, technically, the Canary belong to Spain, only that they are located further to the south. And I will experience everything at the same time! I am not worried about the journey. I feel fear that something may go wrong and I will be forced to spend the summer in Ljubljana.

The yoga teacher confirms the term and I start booking my flight through STA (Student Travel Agency). It does not proceed without complications, a clerk from Koper lets me know that the visa payment has been rejected. How is that possible?

I call the information office where they explain that I do not have 500-euro limit per month. I call the agency again and ask them for payment order. I have to settle it till three in the afternoon, if not, the reservation will be canceled. I have two bank accounts but not enough money on any of them to be able to settle the whole amount. So I drive to the first bank, withdraw cash, run to the second bank, make a deposit and then transfer the amount to the agency. I ask the bank clerk to send the agency the confirmation of payment because it will not reach the agency account before tomorrow. When everything has been settled, I, as wet and nervous as I am, sit down on the burning pavement in front of the car and light a cigarette. This is it; I depart in the middle of July!

Before departure I meet the yoga teacher at the candy store in the middle of the shopping mall to give her a larger part of the demanded payment for my dream holidays, and after that, through Facebook, I meet the man who will be present there to provide organizational support. I connect well with both of them and can hardly wait to join them.

One night I am dreaming that someone came to ask me if I was coming with them. I agreed but I had a feeling that I confirmed too fast. The next moment I wake up with numbness in my left arm although it was resting on my stomach and was not twisted under my ribs. I tell Manja, the upper neighbor, about my dream, but she is not as excited about the mystical experience as I am. She suggests that I should see a doctor in case something is wrong with my veins – so that I do not get a heart attack. But my enthusiasm remains undisturbed and I expect sex down there too. I cannot get rid of thinking about a man's body on mine. There has been eleven months since my last intercourse and I have had enough of voluntary nun-ism. Not only do I buy a new suitcase for my traveling, but also the whole range of cute and comfortable underwear, that is, boxers. Although I do not know how I will carry that out. I do not want to get permanently involved, I am not for short adventures, but I want to have sex again. So how? Who with?

I also start dealing with karmic absolution. During the week when I am meditating on that intention, several former friends and lovers call me or send me a message. Even Matey, and the biker and the businessman, while the Carpenter is sending me greetings from London. Even Jan, who I write a long letter of gratitude to him thanking him for everything he offered me, he was the one to make me really love someone for the first time. I mention with good intention that he should show his softer side to someone else too and that I am convinced that he will find someone to love him in return. He does not respond.

I exchange the gifted golden jewelry and get rid of all presents but a perfect joy at releasing the old and buying the new does not last for long. Upon my return from the cleaning spree the glass on both picture frames that I wanted to have on my walls breaks. The first one with the photo of dolphins under the glass does not even come home undamaged, and the other one with an encouraging motto *Universe makes way for those who know where they are going,* falls down from the wall at home. I hope that glass shards bring luck.

Well, whatever will be - will be, and I am sure that holidays will happen for the greatest good. I ask K about it, while I am purchasing another interesting activation text. This one discloses the wisdom of the masks we are wearing. K is excited about the idea that I invest everything I have into my future and follow my heart which is taking me there. I feel better due to her support, but my financial plans do not go according to the plan. First, the teaching of immigrants ends sooner – the group got too small and they decided to combine two groups, so I remained without one. Tasha appears to be a kind of friend as she really is. I was writing her thesis alone, all weekends and other days when I had free time, finished it in the middle of May while she was posting the photos of rolled dumplings she was preparing. She graduated in June with A, but I will not get the money before I leave for the Canary Islands. This 'happy' news was sent to me at the beginning of July and Alex and I had to interrupt our vacation on Croatian coast because I would not have enough money to spend the whole month close to the African continent. I felt I owe him a vacation because he was supporting me through the last months of our relationship and I wanted to somehow pay him back. The casino got bankrupt and he has been unemployed since the spring. I wanted to pay for a week of camping, but first there was rain, then Tasha, and I do not know what I was thinking. I get nervous, annoying and grumpy in his company regardless of how I force myself to be relaxed and to feel and express unconditional love. I know that he is a great person, but I am repelled by everything on him. It must be the first time in my life that I am happier driving home from the seaside than in the other direction. Well, I am departing in two weeks …

I cannot believe I have succeeded! I am standing at the Venice airport with my suitcase in line for the X-ray examination. I hugged Alex for farewell ten minutes ago – he is really kind to have taken me to the airport! I am holding the air ticket with two stops, the first one in Madrid and the second one on the island of Gran Canaria. I feel great! I am a little scared how it will go. Will I find the exit? Will everything be alright with the plane? Will I arrive in time to catch another flight? Will my yoga teacher be waiting for me at the airport? Are they good people? Will I have a good time? … I feel my heart beating in my chest as never before. But my decision is confirmed by the numbers of the registration box and gate – 15 and 23. My numbers! I know I am not alone, something big is waiting for me.

After one hour I am looking through the window in expectation, the bird view is disclosing the water city. The morning Venice is sunbathing in the sunlight which is shining on the labyrinth of canals and luxurious buildings while the Iberia airline plane is flying higher and higher ...

STATION 8:

THE HEAVEN ON EARTH

Corralejo, 15 July 2010
Dear Journal!

Hey, I am on the Canary Island, Yeeeey! ☺ IT Б HEAVENLY!

The women, including the pilot, have brought me to Madrid yesterday. I was running and running through the airport to reach the right gate in time, boarded the plane, got off the plane because there was something wrong with it, boarded another one (this time with a male crew) and happily arrived at Las Palmas. There I felt the right atmosphere, CRAZY! We walked across the airport to a small plane heading towards Fuerteventura. At the top of the stairs the flight attendants greeted us in cute green uniforms and gloves. They offered sweets and water, free of charge!

I am excited about flying! Taking off is amazing, even more than accelerations on motor bikes! And I got to see the island from the air – veeeery beautiful, surrounded by emerald green water. Dream-like! It seems to resemble the scene from my dreams. Is it possible that I was dreaming about this?

The house is ok, 10-minute walk from the center and the beach. WANDERFUL beaches with the sea of azure color! And a fantastic café with wireless, deckchairs, mini sofas, and white curtains … and a crazy view of the neighboring island.

The yoga teacher, a beautiful black-haired lady, resembling a Vinetou's girlfriend, and her partner were waiting for me at the island airport, they both are ok, same as the third member of the crew who I met personally in the house, Jurij.

Everyone is smoking here, and not only cigarettes, yesterday evening the yoga teacher rolled one with hashish! ☺

On the top of everything, Jurij was celebrating his 34th birthday yesterday, so we drank a few beers.

I wanted to take advantage of being thousands kilometers away from home with the unknown people to create a healthy, spiritual life which includes morning yoga, detoxification of the body, and facial yoga. I wanted to get back home clean of addictions; I prepared myself to release the life I was used to, which of course does not include cigarettes and beer. To express myself truthfully, I expected to meet a bunch of posh individuals who would look at me blamefully if I smoke, and would force me to abstinence. ☺ So, I do not know what will happen to the rehab. ☺

I could not fall asleep at night. I was too excited about the beauty of everything. I got up and wrote a prologue to my book. Yeeeey! ☺ Bravo me!

16 July 2010
Dear Journal!

Here I am, having experienced two enlightenments already.

I could not fall asleep during the night and I was thinking about Odysseus. In the afternoon we were discussing leashes and I was interested in their opinion because I always unleash my dog (who, by the way, I already miss). The doggy here is off the leash all the time, nobody bothers them, but I am constantly being attacked in Ljubljana. A man in the park asked me if the tragedy with bullmastiffs had not taught me anything and that he would call the police. At night I realized that it was easier to control than to trust and that that is the reason for worrying. I had always unleashed him because I felt it was the right thing to do.

I have decided to trust from now on! Trust! Trust the Universe, trust myself! I cannot/do not want to control everything …

The second relief was brought by the acceptance of marijuana. It is obvious that spiritual people use it in moderation too. I was so terrorizing myself … called myself a little junky …. My little shamanic experiences are nothing compared to professionals!

Every day (in the morning and in the evening) I do yoga and I drink a clay beverage every morning, and I have been writing this morning again. Good girl! ☺ The beaches are breathtaking! Love love, love it here!

And yes, cockroaches are everywhere around the town. It is unbelievable how many of this vermines crawling with us on the city streets. ☹

17 July 2010

During another sleepless night I realized why I was buying and wearing black clothes again. A blister which I got a day before arrival shows the same: I want to block the part of myself which enables soooo perfect experiences. I feel that I do not deserve them. That can explain why I feel so awkward when I am around the writer. I seem to have created the distance myself.

18 July 2013

Most of the attendants (except for Jurij with who I socialize most often – he is fun) do not seem satisfied. There is a hidden tension between the yoga teacher and her partner who shows himself in sharp and badly hidden thorns. Their 3-year relationship seems to be ending with a war storm. The writer is not satisfied either, she got ill with angina after she arrived and has not managed to heal herself with natural remedies such as onion, garlic and similar smelly stuff. While vegetarianism is self-evident in the house, and the dishes and spoons are separated from rare food 'contaminated' with dead energy, the problem is in certain vegetables, lactose and gluten, additional dissatisfaction is caused by the house which is located too far away from the sea, the rented car which is not used enough, rare trips and similar unfulfilled expectations.

But I have a heavenly time! I am amazed at the bays and today I visited the neighboring island of Los Lobos. With the writer's publisher and a new member we went for a walk across the island and went swimming in the crystal clear ocean by the long sandy beach from a fairy tale. My God, it is so beautiful! Really! ☺

21 July 2010 – morning

What is going on?

I am confused about Jurij who I feel I have known since ever. We have several things in common:
- He used to wait the tables in a pub where I used to spend my favorite time during student parties. Maybe we met there?
- Before athletics in his teenage years he trained swimming – my excitement at handsome bodies of swimmers does not to be mentioned, and the sport used to be my favorite sport for watching on TV;
- He is into internal design which I adore – I spend a lot of time decorating the rooms where I am in my mind;
- He wanted to attend a high school in Ljubljana where I had my student traineeship;
- He adores Barcelona, but has not had the opportunity to visit it. I was there during my matura excursion;
- We were dealing with the same topic at the same time: I was reading The Dragon Catcher, while he was watching the movie recorded after the book which was based on;
- There were several events that happened to us in the past at approximately the same period;
- We were reading the same books during our childhood, at the moment he is reading Paasilinna, the author I myself have been excited about;
- It has happened several times that he is reading my mind – I am thinking about something and he says something as a trigger for me to express what I have been thinking about;
- We have a similar skin mark at the same spot on our left arm;

337

- We are wearing a necklace gifted to each of us by our mothers;
- He has a younger sister whose is one week younger than me, his parents wanted to give her my name, but a relative was faster and they chose another name to avoid the repetition; his sister has been dating a guy for more than a decade whose grandma is Russian with Ukraine roots (and my late grandma was Ukraine too – isn't that strange?!);
- We both felt, before we arrived, that something would happen here;
- And last but not least … is it a coincidence that the Universe has sent me here with the cheapest air ticket exactly on his birthday?!

I like his loud smile, sneering sense of humor, hazelnut eyes shining from naughtiness, naughty comments and bad jokes.

As that he was calling me when I joined him an hour ago on the terrace, where we both, unable to sleep, smoked a tobacco. I wanted very much to get into his hug but I did not dare. I am not sure that he likes me. He is a person who does not like spirituality, he has joined us because of his student-period friend, the teacher's partner, with who they take care of the house and preparation of dinner, but they are not interested in yoga and other stuff from the field. During our conversation about the hypocrisy of spiritual people it was difficult for me to admit that I have been into healing lately.

I do not want to get involved with him, a sensitive cancer. Although he is affectionate, he would not encourage me at my growing because he is hiding too much – he himself admitted that he was wearing numerous masks, and he is blaming others for his feelings and difficulties. His firm had gone bankrupt and brought a lot of debts. He is curing his wounds here, taking tranquilizers, but the largest energetic minus is his ex-girlfriend, who is still writing him long messages. A very sick ex!

Regardless of everything I am being attracted to him. Why??!

P. S. When I got back to my room and thought about why I had not jumped on him and how nice it would be now to cuddle with him, it cracked strongly in the window frame. Yes, right, I thought. What? Was I supposed to have sex with him? And it cracked again.

Is there someone telling me something? ☺

21 July 2010 – late at night

What am I supposed to write?
☺☺☺☺☺☺☺
I   AM   HAPPY!!!!!!!!!!!!!!!!!!!!!!!!!!!!!!!!!!!!☺☺☺☺☺☺☺
I cannot find the words to describe what I am feeling. ☺ In the afternoon we visited El Cotillo, a little town on the other side of the island, before that we stopped at a paradise bay with the sea of the most beautiful color I have ever seen.

I   HAVE   FOUND   MY   HEAVEN!   ☺☺☺☺☺
OH, I am totally ungrounded … How can I describe my feelings, what happened?

Maybe I can write a story. Yes … ☺

I am gazing at the dark vastness of the ocean and admiring the power of the sea which is hitting the grey rocks which protect the peacefulness of the bay on the other side. I am peaceful, looking at completeness, feeling perfect, sensing harmony …. The water is wonderful, the wind is wonderful, a peaceful bay is wonderful; the huge firm rocks where I am standing are wonderful, the sun is wonderful, I am wonderful. Life is wonderful!

I smile when I remember that I used to stand on similar rocks, but they belonged to Dalmatia and little waves there cannot compare to the power of the ocean. At that time during the conversation about reincarnation I said that I had the feeling that I would reach nirvana in this life. I felt rather excited, but that was nothing in comparison to the harmony I am experiencing now in every part of my being.

If then, when the angels gave me a hint about spending my vacation on Fuerteventura, my home was really the beginning of the rainbow, this place represents its end.

I do not expect anything, I do not want anything, I am not afraid of anything, I am not hiding from anything, I do not regret anything. I feel and enjoy the perfect moment ... without the past or the future. This is it! This is how the HEAVEN ON EARTH feels!

"Oh, look at him," I mumble with the smile on my lips when I remove my eyes from the hypnotic scene in front of me. On the way to 'my cape' Jurij is pushing his way over the rocks and through the pools of sea water which wedged in during the recent high tide.

"Am I disturbing you?" he asks before he reaches me.

"No," I shake my head. "I am enjoying the beauty of the nature. "I say and turn to the waves. I flap my arms and inhale dramatically while imitating the king of the world scene.

"Yes, it is really beautiful. Can I join you?"

What courtesy. "Sure. Welcome to my kingdom." I jump off the rock and point to the towel in the shelter of the rocky nest. Fortunately, there is enough space for the two of us and he puts his towel next to mine.

"Are they getting on your nerves?" He asks. He is thinking of the hosts who brought us to the bay one hour ago, but had a fight during the drive because of inefficient morning sweeping.

"No, it's ok. I find this place more beautiful, so I have made my bed here," I respond with a half-truth. I wanted to be alone to think about my emotions, towards him as well. And I have found the heaven!

"You're right."

We are sitting on our towels, he lights a cigarette and we are staring at the sea.

We shroud ourselves in relaxing silence for a few minutes, then he says: "I've brought a sun cream. You haven't put any on. Here you are."

He is right. I take the offered cream and start spreading it on my legs.

"Can I help you?" he smiles and asks when he notices that I am struggling with a white mass which is not absorbed as fast as it should be. Maybe I put too much of it on my skin. Of course, I accept his help. I adore summer which always offers 'unintentional and coincidental' touches.

He takes the tube and removes the hair from my shoulders. "Have you heard a joke where the oldest daughter visits her parents and informs them that she is a lesbian?"

"No."

He starts telling the joke, but I am not listening. Uh, how his fingers feel good, massaging my shoulders, the back ...

"... I, father," he concludes and is laughing at himself. "You don't like jokes, do you?"

"Not really," I sincerely admit but am laughing together with him.

While he is gently massaging my back he offers some inopportune comments, then his hands reach the area around my bra which is still preventing the idyll. I laugh louder and undo it.

"Here, so that you don't spread on it. I doubt it can get burnt," I say and expose myself without unnecessary frame. It's enough of beating around the bush. If it feels great, it feels great, why would I pretend?

He laughs too. I lean on his chest and his hands are now massaging the skin on my hills.

We are enjoying, I turn towards him. "A kiss?" And I kiss him.

This is how it happened. ☺ We drove to the town and my zen for nirvana or whatever that feeling was lasted and lasted. And what is better than cuddling under the blanket beside the lit pool late into the night? Fortunately, we were soon left alone. The guy is so gentle and not pushy at all. We did not go further than teenage caressing today and it feels GREAT.

I came to sleep in my room. While I was writing this, it started to dawn, I doubt I will close my eyes today. ☺ Anyway,

Who would want to? ☺

22 July 2010

A fairy tale! All is the best! ☺ Jurij is like a dream, I like in a lot! ☺
Thank you, because I have everything that I have wished for! Thank you thank you thank you! ☺
In the evening I was lying in bed and thinking about angels when Jurij's phone rang twice. I regarded it to be a coincidence and started thinking about something else. But after half an hour I was thinking how strange it was that it rang at that exact moment, when it rang again! Isn't that interesting? ☺ Later when I told him about the experience, he said that there were no missed calls neither messages on his phone.

23 July 2010

Days ago new participants joined us, super girls. They both master reiki and one of them is also an astrologer. Today we had a ladies' afternoon. ☺
The three of us went shopping in the town center and later the writer joined us on the beach in Sirena. We sat on the low armchairs at the round table and took out our little notebooks. Before that, we had bought pens with feathers on the top. I got a violet one because everything here seems violet to me. Whenever I close my eyes, in particular during or after yoga, I see this shade of the rainbow. I wanted a blue one too and bought both but offered the blue one to the writer who came without it.
How everything is good for something, isn't it? ☺

The reading of astrological maps followed. Mine shows that I have brought great knowledge from previous lives, and that I need to work with spirituality and on my intuition which is very strong. I do not agree with that totally, but maybe … one day …

My goals in life need to be clarified and relationship with my family needs to be healed. She had noticed my creativity, I should create as much as possible. Is she talking about writing? I asked her about that and she encouraged me with words that when I'll finish with my writing everything will open to me, but before I reach that point I will have to process a lot of fear. No, really? ☺

Each of us received our map, the writer created numerological analyses of our names. With regard to my name, she confirmed the numerologist's, I decided for a strong number and additional name which will strengthen my intuition and expression.

We stayed at the pub the whole afternoon and paddle in the water. Heavenly! What a gift I have offered to myself!!

Besides, I was hugging someone in the evening veeeery tight and passionately. ☺☺☺ Mmmm …

24 July 2010

Today I totally lost it. As soon as I woke up I started cleaning my room which was messy with all the stuff I had been using these days. In the afternoon I was alone and I liked that very much.

I dawned on the fact that I like Jurij very much, more than I would like to. However, based on my emotions, I determined that I was still thinking that I was not good enough …. to enjoy … for someone to love me … also I do not feel that my parents will like me if I do not follow their principles. I do not feel that I deserve to be accepted.

I was lying on the artificial grass by the pool for almost three hours and listening to depressing music on my lap top. And I was crying.

In the evening I was totally ruined. The astrologist opened Osho's book for me and read a paragraph. Ego is looking for what it is familiar with … pain … And I felt better. ☺ But still it's not good enough to enjoy with Jurij as I did previous nights. One moment during hugging I even accused him of thinking about his ex-girlfriend because he was cuddling me with his eyes closed. I did not intend to explain my feelings but there was a situation when I had to choose between three options. Open my legs and pretend to be enjoying, or leave to my room without an explanation, or roughly explain why I was not well.

I chose the last option, and my lover hugged me without saying a word and kept hugging me well into the night. ☺

26 July 2010

What a day!

I am lying on my bed, while above me on the ground floor the lava of blaming is flowing from irritated throats and heating all the house. With full moon the tension reached its peak and all the accumulated dissatisfaction burst into a loud quarrel between the yoga teacher, the writer, and her editor. They are leaving tomorrow because it is impossible to write in such atmosphere. That means that her facial yoga workshop is cancelled and several attendants will not get what we have paid for. But I am not bothered by it.

Today I visited Lanzarote, the neighboring island, without Jurij. He hit a rock in the water and injured his finger, so, he is unable to drive. The rest of us traveled across the water by hydrofoil, rented a car and drove around the island of volcanoes. We visited the National park, the Museum of wine history, and

Cesar Manrique's crazy house. It was great, but I missed someone …

In one hour I am doing midnight yoga, and then we are supposed to go out. Finally! 😊

27 July 2010

OH, MY GOD!
After yoga, only me, Jurij, and one of the attendants went out. Already the first glass of wine took me out of reality. Through my half-closed eyes I only recognized soft sand under my bare feet, enticing sound of the guitar, and the hands which were caressing me, holding me, and leading me to the recognition that I am totally in love.

But, watch this!

In the morning I woke up in the adjacent room – fortunately, in an empty bed , where the colleague, who we totally rejected yesterday, is accommodated.
Alcohol erased quite a large part of the evening, but I do remember that before we went home, I went naked for a swim in the night ocean, and towards the morning I and Jurij slept in the same bed for the first time. In my room!

How did I get there then? Of course, I apologized for intrusion but the yoga colleague said that he did not even notice me on the other bed and that I should not worry. What Jurij thought when he woke up alone, I have no idea. In his typically cynical tone he blamed the full moon in combination with his (bear-like) snoring for my night escape, but he did not blame me for anything. Thanks God …

1   August 2010

I experienced an interesting situation during yoga class today. During the final meditation I fell asleep and the image of Jurij appeared. He said that I would fall??? What does that mean? At the end of meditating I felt numbness in my left arm, the same as at that night in Ljubljana when I was dreaming that someone was asking me if I would go with them.

How strange! Is there a connection? Was he asking me if I would go with them? Why will I fall?!

6 August 2010

Yesterday Jurij and I borrowed a car and went on a trip across the island. There is almost no soil on the island and nothing grows outside of arranged and trimmed gardens. Only volcanoes and sand … Among the Canary Islands this island is the only one to have escaped mass tourism and there are numerous solitary places next to the ocean.

We drove to the south where we watched the Wind and Kite World Cup. The longest European beach, full of surfers. Crazy! Then, we found a dream-like volcano beach, that is, the beach with black sand, where we were dipping in the afternoon and hmmmmm … ☺

We found an even prettier town with the middle age wall where we had a romantic dinner. We ended the evening with the winning party of the world surfing championship. Well, I concluded it with dancing barefoot on the sand in the rhythm of trance music, the selfless gentleman took us home safely.

The impact of the coming departure can already be felt. I am leaving in a week. We both spend certain moments in bitter silence. I have never expected the holidays to be so fairytale-like. I do not want them to end!!!!

8 August 2010

When you think that you have experienced everything!

In the morning my mother's message surprised me. She opened my mail (once again! After all my explaining, quarreling, threatening … asking her not to do that!) and texted me that my primary-school schoolmate invited me to her wedding. I have not seen her for quite some years and she has remembered me? It is true that we used to be the best friends and we promised to each other that we would be each other's maid of honor and godmother to our kids. When she gave birth to her son she forgot about me, but not now, although she only invited me to attend the wedding as a guest.

I got a little confused; she is in serious adult waters, with a steady job, a child, and now husband. And I … like this … I do not even know what Jurij feels about me – although he mentioned today that he would inform his lovers at home not to wait for him anymore.

In the afternoon we went to El Cotillo, this time we visited cliffs and sandy beaches underneath. As that emotional stress that I experienced earlier was not enough, I experienced a physical one too. Waves and the current started pushing me towards the open sea, so I had to try really hard to swim back to the sea shallows and oppose the bombarding of high waves. There I was pushed to the ground so I felt like that I was rolling in a washing machine.

In addition, Jurij argued with other two members and got me into the bad mood too. Before departure I heard them criticizing his slow work and careless cooking, but I will not tell him that. Although I paid for dinner, we ate out, but it was not good enough. He was still in bad mood, and I was becoming sad, so I decided to go to the beach alone. I wanted to go back in an hour or so, but we met half way and went to the center. And we got lost again. Without looking at what the other one was doing, we both took different directions to find a bank machine. He reached me in front of the house when I was getting really angry because once again someone seemed to have betrayed me.

What is happening? First, such harmony that we meet half-way and then such disharmony?

9 August 2010

Last week I gave up yoga, we spend days at the beach, evenings in Sirena pub which is lit by torches at night. Most of the time we are silent, listening to music, drinking red wine, or sipping margaritas, and we have smoked quite a few joints. Nobody has spoken to us because of that – the law permits cultivation of up to five plants for personal uses so they are tolerant with regard to that.

The nights spent dancing is concluded with making love, and later, sleeping outdoors - next to the pool, under the starry and reddish sky, in a tight hug.

I DO NOT WANT TO GO HOME!!!

But I will return home tomorrow, Jurij will get back at the beginning of October. I am writing this after the farewell dinner, while he is washing the dishes, before we go to Sirena for the last time …

STATION 9:

RETURN

The plane is circling above artificially illuminated Venice and starts descending slowly towards the Marco Polo Airport. The night flight does not bring many passengers, so I have all three seats in a row to myself. But I would not notice passengers anyway. My whole being stayed on the island of sleeping fire, in the ocean, between the sand and volcano rocks. In the middle of the lava of emotions there are my man's hands, hugs and words: *"I love you."*

I have found my Heaven, physical and psychological. How can I return to the reality now? A boring job, fake friends, smug and hypocritical co-workers, mean teenagers, a shortage of different things ... To everyday routine that kills any sign of spirit in the body?

I think of my dog and I feel slightly better. I have missed him, I am missing him like crazy! He is waiting for me at the airport with Alex so I am going to hug him in a few minutes.

I do not know what follows but the thought of unconditional dog's love returns my will to live. I remember the people I met at the airport. On the way to Fuerteventura I met a Spanish speaking lady who spends half a year in Brazil and another half at Gran Canaria; on the way back I met an Italian gentleman who moved to Tenerife after twenty years of working at different oil platforms. Did they want to tell me something? Is my future similar to theirs? Will I experience my dream-like traveling some day? Will I build my dream home in an exotic place and visit my home Slovenia from time to time?

I always thought that I would travel to my new life by train, but this time I am traveling by plane. Nothing is as it seems ...

I start thinking optimistically how blessed I am to have had the opportunity to experience so many beautiful things this month. However, all that was happening in perfect conditions, without stress, without obligations ... in the heights of a fairy tale which has ended. An opportunity to actually realize the heights, ground them and anchor in the reality is about to come!

EPILOGUE

A new plane is arriving in four weeks when Jurij returns from Fuerteventura one month earlier as was planned. Our nine-month relationship has given birth to moving to the seaside of Slovenia to live together as a couple, that is, as a triple – a shared care of the dog. Alex was washed away by fleas that come from Kranj several times to dip in the sea.

The beginning is difficult. I love him, but if I had known what I was about to go through without a guarantee for success I would have never started that 'adventure'. Heaven and hell are exchanging places and sometimes I am experiencing all possible traumas at once.

But we are fighting the past and the darkness. Also with each other, everything for the birth of our children – his furniture salon and my book.

About the author

Oneya B. Rajsel was born in Slovenia. In 2008 she finished studies of Slovenian language and Sociology of Culture in Ljubljana with the diploma thesis on female literary characters in modern novels.

She has been teaching children, adults and foreigners Slovenian language for the last 15 years.

Her first short stories were published in a few erotic magazines and *Collection of erotic stories: Touches and promises (2011)*.

She continued with more serious literature. Short story *Try Again and once more and one more time* won the first prize at the *Literature competition in Trieste (Italia, 2012)*.

Novella *The Rainbow Year 2013/3013* has found its place in *the Annual collection of Slovenian fiction Stardust 2012*.

You can read her *articles on her website:*
https://oneya.net/
or connect with her on social media:
https://www.facebook.com/oneyabarbara.rajsel
https://www.instagram.com/oneya.rajsel/

Next book
Her second novel (working title: **How I won the lottery of life**) continues the story about following your dreams and the heroine will grow big time. Phoenix is already waiting to rise from the ashes …

Oneya Barbara Rajsel: Train for Heaven on Earth, finding your path
2. edition

Published in Ljubljana, Slovenia, by ONEYA B. Rajsel
Translation to English: Vesna Leme
Proofreading: Alexander Netuzhilin

Price: 25 €

Oneya Barbara Rajšel, s.p. – Založništvo in izobraževanje
Mestni trg 10
1000 Ljubljana
Slovenia
info@oneya.net
https://oneya.net/
https://www.facebook.com/oneyabarbara.rajsel
https://www.instagram.com/oneya.rajsel/

CIP - Kataložni zapis o publikaciji
Narodna in univerzitetna knjižnica, Ljubljana
821.163.6-31

RAJŠEL, Oneya Barbara
Train for heaven on Earth : finding your path --- : a novel / by
Oneya B. Rajsel ; [translation Vesna Leme]. - 2nd ed. - Ljubljana
: O. B. Rajšel, 2024

Translation of original: Vlak za nebesa na Zemlji
ISBN 978-961-96040-5-2
COBISS.SI-ID 197539587